Praise for *New York Times* bestselling author Lindsay McKenna

"McKenna provides heartbreakingly tender romantic development that will move readers to tears. Her military background lends authenticity to this outstanding tale, and readers will fall in love with the upstanding hero and his fierce determination to save the woman he loves."

—*Publishers Weekly* on *Never Surrender*

"Talented Lindsay McKenna delivers excitement and romance in equal measure."

—*RT Book Reviews* on *Protecting His Own*

"Lindsay McKenna will have you flying with the daring and deadly women pilots who risk their lives… Buckle in for the ride of your life."

—*Writers Unlimited* on *Heart of Stone*

Praise for *New York Times* bestselling author Joan Johnston

"A guaranteed good read."

—*New York Times* bestselling author Heather Graham

"Joan Johnston does short contemporary Westerns to perfection."

—*Publishers Weekly*

"Joan Johnston continually gives us everything we want… fabulous details and atmosphere, memorable characters, a story that you wish would never end, and lots of tension and sensuality."

—*RT Book Reviews*

NEW YORK TIMES BESTSELLING AUTHORS

LINDSAY McKENNA

& JOAN JOHNSTON

WILD MUSTANG WOMAN
&
HAWK'S WAY: JESSE

If you purchased this book without a cover you should be aware that this book is stolen property. It was reported as "unsold and destroyed" to the publisher, and neither the author nor the publisher has received any payment for this "stripped book."

ISBN-13: 978-1-335-03999-6

Recycling programs for this product may not exist in your area.

Wild Mustang Woman & Hawk's Way: Jesse

Copyright © 2019 by Harlequin Books S.A.

The publisher acknowledges the copyright holders of the individual works as follows:

Wild Mustang Woman
Copyright © 1998 by Lindsay McKenna

Hawk's Way: Jesse
Originally published as Honey and the Hired Hand
Copyright © 1992 by Joan Mertens Johnston

All rights reserved. Except for use in any review, the reproduction or utilization of this work in whole or in part in any form by any electronic, mechanical or other means, now known or hereafter invented, including xerography, photocopying and recording, or in any information storage or retrieval system, is forbidden without the written permission of the publisher, Harlequin Enterprises Limited, 22 Adelaide St. West, 40th Floor, Toronto, Ontario M5H 4E3, Canada.

This is a work of fiction. Names, characters, places and incidents are either the product of the author's imagination or are used fictitiously, and any resemblance to actual persons, living or dead, business establishments, events or locales is entirely coincidental.

This edition published by arrangement with Harlequin Books S.A.

For questions and comments about the quality of this book, please contact us at CustomerService@Harlequin.com.

® and TM are trademarks of Harlequin Enterprises Limited or its corporate affiliates. Trademarks indicated with ® are registered in the United States Patent and Trademark Office, the Canadian Intellectual Property Office and in other countries.

Printed in U.S.A.

Lindsay McKenna is proud to have served her country in the US Navy as an aerographer's mate third class—also known as a weather forecaster. She was a pioneer in the military romance subgenre and loves to combine heart-pounding action with soulful and poignant romance. True to her military roots, she is the originator of the long-running and reader-favorite Morgan's Mercenaries series. She does extensive hands-on research, including flying in aircraft such as a P3-B Orion sub-hunter and a B-52 bomber. She was the first romance writer to sign her books in the Pentagon bookstore. Visit her online at lindsaymckenna.com.

Books by Lindsay McKenna

Shadow Warriors

Running Fire
Taking Fire
Never Surrender
Breaking Point
Degree of Risk

Jackson Hole, Wyoming

Out Rider
Night Hawk
Wolf Haven
High Country Rebel
The Loner

Visit the Author Profile page
at Harlequin.com for more titles.

WILD MUSTANG WOMAN

Lindsay McKenna

To all my faithful readers. A big hug back to you!

Chapter 1

Kate Donovan wanted to run and hide—again. In a few moments, the only man she'd ever loved would be picking her up at the halfway house in Phoenix, Arizona, to take her home. Home to the Donovan Ranch just north of Sedona. Her stomach roiled and the butterflies fought with one another as she stood on the porch of the rambling ranch house. Shame ate at her, as it always did.

She had just been released from an eighteen-month prison term when Sam's shattering phone call came, ripping open every other festering wound within her. When she'd been put into prison, only her two younger sisters, Rachel and Jessica, had been there to support her through the embarrassing trial. Kelly Donovan, her drunkard father, hadn't come near her or the courtroom.

He had been too ashamed of her. And now that she was coming home, he wouldn't be there for her, either.

Tears burned in Kate's eyes and she forced them back, as she'd learned to force everything else in the last eighteen months. Sam had called her last night to tell her that her father was dead. He'd died in a head-on collision with a drunk driver the morning of her release. Suddenly the irony of the situation struck her: Kelly had hit the bottle when his only son, Peter, had died in the closing days of the Vietnam War. Kate's brother had been Kelly's whole world. All his love, what there was of it, had been pinned on Peter—not Kate or her sisters. Why should she expect him to be there for her now?

Lips parting, Kate stared down at her plain oxford shoes, long past due for the trash bin. She felt just like that leather—beat-up, stretched beyond the point of usefulness. She felt *old.* Oh, how old she felt! And Kelly's death lay like a numb, heavy blanket over her already deadened senses. Going to a federal pen on trumped-up charges of ecoterrorism had stolen her life from her.

She still knew she was innocent. The FBI, frightened by the extreme views of the environmental group she belonged to, had planted an agent in their midst. And the agent had used her and developed a plan to blow up the nuclear plant outside of Phoenix. The worst part was it had been the FBI agent's idea! Kate had argued against it, but the more militant members thought it was a plan worth considering.

Now she was going home again. And now Kelly was dead. Her father was dead. Hell, he'd never been a father! He'd been a ghost in their lives after Peter died.

Rubbing her wrinkled brow, Kate drew in a deep,

ragged breath. When Sam had called last night—out of the blue—she had been stunned into silence by the sound of his deep, healing voice. She'd never forgotten that first, trembling kiss he'd given her when she was barely a women. And now, at thirty-seven years of age, she still filled with warmth at the memory.

She moved woodenly along the porch, feeling the remnants of the late November heat. The halfway house was designed to give women coming out of prison a few days to adjust to being on the outside once again. Kate was grateful for the space—a room of her own, no clanking and clanging of bars, or the endless noise of women talking.… She shook her head, feeling a little crazy.

Placing a hand on a wooden post that needed to be sanded and given a new coat of paint, Kate stared sightlessly past the brown lawn and the bare cottonwood trees that stood at the end of the property. The house was not in a good neighborhood, and though it was almost noon, the sidewalks and street were empty. Suddenly she felt frightened. Was it her father's unexpected passing that scared her? Or was it that she would be seeing Sam today when she thought she'd never see him again? Both? Probably. She dug her fingers briefly into the wood of the post and felt its dried, splintered texture. Arizona heat sapped the life out of everything. Kelly Donovan had sapped the life out of her.

Kate wanted to feel something at her father's death, but she felt nothing. The numbness that inhabited her had begun with her capture by the FBI agents; it had protected her as she faced the accusations made during the trial, and as she was locked away behind bars. For almost two years, she'd felt nothing. Kate laughed—a short, explosive sound. Well, she was feeling plenty now, but it had to do with Sam McGuire.

Gripping the post, she hung her head and felt tears crowd into her tightly closed eyes. Sam… The memory of their youth, their beautiful innocence as they'd fallen in love was one of the few unsullied things in Kate's life. Another was her mother, Odula, who had died ten years ago of a sudden heart attack. Kate was lucky her mother had loved her and her two sisters with a fierceness that defied description, that Odula had tried to make up for Kelly's behavior as a father, a negative role model in their lives.

Sam is coming….

Opening her eyes, Kate groaned, her gaze pinned on the end of the street, where she knew he would turn to come down to the halfway house. What must he think of her? He'd probably swallowed the FBI's lies, blasted out in the newspaper headlines. He hadn't come to the trial, as Rachel and Laurel had—but why would she expect him to? She'd had no direct contact with him since she'd left the ranch at eighteen years old. Absolutely none. Back then Kelly had been drunk most of the time and Kate was just glad to grab her high school diploma and get the hell off the ranch. After graduation, Sam had married his high school sweetheart, instead. And Kate had eventually left the state entirely to start her own life.

Some life… Once more humiliation flowed through her. She was the oldest of three daughters and she was the one who had managed to screw up her life the most. Rachel had become a world-class homeopathic doctor who taught in London, England, and Jessica ran her own healing-arts business in Vancouver, Canada. Kate had nothing to show for herself—just endless low-paying jobs that she usually got fired from because she was smarter than the guy who owned the business—and she made the mistake of telling him so. Kate the hothead. She'd been that way ever since Peter died. How much she had loved her older brother! They had all grieved deeply for his loss. Only Kelly had never gotten over his son's death like they had.

None of her sisters had stayed at the Donovan Ranch after age eighteen. They had fled just as she had. And why not? Kelly had made it clear he didn't love them or need them or want them around to run *his* ranch. Peter had been the heir apparent, chosen to take over the Donovan Ranch and give it another glorious generation, replete with grandchildren for Kelly. Yep, Kelly had had all his dreams in place—and none of them had ever included his three daughters. Well, his dreams had died with Peter. And now he, too, was gone.

Kate heard a low growl, the unmistakable sound of a heavy truck. Her heart raced as she lifted her head and turned to look down the street. There was a dusty Dodge Ram pickup turning the corner. The truck had obviously seen a lot of hard use and more than likely earned its keep in the ranching world—just like the man in the black Stetson behind the wheel. *Sam McGuire.*

Suddenly Kate felt anxious, more frightened than the day they had pronounced her sentence to the maximum-security prison. Her eyes widened as the truck pulled to a halt along the curb and she saw Sam McGuire for the first time in eighteen years. Her hand slipped from the post and she moved to the front steps. *Sam.* Oh, how she still ached for him! How many dreams during how many nights had she had of Sam kissing her, loving her, holding her? *Too many,* her wounded heart screamed. *Too many.*

Somehow she was going to have to hold herself together. Somehow she'd have to keep from revealing to Sam how she really felt. Too many of life's events stood between them. He was married. He had a son named Christopher, the last she'd heard. That's what Jessica, her youngest sister, had told her in one of the few letters they'd exchanged over the years.

As Sam eased out of the truck and shut the door, Kate couldn't stop her gaze from moving hungrily over him. At thirty-seven years old, Sam looked wonderful. He'd always been tall, almost six foot three inches, his shoulders broad and square. Kate remembered his proud bearing in high school. Even then, he'd had natural leadership ability. He had always walked with a kind of boneless grace, very male, very in charge.

But the years hadn't been kind to him, Kate realized. His square face was deeply lined at the corners of his gray eyes, telling her of the endless hours he'd spent out in the hot Arizona sun. The deep grooves bracketing his mouth told her he'd held a lot of what he felt inside. His skin was deeply tanned, his dark brown hair cut military short.

She noticed he was wearing a clean, long-sleeved, blue denim shirt, the sleeves rolled carelessly up, and a fresh pair of jeans. Kate knew how dirty and dusty ranching work was. Obviously Sam had taken some pains to shave, shower and put on clean clothes before seeing her. Even his boots, tobacco brown, were not the normal scuffed and scarred pair he would wear while working, but were polished and free of dust.

Raising her eyes, she saw that his black Stetson was set low so that she could barely see those piercing gray eyes of his as they met hers. For an instant, Kate felt a thrill of joy, deep and shattering, as their eyes made contact. And then, just as quickly, she crushed those wild, euphoric feelings.

Unable to hold his searching gaze, Kate broke eye contact. She stood there, her head hung, waiting. Would he judge her? Call her a criminal? Kate knew that word had spread throughout Sedona about her prison term. She knew her name was dirt. Inwardly, she tried to steel herself against Sam's accusations, spoken or not. How badly she wanted to look into his eyes again. At the first contact she'd felt only joy. Joy! How long had it been since she'd felt anything? *Too long,* her heart whispered. *Far too long.*

Sam tried to hide his surprise at the woman before him. Kate Donovan, the girl he'd known in high school, had been a winsome creature, wild like the wind. She had been the spitting image of Odula, her Eastern Cherokee mother, with that thick, black mane of waist-length hair that reminded him of a horse's flowing mane. She had Odula's startling blue eyes, so large and innocent with awe over life itself. Taller than most of the girls in high school, she stood at five foot eleven inches by the time she was a senior. For Kate, who had always tried to hide like a shadow, her height was one more thing that kept her from feeling like other girls her age. Now he saw that it still set her apart.

As Sam slowed his steps, he held Kate's intense blue gaze and felt a stunning force wrap around his heart and squeeze it hard.

Never had he forgotten kissing those full lips that were now compressed with holding back so much emotion. His body went hot with the memory—the memory of holding her, loving her, making her his. As a sophomore in high school, she'd given him her heart and virginity willingly. Passionately. And how he'd loved her—he still did. Shaken by the avalanche of emotion that had somehow, over the years, managed to survive, despite all his bad mistakes, Sam felt a keen, crying ache in his heart—for Kate.

It was her eyes that showed him the extent of her suffering. They had always been special, with golden flecks of sunlight dancing in their depths. As Sam searched her gaze now, he found only dullness and darkness. Could he blame her? She'd just been released from prison. A place like that was enough to kill anyone's spirit. He didn't believe Kate was an ecoterrorist. Yes, she was outspoken, brash, and didn't always think things through before acting. But she wasn't a killer as the media and FBI painted her. Kate wouldn't hurt a fly. She was a warm, loving girl who'd embraced life. And he'd loved her for years.

Now, as he slowed to take the steps up to the porch where she stood waiting for him, he felt naked with pain. Her pain. And he tasted bitter remorse in his mouth for what he'd done to her.

She looked so different from the young girl he remembered. No longer did she have that thick, black mane that swirled endlessly around her proud shoulders. Instead her hair was cut very short and clung to her well-shaped skull. She'd had a thin, model's body in high school. Now, as she stood before him in a pair of Levi's and a pink, short-sleeved shirt, he saw she had filled out in the right places, had some meat on her bones.

Sam could feel the internal strength in Kate; he always had. Her body was firm, and he guessed that she'd exercised a lot in the prison just to keep from going insane. How else could she have stood being locked up for a year and a half? Of the three sisters, Kate was the wild mustang among them. Sam had seen mustangs die, literally, of grief when imprisoned in a corral or box stall. Such was their need for freedom, for the wide-open spaces where they could run at will.

Kate was like that—wild, free and untamable. That was why he'd fallen in love with her so long ago. That's why he'd never gotten her out of his mind or heart. And he'd tried.

Studying her oval features, her high cheekbones set off by beautiful, wide-set, sky blue eyes, Sam saw the years of suffering in her face. He saw lines at the corners of her eyes, slight but present. And more than anything, he saw how the corners of her mouth were pulled in, a sign of the emotions she held at bay. He laughed to himself. Didn't he do the same thing?

When he saw the sudden panic in Kate's eyes, her uncertainty, he automatically took off his hat and halted at the base of the steps. He recognized that look of fear. He'd seen it in mustangs when he approached them too quickly. They were wary and distrustful, just as Kate was now. Could he blame her? He'd had so many dreams for them—hell, he'd managed to kill all his dreams and destroy Kate in the process: His heart ached as he saw that deep, ingrained fear in her eyes. What had prison done to her to make her react like that to him? When she was a wild, young filly, she'd been fearless. Bitterly, he remembered how life could make one scared and cautious. He had been stung a couple of times over the years. He no longer felt reckless or fearless himself.

He wanted to say so much, and yet it all jammed up in his throat. Suddenly the red bandanna he wore around his neck felt tight, and trickles of sweat slid down his temples as he played nervously with the edge of his Stetson.

"It's good to see you again, Kate," he said, meaning it. He saw a glimmer of tears in her eyes and felt her desire to move closer. At that instant, all he really wanted to do was open his arms, whisper for her to come forward so he could hold her. Just hold her. He knew that was what she needed, then as well as now. Of all the Donovan girls, Kate had taken the most abuse from Kelly because she'd fought back like the rebellious teenager she was. And she was the most injured by her father's ways. Sam saw that now as never before. So instead of reaching for her, he slowly lifted his hand in welcome. He had to move slowly in order not to scare her into running—again.

Without warning, the past came tunneling back at him, sharp and serrating as a knife blade stuck in his chest, hot and passionate as her breath had been when he'd found her crying outside her locker in the hallway of the deserted high school one evening. Oh, Sam had known Kate was an outsider at school. He'd been the star running back of the football team, while she was a quiet, mouselike sophomore who hid out in the library between classes.

He'd just come in from a very late football practice. Weary, his helmet dangling from his long, bruised fingers, he'd seen a darkened figure crouched beside a locker at the end of the highly waxed hallway. It was almost nine p.m., and there were only a few lights on. Sam frowned, shoved his damp hair off his furrowed brow as he walked softly toward the hunched, sobbing girl.

As he drew closer, he saw that it was Katie Donovan. His heart lurched and his steps slowed. She was wearing jeans and a white tank top, her thick, black hair like a cascade around her shaking shoulders. The sobs coming from her twisted his heart. For so long, Sam had wanted to meet her, but she evaded him every time he tried. Yes, he'd heard the stories about Old Man Donovan. No one in Sedona had missed hearing about his infamous drunks. Sam could understand why the three Donovan girls were like shadows around school. If he had a father like Kelly Donovan, he'd be ashamed, too, and probably hide out like they did.

Sam halted beside Kate, who sat on the floor next to her open locker, her knees drawn up tightly against her, her face buried in her arms. As he leaned down, the light casting long, gray shadows around them, his eyes narrowed. *What the hell?* He saw blood drying on her arm. His gaze traveled to her tank top, where a rusty stain appeared. Shocked, he realized that Kate was hurt.

Without thinking, he took the white towel from around his neck, crouched down and reached out.

"Kate?"

Her head snapped up. Sam heard her gasp. She jerked her head to the right, toward his low, concerned voice. Her red-rimmed, tear-filled eyes widened.

Sam heard himself gasp. His hand froze midair, the towel in his fingertips. Kate's left eye was blackened and swollen. Blood was leaking out of her nose. Her lip was split. Gulping hard, Sam realized someone had beat her up. Who?

"You're hurt...." he rasped, before getting down on one knee and pressing the towel gently into her hand. "Hold on, let me get you some water...."

Still in a state of shock, Sam went to the lavatory down the hall. He found a cup and brought it back, filled to the brim with cool water. Kate refused to look at him as he knelt back down beside her.

"What happened?" he demanded, dipping the edge of the towel in the water. He saw her fighting valiantly not to begin crying again as he slid his hand beneath her trembling jaw. As gently as he could, he wiped the congealing blood away from her soft, full lips, nose and chin. She was so scared. Her eyes were wide with shock and fright. Never had Sam felt more protective—or more angry at whoever had done this to her.

"I—I got thrown off a horse," she rasped.

He grinned a little, one corner of his mouth lifting. "Try me again. No horse is going to give you a black eye and a split lip. You trying to tell me you caught a horseshoe in the face? I don't think so. 'Cause then you'd be dead."

Choking, Kate closed her eyes. "N-no...."

"Here," he said soothingly, dipping the towel again and carefully folding it up. "Put this on your eye."

She did as he instructed.

Sam put his hand on her shoulder. He felt her tremble. She wouldn't look at him. "Heck of way to encounter a girl I've always wanted to meet," he weakly joked.

When Kate hid her face in the towel and leaned heavily against the locker, Sam realized that something was terribly wrong.

"Kate?"

She didn't answer.

Grimly, Sam maneuvered around and placed his hands on her shoulders. She was quivering like a frightened animal. "Kate, what happened?"

She sobbed and refused to look up at him.

Smoothing the curtain of black hair away from her damp, flushed face, he muttered, "Come on, we're getting out of here. Can you walk?"

Sam helped Kate to her feet. He was a lot taller than her, but she was tall for a girl. Slipping his arm around her waist, he allowed her to lean against him, her legs none too steady.

Later, out at the quiet football field, sitting in the bleachers—his arm around her shoulders, her face pressed against his neck—Sam had finally pried the truth out of her. Kelly had beaten her up. Her own father had struck her repeatedly.

Sam sat there till late that night, chilled by the wind off the Mogollon Rim. Kate's words and sobs tore huge chunks out of his heart, and he felt her pain.

In the next two years, Sam would come to know Kate intimately. Would see for himself the trouble between her and Kelly. And he would love her. Wildly. With abandon. Together they would weave dreams. Dreams that he would later smash by his own foolish actions.

Sam's face wavered in front of her. Kate swallowed abruptly and blinked rapidly to make her tears disappear. She stared at his proffered hand, a hand scarred and callused from years of laboring on a ranch. His voice, low and deep, moved through her like a healing salve. The shame that consumed her lessened momentarily, too. He was holding out his hand to her. Was it a gesture of peace? Of welcome? Or was he just performing a necessary social grace? She wasn't sure.

Kate wanted to believe that Sam was welcoming her. But she knew better. He'd never showed up for her trial, never wrote her a letter or tried to call her. Why should he? There was nothing between them now. He was married and had a son. He had a life of his own. He owed her nothing. Absolutely nothing. A two-year high school crush did not make him responsible for her after they'd broke up. As her gaze moved from his strong, square hand up to his barrel chest and the dark hair that peeked out at the top of his shirt collar, she swallowed convulsively. If Sam knew how many torrid dreams she'd had of him over the years, even he would blush. And not much made him blush, as she recalled.

Her gaze ranged upward to his mouth, and she began to feel heat pool in her lower body. It was a warm, wonderful sensation. She remembered that well-shaped mouth as no other; it was wide and quite capable of a wicked, boyish grin. Kate had always loved Sam's rolling laugh and she hotly recalled his mouth closing commandingly over her lips, to fuse them to his own. Now that strong mouth was compressed and Kate grew frightened. She'd seen that kind of response to her before: she was bad news, tainted, an awful person. Yet as she met his gaze, that curious warmth still flowed through her. The sensation caught her off guard.

Kate knew Sam could be a hard-nosed son of a bitch when he chose to be, and usually with reason. But that side of him wasn't present now. His eyes, usually gray and glacial looking, were a warm slate color at the moment, and she could feel her response to him building. She hadn't expected warmth from him. Without thinking, Kate lifted her slender hand and slid it into his waiting one. Sam was just being civil to her because Kelly had died the night before, that was all.

The strength of Sam's hand enclosed hers. Her flesh was damp with fear as she felt the monitored strength of his callused fingers. Heat jolted up her arm at the contact, and almost as quickly, Kate pulled her hand away. If she allowed Sam to touch her for one more second, she'd burst into tears and take that dangerous step forward, falling into his arms.

"Sam..." She choked and broke off for a second. "Thanks for coming to pick me up. You didn't have to."

Shaken, Sam settled the well-worn Stetson back on his head. Kate's handshake had been weak, clammy and unsure. How unlike the Kate he used to know. Anger stirred in him as he wondered how much prison had beaten the life and spirit out of her. There was so much to ask, so little time. Other things had to take priority right now.

"I wanted to, Kate. It was the least I could do. I'm

sorry about Kelly's passing. At least he went fast and didn't feel a thing."

Sam's deep murmur fell over her like a warm, nurturing blanket. Kate absorbed his care like a love-starved child. Standing uncertainly before him, she felt his gaze ranging over her from her head to her toes, and it made her feel painfully vulnerable. Her fingers tingled where he had held hers briefly. Did Sam realize that even now his gentle strength fed her spirit? When he'd touched her, she felt the first spark of hope in many years.

As she risked a quick glance up at him, she wondered if he knew the power and sway he held over her. Probably not. It was her neediness, her love for him that was making her feel this way. If nothing else, Sam always did what was proper. He could be counted on to do the right thing—just as she could be counted on to do the wrong thing.

Grimacing, Kate took a step back. "You've got a life of your own to run," she said. "You didn't have to come and get me, too. I appreciated your phone call last night about Kelly."

Sam moved up the stairs and worriedly assessed Kate. She was pale. Although she had Odula's dark, golden coloring, her skin seemed bleached out. He guessed it was from too many hours spent in the prison and not enough in sunlight. Kate had always been a sun lover. She hated being indoors, and had spent most of her time outside working on the ranch, laying wire for fencing, helping with the cattle or the horses—any excuse not to have a roof over her head. The three sisters had built a huge tree house in the white-barked arms of the Arizona sycamore out in their front yard. Kate had spent many nights sleeping out there under the sky, rather than in her bedroom where such starry beauty couldn't be seen.

"Listen," Sam told her heavily, "I called Rachel in London and Jessica in Vancouver. I told them Kelly was dead. Rachel will be here tomorrow evening. Jessica will come in the next morning. I…" He shrugged. "I took it upon myself to set the funeral for the third morning."

Kate's mouth thinned. "That's fine, Sam. Thank you. I don't imagine there was anyone else there that cared about Kelly's passing."

"No, not too many at this point."

She pinned him with a dark look. "You didn't have to do this, either."

"I worked for Kelly for five years, Kate. I owe the man something."

She shrugged. Sam was that way. He had loyalty to others regardless. Kelly had destroyed any loyalty Kate had to the Donovan Ranch—or to him. Her father had killed his daughters' love, their dreams of being a part of the ranch's growing history. He'd driven them all off. According to Kelly, only Peter had been capable of carrying on the legacy. He was a man. They were women. Women couldn't possibly do a man's job, Kelly had told them repeatedly.

"Who's the ranch manager now?"

Sam shook his head. "No one, Kate."

She glanced at him quickly. How strong and stalwart Sam seemed. She ached to take those few steps and move into his arms. Every cell in her body cried out for his touch. He was so big and tall and solid, as if he could weather any of life's storms and live to tell about it. Well, she'd suffered through one too many storm and had been beaten down once and for all. She felt weak. At this point she was incapable of finding any strength left in her battered soul to dredge up and call her own.

"But… I thought Kelly had a ranch crew—"

"He fired them over time. The last foreman, Tom Weathers, quit two years ago. Kelly was running the entire ranch by himself when he wasn't hitting the bottle."

Grimly, Kate took in a ragged breath. "Yeah, Kelly had a way of firing people, scaring everyone off with his drunken rages. Nothing changed, did it?" She looked at Sam and saw tenderness burning in his eyes. And though Kate hadn't expected that from him after all that had happened, she reveled in it.

Rubbing his mouth, Sam said, "After your mom died, Kelly hit the bottle pretty continuously. Over the years, he did chase off everyone."

"He fired you?"

Sam smiled slightly. "Yeah."

"That was stupid. But then, Kelly was known for doing stupid things." She laughed sharply. "Of course, I'm his daughter and I'm well-known for doing stupid things, making lousy choices, too…."

Sam hurt for her and had to stop himself from reaching out to touch her sagging shoulder. Kate had once walked so proudly. Now he could see she how broken she was. Broken, hurting and badly scarred. "Look," he rumbled, "you're nothing like Kelly, believe me…." Sam caught himself before he said too much. He saw the suffering on Kate's angular features. How badly he wanted to reach out and stroke her short hair, a touch to tell her everything would be all right. But it wasn't the right thing to do at the moment.

"Kate, I know you just got out of prison, and I know you have plans for your life, but right now, one of you Donovan women has to come home. You've got a thirty-thousand-acre ranch to run and no one is there to do it. There's beef to care for, roughly fifty Arabian horses that need tending. You need to come home and decide what you're going to do with the ranch now that Kelly's gone."

She stared at him. "There are no cowhands or wranglers at all?"

He shook his head. "None."

Stunned, Kate stared at him. "But the cattle and horses—"

"I know. I was over there early this morning doing the watering and feeding. I did a little vetting on a couple of Herefords. Probably the last place you want to be right now is on that ranch, but without one of you there, the place is going to turn into a disaster. The animals will suffer and die… I know you don't want that. I can come and help you out a bit, but I've got a job at the Cunningham ranch next door."

"I didn't know…." she whispered. "Oh, Lord, Sam, Kelly never wanted any of us running the ranch…especially me…."

His fingers ached to reach out and touch her. Comfort her.

Kate rested her brow against the post, her eyes closed. She felt the bite of the warm wood pressing into her flesh.

"It's a hell of a time, Kate. You deserve better than

this. You have what it takes to run that ranch. I know you do. But if you don't come home, the ranch is going to die. It's in rough shape, anyway. Maybe, when you and your sisters get together after Kelly's funeral, you'll make a plan and decide what to do with it."

Lifting her head, Kate nodded. "Kelly has probably destroyed the ranch like he has everything and everyone else," she said woodenly.

Sam stood there, feeling every nuance of the rejection and pain her father had caused her. There were times when he hated Kelly for chasing off his children. The sisters had loved the ranch with a loyalty unlike any other he'd seen.

"The ranch is gutted, Kate. You might as well know it now, so there're no surprises when I pull in the driveway. Are you ready? I've got to take you over to the funeral home in Cottonwood first, where Kelly's being laid out, and you have to fill out some papers."

Pain crawled into her heart. For a moment, Kate felt grief over Kelly's passing, despite the fact that she hadn't spoken to him since she'd walked out at age eighteen. All he'd ever told her anyway was that she was no good. A loser. That she'd never amount to anything.

Kate looked over at Sam and found his face deeply shadowed, his mouth a hard, set line, his gray eyes burning with that same tenderness that fed her. "Okay, take me home, Sam. But I'm not staying long. Kelly killed my desire to stay on that ranch one more day than I have to. It was all his and Peter's, and he never wanted us around."

Chapter 2

Sam wondered what was going on inside Kate's head as she sat, seat belt on, looking straight ahead as they drove toward Sedona. For the past hour she'd been silent. How mature and beautiful she looked, yet so different from the teenage girl he'd once loved. Life had a way of changing everyone, he decided.

"You need to know something about the ranch, unless you've been in close contact with someone about it."

Kate slanted him a glance. "I usually got in touch with my sisters once a year and that was it. Since Mom died, none of us had a clue as to what was going on at the ranch." And then, more softly, she added, "And we didn't care, either."

"Kelly made sure of that," Sam agreed sadly. He frowned.

"Do you really hate the ranch?"

She shrugged. "How can you hate the place where you were born and grew up?" Kate waved her hand helplessly as she drank in the sight of the desert surrounding them. They were on I-17, heading toward Black Canyon. From there, they would climb from near sea level to five thousand feet, to the high desert plateau. The tall saguaro cactus that dotted the landscape here would disappear, replaced by shorter prickly pear cactus, which could stand the colder temperatures of winter better than the sensitive saguaro.

"I recall you seemed to love the ranch back then."

"Yes," Kate whispered, "I loved the ranch. I guess in my heart of hearts I still do. In a way..."

"The past has a funny way of looking better than it did at the time?" he teased gently, glancing at her and then focusing on his driving.

"Doesn't it always?"

"Sometimes. Sometimes it gives you hope for making the future turn out the way you want it." Sam shrugged. "I used to have dreams a long time ago. I don't anymore. Maybe you still have dreams...."

His enigmatic answer was too deep for her to delve into. Instead, Kate absorbed Sam's proximity. In the cab of the Dodge Ram, Sam McGuire seemed even larger—and as solid as the truck he drove. He had about as many scars as this vehicle did, too. She noticed them not only on his hands, but on his arms and face as well. Ranching life was hard. Brutal sometimes. It demanded your blood upon occasion. Such as now. They had already talked about the funeral arrangements, having stopped at the funeral home and gotten them mercifully out of the way. Kate still didn't feel anything about Kelly's passing. Maybe it would hit her later.

Her heart was expanding, though, with euphoria. She knew it was because of Sam—his guiding, steadying presence. She stole a peek at his rugged profile. He was not a drop-dead-handsome man. His face was wind worn, sun beaten, his flesh tough and dark. His dark brown eyebrows were thick and straight above those gray, frosty eyes that had always reminded Kate of an eagle's. Those eyes never missed anything and she doubted Sam missed anything now. Inwardly, Kate waited for him to bring up her prison term or in some way use it against her.

Sam hadn't been that kind of man in the past, but things changed, she reminded herself. She wasn't the wild, rebellious fighter of her youth, either, anymore. Questions about him begged to roll off her lips, and finally, she broke the pleasant silence between them.

"You said you work for Old Man Cunningham?"

His mouth twisted. "I'm their ranch foreman. Have been for the past five years."

Raising her brow, Kate laughed a little. "Old Man Cunningham. Who could forget that bristly old peccary?" she said, comparing her ornery old neighbor to the wild pig that ranged across the Southwestern deserts. The analogy was a good one. The boars, which weighed well over a hundred pounds, had savage, curved tusks on either side of their mouth. They had poor eyesight and, if frightened, were known to charge the unlucky person and shred him to pieces. Cunningham was like that. Not only did he wear thick glasses that made his watery blue eyes look huge, he had an explosive temper. He abused everyone verbally, beat up his three sons with his fists and generally made everyone who had to deal with him miserable. Cunningham had the largest spread in central Arizona, over seventy thousand acres, which unfortunately ran alongside the Donovan ranch. Kate couldn't count the times Cunningham and Kelly had gotten into range fights over infractions. It had been ridiculous.

"I'm surprised you traded the Hatfields for the McCoys," Kate murmured wryly.

Sam turned and caught her slight smile. It wasn't much of a grin, but it was a start. He could feel Kate beginning to relax by degrees. How badly he wanted to tell her how much he missed her presence in his life, but now was not the time for such a revelation. "Yeah, well, Old Man Cunningham's last foreman quit on him just as Kelly fired me. I got wind of it and went over and asked for a job."

"Talk about going from the frying pan into the fire."

He chuckled and saw her smile deepen. Kate had a soft inner core to her she rarely let show. But now he was seeing her softness. "At the time, I was saving a lot of my paycheck for my son's college tuition," he admitted. "Cunningham made me an offer I couldn't refuse."

"Oh, I see...." Pain stabbed at Kate. How could she have forgotten that he was married and had a son? Her blind heart still wanted to see Sam as that fifteen-year-old football star she'd fallen so madly in love with—and was still in love with, she reminded herself. How did one erase love from one's heart? Kate had tried in many ways. She'd run from the ranch and from Kelly. And soon afterward Sam had married, at age seventeen, when he'd gotten Carol O'Gentry pregnant. Kate, right or wrong, couldn't stand knowing that her two-year relationship with Sam had been built upon sand. He'd loved Carol all along, she figured. He'd taken the love she herself had willingly shared with him, but his heart had never been hers. Well, that was the past. They were older now and life moved on.

Sam saw the flash of pain in Kate's darkening blue eyes. He felt it. But then, he'd always been in close psychic touch with her. It was as if he sensed more than heard her words, or maybe he read her thoughts from her expression. But Kate wasn't one to give much away in her voice or face or body language. Kelly had probably driven all those normal reactions out of her early on. So Sam had always relied on his feelings and sensitivity where Kate was concerned. He could always pick up nuances in her low voice. Or he would see the gold flecks in her eyes blotted out by some thunderstorm within her, and he knew that she was upset. She was a hard woman to read by most standards, and he was glad he'd gotten to know the soft, gentle, womanly Kate in his youth. That was the woman he'd fallen helplessly in love with until…

Sam frowned, shutting the door on his own bitter, stupid errors. He'd made a lot of mistakes, but the worst was what he'd done to Kate. Maybe now, in some way, he could make up for his transgressions.

"Cunningham is still meaner than a frightened peccary," he told her. "He's in his seventies now, partially blind because of his diabetes, and he still drives his sons into the ground."

"Nothing's changed." Kate shook her head. "He and Kelly deserved one another."

"They were a lot alike," Sam agreed.

"So, how do you tough it out with the old bastard at the Bar C?"

"A day at a time."

Kate laughed for the first time. It felt so good to laugh again. Sam joined her, and she marveled at how that tough, hardened mask on his face dropped away temporarily. It was a precious moment she grabbed and held in her heart. His eyes grew warm, his strong mouth curved, and she reveled in that thunderous, rolling laughter that she'd always loved to hear.

"He's meaner than a green rattler," Kate muttered. "He always beat his boys. I remember going to school and seeing Chet and Bo with strap-mark bruises on their arms. I don't see how they took it."

Sobering, Sam said, "Unfortunately, abuse begets abuse. Chet and Bo are still at the ranch. The youngest son, Jim, is an EMT and firefighter in Sedona. He got out at age eighteen, like you did."

"He was smart."

"Yes," Sam agreed slowly, weaving around some slower traffic on the freeway. "Jim was. He's stationed at Sedona Fire Station #1. He lives in town now. I know he's tried to heal the rifts in his family, with very little luck so far."

"Bet he doesn't go home to visit much, does he?" Kate knew Jim was smart enough to stay out of such a dysfunctional, abusive household, as she had.

"When he was a hotshot with the forestry service up at the Grand Canyon, Jim used to come home once a year, for Christmas, and that was it. Usually things erupted in a fight and he always left sooner rather than later. But he'd always come home again the next year to try and heal the family. He had a girlfriend, Linda Sorenson, who lived in Sedona. He was going to marry her, but that soured, too. Now that he's an emergency medical technician in town, I see him pretty regularly."

"Cunningham is angry at the world and takes it out on everyone. Nothing changes, does it?"

With a shrug, Sam said, "Some things do and some things don't." He glanced at her. "I hope you're prepared to see the ranch. It's pretty much a class A disaster area."

"I'm more worried about getting the livestock water and food."

"I know. When we reach home, I'll give you a hand."

She warmed to his care. "You ought to get a medal, Sam. You don't have to help us."

"A long time ago a certain pretty girl taught me a lot of things. Good things." He slanted a glance at her and saw color rising to her wan cheeks. "I don't think you ever knew how much influence you had on me back then, Kate." Sam wanted to say, *You taught me about loyalty, for one thing. And being responsible.* But he didn't, because he'd been disloyal and irresponsible toward her. His brows dipped as he focused his attention on his driving once more. "Maybe I can return the favor a little now."

Kate drew up one knee and clasped her hands around it. She felt the heat of a blush working its way up from her neck into her face. How long had it been since she'd blushed? She couldn't remember. Sam had that effect on her. He always had. Muttering, she continued, "I'm surprised. All we did was fight during those two years we were going together back in high school."

Chuckling, Sam said, "I'd call them constructive discussions, not arguments. Kelly and you got into hot fights with a lot of yelling. We never did that. And a lot of your anger was because of him, not between us. You had to let off steam somewhere." He shrugged. "I understood you, Kate, and I didn't mind if you got cranky and temperamental every once in a while. I knew what it was like living with Kelly and I saw what he did to you and your sisters...." Sam stopped. The past hurt too much for him to go on. He replayed again that first poignant meeting with Kate at her locker. Although Kelly had fought with Kate a lot, he'd beaten her up only once—that night. Sam had found out later that Odula had given her husband an ultimatum: that if he ever laid a hand on one of her daughters again, she'd divorce him. Kelly had backed down. To Sam's knowledge the rancher never *had* laid a hand on Kate or her sisters again, but he'd mercilessly badgered Kate mentally and emotionally, instead. Sam figured those beatings were no less injurious.

"I guess you and I really didn't fight," Kate replied, studying his harsh profile, his hawklike nose and that chin that jutted out proudly, daring anyone to take a swing. She remembered touching that face, running eager fingers across it, feeling his lips kissing her palm, her arm, her... With a broken sigh, she said tiredly, "That was a long time ago, Sam. Water under the bridge. We've both changed. A lot."

"In some ways, yes, but in others—" one corner of

his mouth crooked a little as he met and held her fearful glance for a second "—you haven't. You're just as pretty as I recall. Your hair is shorter, but your eyes still remind me of the wide, blue sky we live under." Sam stopped himself. He hadn't meant to get intimate with her. Cursing himself for lapsing into how he felt, he added, "But you're right. We all change."

The abruptness of his last comment hurt her. How often during the last eighteen months had Kate remembered all those affectionate words Sam had used with her during their relationship? If he knew, he'd be embarrassed. "I've changed all right."

"The question is," he murmured, "once you see the ranch, will you stay or go?"

"Knowing Kelly, the ranch is probably pretty much destroyed. That's what he did after Peter's death. Then he killed Mom with his drinking. She didn't die of a heart attack. Her heart was broken. There's a difference. Mom had such dreams for the Donovan Ranch."

"And not one of them came true," Sam agreed. Broken dreams. Yeah, he knew a lot about those, too. And he had no one to blame but himself.

"She envisioned a place where all things lived and grew. She hated to see the cattle raised and then slaughtered." Kate shrugged. "So do I."

"You're a lot like Odula," Sam said. "You not only look like her, you have her big heart, as well."

Kate held out her hands, studying her long fingers, the bluntly cut nails. "As a kid growing up, I always had dirty hands. But it was the dirt of Mother Earth under my nails. I loved it. I loved being with Mom out in our huge garden. I even liked weeding." Kate smiled fondly at those memories and clasped her hands around her knee again. "And all Kelly wanted to do was cut down more of the forest on our property, use it for more fencing for more cattle." She shook her head. "I remember times, Sam, that my mom would go for a walk away from the ranch house. I'd find her sitting on her favorite rock behind a juniper tree, crying."

Sam heard the pain in Kate's voice. "Why was she crying?"

"Because, as I found out when I was older and could understand it all, Mom had agreed with Kelly to start a farm, not a ranch. She came from the Quallah Reservation in North Carolina. Her people, the Eastern Cherokee, were farmers, not ranchers. It grieved her to see the cattle slaughtered. One day she told me about her dreams for all of us. When she got done, I cried with her, because our lives had taken another direction instead."

"Kelly's direction?"

"How'd you guess?"

"He was known to be a hardhead."

"You're being kind, Sam. But then, you always were. I was the one who called him what he was."

"Kelly came from this spread. He was a dyed-in-the-wool Arizona rancher, Kate. He didn't know anything else."

"But that didn't mean he couldn't have given in and let Mom realize some of her dreams, too." Angry now, Kate muttered, "He could have given her that apple orchard she wanted. What would it have hurt that selfish bastard to buy five hundred apple saplings and plant them for her? What he did instead was give her for a garden an acre of land that she had to till with the tractor. Trained in traditional healing arts, she wanted an herb garden to make medicines for her family, but he said no. She wanted to take the fruit of the earth and make this place an Eden. Kelly turned it into a perpetual slaughterhouse with the cattle. Everything hinged on those cattle." Grimacing, Kate glared at Sam. "It still does."

"He could have given Odula some of her dreams," Sam agreed quietly. "One person doesn't have the right to destroy the dreams of another." Like he did. He was no better than Kelly.

Kate winced and stared out her window at the dry desert, the prickly cholla, the saguaros that stood like sentinels, their huge arms raised toward the endless, bright blue sky. "Kelly destroyed four women's dreams," she said finally. "It was his dream or no dream at all."

"Maybe if Peter had lived things would have been different."

Shrugging tiredly, Kate said, "Maybe you're right, Sam. But it's too late for all of us. Peter died in a war without reason. Rachel, Jessica and I grew up in a war zone afterward. The war in our house killed my mother. It drove us all away—until now."

Without thinking, Sam reached out briefly and settled his hand on her shoulder. He felt her internal tension through his fingers.

"You're coming home, Kate. The ranch is in bad shape, and I don't know what your dreams are anymore. Maybe you'll sell it off before it goes into bankruptcy. Maybe you'll decide to stay and fight for your mother's dreams and make them come true after all."

Kate shut her eyes, her heart pounding, at Sam's brief touch. His fingers had a strong and steadying effect on her reeling emotions. Somehow, in his presence, her numbed senses were coming alive. She was shocked but grateful. Kate thought prison had destroyed a vital part of her. Apparently it hadn't. Sam was able to bring that part of her out from hiding deep within herself. For the first time, she felt a glimmer of hope.

Lifting her head, she looked into his warm gray eyes. "Sam, in some ways, you haven't changed at all. Hope for the hopeless—that's you. I'm going to let the ranch go bankrupt. I don't have any money—not a cent. Let Kelly's dream die. It doesn't deserve to live any longer, as far as I'm concerned."

Nothing could have prepared Kate for what she saw as Sam drove through the huge entrance gate of the Donovan Ranch. It was a ranch with a hundred-year history behind it. A colorful history. A tragic one. The gate itself had been made by Kelly's grandfather out of large, flat chunks of red sandstone, white limestone boulders and black lava that had been mortared together. The twin towers rose ten feet in the air, joined by a huge black piece curving across the top on which was written Donovan Ranch.

Kate looked hungrily down the rutted dirt road. She knew it led back off the highway for five miles, to the main ranch headquarters. On both sides, she saw cattle ambling about, looking for sparse bits of grass to eat. The cattle looked thin. Almost starved. It angered her.

"The cattle seem in bad shape."

Sam drove gingerly down the road, avoiding the

worst of the ruts. "We've had drought for two years, Kate. There isn't the normal forage available."

"I suppose Kelly didn't supplement with hay?"

"He couldn't. He was out of money. The local feed store refused to loan him any more money. He never paid his bills."

"Do you know how much in debt he was?"

Sam pointed to the glove box. "Kelly kept all his important papers in the rolltop desk in his office. I got them and put them in there. His will is in there, too."

"Kelly never believed in banks or safety deposit boxes, did he?" Kate asked as she opened the glove box. She glanced at Sam.

"Have you looked through his stuff?"

He shook his head. "No. That's not my business, Kate. Maybe when I was ranch foreman it was. But not now."

"So," she murmured, unfolding the will, "how much in debt was he?" Kate knew that all the local ranchers knew a lot about each other's business. There were only one or two feed stores to get grain and hay from, so information was concentrated and gossip was normal.

"I heard a hundred thousand dollars in debt," Sam said almost apologetically. He saw Kate wince. Her lovely, full mouth thinned as she read over the two-page will that Kelly had written some time ago. "The local bank is foreclosing on the mortgage," he warned her. "And unless you or your sisters can come up with a hefty chunk to salve the bank's continuing loss with Kelly, they will foreclose."

Kate skimmed the handwritten document, made out in her father's scrawly, almost unreadable writing. Her heart squeezed in pain. He had made her executor, leaving everything to Kate to dispense with as she wanted. The discovery was shattering. Unexpected.

"I don't believe this," she whispered, gripping the papers with both hands.

Sam slowed as the road began to snake back and forth.

"What's wrong?"

"This is crazy!" Kate held up the will to him. "Kelly's leaving everything to me! Me, of all people. I thought he hated me. We fought so much. He disowned me…."

"I don't think he hated you, Kate. You were a lot like him in some ways. You two had a lot of fights, but I find it hard to believe that a father could hate his own daughter."

"How could he love a daughter who is hardheaded? Stubborn? A daughter with a hair-trigger temper?"

"You are all of those things." Sam glanced at her. "You have your mother's heart, though. And that's where you two parted company. A lot of your arguments with Kelly were over rights for your mother and two sisters."

Kate tried to think despite the shock and pain. "Kelly wrote this a year ago. I was in prison. And he left me everything. How…why?" Tears burned unexpectedly in her eyes, and for once, Kate let them come. Distractedly she wiped at them with trembling fingers, barely able to breathe. "He never came to my trial, Sam. I thought he hated me. That he was ashamed of me. I thought that was why he didn't come. So if he was ashamed, why did he write his will this way? I don't understand it. I just don't…"

As gently as he could, Sam said, "Listen to me, Kate. You're in shock over Kelly's passing. You're probably pretty numbed out from being in prison, which had to be a hell in itself. You haven't had time to come up for air and adjust. Your father just died. You've inherited a ranch that's got a broken back. You're a hundred thousand dollars in debt in a blink of an eye. That's a lot to handle, Gal."

Gal. He'd often called her that as a term of affection when they had gone together so long ago. Kate felt the tenderly spoken word sink into her shaken senses and take the edge off her pain for a moment. Her fingers tightened around the will and the print blurred before her eyes. The jostling of the truck on the endless ruts brought her back to reality.

"Prepare yourself," Sam warned, as they climbed a small hill.

Almost eagerly, Kate looked up. She knew this knoll; just past it the land dropped a thousand feet into Echo Canyon, where there were black walls of lava created millions of years ago when volcanic activity was high. Oak Creek meandered along the bottom. A moment later she saw the layers of red sandstone beneath the white limestone cap of the canyon.

The last mile of the road wound like an angry snake downward.

There was only enough room for a single vehicle. To her right was Deer Mountain, a huge rounded hill covered with prickly pear cactus, junipers and large, smooth black boulders. The mountain got its name because the small deer of the area laid under the junipers and slept during the noontime heat, only to come down the mountains at dusk to drink from the creek near the ranch house before they began foraging.

Down below, Kate caught glimpses of the Donovan homestead. Over the years, many cottonwoods had been planted—her mother's wish, because cottonwoods were sacred to Native Americans. Now the darkly polished leaves of those tall, spreading trees were in fall color and hid the ranch from prying eyes. Odula had loved privacy. Kate recalled the bitter fights her mother had gotten into with Kelly. She'd fought for every tree she'd planted around the main buildings of the ranch. Kelly had refused to help, saying it was a waste, but Odula had wanted the shade and coolness, not to mention the privacy.

Kate recalled helping her mother plant those magnificent cottonwoods that now graced a good ten acres of the ranch's central core. The red, yellow and orange leaves, combined with the red, black and white of the canyon walls, made a kaleidoscope of colors.

"It looks so beautiful," Kate murmured, her voice wobbly as she strained to drink in the familiarity of the place where she had grown up. "I've been gone so long...." And how could she have stayed away? This was such a magnificent place. Her mother had called this canyon Rainbow Canyon, not Echo Canyon as Kelly's forebears had named it. Yes, it was a rainbow of living, vibrant colors. Kate's gaze darted here and there. She saw the many caves up on the wall of the canyon, some of which she and her sisters had played in as youngsters. They'd found many Indian relics, some quite old, but had left them undisturbed.

The memories came flooding back...hundreds of

them, good and bad. Kate found herself drowning in her feelings from the past. As the truck took the last curve onto the flat canyon floor, Kate gripped her hands in her lap, afraid to breathe. Sam had said the ranch's back was broken. What did he mean?

She didn't have long to find out. The cooling screen of cottonwoods gave way, revealing the main ranch house for the first time. Built of a creamy adobe brick, it was a sprawling place, the roof angled just enough so that the little rain they got would run off. Kate remembered the flowers that her mother had once planted around the fence surrounding the main house. Now that fence pitched forward, in dire need of paint and repair, with yellowed weeds growing around it.

Kate's heart beat hard as Sam braked the truck in front of the house. She saw that the windows were grimy and dirty and cobwebs were everywhere. The front door was hanging open, the wood split from a kick or two. Several windows were cracked and some had panes knocked out of them. Kelly's drunken rages, Kate thought, as she climbed out of the truck. She felt as if she were in a nightmare.

To the left of the house was a huge barn. Sam hadn't been wrong about a "broken back"—the ridge line of the roof was sagging badly and several shingles were missing. The barn doors hung askew. The wood was gray and weathered, in dire need of a protective coat of paint. Beside the barn were many corrals filled with Arabian horses—too many for the size of the enclosures. Several of the posts were leaning at an angle and barbed wire, which shouldn't have been used to restrain horses anyway, was rusted and poorly strung.

She felt Sam come and stand at her side. He placed his hands on his hips as she surveyed the horse area.

"Kelly did his own trimming and shoeing on the Arabs," he told her in a low voice. "Most of those animals are down on their heels. That's how long it's been since they've been trimmed."

Kate grimaced. "They have water?"

"Yes, plenty." Sam motioned toward them. "What you're running low on is hay. I'm bringing a truckload over for you tonight. There's no sense in letting these animals starve from neglect."

Kate hung her head. "Sam, you're a real guardian angel. Somehow I'll pay you back. I promise...."

He gazed down at her. "You owe me nothing, Kate. Consider this a gift."

"If Old Man Cunningham found out you were shipping a load of hay over here, he'd hit the ceiling."

Grinning a little, Sam said, "He doesn't know where it's going. And he won't, either. I'll pay him for it. The check will go into his bank account and he'll never know the difference."

Kate turned, unable to deal with his generosity. To the right of the ranch house were five other houses, as well as the outbuildings that housed an aging grader, a bulldozer, a backhoe, two tractors and other farm equipment. She could see all the work that needed to be done. Kelly was a master mechanic, but he'd often left parts lying around, dirty bowls of oil here and there, not to mention greasy rags. Some things never changed.

"You got wheels," Sam said, pointing to a green-and-white Ford pickup that had seen better days. "I checked it before I left to come and get you. It runs, but if I were you, I'd keep an eye on the oil gauge. This thing had blue smoke rolling out of it."

"That truck looks like it's twenty years old," Kate said.

"Kelly never threw anything away. He always repaired it himself. And if he couldn't, it sat."

"The place looks like a dump," Kate said grimly. Gone was the pristine house, the sparkling windows, the white picket fence with bright wildflowers adorning it like a colorful necklace. When her mother was alive, things had been kept clean. The place looked like a garbage pit in comparison.

"I know," Sam said sadly. He cupped her elbow and led her through the gateless picket fence. "The inside of the house is filthy. Kelly lived pretty sparsely."

Kate tried to steel herself but it didn't help. Her mother had kept this old, rambling ranch house neat as a pin, with no dust, no sand on the floor. As Kate entered the broken front door, which hung to one side, she gave a little cry of distress.

The interior was dark. Cobwebs laden with layers of dust hung everywhere, like grayish white chandeliers. The grit of sand crunched under their feet. The oak floor had once been a pale golden yellow; now she couldn't see it for the dust. Odula's frilly white curtains had been traded for dark maroon ones that were drawn shut across each window. The odor of whiskey assailed her nostrils. The smell of garbage sickened her.

When she got to the large kitchen, Kate gagged. Kelly had left food out on all the counters. Sacks of garbage were everywhere. She saw cockroaches scurry away as they entered the room.

"This is horrible," she whispered, gripping the doorjamb and staring into the dark depths. "Horrible. . . ."

Chapter 3

The screeching crow of a rooster very close to the bedroom window awakened Kate from a deep, healing sleep. Wrinkling her nose, she pushed the covers away from her upper body. Burying her head in the pillow, she lay there for a moment without moving. Every bone in her body ached as she felt the fingers of reality tugging at her. The bed was soft. There were no clanking bars, no chatter of women and guards. Just the blessed sound of a damn rooster crowing its fool head off. Her mouth twitched and she slowly rolled over, luxuriating in the bed and the sense of serenity she'd felt ever since opening her eyes.

The ceiling of her old bedroom met her gaze. The paint was chipped and peeling. The brass bed she slept in had been hers since she was a child. It felt good to be back in it—it reminded Kate briefly of being in her mother's arms. The goose-down quilt was warm and comforting across her tall, lanky form. The window was open to the cool November morning and she could hear the soft snort of horses, the whinny of a foal, the lowing of cattle in the distance.

All those animals were her responsibility now. That made Kate sit up. She rubbed her puffy eyes with the backs of her hands. Wearing only a clean T-shirt given to her by the rehab house, Kate pushed herself out of bed and headed down the hall to the bathroom. She'd managed to make the house more livable yesterday. The last thing she'd done before hitting the bed at one a.m. was to clean the kitchen. She couldn't stand filth. And that was what Kelly had lived in. The place was a pigsty. Although the house still seemed gloomy, she felt strangely buoyant.

As she took a quick, hot shower and scrubbed her hair, Kate's thoughts returned to Sam. He'd remained with her all day yesterday, helping her, working his tail off to feed, water and vet as much as he could. He'd also brought enough hay for the next three days to feed the Arabian horse herd.

After her shower, Kate dressed in a pink tank top and a pair of Levi's, then hunted up her old cowboy boots. Someone—probably her mother—had put them in a box. They were ancient, the leather hard and cracked, but they would have to do until she could buy a new pair. One didn't live on a ranch and not wear protective boots. Running her fingers through her damp hair to put it into place, Kate hurried to the kitchen. To her surprise, she inhaled the odor of fresh coffee perking. Who...?

Warily, she slowed down as she approached the kitchen. A radio was playing softly, nice instrumental FM music, the kind she'd missed in prison. All she'd heard there was hard rock, until she'd thought she'd go insane from the raucous sounds. The odor of bacon frying tempted her. Someone was in the kitchen. Mystified, Kate halted at the door.

"Sam!"

He was at the electric stove, a skillet full of potatoes and eggs in hand. "You look a lot better than I feel," he muttered, and turned back to his duties at the stove.

"But—how? I mean, I didn't hear you come in." Kate moved to the coffeemaker and poured herself a cup of coffee. Her heart was beating strongly in her breast, and she tried not to stare at Sam like the love-struck teenager she'd once been. He wore a white cotton shirt, the sleeves rolled up his arms, a faded pair of Levi's, a belt and cowboy boots. The red bandanna around his throat emphasized the thick, corded muscles of his neck. The way his shirt stretched revealed the power of his chest and the breadth of his shoulders. There was nothing weak about Sam. There never had been.

He was clean shaven. She saw where he'd nicked himself on the side of his hard, uncompromising jaw. A piece of paper was still stuck on the wound.

"Dress you up, but can't take you anywhere," she murmured, moving over to where he stood. Gently, she eased the tiny piece of paper from the cut on his jaw.

Sam stood very still. He felt Kate's warm presence so very, very close to him. As her fingers brushed his jaw, his heart thudded hard in his chest to underscore how badly he ached for her touch, no matter how brief.

When she lifted the paper away, he cut her a sidelong glance. Kate's cheeks were a bright pink color. It reminded him of the few struggling pink flowers outside the picket fence. Her eyes… Lord, her eyes were clear, and for the first time, he saw glints of gold in them. Groaning inwardly, he fought the urge to turn and place his arms around her, crush her against him, find that soft, parted mouth and take her. Take her all the way to heaven. He knew he could. He knew that in his heart and soul.

"Thanks," he rumbled.

Kate dropped the paper into the cleaned trash can at the corner of the kitchen sink. "You must have gotten up awful early to get over here."

"A little," he hedged, pouring the concoction onto two awaiting plates. "Come on, let's eat. We've got a lot to do this morning before I show up at the Bar C at eight a.m."

Grateful beyond words, Kate sat down. "This is almost like breakfast in bed."

Sam lifted a forkful of potatoes and eggs and looked at her over them. "That was kind of the plan. I was going to have a 'Welcome home, Kate' breakfast waiting for you down here when you got up. You beat me to it."

Touched, Kate ate hungrily. She was starved, in fact. Ranch food had a taste all its own. Prison food was like cardboard. "The rooster woke me up."

"You might take the woman off the ranch, but you won't take the ranch out of the woman."

Kate watched him eating his meal. Sam's plate was heaped with food, but then, he would be working a good twelve hours today and he needed that kind of fuel.

There wasn't a scrap of fat on his hard, well-muscled body, either. Ranching didn't encourage excess weight. She had none herself, but for different reasons.

Looking around the clean kitchen, Kate marveled at the difference. "This place looks almost livable now."

Sam nodded. "It reminds me of the place when Odula was alive."

"Yes," Kate whispered, suddenly choked up with memories of her mother. "Over the years I've come to realize just how lucky I was to have her as a mother."

"She was special," Sam agreed. He stopped eating and studied Kate's features. He saw the pain and loss in her eyes and heard it in her low voice. "You're so much like her." Kate was the spitting image of her, but Sam didn't say that. She had Odula's dark, good looks, those blue eyes that were so thoughtful and filled with intelligence. Although Kate's black hair was still damp and clung to her shapely skull, she was beautiful, in his eyes. He still saw some of that wild, rebellious mustang in her, although it was deeply hidden.

"I got over here at four-thirty this morning," he said, breaking the silence. "The horses are fed and watered. I let the cattle out of the pens and they can graze for what they can find. This first pasture goes for a hundred acres, so they'll find enough for the next couple of days, until you can get some help here."

"It seems so overwhelming, Sam." She put the fork down and shook her head. "The last thing I remember thinking last night before I fell asleep was that I need money to get this place on its feet. I don't have any. I didn't earn very much while being in…prison."

Being careful not to respond to the word *prison,*

Sam kept on eating. His jaw was still warm where Kate had touched him. She had the touch of a hesitant, wary butterfly, he decided. "Then you're going to keep the ranch?"

Shrugging, Kate continued to eat. "I don't know. I'm waiting to see what Rachel and Jessica say. If we don't have two pennies to rub together among us, the ranch will go into bankruptcy."

"Do you have any idea of their finances?"

Rubbing her brow, Kate said, "No." She saw him frown. "I haven't been very good about staying in touch with them the last two years. . . ."

"But at least you're talking?"

She nodded. "Rachel and I have had our fights, and Jessica, bless her spacy little self, stayed in touch, too. I'm on good terms with them, Sam."

"Good, because right now, if you're going to save your home, it's going to take the three of you, all the money you own and a hell of a lot of elbow grease, time and miracles."

Wouldn't it though? Kate remained silent. She knew so little about her sisters. A letter or phone call once a year had maintained the ties, but she knew hardly anything about how life had treated them. She focused her attention back on Sam.

"Why are you doing this?"

He raised his head and held her soft blue gaze. "Why?"

"Is there an echo in here?"

He grinned a little, wiped his mouth on the paper napkin and put the plate aside. "Why wouldn't I?"

"Don't answer a question with a question, Sam

McGuire. So what if you worked for Kelly for five years? What did he ever do to make you this loyal and helpful to us?"

Sam withheld the real answer to her question. Instead, his mouth curved into a lopsided grin. "Cowboy's code. You help your neighbor when things go to hell in a handbasket."

She studied him ruthlessly, combing his innocent features with her eyes. "I know you better than that, Sam. How about the truth?"

"That *is* the truth," he said gently, slowly getting out of the chair. The wooden legs scraped against the linoleum floor.

"Humph," Kate said, rising in turn. "No one from the Bar C came over here in the last ten years except you." She took her plate to the sink, rinsed it and put it in the newly cleaned dishwasher. Leaning against the counter, she took the mug that Sam handed her. There was such a wonderful familiarity with him. Things had always been so easy between them—until the breakup of their relationship. Kate had had a terrible fight with Kelly one day and, in desperation, she had run way from home, but not before leaving Sam a note saying that she couldn't take it anymore. She'd planned on leaving not because she didn't love Sam, but because at home she was trapped in a bad situation that had no end. She'd left the note at Sam's house, saying goodbye—forever—and then had hitched a ride to Phoenix, truly intent on leaving.

For two weeks, Kate had walked the streets of Phoenix aimlessly, alone, hurting and confused. A policewoman, sympathetic and helpful, had finally picked her up, and Kate went back home. Kelly had tried to be apologetic. Her mother, who had been crazed with grief and worry, welcomed her back with open arms, as did Rachel and Jessica.

It was when she went back to school the next day, her nerves in knots about trying to find some way to apologize to Sam, that Kate had heard the news. In her absence, Carol had walked into Sam's life. Carol had stolen him from her. Maybe that wasn't entirely true, Kate acknowledged. Her own decisions played a key role in all of this. Sam had thought she was gone forever. Carol was pretty, a cheerleader, and Sam was the star of the local football team. It was a natural pairing. And Kate? She was a ranch brat who worked several hours before going to high school and afterward until dark, taking care of the cattle and horses, with her family. She didn't have time for clubs or after-school activities—certainly not cheerleading. But then, Kate reminded herself, she'd never have made it as a cheerleader. She just wasn't the outgoing, bubbly type. She had too much Indian in her; she was too deeply introverted.

"Does Old Man Cunningham know you're over here?" Kate wondered, sipping the fragrant coffee.

Sam leaned back against the counter, leaving about a foot of space between them. "No."

"Do you live at the foreman's house at the Bar C?"

"Yes."

"I don't imagine your wife appreciates you being over here."

He raised his brows and studied her briefly. "She doesn't care."

"Why?"

"Because Carol and I got a divorce last year."

Kate felt the blood drain from her face as she stared up into his dark gray eyes. "Divorce?"

He shrugged and looked away. "You don't need my tales of woe on top of your own right now. After our son, Chris, went off to college in California-Stanford—Carol and I decided that it just wasn't working."

Kate swallowed hard, wanting to know more. But it wasn't the time or place to ask questions. Stunned by his admission, she felt her head reel and her heart pound. Sam was as loyal as they came. What had caused him to consent to a divorce? Looking away, Kate muttered, "At least you stayed together until your son was raised. That's something a lot of couples don't even consider nowadays."

"Yes," Sam said, pushing away from the counter, "and they should. At least, Carol and I did. We agreed that Chris needed that kind of stability."

"So you made the best of it."

Sam's mouth quirked. "We did what we had to do." He paused thoughtfully, then said, "Listen, we need to move about thirty of the Arabs into a new pasture area. Let's saddle up and get it done. That way, it will give you about a week's grace on feed for them."

The familiar, soothing sound of creaking saddle leather, the jangle of a horse's bit, was like music to Kate. She and Sam rode on two of the ranch's Arabian horses as they moved the herd to an upper pasture, much closer to the Mogollon Rim area. The Rim, as they called it, was a huge jutting masterpiece of black lava, red sandstone and white limestone. It rose two thousand feet straight up from the desert floor of the ranch. The north pasture hugged the foot of the Rim and Oak Creek flowed through it, a natural source of water for the horses.

As Kate and Sam rode, their legs briefly touched every once in a while. Kate thrilled to the unexpected contact with Sam. He sat so straight and proud in the saddle, born to the rocking motion of the bay gelding beneath him. The November chill made her feel alive, though she was glad for the denim jacket she wore over her tank top. The air was sweet with the odor of the pine trees that topped the Rim ahead of them.

The huge, carved canyon was over twenty miles long, ending at Flagstaff, and the Donovan spread included four miles of it, so that the canyon mouth actually occurred on the ranch.

Kate loved the canyon area of the ranch. It was a startling contrast to the prickly pear and juniper of the hot desert. The tall Ponderosa pines stood like proud sentinels on the Rim, reminding her of Sam's proud stance when he walked.

The horse she rode was a bay mare named Cinnamon, a long, rangy Arabian looking more like a Thoroughbred at fifteen hands high. She sighed as Cinnamon danced. How good it felt to have the movement of a horse beneath her! How much she had missed this!

"You're looking awful pensive," Sam observed. He saw the joy in Kate's eyes as she turned her attention to him. For the first time, he saw the soft corners of her mouth turned upward, not in. The flush on her cheeks only made her more desirable in his eyes.

"I was just thinking how much I missed all of this," she said, gesturing toward the mouth of the canyon directly in front of them. "How could I have left this place? It's heaven. It really is."

"Sometimes when a caged animal is freed, the taste of freedom is pretty heady."

Kate understood the analogy. Her gaze dug into his, though the rim of his black Stetson was tipped so that she could barely see his eyes. "You're right," she admitted. "I hated prison. I hated everything about it." She inhaled the pine-scented air, the dampness that flowed out of the canyon to the dryer reaches of the desert. And then she regretted her words because she saw Sam's face close. No longer was there that wonderful openness they'd just shared. Internally, she tried to prepare herself for his judgment.

"You're no killer," Sam told her in a low voice, holding her startled glance. "I never believed what I read in the papers about you…about that group you got tangled up with."

Relief sheeted through her and Kate could no longer hold his dark, burning stare. Then she forced herself to look at him again. He deserved her courage, not her cowardice. "You're right," she whispered, her voice raw with emotion. "I did get tangled up with the wrong bunch. They were hotheads, Sam. At least some of them were. Stupid. Just plain stupid. I was stupid, too. But I never was involved in the plans to blow up that nuclear power plant, I swear to you. It was the undercover FBI agent who suggested it and then whipped the men into planning it. I was against it from the beginning, but they just laughed at me."

"So the men who planned it skipped across the Mexican border and you took the fall for them?"

Grimacing, Kate nodded. “Yes, the three men who planned it are somewhere in South America.” Free. Not imprisoned as she had been.

“Sounds like the FBI wanted a scapegoat, Kate. You were at the wrong place at the wrong time and they wanted to make an example out of an extremist environmental group. You got left holding the bag.”

Nodding, Kate compressed her lips. “I didn’t think you’d understand, Sam. I guess I was figuring you would swallow the FBI and newspaper stories.”

Chuckling, he reached over and gently touched her shoulder. How badly he wanted to slide his leather-gloved hand around her tense body and hold her. Kiss her senseless. Forcing himself to break contact, he said, “You and I have a long history, Kate. You’re like a wild mustang. You want your freedom and you want to have your say. Nothing wrong with that. Maybe you made some poor choices about who to hang out with, but that’s all. I remember when a calf or foal would die, you’d cry. I recall a time when the horse you were riding hit a gopher hole and broke its leg. I was with you when that happened. You couldn’t shoot the horse, even to put it out of its misery. So why would I think you were capable of blowing up a damn nuclear power plant that might kills thousands of human beings?”

Tears swam in her eyes and she looked away, trying to get hold of her unraveling emotions. A lump formed in her throat. She was so close to sobbing. Her fingers tightened around the reins as she continued to avoid Sam’s probing gaze.

“I—I just made some very stupid choices with people," she agreed. "I can't kill. I never could. But they wouldn't believe me, Sam." She turned to him, tears burning her eyes. "Do you know how angry and frustrated I was? I was so ashamed. I could barely look Rachel and Jessica in the eye when they came to my trial. I didn't blame Kelly for not coming. I knew I was the worst disappointment in his life…."

Pulling his horse to a halt, Sam turned the animal around so he was facing Kate. Their legs touched, his dark leather chaps against her slim jeans-clad leg. "Listen to me," he growled, reaching out and cupping her jaw. He felt her tremble. "Not everyone is ashamed of you. I'm not—I never was. Yes, there are going to be people in Sedona who have judged you, Kate. But folks who know you will know you are innocent." He brushed his thumb against her cheek where the tears had fallen. The suffering on her face nearly cracked his massive control. As her lips parted and trembled, all he wanted to do was kiss her and take that pain she was suffering into himself. Right now he was stronger emotionally than she was. He knew he could do that for her, but would she let him? Sam was very unsure. The old Kate he'd known well. This was a new Kate—a woman damaged badly by prison, by being unfairly branded as a terrorist. He had no idea what those wounds had done to her—yet. And until he did, he could do little but be supportive and try to nurture her in small ways.

A breath escaped Kate as she closed her eyes and laid her cheek into his gloved palm. How strong Sam felt. She wanted desperately to be in his arms, to once more feel those iron bands closing around her and holding her safe. "I feel like raw meat inside," she continued, unable to look at him. The hot tears beaded on her thick lashes and then fell down her cheeks. "I'm so afraid to go into town, into the feed store, and sense their eyes on me, to feel them judging me, Sam."

"I know," he rasped. "I know."

Pulling away from his touch, Kate blinked her eyes rapidly and then wiped the tears away. "But I've got to do it. I can't keep running and hiding. I started that habit at seventeen. And when I was eighteen, I ran away from this ranch—and Kelly—for good. I've been running ever since. I've made a mess of my life, Sam. I feel bad inside. I'm ashamed. My sisters are successful. They made something worthwhile of their lives. I haven't. I'm the oldest and I've screwed up everything I ever touched."

Sam forced his hand down on his leather chaps. Kate's voice tore at him. She had no idea how much he still loved her—had always loved her. And she wouldn't know, either. He was a failure, too—at his relationship with her in high school, and later with his loveless marriage. Kate would never love him after all the lousy mistakes he'd made. He was the real loser here, but she didn't realize it. All the dreams they'd shared during those two years together were shattered. Gone.

But Sam had to put aside the past for the time being. There was enough going on right now. He knew Kate was suffering over Kelly's death. As much as she hated Kelly, he was still her father, and she had much grieving to do. After eighteen months in prison, she was suddenly free and that had to be causing her a hell of a lot of readjusting, as well. And then to have the ranch going into bankruptcy, to have her roots, her heritage taken away from her—something he knew was so intrinsic to her—made him wonder how she could handle it all.

One thing Sam had discovered early about Kate was that her hellish years growing up with an alcoholic father had made her strong. She had a backbone of steel. Sam knew some steel was flexible and could be tempered by heat and fire, while other steel was brittle and couldn't stand stress at all. What kind was Kate made of? What had life done to her? Had it tempered her strength and courage so that she could bend and weather all of this? Or would she crack under the strain, broken like this ranch was? Sam had no answers. And as much as he wanted to help Kate, he knew the outcome depended solely on her own grit, her spirit to fight back, to reclaim her rightful heritage—no matter what odds were staring her in the face.

"Well," he told her heavily, "I'm no prize either, if you want to look at it that way."

Sniffing, Kate wiped the last of the tears from her face.

"What are you talking about?"

"I made the worst decision of my life by marrying Carol. It was eighteen years of hell. A prison. So, if you made a mistake and spent only eighteen months in a prison, who's the stupid one here?" He grinned a little, trying to lift her spirits.

Kate stared at him, openmouthed. "But—I thought you *loved* Carol."

Grimacing, he took off his hat and rubbed his furrowed brow with the back of his arm. "You talk about mistakes. Kate, when I got your note that you were running away for good, I believed you. I knew how bad it was for you at home, and you'd often told me you thought that running away, leaving Sedona, was the only thing that would help." He stared down at his leather-clad fist. Forcing himself, he looked up into Kate's eyes.

"I got roaring drunk three days later. I'd been in touch with your mother. The police were looking for you. I knew you'd really left this time. Not that I blamed you. . . ." He shook his head sadly, his voice dropping with regret. "A couple of my friends saw how down I was by your leaving. They talked me into going to a party. Carol was there and she was drunk, too. I remember passing out. The next thing I knew, I was on her parents' bed, buck naked, and so was she. I should have had a condom. I should have said no, but things got pretty hot and I had sex with her. Talk about stupid mistakes." He rubbed his jaw. "It was my fault as much as hers. Grieving for you being gone, I was drunker than hell, with hormones raging and no condom. Well—" he glanced at her grimly "—Carol ended up pregnant from that one time. My parents were heartbroken. They had college in mind for me. Instead, I married Carol out of responsibility to our baby."

Kate's heart ripped with pain. Sam's pain. "I'm so sorry, Sam! I never knew. . . . When I left that time, I thought I was running away for good." She tried to take a deep breath, but her heart hurt so much, it was impossible. Her voice was barely above a whisper. "What a mess I made by doing that. I felt horrible leaving you, but I had nowhere to turn. As much as you tried to protect me, Sam, you couldn't. I knew that. Kelly had threatened to come after you, too. He knew we loved each other. I was afraid if I ran to your house, he'd follow me and hurt you, so after leaving that note, I hitched a ride to Phoenix." Shrugging painfully, Kate held his saddened gaze. "I spent two weeks just wandering around. I was so hungry.... I didn't have any money, so I begged for food at the back of restaurants." She sighed. "I'd always thought you'd fallen in love with her and out of love with me because I left you. Not that I blamed you...."

"No, Kate." Sam cleared his throat and looked up at the sky, now alive with high clouds turned a dark pink and lavender as the sun approached the horizon. "I was so damned ashamed of what I'd done—how I'd fouled up my life, college plans, and hurt my parents—that I let you think that. I was just too damned cowardly to really tell you the truth. Until now."

Joy and shock suffused her. Kate stared at his grim features. "And the past eighteen years was to—"

"To give Chris, our son, some stability. I owed him that much. It wasn't his fault we screwed up. As it stands, he's going to college and he'll get a good start in life. I made my bed and I laid in it, Kate. I never was angry at you for leaving me that note. If anybody understood, I did. At least you didn't make the kinds of mistakes I made. You made others, that's all. But nothing worse, in my eyes, than the one I made with you."

He'd been in a loveless marriage for eighteen years. Kate sat in the saddle, her feelings in turmoil, her head spinning with realizations and guilt over her own adolescent rebellion, over running away. By doing that, she'd set both herself and Sam on a course with disaster. "I guess," she murmured, "there's all kinds of prisons, aren't there?"

"Yes," he answered. "The key is to survive them, Kate. That's what you've got to do now. Somehow you have to find the internal strength, the guts, to get through this—Kelly's passing, your responsibilities for the ranch. There's a great burden sitting on your shoulders, a hell of a lot of decisions in front of you. But you're Odula's daughter. You've not only got her blood, and her love of the land, you have her spirit." He swept his arm toward the canyon walls. "I couldn't have survived my time in prison without being on this land. There's something special here, Kate. I don't know what it is, but it has me by the throat and I don't ever want it to let go.

"This land fed me, nurtured me through those years with Carol. I love my son deeply, and I was able to impart my love of this land to him. It's a part of him now, like it's a part of you and me." He sighed, looking down at his hand on the saddle horn. "I hope that you stay here. Stay and try to root yourself here—for a lot of reasons. Some of them are purely selfish on my part. Others are not." He glanced at her through slitted eyes. "You're like a tree torn up, roots and all. Now you're getting a chance to come back, dig a hole and replant yourself. It won't be easy. It'll take back-breaking work. A commitment like I gave to my marriage, really. I don't know where the money will come from. I hope one of your sisters has it."

Shrugging, Sam reined his horse away from hers.

"Come on," he said gruffly, "we've got to get the herd moving. I have to be at the Bar C soon or Old Man Cunningham will fire me for sure."

Chapter 4

Late in the afternoon, after vetting several young Arabians, Kate sat near a long wooden water trough. She dipped her hands into it and splashed her face, finding the water cool and refreshing. Murmuring over the luxury of it all, she straightened and wiped her eyes. This was a far cry from being in prison!

In the corral where she stood, there were twenty young foals, all black for the most part. It was amazing that the broodmares were bay, chestnut, white and gray, but the foals turned out black. Her gaze moved to a barbed wire enclosure away from the mothers and babies.

A black stallion, his coat gleaming in the November sun, paced back and forth endlessly. Gan, which was Apache for devil, didn't deserve such a name, Kate thought. Sam had told her that Kelly had won the black

Arabian stud in a poker game in Sedona with some of his old cowboy buddies ten years earlier—shortly after Odula's death.

Her father had gotten drunk one night and gone to the Red Rock Inn, a famous landmark where cowboys frequently gathered to drink whiskey, smoke and play cutthroat poker. It was on that night that Kelly had bet his entire herd of prized, registered Arabian mares against Ben Turner's black stud. Luckily, Kelly won. But he hadn't won much, according to Sam. The horse, a hellion, was unmanageable. No one could ride Gan. No one could get near him except with a crop or some other protection in hand. The only reason the stud had been kept alive was the fact he could throw black foals a high percentage of the time. And in the world of Arabian horses, the color black was rare, so people paid more money to have one.

Kate's heart went out to the black animal. She decided that the stallion had probably met with heavy abuse in his younger days and had turned on humans as a result. Sam had told her that Kelly, in his drunken rages, would go out and throw rocks and jeer, tease the animal unmercifully. When Sam found him doing it, he'd haul Kelly away from the nervous stallion, which would be shaken and enraged. More than once Kelly had been bitten by the stud. Kate shook her head as she stood there watching the beautiful horse. Kelly had had it coming, there was no doubt.

Sam had left hours ago and she felt the emptiness inside her. Kate already missed his larger-than-life presence. She missed *him,* but was afraid to admit it to herself. Picking up the plastic toolbox containing vetting supplies, she leaned down and slipped between the slats of the fence. The work was endless, but she loved it. Being outdoors again, breathing fresh, pine-scented air and experiencing the dryness of the desert, was far preferable to being incarcerated in a prison.

Her muscles ached here and there; the long horseback ride with Sam had been heaven, but she hadn't put a leg over a horse since she'd left the ranch years ago. Now the muscles in her legs were tightening up. Her arms and shoulders were sore from helping Sam move fifty bales of alfalfa hay from his truck into the barn. But it felt good to be physical again. More and more Kate realized how much she'd missed this ranch, her roots.

When she thought of Rachel arriving tonight, her heart squeezed in fear. Her sister was two years younger than she. In high school, Rachel had been the popular one, voted school president her final year. And despite all her ranch chores, she'd managed to be a member of the debate club, too. Everyone knew and liked Rachel. She was beautiful, Kate acknowledged, with thick, long, brunette hair, dancing green eyes, a willowy figure. And she was smart as a whip.

Making sun tea later, Kate placed a gallon jar of cold water with four tea bags out in the sunlight, then sat down on the porch. It, too, needed a coat of paint. Everything did around the ranch. As she sat there, her arms resting on her knees, Kate wondered how she could revive the place. Hourly, she found herself wanting to save it more and more. Sam was right—her roots, her history, were here. Everything she was and was not came from this old ranch. Now it looked like her—battered and nearly destroyed from years of neglect. She'd nearly destroyed herself with a lot of bad choices, Kate acknowledged. But the circumstances of her life weren't anyone's fault but her own.

The fact that Kelly had left her as executor of the will and owner of the ranch bothered Kate more than she was willing to admit. How many times had he said she'd never be able to run a ranch of this size? That she and her sisters didn't have what it took to do so? So why had he left it to her? Why?

Near sundown, around six p.m., Kate heard a truck pull into the driveway. She wiped her hands on a towel and hung it on a peg. The odor of a pot of chili cooking on the stove permeated the kitchen as she moved through the room. Was it Rachel? Her heart sped up in anticipation.

The knock at the door, which she'd repaired earlier, echoed through the living room.

"Come on in," Kate called from the kitchen entrance.

Sam poked his head in the doorway.

Blinking, Kate halted midway through the living room. "Sam?" He'd said this morning that he wouldn't see her until the weekend.

"Howdy. Sorry to drop by unexpected," he said, standing uncertainly.

Frowning, Kate gestured for him to come in. "That's okay. What's wrong? You look worried."

With a grimace, he took off his hat and entered the room after wiping his dusty boots on the mat. "No more than usual. I just thought I'd drop by and see how you were getting on." If he'd been brazenly honest, Sam would have added, *I had to see you.* And he did. Almost every minute of his day, he'd rerun one of their conversations or visualized the precious smile that shadowed her so very serious mouth. He craved to see more of that dancing light in her eyes. Sam knew he didn't have the right to be here. At all. But he couldn't help himself as he stood there, hungrily absorbing the sight of Kate into his being.

"I was just going to eat some chili. Come on in," she invited. He looked tired, but then Sam had been up since four this morning, put in half a day's work here at the ranch and then gone over and put in eight solid hours at the Bar C. She noticed his jeans were soiled and his once-white shirt was dusty and had splotches of sweat across it. How handsome he looked even now, she decided, as she walked back to the kitchen with him. Automatically, her fingers grazed that spot where he'd cupped her face earlier that morning. The love she felt for him welled up in her, and she was unable to stop it. The feeling was good, strong and grounding. Another part of her, the scared, frightened mustang, wanted to run—again.

Automatically, Kate filled two bowls with chili and took some freshly made cornbread out of the oven. She cut several thick slices and gestured for Sam to sit down at the kitchen table.

"Dinner?" Sam grinned, looking at the hefty bowl of chili filled with onions and green Mexican chilies. The smell was mouthwatering.

"Why not? You've earned it. Wash your hands at the sink and then we can sit and eat. You can tell me over the dinner table what my next problem is."

Once they both sat down to eat, Kate marveled at

how delicious the spicy chili tasted. Her mother's recipe. Mexican food was a main part of their fare, but so was fry bread, cornmeal and a lot of vegetables from her mother's background. By contrast, Kelly liked Irish stew, corned beef and cabbage and plenty of potatoes. All these things drifted back to Kate as she ate hungrily. Sam sat opposite her, eating just as much as she did. He went through half the cornbread, and she wasn't surprised. The sun tea made the meal complete. This was the first meal she'd made at home and it tasted marvelous.

"So," Kate murmured, placing her empty bowl in the sink after eating, "how did your day go? Like mine? Busier than a one-armed paper hanger?"

Sam took one more piece of cornbread, slathered it with butter and squeezed some honey from a plastic container over the top of it. "That sounds about right," he growled, giving her a slight grin. Kate was a damn fine cook, he'd discovered. But then, she was good at anything she set her mind to. As she stood at the kitchen counter, her back against it, sipping sun tea from a glass and studying him, he saw exhaustion around her eyes. Knowing her, she'd worked nonstop. Kate was a worker of the first order. She always had been.

"Listen," Sam said gently, as he wiped his hands on the napkin, stood up and walked over to her. "Why don't you rest a little, Kate? You're looking pretty worn out." Fighting himself, Sam cupped her shoulders. He ached to lean down and kiss her parting lips. He saw the surprise and then the molten longing in her blue eyes. And just as quickly, it was replaced with hurt. How badly he'd hurt both of them. Sam wished there was a way he could apologize enough to Kate on that account.

Kate held herself very stiffly, afraid to move, afraid to breathe. His hands felt stabilizing. Wonderful. How she wanted simply to surrender, lean against his powerful, strong form. Uncurling her fingers, she whispered unsteadily, "Please…"

Sam could smell her clean hair, and he longed to press his face against her head and inhale the sweet fragrance. He felt her tremble violently as he held her shoulders. Allowing his hands to drop back to his sides, he realized she didn't want him to touch her. He'd overstepped his bounds—damn his own selfish need and hunger for her! Moving away from her, he said gruffly, "Look, you have Kelly's funeral in a couple of days. Your sisters will be here. Right now you need them more than me."

Bitterly, Kate turned. She saw the dark, hooded look in Sam's eyes. Her body ached for his continued touch. "They may not want to save the ranch. They may not care anymore, Sam. Not that I could blame them. Kelly ran us off. He made it clear we weren't capable of running a ranch. As far as he was concerned, women were good for only one thing—having kids."

Sam raised his eyes toward the ceiling. "Kelly was old-fashioned."

"He was of caveman mentality," Kate retorted. "He *never* respected the three of us. Hell, he never respected our mother, and she was ten times smarter than he was. But he was too proud, too stiff-necked to listen to her counsel." Kate looked around the kitchen, her voice wobbling with sudden grief. "He didn't think women were worth a plugged nickel. Only a man could run this ranch." Her eyes hardened and she put her hands on her hips. "I swear, Sam, if I can, I'll save this ranch even if I have to kill myself doing it."

Sam knew there was no love lost between Kate and her father. Kelly had made sure of that. "Look," he soothed, "wait until Rachel gets here. You ladies have your mother's intelligence. My bet is that among the three of you, you'll come up with a plan to save the ranch."

When Kate saw Rachel climb out of her rented vehicle, all her fear left her. Whatever their past, it didn't matter at that moment. Her sister was home. Rachel's long, reddish-brown hair was still thick and curly, falling below her shoulders. At thirty-five, she was tall, proud looking and still just as thin and ballerinalike as she'd been as a girl. Slightly shorter than Kate, Rachel wore a long-sleeved, dark green sweater, a black skirt that fell to her ankles and sensible dark brown shoes.

Kate flew off the wooden porch, her arms wide. "Rachel!" she cried.

Rachel smiled tiredly and opened her own arms. "Hi, sis…."

Kate squeezed her hard, tears coming to her eyes as she stepped back to look at her sister. Behind her, the night was coming on, a dark cape over the twilight sky. "I'm so glad you're here."

"Me, too." Rachel smiled unsteadily, tears in her eyes. "How *are* you?"

Kate shrugged. "I'm free of prison, if that's what you mean," she said a little defensively.

Rachel picked up her leather traveling bag from the rear seat, then a black physician's bag. "Let's go inside, shall we? I'm beat from a nine-hour flight across the Atlantic and then a five-hour flight out of New York."

Warily, Kate took the rest of her luggage and led her into the house. "You'd better prepare yourself," she warned.

Somehow, Kate felt responsible for the bad condition of the house as Rachel walked through it to her old bedroom, down the hall and across from Kate's.

"Kelly really let the place go, didn't he?" Rachel said, dropping her luggage on the recently made bed.

"Yes. Everything around here is either broken or ready to fall apart. Are you hungry?"

Rachel pushed her dark hair away from her face. "No…thirsty though."

"Come to the kitchen. I've got fresh coffee made."

Rachel smiled. "No coffee for me. I'm on a homeopathic remedy for grief and coffee will antidote it."

Kate smiled a little, falling in step with her sister. Despite her fears she was glad to see Rachel and already felt the effects of her solid, soothing nature. "That's right, you're a homeopath. I tried to figure out what you did from those once-a-year letters we sent to one another. It's a type of alternative medicine?"

"Yes," Rachel said, "it's a natural medicine discovered over two hundred years ago in Germany, and it's practiced around the world."

"You said you're teaching at Sheffield College near London?" Kate poured her some iced tea and they sat down at the table.

"Thanks, Katie. Yes, I'm one of the instructors

there." Rachel reached out and gripped her hand. "How are *you,* though?"

"I'm home," Kate said simply. "It feels good, Rachel. Really good. Better than I thought it would."

Sipping the tea, Rachel studied her as a comfortable silence fell between them. "I'm talking more about how you're handling Kelly's death. Where are you at with that?"

Rachel's hand was warm and dry as she folded it over Kate's. Kate had always marveled at her sister's beautiful hands. They were so long and artistic looking. Hers, in comparison, were large knuckled with blunt-cut nails and lots of old ranching scars covering them. Moving her gaze back up to her sister's face, Kate saw that Rachel's green eyes were filled with concern, and she tightened her grip.

"I heard it from Sam McGuire," Kate continued. "He called to tell me about Kelly at the halfway house I was staying in when I got out of prison a couple of days ago."

Gently, Rachel said, "How are you *feeling,* Kate?"

Frowning, Kate pulled her hand away. "I'm not feeling anything," she said flatly. "Not a damn thing, and I don't care if it's right or wrong."

"There's nothing wrong with that response," Rachel said. "Grief has many faces."

"I'm not grieving," Kate said, her eyes flashing.

"I am." Her sister sighed. "I took *ignatia amara,* a homeopathic remedy for grief. When Sam called me, I started to cry."

"Why? All Kelly ever did was make *us* cry. I'm not shedding one tear for that bastard after what he did to all of us."

"He was a very injured human being," Rachel said slowly.

"He injured all of *us!*" Kate lowered her voice. "I'm sorry. I'm just upset. So much has happened since I got home."

"Tell me about it?"

How like Rachel, Kate thought, to be the listener. She always had been. Having her here was good. Kate felt less threatened now. Almost relieved. Rachel was the cool-headed one in the family, more like their mother, who had always listened in silence and then chewed over everything internally before speaking her thoughts. Kate, on the other hand, had inherited Kelly's hair-trigger temper, his brusqueness and lack of diplomacy.

"It's almost eight. You have to be dead on your feet," Kate protested.

Shrugging, Rachel smiled warmly. "Hey, I haven't seen you in so long. So what if I'm tired? I'll sleep in tomorrow morning. We have a lot to catch up on, Katie." Looking around, Rachel's voice lowered with emotion. "And I want to know about our home, and what is going on with it."

Kate snorted. "Our 'home' is a hundred thousand dollars in debt and a week away from being foreclosed on by the bank unless we declare bankruptcy. Either way, we're going to lose it."

Chapter 5

The next morning Kate, with Rachel's help, fed the cattle and horses. It was nearly eight a.m. when a small red compact car came zooming down the dirt road of the canyon. The two sisters stood on the porch and watched the vehicle's progress and the huge cloud of dust it kicked up in its wake.

"That's Jessica," Kate said with a laugh.

Rachel laughed in turn and dusted off her hands. "Yep. Jessica's never slowed down." She looked over at Kate. "She's how old, now?"

"Thirty, I think." Kate shook her head, then studied her sister, who had traded her professional clothes for a long-sleeved white blouse, jeans and boots, and braided her hair into two long, thick plaits. They reminded Kate of their mother, who'd always worn her hair in braids prettily decorated with pieces of colorful yarn and feathers. Absently, Kate touched her own short hair. She wanted to grow it long once more to try and reclaim her Native American heritage. "Last night when we stayed up late talking, I got to thinking that we three haven't stayed in touch like we should have. We just sorta scattered like a flock of startled quail and went three different directions."

Rachel nodded. "And to three different countries. I live in England. Jessica lives in Canada."

"Kelly did it." Kate knew she sounded bitter and didn't care.

Rachel reached out and squeezed her hand. "Katie, some day you'll be able to let go of your anger over what Kelly did to us. He did the best he could. He was just a very wounded human being."

"Aren't we all wounded?" Kate demanded, her anger rising. "Just because we are doesn't mean we go around beating the hell out of our kids or pushing them away and telling them they're no good because they happen to be female and not male." Her voice shook and Kate forced herself to take a deep breath. "You're right. I've got a lot of anger."

"I can give you a homeopathic remedy to help you start processing it," Rachel said.

"Maybe," Kate muttered as she watched the red car pull into the driveway. "I'll let you know." She didn't know that much about homeopathy, and thankfully, Rachel didn't push it on her. Right now, they had a ranch to try and salvage. Kate would use her anger constructively this time around. Maybe she would do something right, for once.

She couldn't help but grin as Jessica, who at five foot

six inches was the shortest of the three, came leaping out of the car like a colorful whirlwind in a bright red cotton skirt, a purple-and-pink blouse with long puffy sleeves, and a violet scarf around her neck. The youngest of the sisters had Odula's long, black hair, sparkling gray eyes and Kelly's thin, wiry build.

"Katie! Rachel!" Jessica shrieked, running toward them with her arms outstretched.

Kate laughed and stepped off the porch. Jessica looked so fresh and unscarred by life. Her small, fine features, like delicate porcelain, showed no sign of stress or aging. She was the same little elfin sprite Kate had grown up with. As Jessica threw her arms around her, Kate could smell the perfumed fragrance of some flower.

Rachel joined them, and more laughter, tears and embraces followed. How good it felt to have the arms of her younger sisters around her! Kate felt Jessica squirming like a wildly happy puppy—she was never able to be still for more than a heartbeat. As Rachel's husky laughter fell over them like a warm, welcoming blanket, Kate felt her anger dissolve, replaced by an unparalleled joy surging upward. How much she loved her sisters! And how much she had missed them—their counsel and shining personalities—in her life. As they stood in a small circle, hugging one another, she realized for the first time just how much she'd lost by running away from the ranch. She should have stayed to watch them grow and mature. Would she ever learn not to run?

Finally, when they all separated, Kate looked at them. Rachel had tears in their eyes and Jessica was crying unabashedly. Pulling out some tissues she had in her pocket, Kate said, "Come on, you crybabies, we've got a lot to talk about." She gestured for them to come into the ranch house. "Blot your eyes and let's get down to business or we'll have a lot more to cry about."

Jessica sat with a cup of tea between small, delicate hands, each slender finger of which was ringed in silver or gold. Kate served Rachel a cup of hot tea also, and after pouring herself a cup of strong coffee, she told them the bad news about the ranch, not sparing her sisters the bottom line.

"Kelly left the ranch to me in his will," she told them in a low voice.

Jessica brightened. "Oh, that's wonderful, Katie! You're the firstborn. It should go to you."

"Kelly wanted it to go to Peter," Kate growled.

Rachel reached out and touched Kate's hand. "No matter how much you dislike Kelly, he loved you, Kate, the best he could. I think he showed that by giving you the ranch."

She wasn't willing to agree with Rachel's assumption. "I haven't got two cents to rub together. I'm flat busted." She looked at them, her voice earnest and low with passion. "I love this place. When I first came here, I was ready to let it go, but… I can't now. I can't explain why."

Jessica sighed. "Oh, Katie, this is our home. Our *roots*. How could any of us let it be taken from us?"

"Are you saying you want to save the ranch?" She prayed that they did.

"Why not?" Rachel said, sipping the tea. "This ranch

has a hundred-year history. It has Donovan blood, sweat and tears in the sand. I feel it's worth trying to save."

Jessica removed a wispy lock from her brow with a graceful motion of her hand. "Katie, you may not have any money, but you have heart. I have some money saved from my business. It's not much, but…"

Kate looked at Rachel, who was by far the most successful moneywise of the three of them. "What about you, Rachel? We need money. Do you have any you want to pour into this broken ranch we call a home?"

"I lay awake half the night thinking about that," Rachel admitted slowly, turning the white, chipped mug around in her hand. Her broad brow wrinkled and she slanted a glance toward Kate. "All my life, since I can remember, I've wanted a healing place, a clinic to take care of the poor, the elderly and the babies. When I discovered homeopathy, I knew it was the vehicle for my dream." She shrugged and tried to smile. "That's why I went to England, to get the very best training in the world. That's why I've worked over there, teaching as well as running my private practice. I didn't want to leave the U.S., but I had to in order to get the education."

"So, this clinic," Kate prompted. "Are you building it over in England?"

"No…" Rachel laughed softly. "The other part of my dream was to have it here, on the ranch. Remember how Mom used to tell us she had a dream of a medicine house? A place where she could use her herbs, flowers and poultices on people who needed healing?"

Jessica nodded and smiled tenderly. "Mama *was* a healer. Look at you and me, Rachel—we're in the healing arts. I've got my own natural essence company and you're a homeopath. Both are alternative medicines. Both of us got our training from Mama's herb garden. She taught us everything she knew and we just carried it forward, that's all."

Kate felt like a failure—again. Odula had shown the three of them her healing skills, taught them her tremendous herbal and floral knowledge, and Kate had stupidly walked away from all of it. All because of Kelly. She saw now the mistake she'd made. In getting rid of Kelly, she'd also cut out and run from the good things she'd been given and taught. Thankfully, Rachel and Jessica had not done what she had. But that made her feel even worse. Fighting her own feelings of inadequacy, she looked at Rachel.

"What is your bottom line on this, Rachel?"

Opening her hands, Rachel said, "I can't leave in the middle of a school year at Sheffield. My contract is up December of next year. I could leave at that time, come back here and work with you to try and save the ranch. I have fifty thousand dollars saved."

Kate gawked at her sister. "You're kidding me! That's a lot of money!"

Rachel grimaced. "Katie, that money was squirreled away over a fifteen-year period for my dream of having a homeopathic clinic."

"I've got it!" Jessica cried, pushing her chair away from the table. "I know what we can do!" She whirled around on her tiptoes and clapped her hands. "It's so simple! Rachel, you come back home a year from December. I can make it home by May at the earliest. My company can't be picked up and moved just like that—I have to do some serious planning." Eagerly, she placed her hands on the table and looked at them. "I've got twenty thousand dollars in assets I can give, Katie. Why can't we all come home as soon as possible? Rachel, you can still have your clinic. Build it here, on the property! And I can build my greenhouses and the other buildings I need for the natural essences I make. We could do our work here, at home. Oh, wouldn't that be a wonderful dream come true? Mama always wanted us to stay on the ranch!"

Kate sat there, feeling Jessica's boundless hope. It all sounded so good and so easy. "I guess the only thing I can bring to this deal is my elbow grease," she joked weakly.

Rachel grinned. "You're the one who's going to be working herself to the bone, with us unable to be here to help at first. Besides, Katie, it's your *heart* that's really invested in saving our home. We have money, but so what? You'll be here, working dawn to dusk." Worriedly, she added, "And you can't do this alone, Katie. We're going to need a foreman. Someone who can help you out daily."

"We don't have *that* kind of money," Kate protested. "I've been running some figures in my head. We could sell off half the cattle herd. That would cut down on the needed hay for the coming winter and stop some of the financial hemorrhaging. We could also sell off about fifteen head of the black Arabians for the same reason. They'll fetch a decent price because black is rare and in great demand."

"If we did that," Rachel said, "would it pay off the hundred thousand owed on the ranch?"

Kate grimaced. "No. We can probably get twenty

thousand out of the cattle and horses we sell off. If you put in your fifty thousand, and Jessica her twenty, that's getting us up there." She clenched her fist. "But the bank may want the whole hundred thousand dollars no matter what we try and do."

Rachel nodded. "The funeral is tomorrow morning. How about if I call up the banker for an appointment with him tomorrow afternoon? I can only stay three days and then I've got to get back to England. Let me handle this part of it, okay?"

Kate was relieved. "No kidding. Your diplomacy is a hell of a lot better than mine! Hoof-in-mouth disease, you know?"

Jessica giggled. "Katie, you have other strengths that we don't. Let's all of us use our skills to the best we can. The three of us can do this! I'm so excited!" Her eyes shone with hope.

"Still," Rachel warned, "as soon as I can get the banker to give us some breathing room and refinance the ranch, we need a foreman."

"We don't have the kind of money it would take to get someone, Rachel." Kate sighed. "Foremen are special. They know everything from accounting to calving and then some. I can't just hire some wrangler looking for work."

"You mentioned Sam McGuire last night," Rachel said primly.

"What about him? Can you lure him back from the Bar C to take over here? You know, he worked here for five years. Maybe he wants to come back."

Instantly, Kate was on her feet. The chair she was

sitting on tipped, but she caught it before it fell over. "Sam's got a job already."

Jessica frowned and tugged at a lock of her hair. "So what? Can we lure him away from it? I'll go see him, Kate—"

"You will not!"

Rachel frowned. "Kate, don't get stubborn about this. You need help. Sam McGuire is a known quantity. You're right—we can't just hire some tumbleweed wrangler that drifts from ranch to ranch looking for work. Sam's a hard worker. He's loyal and he's smart."

Panic set in and Kate began pacing the floor of the kitchen. Rachel's argument was on target, she acknowledged as her heart pounded hard in her breast. "But he's already got a good-paying job."

Rachel laughed. "Oh, yes, at the Bar C. Come on, Katie! Old Man Cunningham is a mean old peccary. His wranglers work for a season and then quit on him. He can't keep anyone for long. He's got high turnover because he's grumpy." She grinned mischievously. "I'd like to give him *Bryonia* to sweeten his disposition up a little."

They all chortled.

Rachel shrugged eloquently. "I'm sure Sam would consider coming back now that Kelly's gone. He *loved* this ranch. I talked to Kelly one time on the phone about Sam and he told me that Sam was like a son to him."

Kate halted and stared at Rachel. "He said *that?*"

"Yes, and a lot more, but I'm not going into that now." She eyed Kate. "Do you want me to ask Sam or do you want to do it?"

Swallowing hard, her throat dry, Kate rasped, "No… I'll approach him."

"He's been helping you out ever since you came back," Rachel said gently. "I've got to think he cares about our ranch or he wouldn't have done it."

Standing very still, Kate realized Rachel's wisdom. "You're right," she whispered, "I've got to get out of the way and let the ranch be helped, not hurt by me. Okay, I'll ask Sam sometime after the funeral. He'll be coming to it."

Rising to her feet, Rachel smiled. "Good. Don't look so glum, Katie. It's not the end of the world, it's the beginning. Come on, I'm going to give you some *natrum muriaticum.* I think you need it."

At that moment, Kate felt too enmeshed in the violence of her own feelings about Sam to care about a homeopathic remedy. A huge part of her hoped he would say no to their request. Another part had never stopped loving him, or wanting his daily presence in her life. How could she keep her feelings toward him separated from the hard, demanding ranch activities? He didn't love her. Too much time and hurt and life responsibilities stood in the way, Kate knew. But that didn't stop her from loving him. Even now.

Sam would live in the foreman's house, not in the main ranch house, but that was still too close for comfort. Kate was scared—more than she ever had been before. She'd known fear when the sentence for an eighteen-month prison term was announced by the judge, but this was different—and far more personal. She was afraid that she couldn't keep her feelings private from Sam.

Tasting the fear, she watched Rachel walk over to her homeopathic kit, which sat on the kitchen counter. Her sisters were so solid and normal compared to her. They were successful, had saved money, had dreams and goals, and worked hard toward them, while she'd made a mess of her life.

"Here," Rachel murmured, patting several small white pellets in Kate's hand. "Take these. It's potentized table salt. It's for people who bury all their feelings, Katie."

Wryly, she looked at Rachel. "Me?"

Laughing, Rachel slid her arm around her shoulders. "Yes, you, Miss Toughie. Go on, put them in your mouth and let them melt away. And then take a shower and go to bed. You'll feel better tomorrow morning." Rachel lost her smile. "Tomorrow, we bury Kelly."

"Bless him," Jessica whispered, her eyes filling with tears. "He was such a tortured soul. He's in a far better place now, with Mama."

Kate didn't know what had happened to her emotions, but the funeral for Kelly hadn't been as arduous as she thought it might be. Kelly Donovan was buried on the family plot on the ranch, surrounded by heavy wrought-iron posts that needed painting. Ten other graves were in that rectangular enclosure on a hillside covered with Ponderosa pine. Mercifully, the ceremony was short. The minister said all the right things and then shook their hands and left. Jessica paid him the 120 fee for his services.

Sam McGuire had come and stood next to Kate during the funeral. Afterward, he settled his dark brown

Stetson on his head. Today he wore a dark brown blazer and a white shirt with a big bolo tie sporting a turquoise stone in the center. His Levi's were clean, and he wore his go-to-town cowboy boots, the same ones he'd worn when he'd picked her up at the halfway house down in Phoenix. Kate had watched the warmth of Rachel's and Jessica's welcome for Sam. Her's had been a curt and short greeting in comparison. She chided herself relentlessly. Why couldn't she be just as warm and outgoing as her two sisters? She was a crab compared to them. She always had been. It was her anger against Kelly, Kate decided. Damn him, he'd always ruined her life. Always. And now, as she stood alone under the pines near his fresh grave, she was the one on whose shoulders the responsibility fell to try and save the ranch. Could she do it? They had enough money to probably give them breathing room, but to make a ranch profitable was another thing all together.

Hands damp, she saw Sam excuse himself from her sisters and purposefully walk toward her. She felt heat leap to her face as his dark gray gaze settled on her. He looked grim—she could see sadness in the set of his mouth and in the darkness of his eyes. Sam wasn't the kind to pretend something he didn't feel, Kate thought.

"Want to go for a walk?" he asked, tipping his hat to her.

Kate wished the heat in her face would subside. She'd blushed like this in high school every time Sam looked at her that way. "I guess. . . ." she murmured. Kate knew her sisters didn't need her right now. Rachel was meeting with the banker at two p.m. today and she'd fill them in on whether or not the bank was going to foreclose on them. And Jessica had some of her own business to attend to back at the ranch.

Sam gently placed his hand on her elbow and led her down a well-worn deer path, moving more deeply into the woods. "You look mighty pretty in that dress."

Kate tried to steady her reeling senses. Sam's hand was firm yet careful. He was so strong and tall—like the mountains. But she felt like a raging river without banks right now. "It's not my dress. It belongs to Rachel. She loaned it to me because I didn't have any…."

Sam smiled down at her. The dark blue, long-sleeved dress was conservative and fit Kate well. Small pearl buttons down the front stopped at a white belt around her waist, setting off the white collar. The material was soft and flowing and fell around her slender ankles. Sam noted that she was wearing different shoes, too. Knowing Kate had little money, he suspected Rachel had loaned her them, as well, but he wasn't going to inquire and embarrass her further. He saw the wariness in her eyes. Always the wild, untamable mustang, he reminded himself.

He smiled inwardly. A mustang could be tamed, but doing so took patience and time. He had both. But what gave him the right to try and tame Kate? To try and win her heart again? He was a miserable failure at so much in his life.

"Well," he murmured huskily, "the dress brings out the sky blue color of your eyes."

His compliment went straight to her heart and Kate absorbed it greedily. She tried to think through the haze of feelings and desires that Sam automatically stirred up in her. "Thank you…."

"You ladies talk about the fate of your ranch?" Sam asked, halting beneath a huge pine. He didn't want to drop his hand, but he did anyway. He stood before her, taking her in more fully. Kate's hair had been coiffed, he was sure, by Jessica, who had those feminine skills. A pair of gold earrings with small pearls adorned her delicate earlobes. Even a touch of lipstick graced her lips. But her real beauty was completely natural, Sam thought. Kate was a living, breathing part of this harsh, extreme land that either tore a person apart or built character. Kate had character.

"Yes," she said in a strained voice. She twisted her hands and looked down at them. "Sam, they had an idea. It was this… I mean, no, it's a good idea, I think." Kate took a huge breath and forced herself to look up at his craggy, sun-darkened features. She was so scared. "Rachel thought it would be a good idea to hire a ranch foreman—I mean, to help me—us—because they can't come home for six months to a year from now due to their other commitments. It would be just me. And I don't want to hire just any old person to help me. They felt I should ask you to come to work for us…." She looked away, her voice strained. "We can't pay you what you're worth, but as soon as we got the ranch back on its feet, we could pay you more and more over time."

In that moment, Kate had never wanted anything more than to have Sam say yes to her proposal. The fear that he'd reject her lingered. She still loved him, even if he didn't love her.

Sam took off his hat and ran his fingers slowly across the rim of it. "I see…."

Opening her hands in frustration, Kate blurted, "You

worked here before but it'll be different this time, Sam, I promise. I'm not Kelly. I need someone who's got business savvy about ranching. I've forgotten so much over the years. I need help. It's true that Rachel and Jessica are giving the money, but I can't run this place single-handedly." She earnestly searched his face for some kind of a sign. Right now, Sam's face looked like the craggy cliffs of Oak Creek Canyon—completely unreadable. More panic set in, and she began to talk very fast, stumbling over her words.

"Look, I know I'm an ex-con. I know I have a bad history with people around here. I'm sure you're concerned about your reputation, but I'll try and be good. I'll try to make good decisions and I'll listen. I really will. I know I'm stiff-necked and pop off at the wrong time. But I'm older and I've learned. Please, could you consider it? I'll stay out from underfoot. I'll handle the accounting, the money part of it, and you just tell me what to do and I'll do it—"

Sam gripped her arms. "Kate," he rasped, "stop it. Stop it and listen to me. You don't need to cut yourself down like this."

Helplessly, she stared up at him. "I'm no prize," she said in a choked voice. "I know that. And I'm a hothead. I know that, too. But Sam, this ranch is my *heart.* My *soul.* I'll do *anything* to save it, I'm discovering. But I need someone like you. You're as straight and true as an arrow. You don't lie. You don't play games. I need that kind of man to help me save our ranch…our home…."

His nostrils flared as he stared at Kate's upturned face.

Her cheeks were flushed and he saw the pain and

pleading in her huge, wide eyes—the eyes of a hurt child in some ways, he thought. His fingers tightened slightly on her arms. He had a tough time believing she was asking him to come back to the ranch to help her. For an instant he saw longing in her gaze. For him? How was that possible, after all he'd done to her?

"Rachel said Kelly thought of you as a son. Is that true?"

Sam nodded, still looking into her wide, beautiful eyes.

"Did he mean that? He was so hung up on his grief for our brother...."

Gently, Sam allowed his hands to slide downward. Kate felt good beneath his fingers, though he felt her tense a little. "I think," he admitted, "at some point Kelly realized his grief for Peter had torn the family apart. But by the time he realized that everyone was gone. He told everyone in Sedona I was like a second son to him, and for a couple of years, he was a fairly decent man who didn't hit the bottle too often."

Kate stared up at him. "But the three of us weren't good enough, were we?"

His fingers stilled on her hands. They felt damp and cool in his. "If that was so, why did he make you the owner of the ranch, Kate?"

She avoided his burning look.

"Kelly might not have been one for a lot of truth or honesty, but when it came down to it, I think he was apologizing to you. Maybe letting you know he loved you in his own way by making you executor."

Though pain crawled through her gut, Sam's hands felt comforting on hers. She compressed her lips, her voice low and trembling. "But you said he treated you like a son."

"For a while," Sam reminded her wryly. "He got over that, too."

"How? By hitting the bottle again?"

"'Fraid so, Kate."

"I feel so confused," she whispered unsteadily, and then looked up at him. Kate felt the tenderness of his gray gaze enveloping her like a warm, embracing blanket. She felt his fingers tighten momentarily around hers. "I'm sorry, Sam, I didn't mean to lay all this on you. I know how badly Kelly wanted a son. It's not your fault."

"No insult taken, Kate." He tried to smile, but failed. "I'll give my two-weeks notice today. All right? Stop talking about yourself this way. So you made some mistakes. So what? What's more important is that you've learned from them. I can see that better than anyone else can." He lifted one hand and grazed her flushed cheek with his index finger. The startled look in her eyes caught him off guard. Kate pulled away from him, her hand on her cheek where he'd just touched her. In that moment, Sam realized that she didn't like it—or him. Whatever had been brought to life between them so long ago was really dead and gone.

The pang in his heart felt like a stake had just been driven through it. Settling his hat on his head, he looked up beyond her to the mountain cloaked in pine. Kate and her sisters needed his help. Kate didn't want him back on a personal level—that was obvious. All right; somehow, he'd rein in his feelings for her. He'd work damned hard to keep how he felt about her to himself.

She wanted a foreman, not a lover or possible partner in her life. His mouth compressed. Lowering his gaze, he met her wide, pleading eyes.

"I'll do it, Kate. Did you hear me?"

Still disbelieving, she nodded. "You really will?"

"Yes," he said heavily, turning to go back down the slope, "for you and your sisters."

Kate reached out, wrapping her fingers around his lower arm. "Sam…wait…."

He stood perfectly still. Kate's fingers were warm and soft against his hard flesh. "What is it?"

"If Kelly saw you as a son," she began, searching his somber features, "I don't understand why he didn't leave you the ranch, instead."

Sam pulled out of her grip, because if he didn't, he was going to haul Kate into his arms, crush her against him and take that ripe, soft mouth with his. His lower body ached with need—need of her and only her. More harshly than he intended, he rasped, "Kelly saw me as Peter's replacement, that's all. Don't make anything out of it. I think he loved you, Kate, and leaving you the ranch was the only way he could show you he did."

Kate stood there, still dizzy with realization as Sam walked in long, steady strides down the slope to where the vehicles were parked near the grave site. In her wildest imagination, she couldn't envision Kelly calling any man his son except Peter. Rubbing her brow, she slowly started back down the hill. Her mind spun with more questions than answers. If Kelly had adopted Sam like a son, he'd obviously wanted him to marry one of them, hadn't he? That was silly. They had all left the ranch. What kind of harebrained scheme had Kelly thought up? Sam had worked for Kelly after Odula had died, and Kelly had been hitting the bottle pretty regularly around that time, grieving, she suspected. That was it. Kelly was probably roaring drunk when he'd said those words, that was all.

Still, as Kate stepped carefully around the black rocks sticking up through the carpet of brown pine needles, she was shocked by the implications of her father's words. Who had Kelly seen as Sam's wife? It couldn't have been her, that's for sure. Jessica? Rachel? With a shake of her head, she jammed her thoughts on the matter deep inside her. Right now she had to focus entirely, along with her sisters, on saving the ranch—if the bank would allow it to be saved.

Chapter 6

Kate felt loneliness eating at her. It was exactly one week after Kelly's funeral and her sisters were gone. Already she missed them terribly. Their support as far as the ranch was concerned was enormous. But more than anything, they had helped ease the shame she felt over her recent past. They had listened to her story of what had happened. Jessica had cried. Rachel had told her that something good always comes of bad experience. Kate wasn't so sure. Standing on the porch of her home, watching the sky turn lavender before the sunrise, she wondered how she had remained sane in prison.

This morning, now that the feeding and vetting were done, she wanted to ride out to a particular pasture that needed repairs on the fence. Chet Cunningham had nastily called over and demanded they fix their rotting fence posts and string some new barbed wire to keep their cattle off the Cunningham property. In her leather saddlebags were pliers, wire cutters and heavy leather gloves. Plus a new homeopathic first-aid kit that Rachel had absolutely insisted she take with her. Rachel had even made one for Kate to carry in her truck! Kate had laughed, but she was grateful for Rachel's care.

There were five houses on the ranch property and new guests had arrived two days before Rachel and Jessica had left. Morgan Trayhern, the man who had commanded her brother's company, had been written about glowingly by Peter in a number of his letters to Kelly and Odula before that tragic day he'd died on a hill in Vietnam. Many years later, Morgan had flown in to talk to Kelly about his son's death, and apologize. Now Morgan and his wife, Laura, had asked to come and stay at the guest cabin for a couple of weeks.

Apparently, Morgan and Laura had been involved in a very traumatic kidnapping. Kate was uneasy about the South American drug connection, but had some of her fears eased when she was told a crack Army officer, Major Mike Houston, would be guarding the ranch during their stay. Morgan was recovering from his recent imprisonment and coma. Dr. Ann Parsons from Perseus, Morgan's mercenary outfit, was also on call at the ranch during their stay.

Kate had approved their visit because Rachel had urged her to fulfill the old family obligation. Kate had no reason not to. There were houses available down in the canyon for Morgan and his wife, as well as the major and the doctor. Kate had met Dr. Parsons earlier in the week, and a part of her wanted to mingle more directly because she liked the tall, thin doctor. Maybe it was Ann's large, compassionate blue eyes that drew Kate. Or maybe it was simply because Ann was around Kate's age. Kate had found out via Rachel, who was inquisitive when she met new people, that Ann had been an Air Force flight surgeon and a psychiatrist until Morgan had snatched her from the military and asked her to head up their medical trauma section. Ann was, according to Rachel's whispers, more like a sister to Morgan, which explained in part why she was here at the ranch to take care of him.

Kate walked a long circle around Morgan's other friend, Army Special Forces Major Mike Houston. Part Quechua Indian, with his mother from Mexico, Mike was a big, barrel-chested, square-faced man in his thirties with frosty, dark blue eyes that reminded Kate of a cougar she'd once met up on the Rim. Though Mike's intelligent eyes were not yellow like the cougar's, his huge black pupils seemed to drill right through her, just as the cougar's had on that fateful day. And there was an air of danger as well as mystery around Mike.

Jessica, sensitive as she was, was mesmerized by Mike Houston from the moment she met him. More than once she had drawn Kate aside and whispered that he reminded her a lot of her friend Moyra, who worked at Jessica's company up in Vancouver. Moyra, who was from South America, was a member of the highly secret and mysterious Jaguar Clan, and according to Jessica, Mike had the very same lethal energy around him that Moyra did. The fact that he'd been down in Peru for nearly ten years, working as an American advisor to halt shipments of drugs into the U.S., told Kate a lot about the man.

Kate pooh-poohed a lot of Jessica's psychic information, while Jessica was dying to ask him if he was a member of the Jaguar Clan, but was afraid to. Kate just laughed and shook her head over her little sister's curiosity about the soldier. Though Houston was laid-back, Kate could feel an air of tension around him. It was nothing he broadcast directly, because his mouth would often curve into a casual Texan smile of welcome that would make most folks feel at ease.

As Kate walked to the barn, she saw her two ranch guests out at one of the Arabian broodmare corrals looking at some of the growing foals. Ann and Mike each stood with one foot propped up on the lowest rung of the corral, their arms draped lazily over the uppermost one. Even though they wore jeans and short-sleeved cotton shirts, there was no hiding their military background. As Kate drew nearer, she could see that Mike often stole a swift glance at Ann when she wasn't paying attention. Kate saw the familiar look of longing on his face. She'd seen that expression on Sam's face when he looked at her.

A slight smile tugged at her lips. The major seemed very interested in Ann—man to woman—if she was reading the situation correctly. And why not? Ann was an attractive woman, with shoulder-length hair that fell in a soft pageboy about her oval features. Though the color seemed almost black, Kate saw the reddish gold cast as a slight breeze lifted a few strands in the early morning sunlight. If Ann was aware of Houston's keen appraisal, she didn't show it. Maybe it was a one-way street, Kate thought as she drew close enough to speak to them. Just as her love for Sam had turned out to be. Suddenly, she felt very sorry for Mike Houston. It was hell to fall in love when the other person didn't return the feeling.

"Good morning," Ann exclaimed, turning and smiling at Kate.

"Hi, Ann." Kate nodded in Mike's direction as he turned. That easy Texan smile came to his square face, while those frosty blue eyes warned Kate that this man was a warrior in every sense of the word. "Watching the babies?" she asked, slowing her pace and pointing to the corral, where several foals three to six months old frolicked at their mothers' side.

With a soft laugh, Ann nodded. "I love babies."

"That's good to hear," Mike said enigmatically, turning and watching the foals kicking up their heels.

Ann raised one eyebrow, but said nothing. Her blue eyes sparkled as she met and held Kate's gaze. "How are you doing today?"

Knowing Ann was a psychotherapist as well as a medical doctor, Kate really didn't want to reveal too much. "Okay," she murmured, standing near them, her gaze on the horses in the corral.

"Mmm," Ann said, "one day at a time. I understand."

Opening her mouth, then closing it, Kate realized that Ann *did* understand. If Mike hadn't been nearby, Kate would have been tempted to confide in Ann. But of course, Ann was a guest here. The doctor was here for Morgan and Laura, not her. Changing the subject, Kate said, "Will you go for a ride later?"

Mike twisted his head and grinned. "Us Texas boys

just can't stand not throwing a leg over a good horse." His gaze settled warmly on Ann, who had her back to him. "What about you, Ann? I know you're from Oregon, and you've probably never been around horses much. Would you go riding with me?"

Kate saw the merriment in Ann's eyes as she turned and held the major's teasing stare. She sensed a warmth between them. Maybe Mike's ardor wasn't one-sided after all.

"Just because I'm from Oregon doesn't mean I never saw a horse before."

Mike held up his hands in surrender. "Now, Ann," he drawled good-naturedly, "I didn't say there weren't any horses in Oregon."

Kate grinned. She liked the parry-riposte between them. They made a handsome-looking couple. Mike was like Sam in the looks department, with a rugged, weathered face that had been shaped and molded—sometimes brutally—by life's circumstances. Ann was beautiful in Kate's opinion—even if she was skinny as a rail. That woman could stand some meat on her bones, Kate thought, studying her thin hands—a surgeon's hands. Often Kate had seen her embroidering or knitting out on the front porch of the house where she was staying.

"I think," Ann said seriously, "us folks from Oregon ought to teach you Texas men a lesson in horseback riding." She glanced over at Kate. "Don't you think?"

Laughing, Kate nodded and pointed a finger in Mike's direction. "I think you just stepped into a bear trap, Major Houston."

"Ouch," he jested with a widening smile. "Okay,

the gauntlet has been thrown. I'm just dumb enough to pick it up."

Ann smiled. "You'd pick up any gauntlet that was thrown, Mike, and you know it. And dumb? No, I don't think so. I might accuse you of many things, but that's not one of them."

"Oops, guilty twice over." With a sigh, Houston said, "I guess I'll just have to go saddle up two horses and find out."

"How about if I saddle my own?" Ann said pointedly.

"That's three," Mike said, deflated. "I think I'm getting the message. Not only do women from Oregon know about horses, they know how to saddle them."

Ann winked at Kate. "Not only that, we can ride like the wind, Major."

Kate lifted her hand. "Okay, you two go riding. I'm sure you'll enjoy it. There're two geldings, a chestnut and a bay, on the left side of the barn aisle. They're good, gentle trail horses. I've got some work to do, so I'll see you later."

As Kate walked on past them into the barn, where Cinnamon greeted her from the box stall at the end of the aisle, she heard Mike's deep, husky laughter as he continued to tease Ann. Somehow, Kate knew that Ann would handle that Texas know-it-all cowboy just fine. Mike was intelligent, but Ann had a street smarts that would get him every time.

Kate chuckled, eager to saddle her mare and get to work. Earlier, she'd heard that as soon as Mike was done with his assignment to guard Morgan and Laura for the next two weeks, he was going back down to Peru to continue interdiction activities. She wondered if Ann figured into his future plans.

As Kate reached Cinnamon's stall, the bay mare nickered again and thrust her muzzle over the top, looking for the carrot Kate always carried with her. Feeding the mare, Kate found her thoughts moving back to Ann. Ann had turned her resignation into Perseus before coming to the ranch. Now Kate wondered what a woman like her was going to do after quitting such a high-powered, well-paying job? She'd heard Rachel confide that Ann wanted to work with the poor and underprivileged in Washington, D.C., but Kate wasn't certain that was what the doctor would do.

Patting Cinnamon affectionately, Kate led her out of the box stall, tied her in the aisle and began to brush her down before saddling her. Yes, the day was turning out to be pretty good so far, even if Kate had fence mending staring her in the face for most of it—one of the most dreaded jobs a rancher had to undertake. Still, the day held hope, and this was the first time Kate had actually felt that particular feeling for a long, long time. What would make her day complete would be to see Sam—but that was impossible.

Absorbing the bright blue sky, the dry desert air, the soft scent of scrub juniper that dotted the rocky, red clay and sand, Kate felt peace settling around her. The rhythmic movement of her surefooted horse, the chirping of birds hiding in the dark green arms of the junipers, conspired to make her feel a momentary trickle of happiness. Of late, she'd been slightly less numb inside, which was amazing to Kate. She'd thought her feelings, pulverized by the trial and prison, were dead and gone. Rachel had told her the remedy *natrum muriaticum* would help bring them back. But whether it was the natural remedy or her time on the ranch that had brought her senses alive again, Kate hung on to each fleeting feeling as it arose in her.

The fence line curved up a slope covered with yellowed chaparral, prickly pear and slender stalks of dead grass. The black lava rocks scattered throughout the region poked up through the red clay ground, which was almost as hard as they were. Kate frowned as she noticed some broken strands of wire. Fence mending was hard, dirty work and she was glad the morning was cool. Doing this kind of work in hundred-degree summer heat was blistering and sapping. It wasn't her favorite duty, anyway.

Today Kate wore a red flannel, long-sleeved shirt over a white tank top and a pair of Levi's that were finally getting broken in. Jessica had gone into Sedona one day last week and bought Kate seven new pairs of Levi's, seven flannel shirts in a rainbow of colors, heavy socks to wear with the new pair of cowboy boots Rachel had bought her, and a brand-new black Stetson cowboy hat with a wide brim to protect her face and neck from the powerful sunlight. They'd also purchased several skirts and two dresses, though Kate didn't know when she'd wear them. Her sisters had always been good to her, but now she felt as if she was truly being taken care of by them. Maybe that's why she missed them so much—they were nurturing like their mother had been. How come she wasn't that way? Or maybe she had been at one time, but life had beaten it out of her? Kate was unsure.

Cresting the hill, Kate pulled her horse to a stop and dismounted. The Arabian had been taught to ground tie, which meant that when Kate dropped the reins to the ground, the horse wouldn't move. Pulling on thick, protective gloves, she set to work on the twisted, broken barbed wire. Off in the distance, perhaps half a mile away, she saw another fence crew working—from the Cunningham side of the property.

Kate slowed her step and narrowed her eyes. Her heart sped up. It was Sam and three other wranglers out fixing their fence line. For an instant, she stood very still, transfixed by Sam's seemingly larger-than-life form. He was sitting astride a big, rangy chestnut gelding with four white socks and a white blaze on its face. The blue-and-black checked shirt Sam wore emphasized the breadth of his shoulders and powerful chest. A red bandanna was around his neck, and he wore a denim jacket that matched the color of his Levi's.

Swallowing convulsively, Kate forced herself to get to work. Picking up one end of the barbed wire, she took a twelve-inch strand and twisted it around the broken part. Leaning down, she retrieved the other rusty end and connected them. Though the whole fence line needed to be replaced, as Chet had nastily informed her on the phone, this would have to do for now. At least, until she had more help. Since Sam had given his notice to Old Man Cunningham, he hadn't been over to the Donovan ranch. She couldn't blame him for being cautious. That old bear Cunningham would probably fire him on the spot for disloyalty.

How she missed Sam! How many times had she awakened in the morning, thought of him working with her at the ranch again, and gone into an absolute panic? Often during her twelve-hour workdays the thought of spending more time with him sent her into a spasm of euphoria mixed with fear.

As she connected a second strand of barbed wire, her sensitive ears picked up the sound of a galloping horse. Kneeling on the ground, she finished the connection and then looked up.

It was Sam. Her hands froze on the wire as she watched him riding up the slope toward her like a man born to the saddle. He rode with such ease and grace, his upper body absolutely still, his hips moving with the rhythmic motion of the horse, his long, powerful legs wrapped strongly around the animal. Slowly, Kate forced herself to stand up. She saw the hardness on Sam's face and in those cool gray eyes barely visible below the brim of his black Stetson.

Just getting to see him was wonderfully healing for Kate. She moved to her mare and took off her gloves, stuffing them back in the saddlebag. As Sam drew his horse to a halt, she managed a lopsided smile of greeting.

"Great minds think alike?" she asked, pulling out a thermos of hot coffee.

Sam tipped his hat to Kate. Her cheeks were flushed from work, from the chill of the November air, and her black hair curled around her face, slightly damp at the temples. Did Kate know how beautiful and wild she looked? Sam wondered as he dismounted.

"I think so," he said with a brief smile. Searching

her large, blue eyes, Sam saw some of the darkness he'd noticed at the funeral was gone. That was good. He watched as she poured some steaming hot coffee into the thermos cup. Her hand shook a little. "Chet told me he'd called you up a couple of days ago, griping about this fence line." Sam looked back at his hardworking crew down below. "Thought I'd get this done before I left. I've got two other crews laying new wire and post about a mile down the line."

"He wasn't exactly nice about it," she agreed. "I'm glad your men are fixing the rest of it. I wasn't looking forward to doing this all day." Kate offered him the cup of coffee. He shook his head, but thanked her. Nervously, she sipped the hot liquid, almost burning her mouth. It never failed to amaze her how ruggedly handsome Sam was. Sweat stood out on his furrowed brow and his gray eyes were fathomless, as always. Kate wished she could tell how Sam felt by looking into his eyes, but he was like that rock canyon wall—unreadable. As she stared at his mouth, her lower body tingled in memory of his kisses so long ago. Kate had never forgotten his touch, his strength, or his tenderness with her. For a man of his size and power, Sam had always been exceedingly gentle. She had given her virginity to him and he had cherished that moment with her as something not only special, but sacred. Kate had felt like the most loved woman in the world.

Coloring, she looked away and pretended to be watching the crew below. It was a good thing Sam couldn't read her mind! What would he think of her, a foolish young girl in high school who still had a heartbreaking crush on him when she was old enough to know better? The coffee burned her tongue. She frowned.

Cinnamon's soft snort made her glance toward Sam. He was gazing at her. Instantly, her heart slammed against her ribs. His gray eyes were narrowed, thoughtful and burning with that look—the look she'd never forgotten from her youthful days with him. It was a smoldering look, of banked coals ready to explode into life. It was a look that had come into his eyes when he wanted her, wanted to make hot, passionate, unbridled love with her.

She had to be crazy. Kate chided herself and dipped her head, focusing her attention on drinking her coffee. Sam didn't desire her. That was the past. She'd misread the intent in his eyes, that's all.

"How are you getting along without your sisters?" Sam asked, stroking Cinnamon's mane as he stood beside the mare. He'd seen high color come to Kate's cheeks as she'd dodged his look. Damn, he hadn't meant to give away his real feelings for her. Did she notice just a little how much influence she still held over him? Even though she was dressed in work clothes, they could not hide her femininity, the graceful way she moved her hands or quirked her full lips. No, beneath that wide hat brim was a mature woman's face. A face he wanted to touch with his fingers and retrace to see if he remembered it as well as he thought he had.

Kate shrugged and kept a safe distance from Sam. "I miss them terribly."

"I was hoping the three of you would get along." Sam used his thumb to push his own hat higher on his head.

"Any word from the bank on what they've decided to do with the foreclosure?"

With a slight smile, Kate turned to him. "Thanks to Rachel's diplomatic skills, she managed to talk the bank president into not foreclosing. My sisters have pitched in seventy thousand dollars against the hundred thousand that's owed. I've got a buyer for half the beef herd and I'm sending twenty Arabian yearlings to an auction that will be held down in Phoenix in a couple of weeks. I'm hoping we'll get another twenty thousand."

"Smart move," Sam said. He watched her toss away the last few drops in the plastic thermos lid. "That's good news."

"The best," Kate agreed, realizing she had to put the cap back on the thermos in the saddlebag that Sam was standing next to. She moved slowly toward him. It was then that she noticed the left side of his jaw looked a little swollen and bruised.

"What happened?" she asked, pointing at his hard jawline. "Did you tell Old Man Cunningham you were giving your two weeks' notice and he nailed you with a right cross?" It would be just like him to do that, Kate thought.

Sam saw the wariness in Kate's eyes as she hesitantly approached him and her horse. He stepped back to give her some breathing room and instantly saw relief in her gaze. That hurt him and he wrestled with the pain. "It was Chet," he admitted. "The kid's a hothead of the first order. Cunningham and I got into an argument after I told him I was giving my notice, and Chet walked in on it. The kid took a swing at me and connected."

Kate saw merriment in Sam's gray eyes as she

quickly twisted the cap back on the thermos and tucked it down into the saddlebag. “Somehow, knowing you, Chet got the worst of it in the long run.” She pulled her leather gloves back on.

Chuckling, Sam moved around the head of the mare, his hands resting on his hips as he surveyed his line crew. “He’s nursing a broken nose.”

Laughing, Kate went back to work on the third strand of barbed wire. “Well deserved, I’m sure. He’s the youngest?”

“Yeah,” Sam rumbled, kneeling down beside her and picking up the broken end of a strand of barbed wire. “Mean as a green rattler.” Green rattlesnakes were the most poisonous of all the rattlesnake species in Arizona.

“He was always that way,” Kate murmured as they worked together. Their fingers met briefly. Kate inhaled sharply and dropped the wire. How silly of her! Scooping it back up, she took the other end Sam proffered. He was so dizzyingly close, she had to force herself to remain calm as she twisted the ends together.

“Chet was the youngest and the most spoiled,” Sam continued. He watched her work with quick, smooth efficiency. “For someone who hasn’t been doing ranch work for a long time, you haven’t forgotten much, have you?”

Laughing a little, Kate shook her head. “Listen, so much has come back to me since I got home, Sam, it isn’t even funny. I thought when I ran away at eighteen that I’d forget all of this.” She slanted a glance at him, amazed at how open and readable his face was right now. The flecks of silver in his gray eyes warmed her and so did the careless grin shadowing that strong, wonderful mouth of his.

"You never really left, Gal." Damn! He hadn't meant to call her again by the affectionate name he'd given her so long ago. Sam saw his words have an immediate effect on Kate. Her hands froze in midair for a second. And then she ducked her head and quickly finished connecting the barbed wire. Scrambling to cover his error, he added huskily, "Your heart and soul are here, like you said before. I don't know too many people who can cut those parts out of themselves and survive very long." He eased to his feet and stepped back a little to give her the breathing room she obviously needed.

Shaken with longing, Kate stood up and brushed off her dusty, red-clay-covered knees. "I guess part of me didn't leave the ranch. Not really." She removed a glove and pushed several curls away from her temple. Sam had called her his pet name, Gal. The word had rolled off his tongue like hot honey across her screaming, sensitized nerves.

Moving over to his gelding and picking up the reins, he said, "I'd better get back. Is there anything you'll need in the next week before I come over?"

Touched by his concern, Kate shook her head. "I just need to clone myself and be two people, is all," she said, laughing softly. Sam moved with the ease of a man born to the saddle as he mounted his chestnut gelding. He sat tall and proud in the saddle, his shoulders back, his posture like that of a military officer. Yet there was such ease and grace about him even then.

"Look," Sam said more seriously, "if you run into

trouble or need help, Kate, call me? You've got my phone number."

"Yes, I do. I'll be fine, Sam." She put the pliers back into the saddlebag.

He liked to watch Kate move. Nothing was wasted in her motions. She was always thinking, and he liked that about her, too. Ranch life was hard and ranchers learned to conserve their energy, finding the shortest routes, watching where they put their feet because rattlers abounded in the area. Even in November, which was hotter than usual this year, some rattlers were still out and about instead of crawling in their holes to hibernate the winter away.

Sam paused before turning his horse toward the Bar C. "I may be out of line," he said, catching her gaze, "but I'd like to take you to dinner, Kate." He saw her eyes grow huge with shock. Girding himself for her answer, he pushed on. "I can't take time out from my normal ranching duties right now or Old Man Cunningham will pitch a fit. I'm free after eight. How about dinner down at the Muse Restaurant in Sedona? They've got the best New Orleans lamb in Coconino County. We could talk business strategy. I've got some ideas, some plans I'd like to discuss with you before I come over as foreman."

Her heart skittered. Her mouth went dry. Resting her hand on the horn of the saddle, Kate gazed up at Sam's tall form silhouetted against the sky, and felt warmth sheet through her. "Well..." she murmured, "I don't know.... I haven't been to Sedona since I got out of... since I got home."

Sam understood Kate's hesitancy. Her prison experience was so fresh and she was afraid people would look at her, whisper hurtful things. "Kate, I don't dare come over to your ranch right now. I need a neutral place. I don't need another dogfight with Chet, which will happen if he finds out I was over at the Donovan Ranch."

"I see...." She had to say yes, she realized. This was for the good of the ranch. "Okay," she said a little breathlessly. "I'll meet you there for dinner at eight tonight?" The thought of going out with Sam made her giddy. The prospect was scary. And wonderful.

He tipped his hat, the corner of his mouth moving into a slight smile. "It's a date, Gal. I'll see you then."

Pressing her hand against her pounding heart, Kate watched Sam turn the horse around and trot back down the hill toward his crew. What had she just done? It was for the ranch, she chided sternly. It wasn't a date. But Sam had just called it that. And he'd called her by that endearment, Gal. Her hands shook as she picked up the reins and mounted Cinnamon.

There was no sense riding down the slope to repair the rest of the wire, because Sam's crew was coming to fix it. She turned her mare around and went in the opposite direction. There was plenty of wire to be fixed at the other end. As she rode that way, her mind spun. She had refused to leave the ranch last week when Rachel and Jessica wanted to take her shopping in Sedona. Kate just didn't want prying eyes on her. She was too well-known, her past too fresh and herself too raw to handle those accusing stares she knew she'd get.

Now she was glad her sisters had purchased several skirts and two dresses for her during their shopping spree. At the time, she'd told them the new clothes would probably gather dust in her closet, that she really didn't want to go to town or dress up. Well, now she did. Less than a week later! Kate shook her head. Which outfit would she wear tonight?

Sam couldn't stop staring at Kate as she walked into the Muse Restaurant promptly at eight p.m. She looked stunning in a dark brown corduroy skirt that hung to her ankles and a dark blue denim jacket with deerskin fringe hanging from each shoulder. The jacket was tailored so that it emphasized Kate's slim waist, and there was ivory-colored hairbone pipe, four inches long, on each side of the elk buttons. Around her throat was a five-strand hairbone-pipe choker, and on her ears, she wore long elk-bone earrings decorated with red, blue, yellow and black beads, the Eastern Cherokee colors. The dangling earrings only emphasized Kate's long, slender neck. As she walked proudly, the fringe on her gold deerskin shoulder bag swung gently. Sam smiled. She still looked like an Indian, even with her short hair.

If Kate was worried about other people, it didn't show.

Her shoulders were back, her chin lifted with pride, and her sky blue eyes glistened with gold flecks. He took off his hat as she approached the lobby where he'd waited. As she stepped up to him, he caught a faint whiff of a flowery fragrance. Even though Kate wore no makeup, she was the prettiest woman in the very popular restaurant.

He grinned. "Are you the same Kate Donovan I saw this morning stringing barbed wire?" he teased.

Breathlessly, Kate gazed up at him. "I clean up pretty

good—is that what you're saying?" She gripped the deerskin handbag hard, her knuckles white, she was sure. Caught between worrying what the Sedona townspeople thought of her and Sam's glittering appraisal of her, she felt nothing but panic. Stepping closer to him, however, she felt protected in some ways. In other ways, she did not.

Hat in his left hand, he placed his right hand on the small of her back as the hostess hurried over to seat them. "Gal, you're decked out like a show filly for a class A horse show and you just took grand prize."

She laughed softly at his drawled comment. "Only another rancher would know that was a compliment, Sam McGuire." How feminine she felt!

The look he gave her, that smoldering gray gaze, made her feel deliciously sensual in her new clothes. As they followed the hostess through the restaurant, part of Kate's worry about prying eyes melted away beneath Sam's steadying hand. His touch was healing. Provocative. Necessary to her. Miraculously, as they were seated in a black leather booth in a dimly lit corner, Kate felt her fears of going out in public abate to a large degree.

Sam ordered hot coffee and so did she as they looked over the extensive menu of food reputed to be the best New Orleans cooking in the Southwest. Glancing at him over the edge of the menu, Kate studied Sam. He wore a tobacco brown suede blazer, a crisp white cotton shirt, a bolo tie with a dark green, crystalline stone Kate recognized to be diopside, a mineral found in copper mines. His dark hair gleamed in the light, and his face was clean shaven. He'd obviously taken pains to be at his best. Even his nails were blunt cut and scrupulously clean though a cowboy's hands were usually rough and callused, with the red clay of the Arizona desert under his nails. When he'd guided her to the table earlier, she'd inhaled the odor of soap and that special scent of him as a man.

The low lighting in the quiet but busy restaurant made Kate feel as if she and Sam were the only two people in the world. As she circumspectly looked around, she realized that she didn't recognize anyone. That made her feel relief. No prying eyes. No accusations. Just Sam and her. Together. Alone.

Setting the menu aside, she laughed a little nervously. "I feel like déjà vu."

Sam looked up from his menu. "Oh?"

Shrugging delicately, Kate whispered, "Like we were teenagers again. Kids. Like so many years hadn't gone by."

He put the menu down and held her warm blue gaze. He saw such life in Kate's eyes. And, just as he had in the past, he reached out, his fingers capturing hers. "Some things time can't destroy," he told her in a low voice laced with feeling. "What we had, Kate, was good. The best. I never forgot it. I never forgot you."

Chapter 7

As inconspicuously as possible, Kate pressed her palms flat against the linen napkin in her lap to get rid of the nervous dampness. Sam was too close, too virile, and too many memories of what had been—and would never be in the future—were flowing unchecked. Every time she looked at his scarred hands as they played with his coffee cup, she recalled his hands upon her, loving her; she recalled soaring with him in the beauty of their untrammeled passion. Somehow she had to put a stop to this flood of memories and feelings.

"Is Old Man Cunningham making your last two weeks miserable?" she asked.

Sam smiled a little, enjoying the way the shadows lovingly caressed Kate's oval face. "Chet's the one acting out for his daddy. He's got a busted nose, so I think he'll back off now, but with him, I'm never sure."

"A hothead is a hothead," Kate said wryly, managing a one-cornered smile.

"You're not a hothead, Kate. You're a passionate woman who lives her beliefs and isn't afraid to put her money where her mouth is. Chet, on the other hand, is a spoiled kid gone sour. His daddy has contributed to his continuing ways."

She sighed. "That was one of the things I was worried about when I came back here—what people would think of me. When I realized you were going to pick me up, I was so frightened." Kate met and held his warm gray gaze. "That was silly of me, looking back on it now. You've always given people a lot of rope to hang themselves with. Even back in high school, you never bad-mouthed anyone. You never said they were useless or bad or—"

"You thought I'd think you were bad, Kate, because you went to prison?"

Avoiding his gaze, she nodded. She placed her hands around the coffee cup, her voice low. "I thought the worst. Kelly always said I had a bad streak in me. He blamed my rebellious nature on my mother's side of the family."

Reaching out, Sam laid his hand over hers. "Kate, life makes people misbehave. They aren't born 'bad.' Take a look at that black stallion of yours. Over the years, when Kelly was drunk, he beat that poor animal. When I was there, I put a stop to it, but the stud is mean now, and he doesn't trust humans. That horse is seen as 'bad' by an outsider, maybe, but knowing that Gan got the tar beat out of him, we know he isn't really." Sam smiled and caught her wary gaze.

"Same can be said of you. Kelly had a lot of failings and he usually blamed them on other people when he could. You were firstborn, and you got it in the neck. Don't let him calling you bad keep rubbing you raw."

She pulled her hand from beneath his, the need for him overpowering and heady. "I went to prison, Sam. That will be with me until the day I die. There's plenty of folks around here that won't let me forget it."

"So? Are you going to live your life for them or live life for yourself?"

He was right. She took a nervous sip of the coffee. "I'm running scared. I'm jumpier than I ought to be. What I need to do is forget about what other people think and put that energy into saving the ranch."

Leaning back in the chair, Sam nodded. "That's the spirit. You have time now, Kate. And I'm sure there will be folks who say things about you, or look at you funny, but just keep your back straight, your shoulders squared and walk proud. If you don't, this will destroy you."

"I know…."

Sam leaned forward and placed his hands on the table. The waitress came and they gave their orders. He was privately pleased Kate ordered the same meal he did—lamb, mashed sweet potatoes and a salad. After the salads arrived, he moved to another topic that interested him.

"You know, I don't know much about your sisters' businesses. You said they're coming back to the ranch six months and a year from now, but what will they do?"

Kate played with her salad, her appetite gone. She nibbled on the romaine lettuce half-heartedly. "Rachel is a homeopath. That's an alternative medicine that's practiced around the world and gaining popularity here in the U.S.—again. Rachel said that one out of every five doctors here by the turn of the century was a homeopath. And then the AMA came in and things got more political. There was squabbling in the ranks of homeopaths, and they lost out. By 1940, there were very few left. Now," Kate said more brightly, "there's a goodly number of them in the U.S."

"She's coming back to hang out her shingle in Sedona?" Sam ventured. He enjoyed Kate's company. She was relaxing now and he saw the eagerness and excitement dancing in her eyes.

"Not exactly," Kate hedged, placing the half-eaten salad aside. "Rachel's had this dream of founding a clinic for the poor and the elderly. She wants to practice from the ranch. We've got one building, a real old one, that needs a lot of work, but it could, over time, be turned into a clinic."

"And that's how she'll make money?"

"Kind of… She has had a thriving practice over in London and gets paid well for teaching at Sheffield College. The clinic is going to be on a donation basis, so Rachel won't earn a whole lot."

Sam frowned. "Is her idealism getting in the way of reality? If you three ladies don't pool your resources and add to a common till, you won't be able to keep that place afloat. There're too many maintenance costs involved. The cattle—"

Holding up her hand, she said, "I know, I know…." Kate looked up at the ceiling briefly. "This is Rachel's dream. She's worked a long time to make it a reality. I can't just tell her no." Looking at his scowling features, she added, "I was hoping that when you got over here, you and I could sit down and create a long-range business plan on how to continue making the monthly mortgage payments on that land Kelly bought when we were kids. That acreage is what is hurting us financially. The ranch is paid for in full, but that land isn't."

"Running a ranch daily takes a lot of cash flow," Sam said. "Vet bills alone will eat you alive if something goes through a cattle or horse herd."

"Or drought, like we have right now," Kate agreed. "If we didn't have water rights to Oak Creek, I don't know how the cattle would fare."

"You'd have to sell them off or have them die of thirst," Sam told her.

Kate nodded. "It's funny how all this knowledge of ranching is coming back to me, Sam. I thought I'd forgotten it." She held up her hands. "Look, blisters. My hands have grown soft over time."

He captured one hand. Her fingers were long and he saw red blisters here and there on her palms. "You've been digging post holes?" Many of the main corrals at the ranch were in dire need of being replaced.

With a laugh, she nodded. "Sure shows, doesn't it?"

Grinning, he reluctantly released her hand. "Ranching isn't for wimps," he agreed. Looking up, he saw the waitress coming with their main course. "I don't know about you, Gal, but I'm starved. Let's dig in."

Kate hadn't realized how much fun she would have with Sam tonight. It was as if they were teenagers in love again. He spun story after story over their delicious meal of lamb chops. Sometimes she laughed so hard her stomach hurt.

Sam waved his fork in the air. "Have you seen a black cat hanging around your barn yet?"

Wiping her eyes, Kate said, "Yes, he's like a shadow."

"That's One Ear. I don't know how old he is, but he's been the ranch mascot since the time I was there. I saw him the other day and was surprised he was still alive. One Ear hunts pack rats, exclusively. I don't see many cats living too long doing that, but he's made it an art form."

Kate knew that Arizona had some of the largest rats in the nation—pack rats. They could get to be the size of a cottontail rabbit, and cats often lost the battle to them as a result. Pack rats were a real problem, especially when they found an entrance beneath a house or up into an attic. They would chew through wiring, setting a house on fire while electrocuting themselves, or eat through a wooden frame and drywall. They were highly destructive, not to mention disease carriers of the first order.

"I'm glad One Ear is around."

"You should be. That cat is ornery, but then, hunting pack rats has made him that way. I remember one time Kelly was drunker than a skunk and he weaved his way out to the barn to feed the horses. I guess One Ear was up in the rafters of the barn, going hell-bent-for-leather after a pack rat. Well, the rat lost its balance going across a beam that Kelly was under, and it landed on him. About a split second later, One Ear landed on Kelly's back to get to the pack rat. I heard Kelly shouting and cursing a blue streak and went running out to the barn to find out what was going on."

Sam chuckled. "Kelly was lying in the aisle of the

stable area, twisting, squirming and shouting. One Ear was leaping and hissing. What had happened, as near as I can put together, was the pack rat landed on Kelly's shoulder and made a dive down the collar of his shirt. That black cat was biting, swiping and clawing at Kelly's backside, where the pack rat was trying to hide. Kelly was shrieking and hitting at his back with his hand, and rolling around on the floor, trying to get the cat to quit attacking him."

Kate put her hands to her mouth to stop from laughing too loudly. She loved Sam's face as he told a story; he lost that usual hardness, that implacable look. His gray eyes danced with humor; his mouth hitched into a grin.

"What happened?"

"Well," Sam drawled, wiping his mouth with a napkin and putting his plate aside, "I saw the pack rat zoom out the bottom of Kelly's shirt, which was in shreds at this point from One Ear's clawing attacks. It took off under a box stall and so did the cat. Kelly was lying there in a daze, swearing. His shirt was in shreds. He was a little bloodied, so I took him to the water trough outside and I threw him in it."

"You threw Kelly in it?" Kate's eyes grew round at the picture that presented. Few people ever stood up to Kelly. Obviously, Sam had.

"Better believe it. I got some soap, took off what was left of that rag of a shirt and scrubbed the hell out of his back while he cursed and swore some more."

"Kelly wasn't known to be grateful to anyone," Kate said. "Did he get any diseases from that pack rat?"

"No, just a tread-marked backside was all. After

that, he hated One Ear. He wanted to shoot the cat, but I wouldn't let him. When I got fired, I thought about trying to find One Ear and take him with me, but he's wild and won't go up to a man. It was nice to see him still at the ranch."

"Yes," Kate said with a chuckle, "he survived Kelly, too."

A deep voice interrupted their banter. "Well, well, what's this? The ex-con out on the town?"

Kate's heart squeezed in sudden terror. She looked up toward the source of the male voice. Chet Cunningham stood there leaning against the booth, his nose bandaged, both his eyes blackened. He held a beer in one hand, his dark gaze stripping her.

Sam lifted his head and looked up at Cunningham. "Chet," he said in a low, warning growl, "I'd suggest you amble back to the bar where you came from and leave us alone."

Smirking, Chet raised the bottle to his lips and took a good long gulp from it. Wiping his mouth with the back of his hand, he grinned wickedly. "Now, McGuire, you might be boss on the ranch, but here you're nothing. I don't have to do what you want." He straightened up, lightly touching the bandage on his nose. "You broke it."

"I'll break it again if you don't leave."

Kate's heart pounded in her chest. She felt shaky. Darting a look around, she realized that most of the people in the restaurant were staring at them. Her worst fear had just come true.

Chet took another swig of the beer. "Big, tough bastard, aren't you, McGuire?" His lips lifted in a sneer as he leaned over the booth. "Well, I'm not afraid of you, mister. I never was." He glared at Kate. "You two rattlers deserve one another. Katie Donovan," he crowed in a loud voice. "Man, she's gonna blow up Sedona now that she's home." He weaved backward, caught himself and leaned over the booth again. "Blowin' up a nuke plant, huh? Man alive, you're a terrorist of the first order. Who you gonna take care of next? The bank that owns your broken-down ranch? The hay-and-feed company Kelly owes thousands of dollars to? Hell, you're just like your old man—no good…."

At that instant, Kate felt rather than saw Sam get to his feet. He reached out and grabbed Chet by the collar of his shirt.

"That's enough," Sam snarled, spinning the younger cowboy around.

Kate saw Chet lift the beer bottle in reaction. She opened her mouth to scream a warning. Too late! She saw the bottle smash against Sam's upraised hand as he protected himself from the coming blow. Glass shattered everywhere. Within moments, Sam had dragged Cunningham to the side door and pushed him out.

Hurrying, Kate left the booth and followed them.

"You son of a bitch!" Chet roared, sprawled out on the concrete sidewalk. "I'll kill you!"

McGuire leaned over him and poked him in the shoulder with his index finger. "You get up and I'll break the rest of your face, Chet. Lie there and get a hold of yourself." Breathing hard, he saw Kate approaching. Damn!

Chet glared up at him. "You're a dead man, McGuire. Deader than hell. You just don't know it yet."

Pain began to drift up Sam's left hand where the beer

bottle had struck him full force. Chet had been aiming at the side of his head, and the cowboy could have taken out Sam's left eye if he hadn't reacted when he did. He saw that Chet's round face was red and flushed. Cunningham was so damned drunk he couldn't get up if he tried. More important, Sam worried about Kate, who stood slightly apart, her hand pressed against her mouth, her eyes huge with terror—and pain. A lot of pain. Damn Chet and his big mouth.

Turning, Sam took Kate by the arm and gently steered her toward the parking lot at the rear of the restaurant. He'd get her to the truck, then go back, pick up his Stetson and pay the bill. "Come on," he said, "let's go."

Kate hurried to keep up with his long stride. "I'm sorry, Sam. This was my fault."

"Like hell," he muttered, opening the truck door for her. "Chet's been moody all his life. Me leaving the ranch has made him meaner than usual." He searched her pale features, her broken spirit obvious in her darkened eyes. "I'm sorry this happened, Kate. I really am. Consider the source. Chet's drunk. He's stupid."

"I saw the other people. I saw their faces...."

Angrily, Sam whispered, "Kate, let it go! Stop giving your power away to Chet or anyone else who might think less of who you really are." His adrenaline was making him shaky. He was furious at Chet for hurting Kate. "I'll be back in a minute. Just sit here." He opened the door to his pickup.

Kate nodded and climbed in. She clutched the deerskin purse in her lap. With the door closed, the silence inside the truck was suffocating. Closing her eyes, she tried to deal with the pain that Chet's attack had brought up. In a few minutes, she opened her eyes and saw Sam's large, dark figure emerging from the restaurant. Chet was still lying on the sidewalk, probably passed out. Sam moved around him, heading for the truck, and Kate tried to pull herself together. She didn't want Sam to know just how shaken she really was. He climbed in the driver's seat, and in the gloomy light, she saw his left hand. Dark blood was streaming down his fingers.

"You're hurt," she said in a choked voice, taking several tissues from her purse.

Sam shut the truck door. "Yeah, he got me with that bottle," he grumbled, holding his hand up and looking at it more closely. The blood dripped onto his Levi's. When Kate's hands captured his and she pressed the tissue to the cut, all the anger went out of him. She was leaning against him, close and warm, and her care and attention pulled the plug on his fury toward Chet. Inhaling sharply, he could smell that light, flowery fragrance she wore on her skin. Her soft, thick hair brushed against his jaw as she peered closely at the wound. He felt her breast press against his right arm, her thigh against his. Biting back a groan, he sat very still as she worked to stop the bleeding. His body ached. For her. All of her. In the years since he'd seen her, Kate had matured physically. Now he was wildly aware of her firm flesh against his, the womanly strength, yet incredibly gentle touch of her hands on his.

He hungered for her. As she unbuttoned the cuff of his shirtsleeve and pushed it up his arm, he wanted to lean across those scant inches between them and kiss her exposed neck.

"Sam, this is bad," Kate said, wobbling. "That beer bottle sliced you open. We have to get you to the hospital to get this cleaned up and stitched."

Groaning, but not because of his cut, he muttered, "Let me wrap it in a handkerchief and you can clean it up once we get home."

Kate twisted her head toward him. How close Sam was! She stared, mesmerized for a second, her gaze on his strong, compressed mouth. She saw dots of perspiration on his upper lip. As his gaze lifted and she met his dark gray eyes, a bolt of heat surged through her. Her lips parted. How badly she wanted to kiss him, to feel his mouth once again on hers. And then, just as quickly, she pulled away. How selfish of her at a moment like this—when Sam was hurt—to be thinking of such things.

"Give me your hanky," she said, moving away from him. "And let me drive. You can make it up to me tomorrow by driving me back to pick up my car."

Sam didn't argue, the cut in his hand hurting like hell itself. He climbed out of the pickup, made a couple of tight wraps around his hand with the handkerchief and allowed Kate to climb into the driver's seat. He saw the worry on her face.

"This isn't anything, Kate," he protested as he climbed into the passenger seat.

"Yes, it is," she whispered fiercely. Backing the truck out of the parking lot and driving into the November darkness, Kate felt some of her trembling abate. With both hands on the wheel, she drove away from Sedona. Away from all the staring, prying eyes that had judged her. And Sam had defended her. Now gossip would spread about him. His reputation was unsullied up to now, she was sure. He didn't deserve to be dragged down in the mud because of her own bad name.

She wanted to get back home just as soon as possible. At least at the ranch, there was safety.

"This is going to hurt," Kate warned Sam as she sat down at the kitchen table. Stitching up animals was one thing. Doing the same for a human being unstrung her a little. Sam sat there, his coat off, the sleeve of his shirt rolled up haphazardly on his dark, hairy arm so that she could get a good look at the damage the beer bottle had done.

Sam watched Kate's face. Her brow puckered and her mouth thinned as she gently laid his hand on a clean white towel. Most of the bleeding had stopped by the time they'd gotten home, but a good two-inch gash was laid open on the outside edge of his left hand. He felt the soft coolness of her fingers against the throbbing heat of his hand.

"You know," he told her huskily as she prepared to stitch the wound closed, "every time you touch me, Kate, the pain in my hand goes away."

Taking a deep breath, Kate put on thin surgical gloves so that she wouldn't infect the just-cleaned wound. "I think this cut is making you loco, Sam McGuire."

He grinned a little. "No, Gal, its you—your healing touch." *It's always been you,* he thought. When Kate lifted her head and looked at him, he saw tears in her eyes. She quickly forced them back and concentrated on the task at hand. Sam decided to remain quiet and watch her work. There was such gentle delicacy to Kate.

He wished that she would realize that about herself. Kelly had really hurt her as a child growing up. One day, Sam hoped she'd let those tough, outer walls dissolve so that the old Kate, the real Kate he'd known and loved so fiercely, would emerge.

As she began to stitch up his wound, Sam said in a low voice, "You haven't lost your touch, Kate. Maybe you don't recall this, but I remember times you took care of sick and ailing animals and they always survived. Your two sisters are both in the healing arts. But you're like Odula—you heal with your touch. You don't need a homeopathic remedy or a natural essence." He smiled a little, enjoying her focused care. "A healer. That's you, Kate."

Grimacing, Kate kept her attention on the process. Sam's hand was so large, his flesh work-hardened. She felt each of the thick calluses that over time had built up on the palm of his hand and his fingers.

"Right now, I'd like to punch Chet Cunningham in the nose. What he did was wrong, Sam. You're going to be laid up with this hand a good three weeks. He really hamstrung you."

"Not too much work for one-handed cowboys, is there?"

She glanced up and caught his boyish grin. Returning to her task, she muttered, "Not really. Old Man Cunningham will probably give you walking papers sooner rather than later."

"So?" he teased. "Just lets me come over here sooner and be a crippled cowboy helping you."

She laughed and felt the tension draining away from her. "No kidding! No post hole digging for you."

"But I can use the time and work out a solid business plan for you."

Kate shook her head. "Sam McGuire, I swear if the good Lord gave you mud to work with, you'd find a way to market and sell mud pies and make a profit doing it!"

Chuckling, he leaned back and closed his eyes. Kate's touch was more than healing, it was opening up his heart and letting him hope for a future with her. Not that he deserved a second chance. Sam knew he didn't, but his heart cried out for her still. "Now, Gal, there's always a silver lining to every cloud. You know that."

Glumly, Kate shook her head as she finished. Taking the white roll of gauze, she carefully wrapped the wound. "Hope? I lost that a long time ago, Sam." Soon his hand was swathed in a protective dressing. Pleased with her efforts, Kate sat up and took the plastic gloves off and dropped them in the waste basket. In the bright light of the kitchen, Sam looked a little washed out. She suspected he was in a lot more pain than he let on.

"Rachel gave me this homeopathic first-aid kit," she said, opening it up on the kitchen counter. Pulling out a small booklet, she opened it to read. "She said there's information on remedies that I could use around the ranch, both on people and animals. Let me see if there's one here for you."

Sam sat there, his long legs sprawled out. "My hand feels pretty good now."

"Hmm, here's something." Kate brought the kit over to the table and sat down. "It says for cuts to use calendula. Interesting," she said looking up at him. "That's a flower something like a marigold. Anyway, calendula is for open cuts and lacerations. It helps them heal up faster. The only time it can't be used is in a puncture wound."

"Well, give me some," Sam urged. "I don't want to be crippled for three weeks with this thing."

Opening one of the small amber bottles, Kate poured six or seven small white pellets into his hand. "You're supposed to put these in your mouth and let them melt away."

Dutifully, Sam did as he was told. He didn't care if the homeopathic remedy worked or not. For him, just getting to spend time with Kate was all that mattered. She sat watching him expectedly.

"There. I feel better already."

She laughed and it was a sound without strain. "What a fibber you are."

He joined her laughter. In that moment, he felt that familiar closeness he and Kate had shared with one another so long ago. Some of the color had come back to the high slope of her cheeks. Her large blue eyes were no longer shadowed. Sam thought he saw flecks of happiness dancing in their depths. Because of him? Because they were together? He wasn't sure.

The last thing he wanted to do was leave. But he had to. Rising slowly, he smiled down at her. "I *do* feel better." Reaching out, he grazed the soft, warm skin of her cheek. "But it's because of you, Kate. It always has been…."

He saw her eyes widen—beautifully—and he saw desire in her gaze. For him? It was the first time he'd seen that look since they were in high school. When she placed her hand lightly and tentatively against his chest, his flesh tightened instantly. With a groan, he leaned down.

Kate felt his hand still against her cheek, rough, stimulating and making her want him with every cell in her screaming, hungry body. Without thinking, she flexed her fingers against his chest. How badly she wanted to kiss Sam! Looking up through her lashes, she saw his gray eyes burning with raw need of her. Instantly, her breath caught. She read the intent in his narrowed eyes. He was going to kiss her! Why, after all these years, would he want to do that? Her past was so shameful—how could he want her now? The thoughts dissolved the moment his mouth made hot contact with her parting lips.

Suddenly, Kate didn't care any longer. She lost herself in the masterful power of his searching mouth. His breath was warm and moist as it flowed across her cheek. His hand guided her and tilted her head just enough so that he could fully enjoy her. The taste of him was wonderful, his mouth strong without hurting her. Oh, how Kate had needed his touch! With a soft moan, she found herself a willow leaning against the hard planes of his body. His fingers moved through her hair and she felt his other arm encircling her waist and bringing her against him.

All she'd ever wanted, Kate discovered as she returned his searching, tender kiss, was Sam. The years stood between them and yet, miraculously, they melted away. His mouth curved and followed the line of her lips as they yielded to his sweet, molten assault. Her senses reeled and then exploded outward like the heat flowing through her, making her shaky, making her want him in every possible way. His hands felt strong and steadying against her head, against her bottom as he cupped her body to his. She absorbed his strength and felt his harsh control at the same time. There was no mistaking the fact that he was fully aroused. As she eagerly returned his kiss, lost in the light of explosions moving like a golden haze throughout her, all she wanted was to consume him as he wanted to consume her.

And then reality hit Kate. All the old memories, the shame, the fact that she'd led such a bad life, avalanched upon her. As she pulled away, she realized that Sam's kiss had been born out of the excitement of the night's activities—of Chet's attack upon him. That was all. Nothing more. People often did crazy things after a trauma. Hurt flowed through Kate as she stepped away, her fingers touching her wet, throbbing lips. Her heart was thudding hard in her breast. Her flesh prickled everywhere he had touched her.

As she looked up, she saw the molten look in Sam's eyes. At the same time, she saw a question in his gaze and then disappointment. It was obvious to her that he was sorry he'd kissed her. She wasn't. But that didn't matter, she realized as she took another step away from him.

Sam reached over for his cowboy hat, which rested on the table. His body ached like fire itself. He saw the pain in Kate's eyes, the way she was looking at him. How could he blame her? He'd overstepped his bounds completely with her. There was no way she could want him back in her life on a personal basis.

"I'd better go," he said roughly.

As he moved through the darkened living room,

heading for the front door, Sam cursed himself. Why had he kissed Kate? Why? All it had done was hurt her. What a selfish bastard he was.

Chapter 8

Sam knocked several times at the door to the main ranch house but there was no answer. The light was on in the study, where Kate spent a lot of time when she wasn't at his side working hard from dawn to dusk. By this time, she was usually in bed. When he'd left the barn after tending to a number of calves that had recently been born, he saw the lights at the house were still burning. Concerned, he'd decided to drop by.

Looking up to the sky, he saw white flakes start to come down on the gusts of wind. It was late December now, nearly midnight, and the sky was spitting ice crystals that he knew would turn to snow any minute now. After a two-year drought, all of a sudden rain and now snow were being dumped on them.

After a moment's hesitation, he quietly entered the house and shut the door, taking off his damp hat and hanging it on a peg next to the entry. After he shook the accumulated ice crystals off his sheepskin jacket, he carefully wiped his boots on the rug in front of the door.

"Kate?" His voice rang oddly through the house. Sam waited a moment, sensitive about giving Kate her space, but didn't hear her reply. Ever since that kiss, things had been tentative between them. Sometimes he saw sadness in Kate's eyes. Other times desire—for him. He wasn't sure what was going on, and he was too scared to confront her about it. His gut told him to back off, wait and be patient. Despite his regrets about ruining what might have been for them, Sam found himself hoping for some kind of future that included Kate. He had no business thinking such a thing. His head was clear on why. His heart, however, had a mind of its own. Scowling, he walked toward the office, which was situated on the north side of the house.

The door was open, as always, and the light spilled out into the gloom of the darkened hallway. He placed his hand on the doorjamb and halted at the entrance. His face softened. With the accounting books opened before her Kate was fast asleep. His mouth compressed with concern. Sam knew she was worried about the money. He could see a lot of paper wadded up and littered around the chair where she sat sleeping. Money. Wasn't it always money? The ranch teetered on a thin line between disaster and survival, thanks to mounting feed prices, a drought that had wiped out normal food supplies, a heavy bank debt and constant need for materials for fences and the like.

Kate had her Pendleton jacket hung over the back of the chair. She wore a light pink flannel shirt and a pair of jeans, muddied from helping him calve hours earlier. Her feet were encased in thick, pink socks and her muddy cowboy boots sat on some newspaper next to the antique oak desk. An ache built inside Sam's lower body as he absorbed her soft features. Kate was allowing her hair to grow, and it was slightly curled and ruffled around her face. Beneath the light, he saw the reddish highlights. Her lips… Inwardly, he groaned. Her mouth was one of her finest attributes, in his opinion. So soft and kissable. He ached to kiss her again. If it ever happened—and his heart certainly hoped for that opportunity—it had to be Kate who initiated the kiss, not him. Sam was damned if he was going to be like a thief in the night, stealing from Kate once again. He'd hurt her once and he swore he would never do it again.

Worried about the flush he saw blooming on her cheeks just below her thick lashes, Sam thought about how Kate had been using every bit of her physical strength to keep this ranch going. She was up at four a.m. every day. By ten p.m., she was usually so exhausted she weaved when she walked. On most nights she was in bed shortly thereafter. Yes, he had her pattern of living down pat. The foreman's house sat three hundred feet away from the main house, so he couldn't help but notice such things. His hours were the same as hers, but he was used to the brutal demands of ranching. Kate had just jumped in and was still adjusting.

Sam wanted time with her—quality time. But there had been no opportunities. A series of disasters had occurred as soon as he'd quit the Cunningham Ranch and come over to her ranch. A late thunderstorm had blown up a day after he'd arrived, and lightning had struck nearby, starting a small fire. Fire was always a worry here and the sudden blaze had destroyed three hundred acres before the borate bombers flown in from Phoenix had gotten it under control. All the fence posts had to be removed and replaced with new posts and wire, to keep the cattle from wandering onto Cunningham property.

And then prices on feed shot out of sight, and supplies took a much larger chunk of money. It was as if the bleeding at the ranch changed to a hemorrhage. The effect of the drought in the Midwest, where the wheat, oats and corn were grown, had finally reached Sedona and managing the ranch finances became a juggling act for Kate. She had to rob Peter to pay Paul, as she put it.

The cattle could go without grain, but the young Arabian horses could not if they were to get the nutrition they needed for strong bones in such a desert environment.

How peaceful Kate looked sleeping, Sam thought as he quietly moved closer. He remembered her sleeping in his arms so very long ago. At that time, her hair had been long, halfway to her waist, and he recalled how thick and silky it lay against his chest as she nestled her head in the crook of his shoulder to sleep. An ache spread throughout him at the memory and Sam laughed at himself, stopping inches from where Kate was sleeping. The last six weeks had been a living hell for him. *Hell.* They were so busy trying to keep things going, that they rarely saw one another except while vetting and caring for the animals which wasn't often enough for him.

Sam leaned over and lightly touched the curls near her unmarred brow. His fingers itched to graze the slope of her cheek. *No.* He couldn't. That wouldn't be fair to Kate. He pulled his hand back and allowed it to drop to his side.

When he'd moved into the foreman's house, Kate had helped him unpack some of the boxes. In one, she found the framed photo of Chris, his son. In another, a photo of Carol. He'd seen the look on her face, the pain and sadness as she put the pictures aside. Frustration moved through him. How could he get Kate to understand that he was interested in her? She had shown no overt signs of interest in him, that was for sure. Yet she'd returned his kiss just as eagerly and passionately as he'd explored her delicious mouth.

Releasing a long breath of air, Sam got an idea. He saw the white snowflakes striking the window just beyond the desk. Yes, maybe it would work. Maybe he could devise a way to get Kate to rest, even for part of a day. She desperately needed a small vacation of sorts. Christmas was only two days away and he'd seen two presents sitting on the coffee table in the living room, but no tree was up. Maybe his idea would work.

Gently, he closed his hand over Kate's shoulder and squeezed slightly.

"Kate?" Sam realized just how deeply she was sleeping when she didn't respond to his call. He saw the beginnings of shadows beneath her eyes. She was working herself, literally, to the bone. Matter of fact, she'd lost a good fifteen pounds in the process, from what he could see. The hollow of her cheeks was more pronounced, the flesh tighter against her sloping bones. They were working so hard that they ate on the run or grabbed whatever was easily available. In reality, they needed four wranglers plus themselves to keep this ranch at operating level. Could the two of them continue this murderous pace until next June, when Jessica arrived home?

Sam leaned over, extending his large hand across the soft smoothness of her shoulders. He could feel how firm and physically fit the ranch work had made her. "Gal? It's time to go to bed." He gave her a small shake. Her lashes fluttered and she moaned softly. The beginnings of a tender smile pulled at Sam's mouth as he watched her start to surface from her deep sleep. "Come on, Kate. You can't sleep over the accounting books. You need to get a bath and go to bed…."

Kate felt more than heard Sam's low, vibrating voice. She loved the deep tone of his voice because it always made her feel safe and nurtured. His hand was on her shoulder, gently moving in a slow, provocative circle. Was she dreaming again? Dreaming of his loving her? How wonderful his strong fingers felt against her sore, tired back. Forcing her eyes open, she raised her head. Sam's shadowy features made her blink. Sitting upright suddenly, she felt him remove his hand.

"What's wrong? Does one of the new calves have a problem?" she asked in a muffled tone.

"Whoa, there's no crisis," Sam said, holding up his hand.

He forced himself to take a step back as she sat up and rubbed her eyes. "Everything's fine. I saw the light on in here. It's not like you to be up this late, so I knocked on the door." He smiled a little and rested his long fingers across his hips. "I found you asleep on the books there. It's midnight, Gal. You need to be in bed."

Her skin felt like it was glowing everywhere he'd

touched her. Kate was barely functioning. Her heart, all her sleepy senses, were hanging on Sam's husky voice and his nearness. He rarely came into her house. Blinking to drive her exhaustion away, Kate rubbed her face.

"Oh…thanks, Sam…. I was just trying to find some extra money. I was thinking that maybe I didn't add or subtract right…."

Kate looked utterly vulnerable in that moment as she sat there, her hands curved across her thighs. He wanted to sweep her into his arms, carry her to the bedroom, lay down with her and simply hold her against him until she dropped off to sleep. She needed some holding, some attention, and he knew it. This ranch was extruding every emotion she had out of her. He knew Kate was taking the success or failure of the ranch on her shoulders. It wasn't right, but that's what she was doing. She still felt such guilt over her past that she was probably using the ranch as a way to right old wrongs.

Grimly, Sam said, "I want you to sleep in tomorrow, Kate. I'll get up and do the feeding. Then, when I'm done, you and I are going to saddle up a couple of horses and we're going up into the canyon."

She stared at him. "What?"

He gestured to the ledger books spread out on the desk. "This ranch is bleeding you dry, Kate. I want you to take a day off. Sleep in tomorrow morning, have a nice, leisurely breakfast. I'll drop by when I get the chores done."

She smiled and rubbed her brow. "Sounds like heaven to me, Sam McGuire." And then she studied his harsh, unreadable features. "Why are you doing this? You're working twice as hard as I am."

He matched her smile. “Because you need a down day, Gal, that’s why. Aren’t you a little curious about what we’ll be doing up in the canyon?”

Sam’s teasing warmed her and she laughed a little as she stood up. “Well, yes….”

Nodding, Sam walked to the door. “Good. I’ll see you tomorrow around ten a.m., then.”

“This is beautiful!” Kate told Sam with a sigh. They rode together through the dark green Ponderosa pines, which were covered with a cape of fresh white snow. The storm that had raged throughout the night was the first big snowfall of the season. Bundled in her sheepskin coat and gloves, her black Stetson keeping her head warm, Kate smiled over at him. “Prison took so much out of me,” she confided, absorbing the majesty of the pines as they rode up the snowy slope.

Sam silently congratulated himself on his idea. Behind his black gelding was a packhorse carrying a surprise picnic lunch, hot chocolate in two large thermoses, an ax and enough rope to bring a spruce tree home for Christmas. The weather was cloudy, the sky roiling with dark and light gray shapes. Every now and again a patch of blue could be seen, and even a surprising glint of yellow sunlight briefly shone before the swift-moving clouds swallowed it up.

“Out here,” he told her, “you can not only feel your freedom, you can taste it.” The rushing and bubbling of Oak Creek was to their right as they followed it higher up the hill. The heavy scent of pine filled their lungs and Sam drew the fragrance deep into his chest.

Kate reached out, resting her gloved hand on the arm

of his sheepskin jacket. "This is heaven, Sam. Heaven," she said. How much she wanted to kiss him again! She was afraid to ask. Afraid to explore the possibilities of why it had happened in the first place. More than likely, the kiss had been a knee-jerk reaction after the fight with Chet. If only it had been for other, more important reasons…

Sam's heart expanded powerfully at her touch. Right now, Kate looked like the eager young girl he'd known before life had tripped her up so badly. Her sky blue eyes shone like those of a child. Her soft lips were parted and expectant. The high color in her cheeks simply made her eyes that much more startling and lovely to look at. Despite the fact that he was losing his heart all over again, he grinned at her.

"Start looking for just the right tree to bring home so we can put it in your living room. Christmas shouldn't be celebrated without one."

Sobering, Kate allowed her hand to rest on her thigh. The steady movement of the horse beneath her was soothing and something she loved. She was afraid to ask, but she was going to anyway. Kate had made every attempt to stay on a business footing with Sam, keeping things from getting personal. She was afraid if she dropped that decorum she might make a fool out of herself. She'd seen those photos of Chris, his son, and Carol, his ex-wife, on top of his television set.

"Sam…do you have plans for Christmas Day?"

Surprised, he looked at her. "Why?"

"W-well…" Kate stumbled over her words. "I just thought that—that Chris might be coming home. You said he was on Christmas break from college and I thought he might be—be visiting you for a while."

He shook his head, noting the wariness in Kate's eyes. "No. He's going to visit Carol in New York City."

"Oh, I see. . . ."

"You thought he was coming out for the holiday?" Sam had wondered why Kate hadn't mentioned Christmas to him. It was as if she was avoiding the holiday completely, which wasn't like her. He recalled how much she'd loved Christmas in her younger years. Odula had always had a party, inviting many elderly neighbors who could not afford a holiday meal. The Donovan Ranch at one time had been known for its charity work with the poor and elderly, thanks to Odula. When she died, the gift of charity died with her.

"Yes, I thought you might want to spend time with your family," Kate admitted.

Sam shook his head and watched a huge chunk of snow slide off a nearby pine. The wind was still gusty, and the pines ladened with their white covering, began to lose their adornment. "When Carol and I got our divorce, she moved back East. Back to where she was born—New York. I didn't want Chris torn between choosing one or the other of us for holidays. He decided that every other year he could be with me on Christmas. This year, he'll be with Carol and her family."

"I see. . . ." Kate saw a blue jay flit between the pines, its call loud with warning. The horses were beginning to climb steadily, their breath white like steam, shooting from their nostrils.

"How about you?" Sam asked. With the banks of Oak Creek on one side and a heavy brush barrier on the other, they had to ride close together, their legs touching now and then. He didn't mind the closeness and Kate seemed to like it, too.

"Me? Oh… I just arranged for a beef to be sent to the mission in Cottonwood so they would have food to serve to the homeless over Christmas. That steer you took to the packinghouse in Sedona last week is the gift I'm giving them. They're trucking it down this morning to the mission."

He smiled warmly. "Just like your mother."

Blushing, Kate avoided his hooded gray eyes. She heard the emotion in Sam's deep voice and his approval of her charity. "I want to try and bring back some of the traditions we had when Mom was alive. There's no way we can open the ranch up this year to the elderly. But maybe next year… I always loved being able to help the old ones. They don't all have relations nearby to celebrate with them this time of year. We always had a great time. I know the three of us always looked forward to Christmas Day and all."

Sam remembered very clearly about those times. He'd been part of that special celebration himself when he was going steady with Kate. Odula and her three daughters had worked endlessly in the big kitchen, roasting turkeys, making pot roasts with all the fixin's for the thirty or forty elderly people who would be bussed out to the ranch to enjoy a real family dinner with them. Even Kelly would straighten up his act, get cleaned up and behave.

In that moment, Sam felt the sharpness of his love for Kate. It had never died. It had just hibernated all these years.

Waiting. Just waiting. The joy he heard in her voice as she spoke about helping the elderly, and the golden light dancing in her eyes, made him realize how much he'd missed out on because of his own stupid moment of drunken need. Disgusted with himself, Sam wished he could change the past. He wanted a second chance with Kate.

"Odula's spirit lives on in you, Kate. She'd be proud of you," he murmured.

"Thanks, Sam. I'm beginning to realize how much of my mother is in me and how much I never let grow outside of me." She gestured to the snow-laden pines that surrounded them. "We *always* came up here for a Christmas tree as a family every year. I loved it! All of us on horseback, with a couple of packhorses. We made a picnic and day of it." Her voice grew heavy with feeling. "And you remembered this, didn't you? I'd forgotten. I've forgotten so much that's important…."

He pulled his gelding to a halt and dismounted. Without speaking, Sam placed his hands around her waist and lifted her off her horse. Bracketed by the animals as they were, the movement brought them together. Sam took off his heavy gloves and framed Kate's upturned face. The hope of the world lay in her widening eyes. Wordlessly, her lips parted, just begging to be kissed by him. A fire raged, barely in check, within his aching lower body. He felt the smooth warmth of her skin beneath his hands as he looked deeply into her eyes.

"Maybe a lot of things have changed, Kate," he rasped, feeling the movement of the horse pushing her fully against him. "But people's hearts hold memories. Lots of 'em." He managed a wry, one-sided smile. "My reasons for doing this are plenty. You've been working yourself to the bone. You've lost a lot of weight and I'm worried about that. And your family's traditions are important." Looking deeply into her glistening eyes, he continued, "I feel that in some small way I can help you get back in touch with some of those parts of yourself. Let me help you when I can. I've hurt you once. And God help me, I've never been so sorry. This time around, Kate, I'm going to try and be a positive influence in your life, not one that rips you apart like I did before. If you could just trust me a little, Gal—just a little..." He grimaced and scowled. "I know I'm asking for the moon. You have every right to tell me to go to hell and never look back. I can't change the past, but I can make sure the present is different—better—for you...."

His rough, callused hands felt so steadying, so right to Kate. Completely off guard because Sam had only been this intimate with her once since she'd come home, Kate pressed against him, feeling the heat and vibrating strength of his powerful body. She heard his words, understood them too well, and allowed his raw emotions to blanket her in those moments out of time. Without thinking, she lifted her hands and enclosed his as they lay against her face. Hot tears spilled from her eyes, trailed down her cool skin and laced through his fingers.

"Don't you realize how good you've already been to me?" she said in a wobbly voice. "You didn't judge me when I came out of prison. Without you, Sam, this ranch would have fallen flat on its face. Look how much you've done." Sniffing, she gave him a trembling smile, becoming lost in his dark, stormy gaze. "The past is done, Sam." She saw a flare of some unknown emotion in his eyes and his fingers tightened briefly against her flesh. "I don't bear any grudges, believe me. We both made mistakes."

Taking a deep, shaky breath, Sam nodded. "What I did to you, Kate, is unforgivable…."

"You thought I had run away for good," she whispered, allowing her hands to move to his upper arms. "I can understand why you got drunk that night. We loved one another and what I did to you wasn't right. I know that now—hindsight's always twenty-twenty, isn't it?" Her mouth stretched into a sad line. "You made love to Carol out of grief, Sam. That's something else I know and can understand now that I'm older, more mature. I'm sure you weren't expecting her to get pregnant. It probably came as as big a surprise as any you've ever had." She sighed, looking up at him. "At least, you did the right thing. You were responsible to her—and your son. I really admire that, Sam. It says a lot of good things about you. Even though you made a mistake, you rectified it."

Standing here, protected from the chill of the winter air by the warmth of the horses, Kate absorbed the heady scent of the pine and Sam's hands upon her face, and felt as if all her dreams had come true. She reveled in his attention and the care that radiated from him as it began to heal another old wound in her heart, whether he knew it or not.

Using his thumbs, Sam wiped the remnants of tears from Kate's cheeks. Allowing his hands to fall across her proud shoulders, he sighed. "You're right—I didn't fall in love with her," he rasped, holding her gaze. He saw her eyes widened with surprise. "I was shocked by the note you left, but I knew this had been building for a while. Mustangs run when they're threatened, and Kelly had pushed you as far as you could go. Something had to give. And like you said, hindsight is always twenty-twenty." He grimaced. "You ran. You had no choice. I felt so damned helpless. I couldn't protect you from Kelly, or from the hell in that house you had to live in. When I got the note, I knew you meant it. I loved you and I understood, but it made me reel. I got drunk. I did some stupid things. Things I've paid part of my life to try and correct." His hands tightened on her shoulders.

Digesting his admission, Kate studied him in the soft silence of the forest, letting the bubbling sounds of Oak Creek sooth some of her wounded feelings. "You're letting me off too easily, Sam. If I hadn't run away in the first place, none of this would have happened."

Harshly, he whispered, "You saw no other choice at the time, Gal. I never blamed you for what you did. I understood why you did it. I might have been stupid, Kate, but I wasn't going to do what some guys did if they got a girl pregnant. I wasn't going to walk away and pretend it didn't happen." Anger tinged his words. "I really screwed up. I had the best thing in the world, and in one night, I threw it away." His fingers dug into her jacket. "I threw what we had away, Kate, and I've been the sorriest bastard ever since. I take responsibility for my choices. Being drunk was no excuse. Having had a lot of time to look back on it, I realize I was an egotistical fool. I was the star running back of the football team. I liked all the attention Carol gave me. She'd been following me around all year and I liked her attention a little too much."

Standing there against Sam, Kate felt his anguish. "Teenage hormones and a swelled head to boot?"

He nodded and held her wounded gaze. "Yes. A bad combination. Hell, Kate, at that age, what did we know? I didn't realize I already had the woman I wanted to spend a lifetime with. I was careless, and I thought I knew everything. I played with fire and it burned me. Worse, it burned you, too. If I could do it all over again—but hell, it's too late."

"Did you *ever* love Carol?" Kate asked faintly. Her head swam with the question. How could anyone live for eighteen years with someone they didn't love? That seemed like a horrible prison sentence to her—far worse than the one she'd endured for eighteen months. In one way, Kate was aware of Sam's loyalty and responsibility. Maybe it was his ranch upbringing, where kids were taught from the time they were born that their actions and words carry weight, that their decisions have consequences, and that if they start something, they have to finish it. Maybe it was the code of the Old West, where a man was his word. Where any decision was accepted with the full weight of responsibility to go with it.

Sam allowed his hand to skim the sleeve of her coat. "No. Not real love..." Not like the love for Kate he'd continued to carry in his heart like a torch that refused to go out.

"What a horrible sentence," she whispered.

"Don't feel sorry for me, Gal. I brought it on myself. Carol and I learned to be friends, instead. We had a lot of rough times and we worked on them together. I admire her, too, for what she did for Chris. It says a lot about her commitment and responsibility to the situation." Sam captured Kate's gloved fingers. "What I feel bad about, what I want to repair between us, is what it did to *you*. Somehow I want to make up for all the pain I've caused you, Kate." His mouth became a slash of pain because of all he felt over his stupid actions and decisions. "You were the innocent one in all of this. I saw what life did to you. You ran away from home once and for all soon after graduation. Right after my wedding. You see, I knew your *real* reason for leaving. You left because I'd married Carol."

Feelings surged up through Kate, and she felt a lump growing in her throat. She wrapped her fingers tightly around his, her other hand resting on his massive chest. "No, Sam," she whispered brokenly, "I didn't leave because you married Carol."

He raised head and studied her intently. "You didn't?" They had been two months away from graduation when everyone in school found out that Carol was pregnant and he was going to marry her. It took only a day for the gossip to fly around the school. Then Sam never saw Kate again. She became like a shadow at school and avoided him completely. They had never gotten to talk after that.

"Only my family knows the real reason why I left, Sam. Kelly was drunk all the time. He and I got into the worst argument we ever had when the police brought me home from Phoenix." Kate moved away from Sam, to her horse, and picked up the reins from the snow-covered ground. Her hands shook. "You never knew what happened, Sam. No one did." She couldn't look at him. Instead, she looked at the tall pines behind his massive frame. "Kelly was afraid all along that you and

I were going to run off and get married someday. He said I needed to go to college first and get the education that he never got. This happened the day before I found out you were going to marry Carol. Anyway, Kelly and I got into a yelling match. I told him I didn't want to go to college, that I wanted to stay on the ranch and keep learning how to run it. He got angry. Angrier than I'd ever seen him in a long time. He accused me of going to bed with you—which I had. Before, I'd always avoided telling him and Mother the truth. But that time I did."

Sam stood very still. He saw the anguish in Kate's face as she held the reins tightly in her fingers and stared down at them.

"What did Kelly do to you?" he asked hoarsely.

"It wasn't pretty," Kate admitted hollowly. "He slapped me across the face and sent me flying."

"That son of a bitch."

"My mother came running in, saw what happened, and she flew into Kelly like a hornet." Kate touched her nose. "That's why it's crooked. He broke it when he hit me."

Sam's hands clenched into fists. "That's why I never saw you again at school? You never showed up for the graduation ceremony, either. I was looking for you… but when I called your house, I got Kelly. He told me to never call again or try to come out to the ranch to see you. He said if I did, he'd shoot me on sight. I took him at his word."

With a strained laugh, Kate nodded and turned to him. "Yes, Kelly was good for his word, wasn't he?" The rage banked in Sam's eyes surprised her. His mouth was set and his hands were clenched in fists at his side.

"Rachel, bless her, said nothing at school. We were all too ashamed of it, anyway. She got my assignments, my books, and I finished out the last two months of school at home, on the ranch. Kelly never told me you tried to call me." Kate opened her hands. "What a mess, huh? I got my diploma and left the next day. I took a job in Santa Fe, New Mexico, as a waitress. There, no one knew me. By that time, my nose was healed up. I tried to start a life on my own...."

Wearily, Sam walked up to her. She stood alone, suffering, so proud and so distant from him. "I'm sorry, Kate. So damned sorry. I didn't know any of this...."

She twisted to look up at him and saw the agony clearly written on his features. "After I left home I learned a lot of things over the years, Sam. Especially about having an alcoholic parent. All of us, in our own way, supported Kelly's drinking. We enabled him to carry on and hid from the world the best we could what his drinking did to us."

"It wasn't a secret around Sedona," he muttered.

"Yes, and over time, it just got worse and worse."

A shudder worked through him. "Kate, I'm sorry. For everything."

Her mouth curved faintly as she held his saddened gaze. "I know you are, Sam. You are a good man. You married Carol out of responsibility, not love, in order to give Chris a home and two parents. You yourself were raised by your dad when your mother died giving you birth, so I can understand how important it was to you that your son got the things you didn't."

He nodded. "That's how I felt, Kate. I never knew my mother. I didn't want Chris to grow up without two parents. I knew what it was like and I can't forget the hole that's still in me because of it."

"So you walked into a prison where there was no love, to give him that gift." She shook her head. "I don't think I would've had the guts or the heart to do that, Sam. I admire you for it. I really do."

"I don't regret my choice," Sam said. "Chris is a great boy and I love him as much as life. Carol was and is a good mother to him. We made an agreement early on to do the best we could for his sake." Looking up, Sam saw a bald eagle skimming the tops of the pines along Oak Creek, looking for a noon meal of trout. "She was never happy out West. We agreed a long time ago to divorce once Chris left for college. Our duties to him were over at that point, and he's old enough to understand why we got a divorce. Carol's always wanted a career in photography and now she's got one back in New York City. All's well that ends well."

Kate studied him, aching to reach out and touch his clenched jaw. "What about you, Sam? Are you happy? Are you living your life the way you dreamed about doing? Or maybe you don't have dreams like Carol did?"

He raised his head, a sad smile lifting one corner of his mouth. "My dreams died when you left, Kate." He saw her return his smile, hers soft and edged with shyness.

"Surely you must have at least one left?" she asked.

He shrugged painfully. "None, Kate. I had one hell of a great life when I was a kid in high school. You and I dreamed together of getting married, having a ranch and kids.... Well, that was a long time ago."

Kate nodded, the silence falling gently between them. "If you could dream," she whispered, "what would it be about now?" She held her breath as she watched him wrestle with her question.

"I don't deserve to dream, Kate."

Reaching out, she touched his arm, her fingers curling across the sheepskin coat. "Yes, you do."

Her touch was galvanizing. In that moment, Sam was ready to risk it all. The words came out choked and low. "Then I'd dream of having you back in my life again."

The emotion behind his admission embraced her. Kate saw hope burning in the depths of his gray eyes. "You—would dream of me back in your life?" She found that impossible to believe.

With his thumb, Sam pushed the brim of his hat upward an inch or two on his brow. The startled look on Kate's face said it all. "Am I a nightmare to you, instead?" He held his breath even though he'd asked the question teasingly. What if she said yes? Then the rest of his hope would be destroyed—forever.

Tears burned in Kate's eyes. Wordlessly, she leaned upward and placed her hands flat against his chest. She saw surprise, then joy followed quickly by desire, in his widening gray eyes. Her heart cried out for him, despite all the pain, the past mistakes they'd made that had convoluted and stained their individual lives. Parting her lips, she pressed them against the hard line of his.

Instantly, she felt Sam's returning hunger, his mouth shamelessly taking hers, molding, melding her tightly against him. This time the kiss was not tender or gentle. It was taking, giving, sharing a desire whose flame had never died out over time. Her breath became short as he took her, his hands sliding behind her, pressing her solidly against his hard, trembling body.

The coldness of the air, the moisture of their breath, the moan that came up from her throat, all combined in a whirlwind of sensation. She slid her fingers along his freshly shaved cheeks, felt the warmth and sandpapery texture that was Sam. He smelled of pine and snow and that very special scent of him, only him.

This time there was no holding back with Kate. She had her answer. Whatever was left of their old love was still alive. Her arms slid around his thickly corded neck and she ached to feel his skin against her own. As his hand moved and caressed the side of her breast, she trembled violently. Oh, how long had she gone without his touch? His exploring, searching hands slid down her body, eliciting fire she longed to share with him.

The soft snort of the horses moving restlessly nearby brought Kate back to her senses. In a daze, she felt Sam's mouth leave her own wet, throbbing lips. As she lifted her lashes, she saw the burning, molten desire in his eyes, his face inches from her own. His breath was warm against her face. Weakly, she curled her fingers into the sheepskin collar of his coat to keep from swaying. Her senses reeled, awakened from some deep slumber. An ache between her legs told her how badly she wanted Sam.

"I…" she began unsteadily. "Sam…"

"I know," he rasped, drawing her against him again. His heart thundered like a freight train in his chest. He felt tied in a burning, painful knot of need for Kate. His mouth tingled with her softness, her womanliness. She was as eager and starved for him as he was for her, he discovered. That was heady knowledge. Sam had never expected such a gift from Kate, and he was stunned. He didn't deserve it—at all. Yet the generosity of her heart was overwhelming, and this time, there was no mistaking her intent. She had kissed him. It had been mutual. Sizzling. Needed.

Wryly, he looked down at her, one corner of his mouth lifted. With his fingers, he smoothed some strands of hair from Kate's flushed cheek. "I think we're upsetting our horses, don't you?"

Laughing self-consciously, Kate felt a fierce welling of love tunnel up through her. In that moment, Sam look twenty years younger, like the football star she'd fallen hopelessly in love with so long ago. His gray eyes were lighter and the joy in them thrilled her. Giddy, she said in a softened voice, "I think we've embarrassed them by our unexpected behavior."

Chuckling, Sam was delighted to see Kate return his touch as she grazed his hard jaw with her fingertips. The intimacy was nearly his undoing. He wanted to love her so damn badly he could taste it. He wanted to make up for all the years of pain he'd given her. Yet he was older and wiser now, and he also knew that waiting was not their enemy, but their friend. If Kate loved him anyway near as much as he did her, they had all the time in the world to discover and then explore it—together. To blindly rush in, driven by guilt or hormones, wasn't what he needed right now—he'd done that once and paid dearly and he wasn't about to do it again. That knowledge and experience gave him the ability to smile warmly down at Kate.

"The horses might be embarrassed, but I don't think

we are. Are we?" He said it lightly, teasingly. There was no way Sam wanted to burden Kate or make her feel angst over their unexpected kiss.

Heat stung Kate's cheeks as she absorbed Sam's warm, caring look. It passed right on through her to her wildly beating heart, thrumming with untrammeled joy. Just getting to touch Sam was such a gift to her.

"No," she whispered, meeting his smile with one of her own. "I don't think we are."

Sam tore his gaze from her upturned features. Kate's eyes were alive with happiness. No longer was there wariness in them, or that darkness he'd seen so often since she'd gotten out of jail. Still holding her, he moved out from between the horses. "Look up there," he said, pointing to a good-looking spruce about two hundred feet up the snow-covered hill. "What do you think about that one as a Christmas tree?"

Kate was grateful for his return to less significant things. She needed time to feel her way through what had just occurred between them. Right now, her knees still felt a little like jelly. It was wonderful to just lean against Sam, to have his arm protectively wrapped around her shoulders.

"Yes, that looks like a good tree," she agreed a bit breathlessly.

"Good," he said, slowly releasing her and moving to the packhorse to retrieve the ax. "Let's get on with this Christmas celebration, shall we?"

Chapter 9

Kate couldn't still her excitement as the five-foot-tall blue spruce was set upright in the living room of the ranch house. They had gotten home by two in the afternoon, and by three the tree was up in the corner. A fire burned brightly in the red sandstone fireplace on the other side of the room.

"This is just like in the past," Kate said breathlessly as she brought out the Christmas ornaments from a closet in the hall. How familiar it felt to go to that closet and find the decorations there. Odula had taught them all organization, and everything in the house had a nook or cranny of its own. Placing the boxes on the davenport, she smiled up at Sam who was brushing off his hands.

Her body tingled in memory of his hands, his form, pressed against hers up on the mountain. Something magical had happened in those moments. Something that had set her heart singing.

"There are traditions that ought to be faithfully kept," Sam agreed. He peered into one of the boxes, where colorful ornaments sparkled back at him. "I wonder how many years these bulbs have been unused? The five years I was here at the ranch, Kelly never celebrated Christmas once."

Surprised, Kate began to string the lights on the tree, after trying them out and finding they still worked. "He didn't?" Sam came over to help her, picking up the other end of the lights.

"No, he'd get roaring drunk, sit on this couch and stare moodily into the fire." Sam wound the lights around the tree while Kate attached them here and there. The two of them worked in close proximity, their hips or arms touching occasionally. He savored each grazing touch.

"Probably remembering," Kate said sadly.

"If I were in his shoes, I'd be doing that," Sam murmured. He stood back while Kate plugged in the lights, illuminating the tree with colors. Nodding, he said, "Perfect."

Kate handed him a box of ornaments. Everything was perfect because she and Sam were spending time together once again. Over the past six weeks, they'd rarely seen one another except at work. "Did Kelly ever talk about us?" she ventured softly.

Sam set the box on a nearby chair. His hands were so large, the ornaments so small and fragile in comparison. Carefully, he began to hang them, one by one. "After Odula died, he went into a deep depression that lasted a year, from what I heard. He lost most of his wranglers in that time, staying drunk and firing them for no good reason. I was still working up at the Maitland Ranch near Flag, so I heard this stuff secondhand."

Sam picked up the silver star. "Kelly kept hiring and firing wranglers. He got a real reputation for drinking, exploding like an angry old peccary and firing the next poor cowboy that happened to have the bad luck of crossing his path." Sam frowned and placed the star carefully on top of the tree. When it slipped, he caught it and gently affixed it so that it remained upright.

"When he hired me about four years later, the ranch was a disaster site. I made a deal with Kelly—I would handle hiring and firing wranglers and he would stay out of my territory and keep the books." Sam grimaced. "That was a big mistake, but there was nothing I could do about that. He owned this place, I didn't."

"And so, at Christmastime, he'd just drink?"

"He'd never put up a tree and yes, he'd hit the bottle. He was lonely, though. After the chores were done, he'd invite me over for a drink."

Kate watched as Sam carefully placed another ornament on the spruce. "Did he—did he ever talk about any of us? My sisters?" she asked again.

Sam met and held her gaze. He saw the pain in Kate's eyes. "Plenty. Kelly was a storyteller. You know that. I'd sit here with him drinking my beer in front of the fireplace while he bragged on about you three girls."

Gawking, Kate whispered, "Bragged on us?"

"Yes." Sam stood back, appraising the tree. Slanting a glance at Kate, who looked stunned, he murmured,

"Especially you. He loved you in his own way, Kate. I know you don't believe that, but he did."

She bridled. "A twisted love," she muttered, retrieving the boxes of bright silver icicles to hang on the branches. Handing Sam a package and taking one herself, she sat down to open it.

"He loved you the best he knew how," Sam said, sitting on the couch next to her. When Kate's mouth became fixed in a hard line, he added, "I'm not defending him. He had no right to strike you like he did, Kate. If I'd been around, I'd have decked him, drunk or not."

"It was the last time he ever touched me."

"Well, he'd done enough damage by badgering, manipulating and taunting you girls as you grew up."

"He thought we were boys, not girls. He didn't want little girls running around. He'd wanted four strapping sons instead."

"That was Kelly's loss," Sam growled. "The three of you are pretty special in my book."

"Rachel and Jessica are. I've managed to screw up my life every step of the way."

"Kelly rode you the hardest," Sam countered quietly. "He used to sit here and talk about how hard he'd been on you. How he had to be hard on you to make you into a strong woman so you could run this ranch someday after he died."

Kate's hands stilled on the icicles. "I was Peter's replacement?"

"Yes. I think Kelly thought he had to be brutal and tough toward you all the time in order to teach you how to run this place." Sam sighed. "He was wrong. You don't train children by beating them. All that does is scare the living daylights out of them and they do one of two things—rebel or run."

Kate stood up and began placing the icicles on the tree. Her gut was tight with nausea and grief. "I did both."

"You could have done worse," Sam chided, slowly easing to his feet. He held her angry gaze as he walked over to the tree in turn.

"Like what? I rebelled against him from the time I was old enough to know that how he was treating me was wrong. And when I could, I ran as fast and hard as I could away from him." She looked around the room, her voice softening. "Away from here."

"What happens when you continuously beat a horse, Kate?"

"It'll either cave in, its spirit broken, or it'll fight back."

Sam hung some tinsel near the top of the tree. "I've always seen you as a wild, free mustang." His mouth pulled into a slight smile and he slanted a glance in her direction. "Right or wrong, I still do. Kelly beat you verbally and whipped you emotionally all your young life. You had those two choices staring you in the face. Somewhere in your heart, you knew Kelly wasn't going to ease up on you and treat you like an adult when you were eighteen. Maybe you sensed it. After he broke your nose in that fight, you knew you had to run. If you'd have stayed, it would have gotten worse."

"That I did know," Kate confided, slowly hanging the last of her tinsel on the tree. "I knew if he could hit me once or twice, he'd hit me again. I got tired of feeling like a target."

"He didn't see what he was doing to you. He thought he was grooming you to take over the ranch someday."

"He never told me that, Sam." She stood in the center of the room, feeling frustration and anger.

"Kelly didn't know how." Sam walked up to her. Kate's cheeks were flushed from the warmth of the fire. Several errant locks of hair dipped across her worried brow. "He sat here telling me how good a rider you were. How smart you were with the accounting books. He was proud of your straight A average in school, Kate. He dreamed of you going on to college and then coming back here after graduation, when he was going to hand over the daily running of the ranch to you."

Startled, she stared up at Sam's features. "If that's so, then why didn't he ever call me or write to me and tell me that? I kept in touch with Mom by phone and letter all those years. He knew where I was, what I was doing."

Reaching out, Sam tamed those unruly tendrils back into place. How badly he wanted to slide his fingers through her thick, silky hair. But he resisted. Barely.

"Pride, I think, stopped him. Stiff-necked pride," he told her, watching her eyes grow velvet with his touch.

"Damn him!" Kate whispered, tears flooding into her eyes. "It was his way of getting even with me for running away."

"No, I don't think so. In the later years, when Kelly had time to reflect on how he'd ridden you into the ground, I think he was feeling pretty guilty. And I don't think he knew how to tell you that or to say he was sorry." Sam reached out and placed a hand on her slumping shoulder. "If you had been here those five years like I was, you'd have seen photos of all you ladies on the television set. If anyone came to the ranch, Kelly bragged on about the three of you any chance he got. Some of the neighbors got tired of him saying the same things over and over again."

Sam smiled fondly in remembrance. "Believe me, Kelly was proud of you, Kate. He kept a shoe box in his bedroom that had all you girls' report cards in it. On some nights when I was in the office working on the books, he'd bring the box in, sit down and start pulling up different report cards, talking in amazement about all the subjects you three had taken and how smart you were."

Sam's hand felt steadying to Kate. She hung her head and ached to step into the circle of his arms once again. Somehow, she knew he'd hold her if she wanted. Her stomach hurt with pain and unrelieved grief and anger. "It was all so senseless," she whispered brokenly. "Damn him for not telling us these things."

Gently, Sam rubbed her shoulders, feeling the tension gathered in them. "Kate, give yourself some time. A lot's happened since you left. There's more to tell, but I don't think you're up to hearing it yet."

Sadly, Kate nodded. "Probably not, Sam. So Kelly loved us, but he didn't have the guts to tell us that to our faces. Wonderful. So the three of us have suffered half our lives because he was a coward and couldn't reach out to give us a hug or kiss us on the head." She pulled away, afraid that she was going to raise her arms and throw them around Sam's neck, seeking refuge with him. "You're right, Sam," she whispered bitterly, "I'm not ready to hear much more about Kelly and his drunken exploits." She turned and looked at the tree, her voice raw and unsteady. "All I want—need—is my family back. I can hardly wait for Rachel and Jessica to get home. I want things the way they used to be, only better this time. Much better."

Sam studied her profile and the anguished set of her lips. "The past can't be changed, Kate. But you can change the present and plan for the future." He managed a slight smile. "You three ladies have a hard road ahead, but my money's on you to save this ranch and rediscover your roots."

Kate wasn't so sure of victory, but she didn't say so. Resting her hands on her hips, she looked over at him.

"I'm planning a turkey dinner with all the trimmings tomorrow evening, Sam McGuire. And then I'm going to open the gifts my sisters sent me. Just like we did every Christmas night. Would you like to join me? I'm not going to be like Kelly. I won't tell you I like being alone on holiday. And I'm sure as hell not going to hit the bottle to make up the difference. What do you say?"

He saw the defiance burning in her eyes. Here was the Kate he knew from long ago, the mustang, wild and free. Her spirit might be badly beaten, but Kelly had never broken her. He grinned. "I wouldn't miss it for the world, Ms. Donovan. What time is dinner?"

"Right after we get the animals bedded down and fed for the night."

"Six p.m. I'll be there," Sam said, picking up his hat and shrugging into his sheepskin coat. "With bells on," he promised huskily.

Sam followed Kate into the living room after the tasty homemade meal of turkey and trimmings. He wore his Sunday-go-to-meeting clothes—dark brown slacks, a dark suede blazer, a freshly pressed, white cotton shirt and a bolo tie. Having taken extra pains to shave closely before coming over for dinner, he'd nicked himself once or twice. But the extra care had been worth it. Especially now that he was alone with Kate once more. He held a wineglass that she had just filled with sparkling grape juice. Unlike her father, she never touched alcohol. Odula had raised them to realize being Native American meant they would never be able to drink.

As he moved toward the tree, he noticed the dancing firelight reflected around the darkened living room. The lights on the tree were festive, and he felt happier than he could ever recall. The dinner had been intimate. And Kate looked beautiful in a dark pink corduroy skirt that fell to her ankles. A fancy white blouse with lace at the throat brought out her natural color, and the red velvet vest she wore over it heightened the bright color in her cheeks. He saw her frown and stop midway to the tree, where she was going to open the presents from her sisters.

"What's this?" Kate demanded, pointing beneath the tree. There was a third present there—one she did not recognize. And then she realized Sam must have put it there when she wasn't looking. She glanced over at him. He was smiling at her with his dark gray eyes.

"You're pretty sneaky, Sam," she accused, setting her wineglass on the mantel and moving to kneel on the red-and-green material that served as a colorful skirt beneath the tree.

"Now, I wouldn't say coyote sneaky," he remonstrated. "Clever, maybe?" In many Southwestern tales, the coyote was known as the ultimate trickster. Most ranchers saw them as sneaky. The Native Americans, however, saw the coyote as sacred and felt that tricks needed to be played on humans sometimes to teach them invaluable lessons.

Familiar with the tales, Kate chuckled, settling down and rearranging her skirt around her. Leaning toward the back of the tree, she pulled out another gift. “Maybe you’re right. Here, come and join me. Santa Claus left something for you, too, I think….” She pretended to be studying the card on the long, rectangular gift.

Sam crouched down nearby, his body almost touching hers. He reached out and took the red foil package with a glittering gold ribbon. “Talk about sneaky,” he exclaimed, his fingers touching hers in the exchange.

Chortling, Kate smiled up at him. “Once a coyote, always a coyote.”

“Now you’re a coyote,” Sam drawled, studying the gift with obvious pleasure.

How close he was. And how incredibly handsome! Her gaze dropped, as it always did, to his strong, powerful mouth. Catching herself, Kate pretended to be interested in the gifts. She wanted to tear into Sam’s gift first, but that wouldn’t be right. So she picked up Rachel’s large present and drew it into her lap. Not bothering with protocol, Kate eagerly tore into the gift, the lively green foil flying around her.

Sam watched Kate’s animated features. She was like a kid again—exuberant, enthusiastic and completely spontaneous. This was the old Kate he knew and loved. He saw her smile blossom as she opened up the box to view the contents.

"I figured as much," Kate said, "a *big* homeopathic kit." She pulled out a huge white plastic container about the size of a bread box. Opening it carefully, she pulled out one of the five shelves. At least thirty small amber bottles, all with Latin names on them, stared back at her. "I think Rachel wants to make sure I have enough homeopathic remedies on hand to treat the whole world," she said with a laugh. Fingering some of the bottles, she added, "Rachel said we could use the remedies on animals, too. She said in a letter that we could save a lot on vetting bills if we switched to this type of medicine instead."

"Why not? If it's cheaper and it works, it's a good idea," Sam agreed. He leaned over and gave Kate the next gift. This one was from Jessica.

Opening it quickly, Kate smiled with pleasure. Inside the box were several colorful packages. One was a bath salt made from purple cone flower, another was bergamot bath oil. As well as a sponge, there were four bars of handmade soap that had the scent of jasmine. Kate read the card out loud. "You're going to need long, hot soaks in the bathtub at night after those hard days you're putting in. I make all these things by hand and sell them through my company. Enjoy them. Let them heal you after a tough day. Love, Jessica."

"How about that?" Sam said, looking through the many gifts. "Your sister is really creative."

"Yes, she is," Kate murmured, proud of her little sister. She picked up the bath salts and looked at the design on the front of it. "Mother Earth Flower Essences. That must be the name of her company." She laughed a little and fingered the blue turtle with a colorful array of wildflowers sprouting out of its back, a smile on its face. "This is just like Jessica. She *loves* turtles! Growing up, she always had one as a pet—an old desert tortoise that used to hang out near the watering trough in the north pasture. I remember she would take cut-up fruit and lettuce leaves to it every day or so without fail." Shaking her head, Kate whispered in a choked tone, "Isn't it funny how all the things we did as kids can later turn into something beautiful and meaningful like this? It's just amazing to me."

Reaching out, Sam picked up his gift for her. "I think you're right," he murmured. "Here, this isn't much, but I hope it brings a lot of the past back to the present, Gal."

Curious, Kate accepted the gift. It was a very small box. Sam had tried to wrap it the best he could, the ribbon slightly askew, the corners of the paper sticking out here and there, as if the gift was put together at the last minute. "You didn't have to do this, Sam."

He smiled enigmatically, his arms resting on his knees as he watched her face. "I've been wanting to give you this gift for a long time, Gal…."

Mystified, Kate opened the tiny box with trembling fingers. "What on earth could it be?" she wondered aloud.

He chuckled indulgently. "Open it and find out."

Tossing the paper aside, Kate slowly removed the lid. Her brows knitted. Inside was a piece of lined paper, cut lopsidedly and then folded. "What are you up to, Sam McGuire?" She picked up the paper and put the box aside. In the dim, dancing light, she could barely make out his scrawl. Holding the note closer, she read, "Go to the truck?"

"Yup."

Stymied, Kate tried to read the second line. "Sam, your handwriting is the pits. What on *earth* does this next line say?"

Placing his hand beneath hers, he helped her stand. "It says," he continued, as he steered her toward the door, "to go to my pickup, to the front seat. There's something waiting there for you."

The coldness of the night air hit Kate as she followed Sam out onto the damp, dark porch. It had quit snowing hours ago and she could smell the pungent fragrance of the juniper wrapped in snow blankets as they stepped off the porch. Sam's big red Dodge Ram pickup sat a few feet away.

"You're being a coyote again, Sam." Her heart sped up as he kept his hand on her arm and led her to the door of the truck.

"Don't get all upset, Gal. Just open the door. Your Christmas gift is in there."

In the dim light from the ranch house window, Kate opened the door. She heard a little yap and her breath snagged. From the floor of the pickup, which was covered with newspapers, a little black-and-white form leaped right at her. She heard Sam's indulgent chuckle as the puppy, a New Zealand collie, jumped up on the front seat.

"Oh!" Kate breathed. The puppy wasn't more than eight weeks old, her black, shiny eyes like buttons, her mouth open and already gnawing on Kate's outstretched fingers. "A dog!"

"Not just any dog," Sam said, leaning over her shoulders as she scooped the puppy up into her arms and held it against her breast. "Remember how Zeke, your cattle-heeling dog, died when you were eighteen? He was New Zealand bred, and your mother had bought him fifteen years earlier. Zeke was the best cattle-heeling dog I'd ever seen." Sam smiled as Kate gazed up at him, tears in her eyes. "Right now, we can use every able body we've got, Kate. Having a collie will help a lot, especially moving those cattle from pasture to pasture. Of course, she's got to grow a little first."

Kate stroked the puppy's black-and-white-peppered fur. "She's cute, Sam."

He was so close. So wonderfully close. Kate felt comforted even as she recalled Zeke's death. At fifteen, the old dog had been a little too slow when one of the Hereford bulls got nasty. Zeke had been nipping at the animal's hind legs when one good kick had sent him to his death.

Kate closed her eyes, tears matting her lashes. She felt the warmth of the little puppy wriggling happily against her, felt her tiny pink tongue licking her fingers. "Oh, Sam," she whispered. Blindly, she turned and threw her free arm around his broad shoulder. Being careful not to crush the puppy, she leaned up to kiss his cheek.

In that instant, she felt Sam tremble. Without warning, his arms came around her, pulling her even closer, though he, too, was careful not to hurt the puppy. Leaning down, he intercepted Kate's kiss. Instead of finding his cheek, she found his mouth instead. Her world exploded. His mouth took hers, molded her to him. A soft moan came from her as she placed one hand against his chest. She felt his arms leave her, his hands settle on the sides of her face to angle her to better advantage and continue the breath-stealing kiss.

His mouth was cajoling, strong and consuming. A fire sparked and ignited hotly between them as he slid his lips along hers. Kate felt his warm, moist breath against her face. Her fingers curled against his chest as she returned the power of Sam's kiss. Instantly, she felt him tremble again. A groan, or maybe it was a growl, came from deep within him. She felt his fingers slide through her hair, cherishing her, stroking her as if she was some beautiful, fragile thing. Each stroke of his fingers against her scalp incited more heat within her. The beat of his heart felt sledgehammer hard beneath her palm. His breathing was erratic. So was hers. His mouth was commanding, her response hungry.

It felt as if a volcano, simmering deep inside her, had suddenly exploded. A hot, scalding heat flared upward through her, making her acutely aware of every inch of her skin beneath the clothes she wore. Her breasts tightened as his hands moved restlessly from her hair down her face, following the line of her neck and shoulders. She moaned as his hands brushed the sides of her taut breasts, which screamed out for his touch.

"Kate," he groaned. He couldn't get enough of her mouth, of her. She tasted sweet and tart to him. The eagerness of her response tore at his disintegrating control. Sam slid his hand around her hip, pinning her lower body to his. He let her feel the hardness there, the desire that raged within him. "I need you," he rasped against her mouth. Her lips were wet, soft and pliant beneath his, begging him to go deeper, to explore more of her.

"I need you…." His words were lost as she returned his kiss, her tongue tangling with his.

The world closed in on them, the only sound their ragged breathing, the only sensation their hands touching, exploring one another. Kate was consumed by an inner fire Sam had ignited. His mouth was as she remembered from that morning up on the Rim—strong yet tender, directing without controlling. Each time he slid his lips against hers, a little more of her crumbled. Each trembling touch of his hands upon her face, her breasts, her hair, made her knees grow weaker and weaker beneath the onslaught. For that instant, Kate felt as she had when they were teenagers. She remembered that same hungry, exciting exploration of their bodies with their hands, their mouths….

The puppy whined and struggled, caught between them.

As if drugged, Kate pulled away from Sam, her other hand holding the puppy close. The tingle of her lips told her how powerfully Sam had taken her. Dazed, she stepped back, her knees wobbly. They were both breathing hard. His eyes were like glittering ice shards as he studied her in the intervening moments after their unexpected kiss.

"Time…." Kate whispered unsteadily, reaching up and touching his lips. "I need some time, Sam…."

Chapter 10

Kate sat on her bay mare, Cinnamon, overlooking a herd of Herefords recently moved to a new pasture that butted up against the Mogollon Rim. The towering ridge, a wedge of red sandstone topped with white limestone formed a watershed of sorts. Luckily, the high country on the rim got enough snow to fill the lakes and reservoirs there. However, rains that were supposed to come and feed the parched desert lands thousands of feet below it had never arrived that year.

Cinnamon snorted softly and switched her tail. The mid-March sun was bright and warm. Kate reveled in it. Down below, she saw Sam urging the stragglers into the pasture area. *Sam.* Her heart contracted as the memory of his branding kisses seared through her—just as it did every time the recollection came unbidden to her. Automatically, her fingers tightened around the leather reins.

She smiled a little, watching Pepper, the New Zealand collie that Sam had given her for Christmas, race around, nipping at the heels of cows that were lagging behind and calling for their wandering, errant calves. Not quite five months old, Pepper was already being faithful to her genetic background. In Australia and New Zealand, the dogs were prized for their ability to herd and keep sheep together. Here in the U.S., they were excellent at helping a cowboy move a herd of cattle.

Dismounting, Kate checked the cinch on her saddle. It felt looser than normal. Maybe because she'd tossed and turned so much last night, she hadn't been as careful or thorough as she should have been with her equipment this morning. Nudging aside the rope that hung from the leather-covered horn, she lifted the stirrup back over the saddle to take a better look. Sliding two gloved fingers under the soft cotton strands of the cinch, she decided it seemed tight enough. Oh, well, it must be her imagination.

Dropping the stirrup down against Cinnamon's barrel, Kate remounted. She heard an approaching horse and knew it was Sam on his big chestnut gelding, Bolt. Inevitably, her heart started skipping beats in anticipation of his nearness. Because the demands of the ranch were widespread, they rarely saw each other. This morning was especially wonderful because for a few hours they got to work together.

Sam pulled his Arabian gelding to a halt. Even though it was only ten a.m., he was sweating from the work. Taking off his hat, he wiped his brow with the back of his sleeve and studied Kate, who smiled at him in silent greeting. Her hair nearly touched her shoulders at the back now, soft and slightly curled. It didn't matter if she wore a Stetson, jeans and a long-sleeved shirt, she couldn't hide the fact that she was all-woman. Every now and again, the memory of their stolen kisses burned brightly within him. It had kept his hope alive these past three months. Did he really dare to dream the impossible—that someday Kate might love him as he had always loved her? Over the past few months, Sam had watched as Kate slowly began to shed her shell. She was not only opening up to him a little at a time, she was also much surer of her role on the ranch and more confident that she could save it. Yes, time was on their side, there was no doubt.

"We're done, Boss. Mamas and babies will be glad to munch on that green grass down below." He twisted around in the saddle and watched the herd of three hundred Herefords. Half the cows had already birthed their calves. The other half would be dropping their babies in the next month. It was a demanding time on the ranch right now. Usually, cows could calve without problems. But when there were problems, someone had to be nearby. The pasture was an hour north of the ranch, which meant one of them would have to drive out during the daylight hours at least two to three times a day to check the herd. Losing a calf meant losing a lot of money, and right now, Sam knew they were hitting bottom again financially.

Kate studied Sam's darkly tanned, glistening features as he settled his hat back on his head, his eyes glittering with some unknown emotion. She felt her body respond hotly to his gaze and she could practically taste her hunger for him. Only this time, she wanted to go all the way. To love him with all the fierce passion that clamored restlessly within her. Maybe that's why she wasn't sleeping well at night. How could she with the memory of the searing kisses they'd shared burning in her heart and mind?

Sam gestured to her horse. "Cinch problems?"

"It felt a little loose was all," Kate said. "Must have been my imagination." She gloried in the warmth of the sun on her back. With a sigh, she whispered, "Isn't this beautiful, Sam? A bright blue sky, temperature in the high sixties, green grass like a carpet under our feet and the smell of the pine nearby..." She closed her eyes and then laughed. "I sure wish I could bottle all of this up and wear it!"

Grinning, he moved his horse to parallel hers, their cowboy boots occasionally touching as the animals shifted. What he was looking at was beautiful: Kate Donovan on horseback. Since their stolen kisses, she'd been far more expressive with how she felt. Maybe she was beginning to trust him a little. He hoped so.

"Days like this ought to be bottled and sent east," he agreed, lifting his leg up and over the saddle horn. Leaning his elbow on that leg, he looked down to see Pepper panting happily between them. The dog was small, maybe all of twenty pounds, and Sam didn't know many creatures brave enough to plop down between huge horses with such trust.

"That dog of yours is turning into a good heeler," he told Kate, catching the dancing warmth in her blue eyes. He drank in the soft, upturned corners of her mouth. There was no question that Kate belonged out here, on the ranch. Somehow, being home was helping her to heal a lot of open wounds from her past, too. For that, Sam was grateful.

"Pepper's going to be great," Kate agreed. She leaned over the saddle, her hands outstretched. "Come on, Pepper," she called.

Instantly, the puppy leaped upward.

Kate caught her dog and hefted her up into her lap. She positioned the puppy carefully between her thighs so that she had a safe place to sit. Chuckling, Kate avoided Pepper's pink tongue and patted her head.

Kate and her dog and her horse. It was all so natural, Sam thought as he watched her laugh and play with Pepper. The dog adored her. Who wouldn't? He sure as hell did. As a matter of fact, he envied Pepper—at least Kate allowed the dog to get close to her. He turned away and momentarily scowled. Although his gaze was on the red-and-white Herefords that dotted the green pasture below, his mind and heart were elsewhere.

How many times had he awakened at night from torrid dreams of making love to Kate? He wasn't sorry at all for those rare moments when they could share an intimate kiss. Each was leading to more exploration, more trust and deepening intimacy between them. He *wanted* to taste her, feel her, share her breath, her caresses. In some ways, the kisses were softening Kate and making her more accessible. In other ways, she avoided him like the proverbial plague. Sometimes, without thinking, he'd get too close to her and she'd automatically step away from him. Sam didn't blame her. After all, he'd betrayed her once and he knew that the hurt was a tough wall to dissolve between them. Kate had to learn she could trust him not to leave her in the lurch again—that he would always be there for her.

Wiping the sweat collecting on his upper lip with his gloved hand, he furrowed his brow more heavily as he watched the cattle below. Sam released a long, ragged sigh, then he straightened in the saddle and lowered his leg. Picking up the reins, he looked over at Kate and Pepper. There was such life shining in Kate's sky blue eyes, in her smiling, parted lips as she stroked the puppy's head. "I've got to get back. Need to pick up sweet feed at the mill. Charley's got the order ready for us."

"Oh..." Kate quickly let Pepper slip gently back to the ground. "You're right. We can't take breaks like this too often." Picking up the reins, she clucked to Cinnamon, who headed back down the knoll at a brisk walk.

Sam joined her, keeping his horse a few feet from hers so that their boots or legs wouldn't accidentally touch. They headed for the big aluminum gate at the south end of the pasture. "Is there anything you want in Sedona while I'm there?"

Since Chet Cunningham had embarrassed her at the restaurant, Kate had not gone back to town. Sam understood why, but he also knew Kate couldn't keep herself locked up like a prisoner at the ranch for the rest of her life, either. If she wanted anything, she handed him a list and he picked up the items for her. Shopping for groceries wasn't one of his favorite things, but he did it anyway. He knew Kate was afraid to meet too many accusing looks if she ran into townsfolk in the aisles. Someday, that wound would scab over, too.

Stealing a glance at him, Kate said, "I thought I

might ride into town with you. There're some things I'd like to pick up at the saddler in West Sedona."

Unable to hide his surprise, he stared at her.

"It's about time, don't you think?" Kate asked wryly.

"The time is right when you feel ready to tackle it, Gal." At least he was able to call her by this endearment. And every time he did, he saw Kate's tender reaction. That was all he could do right now. He couldn't touch her or kiss her anytime he wanted—at least, not yet. But the friendship and trust they were establishing was a good foundation.

"I'm such a coward at heart, Sam," Kate said with a sigh, waving her hand helplessly. "I know I've been hiding out here, using the ranch chores as a convenient excuse. Jessica read me the riot act on the phone the other night. She made me mad, but she was right."

"About what?"

"How I was letting Chet Cunningham, one person in ten thousand in Sedona, stop me from living my life fully."

Sam grinned sourly. "That little space-cadet sister of yours has her head screwed on straight."

With a laugh, Kate leaned down and patted Cinnamon's sleek neck. The horse automatically arched a little more in response. "Jessica *seems* to be spacy and ungrounded, but she's not."

"She reminds me of a leaf falling off a tree at the whimsy of the wind."

"Yes, but every leaf knows where it's going—to the ground." Kate grinned. "My little sister is flighty, but she's practical."

"Part of your mother's gift to all of you," Sam agreed

congenially. The aluminum gate was double locked, so he dismounted and walked up to it. "You three ladies all have the genius of common sense," he told her, opening the gate and moving him and his horse through it.

"Mom could make a silk purse out of a sow's ear," Kate agreed with a laugh. She clucked to Cinnamon and moved through the open gate, with Pepper at the mare's heels. Kate watched as Sam carefully double-checked the gate to make sure it was secure. If the cows and calves got out, they could wander over nearly five thousand acres of desert unattended, and that wasn't such a good idea right now.

Kate enjoyed watching Sam as he mounted again, his actions graceful and confident. Giving her a significant look, he brought his horse into a walk next to hers. "So Jessica badgered you into coming to town with me today?" He would have wished Kate wanted to ride in the truck with him on her own accord, but that was pretty selfish of him. Wounds from the past took time to heal and he just had to dig down deeper in himself to find patience.

"Mmm, maybe not badgered. She sent me one of the natural essences she makes for her company. Matter of fact, it comes from broom snakeweed," Kate said, gesturing toward the desert. "It comes from right here. All that yellow-flowering brush."

Raising his brows, Sam said, "That's a pasture weed out here." Snakeweed was a prolific plant that during the spring rain would burst into life, with hundreds of tall, green arms and a cloud of little yellow flowers on top. The wind would pick up the fragrant scent, one of Mother Nature's perfumes. It smelled nice, but it also discouraged grass growth, so it wasn't a favorite of ranchers. But there was no stopping snakeweed, so one learned to live with it.

"I know," Kate said with a laugh. "Jessica said she made that essence several years ago when she was visiting a friend in Tucson. She told me it was a medicine that helped a person confront his or her fears. I've been taking four drops four times a day for the last couple of days and I have noticed I'm not as scared as I used to be when I thought about going into town."

"So, it helps with a person's fears, whatever they might be?"

"That's what Jessica said." Kate shrugged. "Seems to be working. My stomach doesn't clench into a knot when I think about going into town."

Impressed, Sam said, "She's really got something with that stuff of hers, doesn't she?"

"Listen, Jessica's natural essences are used around the world by people who don't want to use drugs. They're natural, and they work. At first, I was like you—unconvinced. But she's so enthusiastic about them and what they can do to help that I had to try them. She says she has another natural essence that cures depression."

"That's pretty heady stuff," Sam agreed. "Trade in your antidepressants for a little one-ounce bottle of a flower essence, instead. I'd do it, too."

"Besides, it's cheaper, safe and has no side effects," Kate added. "Drugs can't compete with that, and that's why her products are just flying off the shelf."

"And Jessica's money is helping to sustain the ranch," Sam noted. Faithfully, every month, the two sisters sent checks. Without those life-giving infusions, the Donovan Ranch would again fall behind in mortgage payments, and the bank, this time, wasn't going to be lenient. In Sam's opinion, the bank would foreclose without a bat of an eyelash. The banker, Fred Smith, was a good friend of Cunningham's, and over the years, the grizzled old rancher had made no bones about wanting to scoop up the Donovan ranch if the bank did foreclose. Then the Bar C would be the largest ranch in the State of Arizona.

"Yes," Kate said with a sigh, "thank goodness for their checks." And their weekly phone calls to her. How she looked forward to Sunday, when telephone rates were cheapest. She would spend at least half an hour talking with each of them, catching them up on ranch news, where they stood financially, and sharing how their personal lives were going. Next to being with Sam, Kate looked forward most to those life-giving phone calls from her sisters.

As the ranch house appeared in the distance, Sam gazed over at Kate, who had lapsed into deep thought, her face serene. "Why don't we take lunch in town?" He looked at the watch on his dark, hairy wrist. "It's nearly eleven a.m."

Startled by the suggestion, Kate felt heat rush to her face. "Where?"

"The Muse Restaurant?" he drawled good-naturedly.

Laughing, Kate said, "The way I feel right now, the Muse would be fine, too."

"The Muse has the best barbecued pork ribs in town…."

Matching his grin, she said, "Why not? I'm like a

starvin' wolf." Then she patted her lean rib cage with her gloved hand.

"You got a deal. We'll pick up the feed and then stop at the Muse for lunch and go to the saddle maker afterward." Sam could barely keep the joy out of his voice. At last! Kate was moving forward again, growing and reaching out. This time he hoped like hell Chet Cunningham was nowhere to be seen. Usually the cowboy frequented Bailey's Bar in West Sedona. His appearance at the more posh establishment months ago had been a real fluke. Chet got into his share of brawls down at Bailey's, had seen the inside of Sedona's jail a number of times and had gotten out only because of Old Man Cunningham's power in the community. Well, it was noon, and Chet and his brother were probably riding the range, nowhere near Sedona, Sam hoped fervently.

Kate wiped her fingers on a linen napkin and grinned across the table at Sam. "This was a great idea. These ribs were good. I made a real pig out of myself." She looked at the scattered bones left on her plate. She'd eaten as if starved, but she knew that was because when Sam was with her, she relaxed. Since prison, her appetite wasn't consistent, but when Sam was around, she ate well. When he wasn't, she picked at food, not really hungry at all. And having lost twenty pounds in prison, she needed to gain them back in order to do the heavy, demanding ranch work.

Sam set their plates aside. The Muse was full of patrons, the waitresses hurriedly making trips between the tables and the kitchen. He and Kate had gotten a table for two against one wall, near a hat stand covered with cowboy hats. Earlier, when they'd arrived, Sam had cruised the bar area to make sure Chet Cunningham or his more obnoxious older brother, Bo, weren't in there drinking. Fortunately, they weren't.

"Let's head down to the leather shop," Sam said.

Scooping up the bones into a doggy bag for Pepper, Kate nodded and stood. "I'm ready." She was aware of several locals looking at her from time to time, but the broom snakeweed essence she was taking—and Sam's reassuring presence—took the edge off her normally nervous response to such curious stares. How proud Jessica would be of her progress. Coming into Sedona for the first time in nearly four months left Kate feeling really free. As she walked with Sam out the front door onto the patio filled with bright-colored flowers in terra-cotta pots, she realized how much she had been a prisoner of a different sort. And worst of all, she'd sentenced herself this time to hiding on the ranch.

Sunlight glanced down through the branches of the fernlike mimosa trees that bordered the patio outside the restaurant. She felt Sam's hand on her arm, and inwardly she tensed, but only for a moment. More than anything, she ached for his unexpected touches and those times when they could be together and share a warm, escalating kiss.

Kate wished she had the courage to tell Sam that she was dangerously close to surrendering completely to her emotions and letting go, that she was longing to love him completely. His kisses were like a teasing dessert, a promise of sweeter things to come. As he slipped his hand under her elbow, her skin tingled pleasantly, and she looked up at him. The dark gray of his eyes gave no hint of emotion, but his fingers tightened briefly around her elbow. How could she tell him she wanted more of his touches? That she wanted the kisses to move to a new, exploratory level? Sometimes she chastised herself for being such a coward. But at least this time she wasn't running. She was making a stand and a commitment to the ranch—and to herself. Kate knew that Sam's presence was very much a part of her being able to do that. He fed her strength and belief in herself.

Kate stepped off the red flagstone steps to the asphalt parking lot. Perhaps she needed to sit down and talk to him of her fears, her assumptions and her dreams. Maybe it was time. He deserved her honesty, not her cowardice.

Fay Seward was at a sewing machine when Sam and Kate entered the small leather store where everyone in town got their saddles, bridles and harnesses repaired.

"Howdy, Sam," she called as they entered. "Well, hello there, Kate. I'll be with you in just a sec..."

"Thanks, Fay," Sam murmured, tipping his hat toward her.

Kate smiled a greeting at the shop owner. Wearing wire-rimmed glasses that gave her a school-marm look, Fay was in her early fifties, her short, ginger-colored hair in tight curls around her oval face. Kate admired Fay's neat appearance despite the fact she worked at a man's job. As Kate wandered through the small shop, breathing in the wonderful smell of clean and rubbed leather, she gazed at all the new horse headstalls hanging on one wall, the new and used saddles sitting around on pine boxes with wheels. Fay's creativity could be seen everywhere. Some of the headstalls had brow bands of woven horsehair, black and white against the tobacco brown or chocolate color of the leather. She stroked several gently and relished the soft suppleness of the leather.

"Take a look at this," Sam called from the other side of the room. He pointed to a black saddle that had the center of it cut out.

Sauntering across the old, creaking wooden floor, Kate eyed the unusual saddle. "What kind is it?" she asked, running her fingers lightly across the polished black leather.

"It's a U.S. Army make—the McClellan cavalry saddle," Sam told her, examining the brass fittings mounted on the front of it. "And look at this—it was made in 1918. Fay must have sewn new leather straps on it."

"Who would ride such a thing?" Kate wondered. The saddle had a high pommel and cantle, but no horn. It would be useless to ranchers. There would be nothing to twist a rope around when they'd lassoed a steer.

Chuckling, Sam knelt down and closely examined the fine workmanship Fay had put into it. "Probably belongs to one of the Civil War reenactors from Camp Verde." He glanced up at her. "They've got an entire unit of men who wear Civil War outfits, go through the old cavalry drills. And," he continued, easing upward and patting the saddle affectionately, "they use equipment from that era on their horses. The McClellan was made during the Civil War and used up until the army traded tanks for horses after World War One."

Kate admired the saddle. "A lot of history here, isn't there?"

Sam was going to say yes when he heard the door open. Looking up, he instantly narrowed his eyes. In walked Chet and Bo Cunningham. Damn! Baby-faced Chet, his cheeks always red so that he looked like he was blushing, broke into a gleeful grin.

"Well, lookit what the cats dragged in, Bo. . . ."

Kate froze. Her heart shattered. Chet Cunningham! She'd recognize that high nasal twang of his anywhere. Looking over at Sam, she saw his face become a thundercloud of anger, his gray eyes slitted and menacing. Slowly she turned to face her torturer. To her dismay, she saw Bo Cunningham standing beside the short, wiry Chet. Bo was around thirty-one, ruggedly handsome with dark hair like his father, and flashing black eyes he got from his Apache mother. Kate had never liked these two while growing up, though they all went to the same school together. The only Cunningham she liked was Jim, though she rarely saw the son who had gone on to work for the EMT. The other two brothers were nothing but trouble looking for a place to happen.

Kate felt Sam move closer to him. Much closer. She felt protected though she could feel the tension radiating around him. A chair scraped along the wooden floor and Kate's attention wavered. She saw Fay Seward frowning as she moved to the oak counter.

"You boys don't have anything in here to pick up, as I recall."

Chet grinned and swaggered over to the counter. "Miss Fay, how are you this fine day?" He tipped his hat to her in a dramatic motion.

Bo, who was built like his father at six foot three inches tall and more than two hundred pounds, kept his black gaze on Kate. "We're just passin' through, Miss Fay," he said in a low, soothing voice. His mouth twisted like barbed wire as he turned to Sam. "Saw your Ram pickup out front, McGuire. Thought we'd drop by and see how things were goin' at the Donovan Ranch." His smile hardened as his gaze pinned Kate viciously. "Looks like you got what you always wanted, Sam—the Donovan Ranch and that wild ex-con of a girl you were always moonin' over ever since she ran away in high school." He chuckled and moved over to the counter next to his brother.

Kate swallowed hard. From somewhere deep within her, she found her voice. It was low and husky when she spoke. "Bo, you and Chet are nothing but rattlers with nothing good to say about anyone. Time hasn't changed either of you in the least."

Bo spread his arms on the counter, staring at her from beneath the low brim of his dark brown, dusty Stetson. His mouth worked into a sneer. "Hey, Chet, listen to her crowin', will you? Now, neither of us have spent any time in a prison and yet here she is, chiding us." He chuckled.

Chet laughed, too. He raised his beat-up, sweat-stained straw hat off his head and scratched his black hair. "Katie Donovan always thought she was better than us. Always had her nose stickin' in the air at high school. Remember that?"

"Sure do," Bo drawled. "Miss Nose-in-the-Air. That's what we called her." His mouth twisted more. "Eighteen months in the pen didn't change her at all, did it?"

Kate was ready to take them on verbally, her anger

soaring. Before she could, she felt Sam brush by her shoulder, his rage barely contained as he strode toward the two younger men. Worried that a fight might break out, Kate moved quickly in turn. Then she saw Fay pick up a baseball bat from beneath the counter.

"No," Fay growled at the Cunningham men, "if you two think you can come in here and bad-mouth payin' customers in *my* establishment, you got another think comin'. As if you two have any room to talk! Both of you boys have been in and out of Coconino County Jail more times than I've got fingers and toes. You quit pickin' on Kate. She served her time. It's done. It's the past, so you let it lie." She laid the baseball bat circumspectly on the counter between them, her hand over it, staring down the Cunningham men. "What'll it be, boys? A lump or two on your head if you keep shootin' off your mouths, or leavin' while your heads are still attached to your shoulders?"

Sam halted halfway to the counter. Automatically, he put his arm out to stop Kate from moving around him. His fingers bit deeply into her arm and he felt her trembling with rage, and he waited. This was Fay's establishment and her territory. She was tough but fair, and if she could handle the Cunninghams, he wouldn't step into the fray. But if they continued calling Kate names, he was going to settle the score with them outside—once and for all.

Bo eased into a standing position. He threw back his broad shoulders and chuckled. "Now, Miss Fay, we don't mean you no harm." He gestured toward Sam. "Nah, we're just droppin' by to say howdy-do, is all."

He tipped his hat to the older woman. "We'll be leavin' now, nice and peaceful like. Chet?"

Chet grinned and followed his older brother out of the store. "Sure thing, big brother. We got some hay to pick up at the feed store." He tipped his hat respectfully in Fay's direction. "Ma'am? Have a nice day."

The door shut with a slam.

Kate released a broken sigh of relief.

"Those damned boys never grew up," Fay snarled, putting the baseball bat beneath the counter once again. "Old Man Cunningham spoilt those two varmints but good. Bad milk gone to sour if you ask me." She looked over at them. "I'm awful sorry, Kate and Sam. Try and consider the source and let it be like water runnin' off a duck's back, will you?"

Easing her fingers from Sam's upper arm, Kate felt his thick, hard muscles. He was as solid as the Mogollon Rim. Managing a weak smile, she said, "Thanks, Fay. This wasn't your fight. Chet has been gunning for me ever since I got out of…well, since I came home."

Snorting, Fay flashed an angry look toward the door. "Those two need their heads banged every once in a while to keep 'em in line. Chet hasn't a brain in that empty skull of his and Bo's more dangerous than a rattler." She walked briskly over to the wall of headstalls. "Come on, I've got those two bridles fixed for you, Sam. Here they are."

Relief washed through Kate as Fay went about the business at hand. Gratefully, she paid for the headstalls, glad that Fay didn't mention her prison past. The older woman treated her like she would anyone. And best of all, she had stood up and defended her. Kate hadn't known Fay well growing up, but she was coming to appreciate her forthright manner.

"Thank you," Kate murmured as she handed her the cash. "For everything...."

Fay placed the headstalls in some brown wrapping paper and tied it up with string. "Teenagers in men's bodies if you ask me. Testosterone for brains. They don't think with their heads, they think with what's between their legs." She handed Kate the package. Squinting her blue eyes, she jabbed her brown, stained index finger at Kate. "Don't let a few snakes in the grass make you feel badly, young lady. Hell, no one has a clean past. I spent time in a local jail once for beating up my husband because he was beating up my daughter. And I've made a lot of decisions I ain't proud of, either. We've all got pasts. What you need to do is let it go. Walk proud, with no apologies." Her glance cut to the door. "Especially to the likes of those two troublemakers. Folks around here will judge you on what you do now, on a daily basis, if they've got any brains."

Barely able to stop from chuckling, Kate kept a respectful and somber look on her face. "Thank you, Fay. You're a wonderful teacher."

Taking off her glasses, Fay tenderly rubbed the bridge of her nose with her fingers. "Then take it to heart, missy." She put her glasses back on and looked over at Sam. "And you stop being so defensive about Kate, here."

Chastened, Sam had the good grace to blush under Fay's squinty-eyed look of censure. "I got a little tense," he admitted.

"I saw you cock your fist. That's why I went for the

baseball bat. It makes for a real balance in a fight. I was countin' on you being smarter than those two rocks-for-brains, and holding your ground."

His mouth pulled into a sour grin. "Miss Fay, I would *never* think of starting a fight in your establishment." And he wouldn't. Fay Seward was known to be crusty, combative and downright cantankerous if she was unfairly disturbed. Every rancher in the territory knew that. And she was famous for her baseball bat. More than a couple of cowboys had tasted the bat's infamous reputation.

"Humph, you'd better now. Kate's got two legs and a brain in her head. She can speak up and defend herself." Fay's eyes flashed. "You're behavin' like a mongrel dog that's found his lifelong mate. Don't be like those two boys and let your brain turn to mush just 'cause you're emotionally in over your head."

Kate bit back laughter. She saw Sam's brow draw down in displeasure, but he didn't get defensive.

"Yes, Miss Fay," he murmured politely, and tipped his hat to her. "I'll come by for that saddle sometime next week?"

Fay twisted around, searching for the saddle that needed repair. "Yessir, you can come by next Friday. I'll have new straps and a cinch for it by that time. Good day to you both."

On the way home, Kate mulled over the entire sequence of what had happened in Fay's saddle shop. What had Fay meant when she said Sam was acting like a mongrel dog who had found his lifelong mate? She risked a glance at his harsh profile as he drove up 89A out of Sedona. Just as quickly, she moved her gaze out the window to drink in the juniper and desert pine that dotted the red sand earth. Wasn't his protective stance a normal, natural thing? Fay didn't think so. And what about Bo Cunningham's comment that Sam had what he'd always wanted—the ranch and her? That comment didn't make sense, either. Or did it?

Chapter 11

Early, unexpected April heat swept across the desert expanse, parching everything in its path. Kate felt a fine tremble of tension run through her as she sat on her Arabian mare, eyes squinted against the strong noon sunlight. She pressed her calves to the bay, and instantly, Cinnamon broke into a slow, controlled lope. Ahead of her, moving up a sandy slope littered with multicolored pebbles, Mormon tea plants that towered eight to ten feet tall and prickly pear cactus, was Sam. He, too, urged his rangy gelding, Bolt, into a lope.

Today they were gathering the three Hereford bulls from their collective pasture, to move them to three new pastures where they would each have a harem of cows to impregnate for the next year's calf crop. They'd decided to leave Pepper home for this job, as it was much too dangerous for a young puppy. Handling bulls was never easy work. It was hard, dirty and dangerous. Worse, neither Sam nor herself knew these bulls. Kelly had bought them after Sam had left the ranch. One of the things a rancher needed to pay attention to was the personality of a two-thousand-pound bull, which weighed twice as much as a horse. Sam and she had watched the bulls and gotten an idea of their temperament, so that when it came time to herd them, they could be prepared as much as possible for any exigency plans.

Even so, Kate had had a bad feeling when she woke up at four a.m. that morning. The moving of the bulls had been put off until it could no longer be ignored. Two people on horseback handling three bulls wasn't enough to get the job done safely. But they had no choice. These bulls were restless. They could smell the cows in season and were frustrated because they hadn't been able to breed. Bulls were not oriented by herd instinct. Once a bull smelled the scent of cows, he could break off at a moment's notice, hurtle his massive body right through a startled horse and rider and kill them in order to get to the cows.

Today, Kate wore leather chaps, as Sam did. The chaps were wide and flared at the bottom, covering part of her dusty, cracked cowboy boots. If a bull decided to take off, she or Sam could be brush popped through thickets of cutting chaparral, slammed into the long, crochet-needle-size spines of a Mormon tea bush or worse, be run into a five-to eight-foot patch of prickly pear cactus. The leather would be a good guard against abrasion, up to a point.

Flexing her gloved fingers on the reins, Kate felt Cinnamon move nervously beneath her, picking up on her tension. The sun beat directly down on them as they spotted the bulls just below the base of the hill, foraging for almost nonexistent grass. Spring was supposed to yield several inches of rain to feed the dry, arid land, but so far it hadn't. Now food was more sparse than ever and the bulls had ranged over a much larger area in order to survive. It would make herding them even longer and more difficult.

"There they are," Sam said, glancing at Kate as she pulled up beside him. He saw the grim set of her lips. She wore a red bandanna around her throat, protective chaps and gloves, plus a special long-sleeved, heavy twill shirt that would to a degree protect her flesh from brutal contact with Mormon tea and chaparral. Her face glistened; her sky blue eyes narrowed, intent upon the bulls.

He wasn't feeling too easy, either. Today they both wore pistols—Colts—around their waists. If a bull got mean and charged, it might have to be shot in order to save their lives. When blinded by the mating lust, a bull was a ton of raw testosterone and adrenaline on the hoof.

Sam rested his hand on the low-slung holster that held the Colt. Earlier, they'd put bullets in the chambers, locked and loaded them and put the safety on. Riding around with a bullet in the barrel of a pistol wasn't something he liked to do, but there wasn't much choice. If he knew the personalities of the bulls better, he might be feeling less tense. Therefore, out of a lifetime of experience, Sam treated the bulls like C-4 plastic explosives just waiting to go off at him. Or worse, at Kate. Worriedly, he assessed her. She seemed easy and relaxed in the saddle, but he saw tension in the line of her mouth.

"You sure you want to do this?"

She quirked her lips. "No, but I didn't see anybody else volunteering." Patting the bulging saddlebags behind her, she added, "I've brought two first-aid kits—one with dressing and bandages, the other that homeopathic kit Rachel sent—just in case."

Scratching away the sweat trickling down his cheek, Sam nodded. "Good." He sincerely hoped they wouldn't need either one of them. "We'll probably look like a couple of pin cushions before this little dance is over."

"Chaps will help."

"Help, but not stop all of those cactus spines." He motioned to the landscape stretching before them. Thousands of Mormon tea bushes stood with their arms full of greenish yellow needles. They reminded him of long crochet or knitting needles, sticking out all over the bush as if it were a giant pin cushion. "This is a bad area. Keep your face protected, Kate. I don't want you to lose an eye to one of those damn bushes." He hated Mormon tea. It was far more dangerous to a human and horse than the prickly pear patches that proliferated on the red, sandy desert.

Except for protective wrappings on their vulnerable lower legs, the horses had little way to defend themselves against hostile plants and bushes. The gelding Sam rode was long-legged, rangy and savvy. From years of experience, Bolt knew how to avoid these dangers. And the Arabian Kate rode was trail trained, also. These horses were smart and they knew how to read cattle. Sam knew his horse had plenty of experience with testy, dangerous bulls. He wasn't sure that Cinnamon had any such experience—and that put Kate at great risk. A horse not expecting to get charged by a bull could freeze—and leave it and its rider a handy target. If Cinnamon was used to docile Herefords and had no experience with the cantankerous behemoths, that was a high risk. But what else could Sam do?

He had known Donovan horses that had bull-herding experience, but when he returned to the ranch, they were all gone. And Cinnamon was new. He'd watched the mare and knew she had a good head on her shoulders. Her response in other situations had been steady and controlled. But bulls could scare even the most levelheaded of horses if they made a split-second charge. A horse could freeze or could leap to one side to avoid being struck. Worse, if Kate asked Cinnamon to make a swift countermove, and the mare, because of inexperience, didn't trust her mistress in the dangerous situation, they could be injured or killed.

It was very important that a ranch horse trust its rider completely. One wrong move, one misstep, could get them killed. There were places on the Donovan Ranch that could only be reached by taking the canyon walls. If a horse did not watch where it was placing its feet or heed the signals of the rider's legs or the reins, they could both slip to their death.

Scowling, Sam studied the three red-and-white Hereford bulls. Luckily, they'd found some pretty good patches of yellowing grass beneath a large stand of Mormon tea and they were closely grouped. That was unusual, but he hoped it was a sign of good things to come. He pointed his gloved finger at the bull nearest them, the largest one with the red ear tag hanging off his left ear. The bull lazily flicked at the flies buzzing around his massive head. "Let's call him One Horn. He's the biggest. I'll take him on. That next one, the middle-sized one, will be Red. The smallest over there we'll call Whitey."

Names would help them when they called out instructions or orders to one another. Red was a muscular powerhouse, his small eyes regarding them suspiciously even now. Sam didn't trust that son of a bitch, either. Whitey was the smallest of the three bulls, and looked the least interested in their approach. One Horn had one of his horns missing, and the other was deformed and thrust upward like a twisted dagger waiting to impale some unlucky soul. Sam didn't like horned Herefords. He'd argued against purchasing them, but Kelly had liked the old traditional Hereford breed with horns.

A Hereford's horns normally were small and curved inward toward the bull's face, which made them a lot less dangerous than other breeds of cattle to a cowboy who had to herd them. One Horn's straggly appendage was like a razor-sharp knife. A savage head toss by One Horn would be like experiencing the cut of a saber. The bull, if angered, could slice and gut open a horse chest to flank in one horrifying motion. It wasn't a very pleasant thought.

Kate's Arabian mare weighed only eight hundred pounds. Sam's gelding was a good four hundred pounds heavier—not to mention a lot taller. Herding bulls with heavier horses was smart because a bull could bump a horse and the horse could stand its ground and not get tossed around like a tumbleweed. Bolt was built like a proverbial tank, with a lot of width across his chest, heavy hindquarters for getting his rear legs solidly beneath him, enabling him to turn on a dime, and a long barrel that gave him the ability to reach a long, ground-eating stride very swiftly.

"None of them look very pleasant, do they?" Kate asked wryly, sitting up in the saddle and stretching her legs. In a few moments they'd be working hard. Once they got the bulls together and moving in the same direction, there could be no stopping or resting—or the bulls would scatter like leaves on the wind, and the herding process would have to begin all over.

"No," Sam growled. He gestured toward the bulls. "Watch One Horn. He's eyeing us. I looked at the breeding records in your office on these three bulls and he's the oldest. That means he's got more experience."

"Translated," Kate said grimly, "it means he knows how to down a horse and rider if he gets a mind to."

"Yes," Sam agreed unhappily. Reaching out, he gripped her upper arm momentarily. "If I yell an order to you, Kate, just do it. Don't wait, don't analyze, all right? You've got to trust me enough to know that I know what's right if these bulls get riled."

She smiled a little and reveled in the firmness of his hand on her arm. "I trust you with my life, Sam McGuire." The tenor of their relationship was continuing to evolve, their exchanges more open, filled with personal warmth. In the last month, Kate had initiated a touch now and then—not often, but it let him know that she was reaching out to him. He'd gotten the message. Now and then, in return, he would touch her. Usually in moments when he was worried for her safety. Like now.

Sam released Kate's arm, his gaze resting on her blue eyes flecked with gold. Yes, things were moving the right direction with her as far as he was concerned. The energy between them was one of friendship now and ripe with sexual tension. The next step would be a heady one to take, Sam thought as he pulled his hat down tightly so it wouldn't fly off once they got started herding these contrary bastards. In time, if everything went right, he knew Kate would let down her guard and trust him. In time, she might trust him enough to learn to love him once again—as he loved her.

"Let's move nice and easy toward them," he said from between tight lips.

Kate nodded tensely and rode at his side. Her heart skipped a beat as One Horn snapped his large head up toward them. He had small, beady eyes. Evil eyes, in Kate's opinion. There was an old horseman's saying that the smaller the eyes on a horse or steer, the less brains it had and the more dangerous it could be. The larger the eyes, the more intelligent it was and therefore easier to work with.

Upon Sam's command, they separated and quietly moved around the three bulls. Kate saw massive amounts of drool hanging in long, glistening strings from One Horn's white muzzle as he studied her. A chill crawled up her spine. Her hands automatically tightened on the reins and she gripped the barrel of her horse more securely with her long legs. Cinnamon sensed her tension and snorted, her own attention on One Horn.

To Kate's relief, One Horn grudgingly turned as Sam approached him, just like a docile steer or cow would. Cinnamon was trained for leg commands, and Kate pressed her right leg against the animal's side, turning left to cut off the other two bulls, which were beginning to go in different directions, away from One Horn.

Instantly, the bay responded and pebbles flew from beneath her rear hooves as she made the cut. Good. Red and Whitey stopped their escape plan and moved back toward Sam and One Horn. Releasing a breath of air, Kate kept her horse reined in. If one of those bulls decided to charge, she knew it could turn its massive body and come hurtling at her in a split second. She needed to keep her distance in order to react in time and get the hell out of the way.

In her gloved right hand, she held her coiled rope. Not that they would ever try to lasso a bull—that would be foolhardy. With a bull's power and weight, he'd yank a cowboy straight out of the saddle. If the saddle cinch didn't break and shred under the bull's strength, the horse could be pulled off its feet and dragged along, too. No, the rope was for making occasional slapping sounds against her leather chaps, but that was about all.

For two hours they kept the bulls in a slow-moving, loose-knit herd. The rocky, cactus-strewn hills came and went. Kate was beginning to relax. Soon the breeding pastures would be coming up. She noticed that the bulls were lifting their noses more often to the air, testing it for the odor of cows in season and that they had picked up their pace to almost a trot. This was where it could get dangerous. No fence on earth could stop a bull if he chose to plow through it to get to the cows. The breeding pastures were smaller, the posts eight feet high with six strands of barbed wire, designed to detour a bull. But that's all the fence would do.

"Kate!"

Sam's voice thundered at her, interrupting her errant thoughts. Startled, she jerked her head and saw him pointing up to the right of him. A Hereford cow was loose. "Oh, damn," she whispered in a strained voice. Automatically, her hands tightened on the reins. Cinnamon tensed, waiting for a command.

The cow mooed plaintively toward the three approaching bulls. Kate knew without a doubt that the animal was in season. And she also knew that all three bulls had caught the hormonal scent on the air and were going to try and race one another to get to her first in order to breed with her. Double damn! Of all the things Kate imagined could happen, a loose cow wasn't one of them. She saw Sam swing Bolt abruptly. One Horn made a bid to veer off to the right toward the cow.

"Get to the cow!" Sam shouted. "Get her herded back to the pasture!"

It was a brilliant plan, Kate thought. Sam's experience over her own lack of it was obvious. Yes, get the cow herded up ahead of the bulls and they'd follow like mesmerized kids behind the Pied Piper. Sinking her heels into Cinnamon, she made the mare leap to the right. Dirt and stones flew as Kate galloped hard toward the cow half a mile away. Out of the corner of her eye, she saw One Horn toss his head ominously as Sam slapped his coiled rope against his chaps, warning the bull to go back and join the other two.

Kate had no time to watch. Hunching low, her hands against Cinnamon's sweaty neck, she rode at a dizzying pace toward the cow. The Arabian's small size allowed her to weave around the Mormon tea and cactus with finesse and ease. Cinnamon's ground-eating stride thundered beneath Kate. The wind whipped past her, the horse's black mane stinging her face as the mare ran. Up ahead, Kate saw the cow move toward the breeding pastures. Good! This was going to be easier than she'd thought. The cow could've turned contrary and headed straight to the bulls instead, causing all kinds of hell to break loose. If that had happened, the bulls would begin to fight one another, causing serious injury and maybe death to one or more of them. Tens of thousands of dollars spent on a good breeding bull could be lost in a moment like this. Kate didn't want that to happen.

Just as she crested the hill, she heard a bawling and bellowing behind her. The cow was trotting quickly toward the breeding pastures, no more than half a mile away at this point. Jerking her head to the left, Kate pulled her horse to a skidding stop.

"Sam!" Her cry careened down into the gully area between two hills, where he rode with the three restless bulls. *"Nooo!"* She saw One Horn toss his head and charge Sam. Without thinking, Kate sank her heels into Cinnamon. The mare hurtled back down the slope. Kate's heart slammed into her chest as One Horn bore down on Sam.

With a grunt, Sam jerked Bolt to the left as One Horn lifted his massive, drooling head and charged. Despite his heft and size, the bull moved like lightning. Bolt dug in his hind legs, throwing all his weight to the right. Sam stayed with the big gelding, his gaze pinned on the swiftly moving bull. Spittle flew up around One Horn's face and caught on the twisted horn, which glittered like a deadly knife.

Bolt knew what to do—he headed away from the bull at full speed. Sam felt his horse using every ounce of strength to create distance between them.

One Horn bawled angrily and made a sharp move to the right, to head them off.

Damn!

A small gully, cut deep and wide by thunderstorms and flash floods year after year, loomed before them. It lay at the bottom of two bracketing hills. Sam heard Kate's cry but he had no time to look up. A huge stand of Mormon tea appeared to the left of them, just before the gully. On the right was a five-foot-tall patch of prickly pear. The gulch walls were too steep for them to cross it at a dead run. If Bolt tried to leap across and scramble up the steep, rocky hill, he'd never make it.

The choices were few. Sam twisted his head. One Horn had read the situation correctly. Determined to cut them off, he was hurtling toward them, bawling, the spittle streaming out of his open mouth, his eyes red with rage. Sam began to pull back on the reins to signal Bolt not to try and make that deadly leap. The horse could break his neck, and so could Sam once Bolt, who was going too fast to negotiate the rocky hill properly, smashed into the other side.

Again Sam heard Kate's cry, this time closer. Where was she? No time to look. Where to go? The gulch and hill loomed before him.

Without warning, Sam hauled the reins against Bolt's thick, sweaty neck.

Instantly, the big gelding responded. The action threw them into the stand of Mormon tea. Sam tried to protect his face as the horse slammed full speed into the thick, tough greenery. The heavy branches scraped against him but that was the lesser of two evils. He heard Bolt grunt and stagger to the right as the horse lost his footing and they slid into the stand. One Horn bawled. The sound was right on top of them.

Bolt grunted, his hindquarters skidding across the sandy desert and sharp rocks. Sam hung on with his legs while trying to unstrap the Colt from his left hip. They had slid completely, like a baseball runner into home plate, into the thick stand of Mormon tea. The long, stabbing needles mercilessly gouged at horse and rider. Sam felt the jabs, but there wasn't time to focus on the pain. He heard the crash of One Horn following closely behind them.

Bolt, his hind legs beneath him now, was breathing hard. There were at least a dozen puncture wounds in the horse from the Mormon tea and the gelding's chest ran red with trickles of blood. As he directed Bolt to move swiftly out of the grove, Sam glanced behind them. One Horn was coming through the Mormon tea like it was a Sunday walk in the park, plowing the ten-foot bushes aside with his massive weight. Sam saw the killing rage in the bull's eyes, and in that second he knew that one of them was going to die very shortly.

Bolt also seemed to realized that this was a life-and-death confrontation. The horse spun to the left, the shortest way out of the grove. Dirt flew in all directions beneath the powerful, hammering strides of the animal. Once they cleared the bushes, Sam caught sight of Kate, her face white with terror. She was heading right toward One Horn, her coil of rope lifted toward him.

"No!" Sam shouted hoarsely. *No good! Damn!* Bolt

weaved to the right in one smooth motion, his long legs eating up the distance between them. Kate couldn't take on that bull! But that's exactly what she was doing. She was trying to get One Horn's attention away from him and transferred to her. Damn her courage! Sam's lips lifted away from his teeth as he leaned forward, asking for every ounce of Bolt's power in order to close the distance. One Horn was torn between his moving targets. He slowed a little, looking first at Kate, then at Sam. But it was Kate's shrill scream that enraged the bull the most. In one lightning move, One Horn twisted to the right, bawling out his challenge and bearing down on Kate.

The ground was uneven—soft here, hard there. Bolt negotiated the terrain as he carried Sam closer. Cursing, Sam managed to get the Colt out of the holster. Trying to unsnap the safety while his horse was barreling down the side of the slope was nearly impossible. He kept missing the catch again and again. There was no way to stop One Horn now. They were trapped in a small area, the rocky hills acting like prison walls that refused them the room they needed to get away from the infuriated bull. The only way out of the situation was to kill One Horn before he killed one of them.

Kate sucked in a breath as One Horn suddenly spun around and bore directly down on her. Cinnamon reacted first, leaping to the right, her feet sliding down toward the narrow gulch. *No!* Instantly, Kate threw her weight to the left, and the horse steadied. Kate could hear the grunting, sucking sounds One Horn made with each galloping stride he took closer to them. Sam's voice thundered, but Kate couldn't make out what he was yelling. The bull was less than fifty feet away, his small, red eyes fixed on her. Drool streamed out of both sides of his mouth as he lowered his head to charge. The wicked horn glinted in the sunlight.

With a cry, Kate slapped her rope against the horse's rump. Cinnamon leaped forward, startled, and they galloped parallel to the gulch. Up ahead, a large patch of prickly pear loomed. She suddenly saw One Horn change course. He was trying to force her and the horse into the cactus patch or down into the narrow gully. The bastard! The bull was determined to kill them. And that realization startled Kate as nothing else.

Cinnamon realized the bull's intent, too. The mare was breathing hard, trying to outdistance the accelerating beast. Kate knew that the hill, covered with black lava and cactus, could be negotiated, but not at this speed or angle. She might take a horse up that steep face at a slow walk, but not at a wild, headlong gallop. Her choices were few. If she tried to go left, One Horn would intercept her.

For Kate, the only choice was the huge prickly pear patch looming before them. It was a good five feet high at the lowest point, and at least fifty feet deep. She knew now that One Horn was counting on the fact that she wasn't going to run her horse through that patch. But he was wrong. Gathering up the reins, Kate synchronized each movement of her body with Cinnamon's stride. In seconds, they were riding as if they were literally a part of one another. The mare steadied under Kate's hands and guidance.

Gripping her legs tight against the horse's barrel, Kate heard One Horn's breathing coming up fast behind her. She knew there was less than five feet separating them. She would have to jump the patch. Or try at least. Kate was hoping that the bull wouldn't plow through the cactus, being too old and wise to the pain the sharp spines caused. Would he stop? Would Cinnamon trust her and make the jump? The horse could refuse and skid to a halt, trying to escape to the right or left instead. If she did that, Kate knew, One Horn would kill them.

Everything slowed down for Kate. She felt each jolting, thundering movement of the horse, felt the hot sun beating down on her, tasted fear in her mouth and felt sweat stinging her eyes. Prickly pear branches grew at all heights, some five to six feet in the air. Would her small mare be able to jump not only far enough, but high enough? Kate didn't know. But she had to ask for a life-and-death effort from the mare. She placed her gloved hands on the sides of the animal's slick neck, the reins tight as she aimed for the narrowest point of the cactus patch. Applying pressure to the animal's sweaty, heaving sides, Kate signaled the horse to pick up speed in preparation to jump.

The wet mane stung Kate's face as she lifted her butt off the saddle, trying to give Cinnamon every chance to use her hindquarters to power them up and over the patch. Kate felt a moment's hesitation in the mare. Instantly, she pressed Cinnamon with her legs. The mare responded. If the Arabian didn't clear the patch, Kate knew it could badly injure them. Depending upon how the horse fell, Kate might be killed, too. In those slow-motion moments before she asked the Arabian to leap, Kate's heart centered on Sam. How she loved him! She swore that if she got through this alive, she'd tell him that.

Kate felt Cinnamon lifting her front legs as the horse began to leap. Everything began to swirl like a surreal picture in front of Kate's eyes and she pinned her gaze on the landing point. She heard Cinnamon grunt as she powered off the desert ground. They were airborne! Never had Kate sat so still. She felt her horse stretching, stretching forward. Then Cinnamon's legs and hooves tucked deep beneath her belly. Kate knew that if she moved in any way, she could throw the horse off and they could die. She saw the five-foot-tall cactus flash beneath them. The Arabian grunted as it grazed her, her tender belly scraped by the needles.

The bawling of One Horn shattered Kate's concentration. She had no way of knowing whether the bull was following them across the patch or not. Her eyes widened. Her lips parted in a cry. Cinnamon suddenly stretched her legs forward, her black hooves aimed toward that clear patch of ground. Were they going to make it? Her breath jammed in her throat.

Yes! Cinnamon cleared the patch by half a foot! The horse landed hard and Kate was thrown violently forward. Instantly, she threw the reins away to give the horse its head so that she might come out of the ungainly, off-balance landing. Too late! Kate knew Cinnamon had overstretched herself, giving all she had to save them. The mare's front knees buckled. Kate leaned way back, her spine touching the horse's rising hindquarters. Cinnamon was going to flip end over end! Fear engulfed Kate. With a cry of surprise, she allowed the forward momentum to rip her out of the saddle. Instead of hurtling over the horse's head, which would leave her in the path of Cinnamon's hooves, Kate pushed away with her legs. She tucked her head against her body as she flew through the air.

In seconds, Kate slammed into the hard, unforgiving ground. She heard Cinnamon grunt heavily off to her right and felt the ground shake as the horse landed in turn. Rolling to distribute the shock of the fall, Kate kept her arms tight around her knees. She heard several gunshots fired in rapid succession as she landed in a Mormon tea bush. Pain shot up into her back and she suddenly stopped rolling.

Straightening her arms and legs, Kate scrambled to her feet and anxiously looked toward the patch. Her eyes widened enormously when she saw One Horn staggering around in the middle of the cactus, his head bloodied. Sam was astride Bolt, his Colt aimed at the crazed bull. On wobbling legs, Kate watched the bull resist the bullets placed in his brain. Then One Horn's red-eyed gaze settled on her. Foam and spittle mixed with pink and red bubbles of blood running out of his mouth. He bawled in fury. Flailing, he fought to move toward her. Kate froze with shock. The bull was dying, but still trying to reach her!

She heard the Colt bark two more times in quick succession and saw One Horn's head jerk upward at the first shot. His forward progress stopped. The second shot felled him. He grunted, flung his head up in a twisting motion and crashed to the ground, only ten feet away from where Kate stood.

Chapter 12

Kate turned drunkenly to check on her horse. Cinnamon stood alertly, shaking off the excess sand after her fall. The mare seemed fine despite the almost deadly leap she'd made.

"Kate!"

Dazedly, Kate turned back toward Sam's voice. She watched him ride the gelding around the cactus patch, his face stony, his flesh glistening with sweat, his eyes dark and fathomless. Bolt's hindquarters lowered as the gelding slid to a stop, and sand flew up in sheets around them. Sam dismounted, his gaze pinned savagely upon her.

"I—I'm all right." Kate wobbled as he ran up to her, his hand outstretched. But she wasn't, and she knew it. She had nearly died. One Horn had plowed through the cactus patch after her. And Cinnamon had fallen. The bull would have gored her to death in the sand right where she stood if Sam hadn't shot him.

Sam reached out, his fingers closing over her shoulder. "Kate…you're white as a sheet," he muttered tightly. "Broken bones?"

"No…" Kate closed her eyes, a ragged sigh escaping her lips. "Oh, Sam…" She leaned forward, lifting her arms and sliding them around his neck. He was hot, sweaty and dirty, but she didn't care. At this moment, all she wanted was him and the sense of safety he'd always given her. She wanted to sob out her love for him, and the words were nearly torn from her as she collapsed into his arms.

"Come here," he rasped hoarsely, wrapping his arms around her. Crushing Kate against him, Sam steadied her against the hard angles of his body. She fit perfectly and he groaned as her head rested against his jaw. He felt Kate trembling, and it got worse the longer he held her.

"It's all right," he breathed huskily, turning his head and pressing his mouth against her damp, gritty hair. "Everything's going to be all right, Gal. I promise you…." He felt Kate moan as he pressed a not-so-innocent kiss to her temple. She shifted and lifted her face to him. He saw tears swimming in her dark blue eyes, saw the terror in them—and something else…. For those few seconds, Sam couldn't believe what he thought he was seeing. He remembered that look from so long ago. Did he dare hope?

"I almost died," Kate murmured, holding his stormy gray gaze. "I could've died and never told you, Sam…." She choked on a sob and moved her hands to his face.

"I love you… I never stopped loving you! I could have died just now and you'd never have known—"

Her words were caught by his descending mouth. He captured her lips fully, his mouth hot, hungry and seeking. Sinking fully against him and allowing Sam to take all her weight, Kate surrendered to him. Tears streaked down her cheeks, met and melted into the line of their mouths as they devoured one another. She'd almost died! Eagerly, she returned his powerful, molding kiss with equal need and fiery hunger. She could smell his masculine scent, taste his fear, feel the roughness of his beard scraping against her face. She suddenly remembered all those wonderful things about Sam that she could have never have experienced again if One Horn had gotten to her before Sam had killed him.

Knees wobbly, Kate tore her mouth from his, breathing hard. She gripped his arms to steady herself. Apologetically, she met his stormy, silvery eyes. She'd known this man before—the raw hunger in his eyes, the cajoling strength of his mouth upon hers, the roughened tenderness of his hands upon her body. "Sam," she whispered, "I—I think I'm going to faint…."

Kate awoke slowly. She felt the heat of the sun on her body, heard the soft snort of horses nearby. More than anything, she felt a damp cloth being gently dabbed across her brow where she lay. Lashes fluttering, she forced her eyes open. The cool cloth felt so good. She was hot, her skin sore and gritty. As her gaze focused, she realized belatedly that Sam was kneeling over her. And even more belatedly, Kate realized with embarrassment that she'd fainted.

"Just lie still," Sam urged quietly. He poured a little more of the precious water from his canteen into his bandanna and wiped the sides of her face. Her eyes were half-open and filled with confusion. He saw her lips twist wryly.

"I don't believe it. I fainted. I've never done that, ever…and I've been in a few tight spots before. I must be getting old…."

Her voice was wispy and weak, completely unlike her. Sam placed the bandanna across her furrowed brow and unbuttoned the two top buttons on her shirt, pulling her collar wide. He'd removed her gloves and set them nearby, propping up her feet so that the blood flowed back into her head and upper body.

"Almost getting killed brings on a lot of reactions," he grunted.

Kate's lashes dropped shut as Sam carried her out of the sun and placed her beneath the spreading arms of a mesquite tree. Languishing there, grateful for his care, Kate slowly realized that she'd told Sam she loved him. Instantly, she opened her eyes and stared up at his hard, uncompromising face.

"The horses…are they okay?"

"Fine. It's you I'm worried about."

Pushing herself up on one elbow, Kate managed a broken smile. Sam helped her sit up and she leaned her elbows over her knees, hugging her head between her legs. Color was rushing back to her face now, and Sam knew she'd be all right. He tucked the damp bandanna into her hand.

"Keep wiping your face down and cooling off." He rose to his feet.

Kate looked up and did as she was instructed. Sam went over to Bolt, who stood no more than six feet away. She wanted to cry as she saw about a dozen puncture wounds across his massive chest from his run through the Mormon tea. Trickles of drying blood made vertical stripes across his powerfully muscled body. Sam spoke gently to the gelding as he slowly ran his hand over the animal's chest in examination. Every once in a while Sam would jerk out a thin, needlelike spine causing Bolt to flinch.

Getting to her feet, her knees still a little weak, Kate moved over to Cinnamon, who had sought the shade of the mesquite tree as well.

"Let me check her over," Sam said from behind her, his hand settling on her arm. "Sit back down, Kate. Just rest a minute."

Ordinarily, Kate would have protested, but the sand and the shade looked awfully inviting. "Okay…"

She watched as Sam discovered at least thirty cactus spines in Cinnamon's belly, where she'd brushed the prickly pear in her lifesaving leap.

Sam crouched down, carefully picking the spines out one by one. Cinnamon never moved a muscle. "She did one hell of a job jumping that patch. I didn't think she would make it." He glanced over at Kate. She had gone pale again and he saw her lips compress at his statement. "Bolt *might* have made it, but I never thought this little bay Arabian could do it. When I saw you make the decision, I thought you were dead."

Kate wiped her brow with her trembling hand. She was still amazed at her reaction to the event. But then, she reminded herself, she'd never been the target of a two-thousand-pound bull intent on killing her, either. "I didn't have a choice. Cinnamon knew that."

Sam patted the mare affectionately after he'd removed all the spines from her belly. "She saved the woman I love," he told her huskily.

Kate swallowed hard as she watched Sam approach her. Her eyes filled with tears as he knelt down on one knee and touched her cheek, cupping it and making her look directly into his eyes.

"I'm going to tell you something, Kate. And maybe it's too soon and I'm out of line, but I just damn near lost you, so I'm saying it anyway." He held her glistening blue gaze as her tears trickled downward, meeting his palm as it lay against her cheek. "I never stopped loving you either, Gal. Not *ever.*" Sam bowed his head, emotions overcoming him. When he got a hold on them, he looked up again, his voice oddly husky. "You've got more courage than brains in your head, you and that little horse you ride. My God, I thought you were crazy for coming back down that slope after us."

Surprised, Kate whispered, "Sam, One Horn had you trapped! What else could I do?"

His mouth twisted into a half grin. "Stayed up on the knoll and watched, you crazy woman."

Incensed, Kate sputtered, "Like hell, Sam McGuire!"

"You came down because you love me."

She stared into his stormy gray eyes and realized how upset he was. "Yes, I did. I didn't see any other options, Sam."

"When I saw you come riding hell-bent-for-leather down that slope, sand and gravel flying, my first thought was that you were crazy, until I realized why you were really doing it." With a heavy shake of his head, Sam rasped, "Kate, you're the bravest woman I've ever known. I think you knew One Horn would go after you. Didn't you?"

She shrugged helplessly and slid her hand against his roughened one. "If he didn't, *you* were going to be killed." Her voice cracked. "I—I couldn't stand the idea of that. I just couldn't…."

Pushing aside the damp strands of hair that clung to her cheek and temple, Sam whispered unsteadily, "I know… I know…."

Sniffing, Kate said, "All I could think about, Sam, was you—what we'd had a long time ago. When you came and picked me up at the halfway house, I felt so many things. I never stopped loving you even though you married Carol. It was probably just as well Kelly broke my nose and I missed those last six weeks of school. I couldn't have stood seeing you in the halls or the cafeteria…anywhere."

Sam eased back on his heel and watched Kate fighting her tears.

"And I never got to tell you back then the *real* reason why I married her," he rasped apologetically.

"You tried and Kelly stopped you," Kate whispered, wiping her tears away with her fingers. "It was just as well, Sam. You did the right thing. It's all in the past."

"Well," he murmured, his fingers grazing the slope of her dirty cheek, "what I'm interested in is you, me and our future, Gal." He lifted his head and watched the two bulls, which had found some dried grass in the gulch and were grazing peacefully. Turning his attention back to Kate, he smiled tenderly down at her. "We got some unfinished business to attend to first before we can really sit down and talk. You up to helping me herd these two thickheaded bulls to the pastures?"

Kate put out her hand as Sam rose to his full height, drawing her up with him. Warmth flowed through her fingers and up her arm as he held her hands, momentarily erasing all her aches and pains from the fall. "You know I am," she answered. "This isn't the first time I've been thrown off a horse, Sam McGuire. It won't be the last." Kate saw a one-cornered grin tug at his wonderful mouth. A mouth she wanted to kiss endlessly until the last breath left her body.

He led her over to Cinnamon, picked up the reins and placed them across the animal's neck for her. "Climb on," he told her, and helped her mount by cupping her elbow to steady her. Kate was quickly bouncing back from the incident. He saw the light shining in her eyes and the love there—for him alone. Sam felt like he was walking on air. Nothing else really mattered, but they had to keep their heads and get ranch work done first.

Giving Bolt a well-deserved pat of thanks, he remounted his rangy gelding, pulling the brim of his hat low on his brow to protect his eyes from the blistering sun overhead. He watched Kate rebutton her shirt, tug her leather gloves back on and settle her black Stetson firmly on her head. What a brave, gutsy woman she was. With a shake of his head, Sam moved his gelding over to where she sat.

"Let's go, Gal. After we get these bulls put away, I want to go home and get these horses cared for properly."

Kate nodded. The horses were their very next priority. She leaned over and gave Cinnamon an affectionate pat on the neck. "Let's go," she whispered. The animals' wounds would be cleaned, and then the horses would be washed down with a hose and carefully examined for any other cuts or cactus spine. Finally they'd be rubbed down, given a good ration of oats and released to the corral for a well-deserved rest.

As they moved the two remaining bulls out of the gully and up the steep slope of the hill, Kate's heart flew like an eagle soaring in that dark blue sky above them. Sam loved her. He'd said the words that she'd dreamed about so many lonely nights throughout her life. Barely able to deal with her wild flood of emotions, Kate forced herself to focus on the bulls. The danger wasn't over yet. Bulls were never to be trusted. Tonight, when the last of the demanding ranch activities were finished, she would have a long, searching talk with Sam—about their future. Never had anything been more tantalizing or hopeful in Kate's life.

The lights were low at the ranch house as Sam approached. It was dark now, nearly nine p.m. Ranch chores were not only demanding, but long. With only two people to do the work of six, it was a harsh way to exist, but he really didn't mind it. Freshly showered, shaved and wearing a clean set of clothes, he climbed the wooden porch steps two at a time. Taking off his hat at the door, he knocked against the screen. Soft, low music drifted from the front room as he walked. Kate come around the corner.

He couldn't help but smile in approval. She was dressed in a soft pink cotton skirt that fell to her ankles. The short-sleeved white blouse she wore had lace around the neck and exposed the delicious curve of her neck and collarbones. Her hair was washed and hung in soft curls just above her shoulders. She was beautiful.

"You clean up pretty good," Sam said in greeting as she opened the screen door to allow him entrance. He saw a flush creep into Kate's cheeks. She smiled shyly, a smile that tore at his heart and touched his soul. Here was the Kate he'd known as a teenager, but all grown up. Her sky blue eyes danced with warmth and welcome. When she reached out and slid her fingers into his, he gave her a tender look.

"I can say the same of you, cowboy. Come on in…." Kate felt a flutter of nervousness as she led Sam into the semidarkened living room. The music soothed her, as did Sam's long, easy stride beside her. She felt his fingers flex more strongly against hers. It was a small gesture, but an important one. His dark hair gleamed from a recent shower, and Kate was surprised to see he'd shaved. Generally, by this time of night, Sam's five o'clock shadow gave him a dangerous look. He wore a clean set of Levi's and a white, short-sleeved cotton shirt. Dark hairs peeked out at his throat, emphasizing his blatant, powerful maleness. She ached to love him, ached to become one with him.

As Sam settled on the couch next to Kate, she turned to him and tucked one leg beneath her, relaxing fully with him.

"Can I get you anything to drink?" she asked, realizing she was forgetting her manners.

Chuckling, Sam shook his head and gathered her hands into his. He liked having her leg tucked against his thigh, the pink of her cotton skirt outlining her firm, strong body beneath it. "No, Gal. Everything I've ever wanted I'm holding right now." He lost his smile and looked deeply into her eyes. Sam felt Kate's nervousness and the fine tension in her fingers. "We don't ever have much time around here," he began huskily, "and I don't want to waste it on preambles." Searching her shadowed features, he saw her lips part. Lips he wanted to capture and make his forever.

"I've got something I wanted to give to you for twenty-some years," he said, releasing her hand and digging into his jeans pocket. Producing a small, ivory-colored box, he slid it into Kate's hand. "Go ahead, Gal. Open it up."

Shocked, Kate stared down at the small cardboard box, which had yellowed from age. She stole a glance at Sam. His face was grim. She saw pain in his eyes and tension at the corners of his mouth. Stymied, she placed the box on her lap and carefully pried it open with her trembling fingers. Even in the dim light, she saw the beauty of a small, slender ring inside. Gasping, she removed the lid. There, nestled in the center of the box, was a sterling silver ring with blue turquoise set in a channel setting.

"Oh, Sam...." She touched the ring gently with her fingertips.

He turned and placed one arm on the couch behind her. "It was the wedding ring I was going to give you after we graduated, Kate. I had it made by one of our Navajo friends up on the Res. I told her I wanted a ring with no edges or anything that could catch on something. Around here, with ranch work, jewelry takes a beating." He smiled at her, at the tears glimmering in her eyes. Taking the ring out of the box, he picked up her left hand. He saw the bruises and cuts on her skin from today's near miss with death. Gently, he eased the ring on her fourth finger. It fit perfectly. That was a miracle to him, after all these years.

"I had planned to ask you to marry me the day after graduation, Gal," he told her in a low, off-key voice. "I had everything set. I had a part-time job up at the Maitland ranch waiting for me. I'd signed up to go to the university there. I'd planned on working during the day and going to school at night to earn my four-year degree. I'd talked to Steve Maitland, the owner, and he'd promised you a job if you wanted one. I'd even gone so far as to sign a lease on a little apartment up in Flagstaff. A place where we could settle in and make our first home."

"Oh, Sam…." Kate cried softly. She pressed her fingers to her mouth. Pain surged through her—the pain of a broken past. She saw him shake his head and felt him holding her hand gently with the ring around her finger. A wedding ring.

"I blew it," he rasped. "One night. One drunk. One mistake that cost me you. I know your running away wasn't the fault of my actions. But if I'd been more mature, less the egotistical football hero, I'd have waited for you and not fallen into Carol's arms because I felt sorry for myself."

Sam lifted his gaze and held Kate's. Her hand was damp and cool inside his warm, dry one. "Kate, I can't undo what happened. I was hoping when you came back that maybe, just maybe, there was a chance for us.

It was a crazy wish that refused to die in me all these years. And since you came home, from time to time I thought I saw love for me in your eyes. Most of the time, I thought it was my imagination, because I wanted you so badly. But today—" he breathed raggedly "—today I knew. I knew without a doubt of your love for me. You proved it in a way that I never expected. There aren't too many women on a little bay horse that would take on a one-ton bull to save the man she loves, is there?" His mouth stretched into a tender smile.

Shaken, Kate sniffed. "I never thought of it that way, Sam. I knew you were in trouble. I couldn't stand the thought of you being killed by that bull. I had to do *something*."

Releasing her hands, Sam cupped her face and looked deeply into her teary eyes. "And you did. That was when I knew, Gal, that you loved me beyond your own need to protect yourself. The ring is yours, Kate. It's always been yours. I want you to keep it. I know we just got back together and I know we—you—need more time." He stroked her cheek with his roughened fingertips. "That's a wedding ring, Gal. It's my pledge to you. Someday, when it's right for you, I want to marry you. I want you to share my name. To share our future—together...."

Whispering his name brokenly, Kate leaned forward, sliding her arms around his strong neck. She felt Sam's arms lock around her, and the air rushed out of her as she buried her face against his. "I love you so much I ache," she whispered unsteadily. "Love me, Sam...just hold me and love me. It's been so long... I need you so badly—so badly...."

Within moments, Kate felt herself being lifted off the couch and into Sam's arms. Contentment thrummed through her as he walked down the hall to her bedroom, to that old brass bed with the colorful quilt across it. Moonlight sifted throughout the lacy curtains at the window, a warming breeze moving the filmy material now and then. As he laid her down on the bed, his large hands bracketing her head, she looked up, up into his dark, stormy eyes filled with desire—for her.

It was so easy to lift her hands, place her fingertips across his barrel chest and open his shirt, button by button. With each of her grazing touches, she saw him wince. But it wasn't a wince of pain; it was the raw pleasure of her touch he was absorbing. The moonlight carved shadows against Sam's hard, weathered face. Her lips parted as his hand moved slowly downward to caress and cup her breast beneath the soft material of her blouse, his own touch evocative, teasing. A small moan escaped her.

His smile was very male as she helped him off with his shirt. Her fingers trembled badly on the belt buckle, so he helped her with that. Instead of shedding his jeans, he turned his attention to her as they sat on the bed next to one another. His fingers burned a path of need as he outlined her collarbone beneath the lace.

"You're a wild and beautiful mustang, Kate," he rasped as his fingers trailed downward. "Let me taste your wildness, woman..." Then he leaned forward, capturing her parting lips. He took her hard and fast, pulling the breath from her. His callused hands caressed her breasts, and a cry of pleasure rippled through her, a cry of mounting, fiery need. He coaxed off her blouse and she saw him smile as he explored the silky quality of her white camisole. In moments he'd eased that from her, too. Her breath became ragged and her hands moved of their own accord across his massive chest. With each touch, she felt his muscles bunch and harden in response. She was barely aware of her skirt being pulled away from her ankles. His hands slid provocatively up the expanse of her thighs and she lay back, her lashes closing.

A hot weakness enveloped her as he followed the curve of her thighs. As her silky panties were eased away her skin burned with need of Sam's continued touch. She felt him shift and move, and she looked up appreciatively as he stood beside the bed and got rid of his Levi's and briefs. Her mouth went dry as she stared up at his strong male form. Sam was nothing but hard muscle shaped and formed by the unforgiving land and harsh weather. She saw many white scars over his body, reminders that ranching was tough and demanding and took more than a pound of flesh from those who rose to the challenge. As Sam eased back down beside her, she gloried in him, in his embrace.

She felt his insistent hardness pressing against her flank as he settled next to her, his arm beneath her head. Stretched out beside him, she turned toward him, a soft smile on her lips. Grazing his cheek with one hand, Kate could feel the brand-new stubble prickle her exploring fingertips. "I love you, Sam McGuire," she whispered, "with all my heart, my soul. I always did. I always will…." Then she sought and found his hot, hungry mouth, pressing herself against him. Her breasts met his chest, her hips grazed his and she felt his maleness meet the soft curve of her abdomen. Sliding her arms around his neck, she felt the ragged beat of his heart against hers, felt the iron bands of his arms encircling her, crushing her against him.

Taking, giving, his mouth slid wetly across her lips. The heat of his tongue thrust into her mouth and she moaned. Her thighs parted and she felt the delicious weight of him move on top of her. It was so right. So natural. She clung to his male mouth as she felt his hand slide beneath her hips, raising her just enough to welcome him into her awaiting depths. The ache in her lower body intensified almost to pain in those fleeting, heated seconds before she felt him move against her. Her nipples hardened against the wiriness of his chest hair. She moaned and flexed her hips upward to receive him fully. Unconditionally. No longer did she want to wait. She wanted him. All of him. Now. Forever.

The power and heat of his thrust made her arch her spine and throw back her head. Her cry shattered the silence, but it wasn't one of pain. It was one of glorious welcome. She felt the grip of his hands on her hips, guiding her, establishing the rhythm. In moments, they were melting into one another and she felt his body cover hers like a hot, hard blanket. She looked up as he framed her face with his hands, up into his stormy eyes glittering with love. She felt each thrust, moved with him, took him more deeply into her with each fluid movement. The ache turned to fire, and then to a burning longing. She saw a partial, triumphant smile tug at his mouth as the heat within her exploded violently, in a rush, like a volcano too long lain dormant.

Crying out his name, she gripped his damp, tense

shoulders, her body pressing against his as the liquid heat flowed powerfully through her like lightning striking during a violent storm. Only the storm was one of raw need for Sam alone, the desire to feel his maleness mated with her femininity once again. She clung to him, gasping. He whispered her name, found her mouth and took it relentlessly as he thrust his hips more deeply, prolonging her pleasure. Moments became sparkling rainbows of color and light beneath her closed eyes as the heat peaked and then began to spread throughout her taunt, quivering form. Then she felt Sam turn rigid, a groan tearing from him, his hands capturing her face and holding her beneath him.

A few minutes later, he moved aside and then brought her up against him. They were breathing raggedly, and he could feel Kate's heart beating against his. He absorbed her soft, cool touches—on his face, shoulders and arms. How good she felt in his embrace! Opening his eyes, Sam stared into her blue ones, which danced with gold flecks of joy. He knew it had been good for her. He had made himself a promise that when it came time to love her, his needs would be secondary to hers. Kate was the one who had suffered all these years. She deserved the best from him now. No longer was he the selfish, egotistical football captain. No, he was a mature man who had made plenty of mistakes, and somehow he was going to make up for every one. One small gift was to make sure she enjoyed their lovemaking as much as he did.

Lifting his hand, Sam brushed several tangled strands of hair away from her damp, flushed cheek. His words came out low and husky. "I love you, Gal."

"I know that now," she whispered, touching his cheek. Kate felt her body tingling in the aftermath and she absorbed the pleasure of just being in Sam's arms, pressed against his hard, muscled form.

He ran his hand lovingly down her rib cage and across her hip. There wasn't an inch of fat anywhere on Kate. Ranching life guaranteed that. He saw the ring on her finger, the moonlight making the silver glint for a moment. Catching her hand in his, he brought it against his chest. "Just tell me that we have a chance, Kate. I don't want you to think that I'll bed you and that's it. Someday I want you for my wife. When you're ready."

Closing her eyes, Kate rested her brow against his chin.

"I never thought," she admitted hoarsely, "that you would ever be my husband, Sam. I've dreamed it over and over throughout the years, but I never thought..." She lifted her head and sighed softly. "This is all so new for me...."

"I know it is," he rasped. "Take your time, Gal. We've got it now.... You're home. You're where you belong. And you're with me...."

partly beneath the shade of an old cottonwood, near the rear of the red flagstone house that Jessica would live in. Jessica had sent him dimensions, details and the money to buy the necessary items to build a house for "her girls," as she called her orchids. Pleased with his work, he glanced toward Kate, who had helped him. His body held a warm glow and his heart became suffused with love for her. She stood so proudly and tall as she surveyed their mutual handiwork. It made him feel good that she thought so highly of his skills.

The June sun had risen at five-thirty, its golden rays starting to heat up the land. There were no clouds in the flawless turquoise sky. The scorching drought would continue for another unrelenting day. They would have to wait until July, when the monsoon rains arrived, driving thunderstorms and moisture out of Mexico sweeping northward into Arizona. Hopefully, plenty of rain would fall. Worried about the slowly lowering water table, a huge lake that lay beneath the Sedona-Verde valley, Sam picked up his toolbox.

"Breakfast about ready?" he teased, placing his arm around Kate's waist. They walked slowly toward the ranch house. What they needed was enough money to hire a full-time cook and housekeeper. Both of them ended up doing housekeeping chores, but haphazardly at best. Their fourteen-hour days were wearing on them after six months without help. Jessica would be a welcome addition, but Sam knew she would have to work hard to get her company set up, fill orders from around the world for her natural essences, and pay her own bills. Still, he felt Jessica's ebullient, bubbly presence would further heal Kate of her past wounds, because she was very close to her little sister.

Automatically, Kate fell into step with Sam. He always shortened his long, rolling stride when he was walking with her. He was always sensitive to her needs, she thought as she leaned against him, resting her head briefly against his shoulder. “We’re so lucky....” she whispered, a catch in her voice as she looked up. Drowning in his tender gaze, Kate tightened her arm around his waist.

“The luckiest,” he agreed huskily, leaning over and pressing a quick kiss to her flushed cheek. He saw her eyes dance with joy. So much of the old Kate was unfolding daily before his eyes. Sam knew it was because their love was allowed to take root once more and thrive. This time he was older and wiser. This time he wouldn’t throw away the woman he loved.

They walked around the ranch house after he put his tools away. It was still early and he could hear the lowing of the cattle, the soft snorts of the Arabians nearby. Overhead, Sam heard the shrill call of a red-tailed hawk. Looking up, he saw two of them and pointed them out to Kate.

“Husband and wife,” he said. Red-tails mated for life and this pair nested on the black lava cliffs above the ranch house.

Kate shielded her eyes with her hand as she watched the two hawks circling lazily five hundred feet above them. “They’re catching the rising thermals.”

Sam placed his arm around her shoulder and watched the birds gracefully flow on the unseen heat currents starting to rise from the earth as the sun grew warmer.

"The Indians would say it's a good sign. They're in the East."

Kate nodded. "East is the direction of new beginnings. Creation."

"Jessica's coming," he said, grinning.

Kate nodded and relished his closeness, his protective arm around her shoulders. "Jessica is so close to Mother Earth."

"I think that of the three daughters, Jessica has your mother's close connection with the soil." He looked at Kate. "Not that you don't, but it's expressed in a different way."

She nodded. "I always used to worry about Jessica. She was so flighty and couldn't ever finish anything she started. Something would catch her eye and she'd take off in this direction or that. I often wondered what she'd grow up to be."

"She runs her own company," Sam murmured. "I'd say she's pretty steady and has a good head on her shoulders despite her wandering ways."

Laughing, Kate agreed. They walked toward the ranch house. She would make them a hefty breakfast and then they'd begin the daily chores of feeding the animals. Today the blacksmith was coming out to trim thirty of the Arabians' hooves. At six dollars apiece, the bill would run up quickly. In his spare time, Sam would do trimming, but he was spread thin as it was, with the weight of the ranch falling on his shoulders.

"Jessica's so excited about coming home," Kate said as they climbed the wooden steps to the porch. "When she called last night, she was worried her orchid girls wouldn't make the trip. I guess they need moisture in the air and the temperature can't be too hot or too cold."

Sam opened the screen door for her. "Coming to Arizona is going to be hard on them."

"Jessica thinks she can manage it with that greenhouse we just built."

"It sounds like she's going to need a full-time helper," Sam said, taking off his hat and placing it on a wooden peg behind the door.

Kate took her own hat off and hung it beside his. Both were dusty, beat-up and desperately needing a good cleaning. Money was tight. Hats weren't high on the list of priorities.

"She said that she's going to have to hire someone to help her, and we're to try and think of someone who might fill the bill." Kate went to the kitchen. While Sam went to the fridge to get the bacon and eggs, she retrieved the cast-iron skillet from a cabinet next to the stove. Their morning routine was wonderful and she loved working closely with him. He'd shred the cheese for their omelets, cut up red and green peppers, chop up some onion and broccoli while she got the eggs ready for the skillet.

"I've got an idea," Sam exclaimed, placing the eggs and slab of bacon on the counter next to Kate. He pulled the rest of the items from the refrigerator and shut the door. Washing his hands in the sink, he said, "There's a half-Navajo, half-Anglo by the name of Dan Black who *might* be the person Jessica's looking for. He's Indian, has close ties to the land, understands and accepts like Jessica does that plants have their own spirit and energy."

Kate nodded and broke a dozen eggs into a big blue ceramic bowl. "Dan Black—that name is sure familiar. Where have I heard it?"

"The Black family up on the Navajo Reservation," Sam told her, wiping off his hands with a towel. He picked up the grater, unwrapped a block of sharp cheddar cheese and methodically began to shred it. "His mother is a real famous Navajo rug weaver. She just received an award of recognition at the White House for her artistry. And Dan is one hell of a wrangler. We can use one. Besides, Gan needs to be gentled and trained. Right now, he's dangerous to everyone."

She put the bacon in another skillet. "If I remember right, they called Dan the 'stallion tamer'?"

"Yes, he's got a good reputation for taming wild mustangs, especially mean studs like Gan."

"So what're his bad points?" Sam was excellent at assessing people.

His mouth quirked. "He's got a few problems."

Kate glanced at him and poured the beaten eggs from the bowl into another skillet. "You're hedging, Sam."

Quickly cutting up the vegetables for their omelets, Sam said, "He was in the Marine Corps for a long time. He went through the Gulf War, Desert Storm. They medically discharged him after that."

"Why?"

"Mental problems."

Kate rolled her eyes. "Mental problems? And you want to hire him to work with Jessica and tame Gan?"

"Now, calm down," Sam murmured, placing the vegetables in a bowl so that Kate could add them to the cooking eggs. "He's not crazy, Kate. Just a little introverted and a loner since coming back, that's all."

"That's nice to know. We have enough problems keeping this ranch afloat without hiring someone who has mental-health problems."

"I knew Dan over at the Maitland ranch in Flagstaff. He worked as a wrangler for me before joining the Marine Corps. He was a hard worker, took orders well and took pride in his work," Sam said, watching her cook. Kate's black hair was brushing her shoulders now. It made a beautiful frame for her incredible sky blue eyes, which he regularly lost himself in when they made wild, unbridled love. "I haven't seen him of late, but I did see him right after his discharge. I think he's got PTSD."

"Post-traumatic-stress disorder?" Kate put the lid on the omelets to let them cook for a moment and turned her attention to the pan of bubbling, fragrant bacon.

"I think Dan's problems are controllable. He was a pretty outgoing young kid at Maitland's ranch. The war changed him."

"What war doesn't change a person?"

He nodded. "Let me do some snooping around about Dan. Fay Seward, the saddle maker, knows the family real well. I might stop in there and have a chat with her."

"If I had my way," Kate said, scooping up the finished omelets onto plates that Sam retrieved for her, "I'd hire people with Indian blood in them. They never lose their connection with Mother Earth. They have a harmony I want to reestablish here."

Sam put the plates on the table and poured coffee into some white mugs. "I don't have any," he teased.

Kate sat down and grinned. "You're Native American in your heart."

"*You* have my heart, Gal."

She loved this time of morning with Sam. They sat with their knees touching beneath the old wooden table. How many times had Kate looked at the ring she wore on her left hand? She wanted to marry Sam after all her sisters were home. Jessica would arrive in May, and Rachel would be home in late November, or early December at the latest. Already the three of them were planning for Kate's coming wedding. It wouldn't be an expensive event, but a small, quiet one. Money was hard to find, and Kate certainly wasn't going to spend it on the wedding gown she'd dreamed of so many years ago. Sam agreed to the wait in order to meet the driving demands of the ranch.

"That's got hot peppers in it," she warned watching Sam as he spread salsa over his omelet.

"Makes it good."

Grinning, Kate said, "Mexican food is the way to *your* heart, cowboy."

Chuckling, Sam dug into the omelet. "Guilty as charged. I was raised on the stuff."

Who wasn't out in Arizona? Kate smiled and absorbed the taste of the omelet.

"So," Sam murmured, "your sisters got the details of our wedding worked out yet?"

Kate grinned. "Most of them. Rachel is so glad we're waiting until she can be here as the maid of honor. I don't know who is more excited, them, you or me."

He felt a bit of heat in his cheeks. Kate's eyes danced

with merriment. Stilling the fork, he caught her gaze. "I probably am."

"No, I am." Kate laughed, thrilled with the thought that by the end of the year she would be Mrs. Sam McGuire. The idea always made her feel euphoric. She saw the happiness reflected in Sam's gray eyes, too. She picked up a piece of bacon and thoughtfully chewed on it.

Sam sipped his coffee, his gaze resting tenderly on Kate. "One time after we made love, early on, you told me that you had all these dreams about a big wedding. You had the dress all picked out. You showed me that scrapbook you'd made up when we were going together in high school. You put it together, dreaming of marrying me someday. I know you and your sisters are pinching pennies and you're not going after the wedding you really wanted."

A rush of love flowed through her as she saw Sam's gray eyes grow tender. How much she loved him! Kate had always imagined what it might be like to be married to Sam, but never in her wildest dreams had she thought it would be possible—or this wonderful.

"It would cost too much to put on the wedding I'd originally planned, Sam. It's okay. Really, it is. Don't be giving me that look. I can do a lot on a shoestring, believe me."

She watched him shake his head. "No, I want to see you have the one I saw in your scrapbook. I've been giving this a lot of thought and I think I've come up with a way to have it happen. Let's sell one of your best broodmares. She should fetch at least five thousand dollars. That should be enough for that fancy dress you showed me from your scrapbook." He saw the tears gather in Kate's eyes. How soft and loving she'd become in the past months. The change was startling and wonderful.

Wiping her eyes with a look of embarrassment, she said, "I never thought of that angle." The fact that he wanted to give her a beautiful wedding dress instead of what she was planning on wearing—a cream-colored wool suit—made her love him even more fiercely.

"That's my job," Sam drawled, giving her a one-cornered smile meant to tell her he loved her.

Kate closed her eyes. "I've always dreamed of a beautiful white wedding dress like that...."

Sam nodded, feeling his heart expand with joy. Kate's voice reflected her sudden enthusiasm. Jessica coming home made Kate happy. She could hardly wait for her "Little Sis" to arrive. "Well, let's see what we can do then, about expanding plans for that big wedding you always dreamed of instead of the shoestring-budget one, shall we? We might be living hand-to-mouth right now, but things could change by the time your sisters get home. Besides, dreams need to be fulfilled." Especially Kate's dreams. Sam had stopped dreaming long ago and Kate had already given him back that gift. He could do no less in trying to fulfill her dreams, too.

Kate knew that with the ongoing drought, any bit of excess money they had saved was being eaten up in feed bills to keep the cattle from starving. "Okay," she whispered. "I'd love to wear a dress like that for our wedding day." How thrilled Jessica and Rachel would be about this news! She saw the love in Sam's eyes, his thoughtfulness toward her sending a wealth of emotion through her.

Slowly rising, Sam picked up their plates, took them to the sink and rinsed them off. "Good. Then it's settled. I've already got a buyer for that one black broodmare." He silently congratulated himself for giving Kate another gift she so richly deserved. He'd taken one look at the scrapbook that she'd pulled out and shared with him many months ago, and had realized the depth of her love for him was more than he thought possible. Kate had cut out photos of the dream house she'd wanted as their home, a lace-and-pearl adorned wedding dress, the white-and-purple orchids for the bouquet she'd wanted… They'd been the dreams of a young teenage girl, dreams that he aimed to fulfill because he loved her. She was giving him a second chance. He wasn't about to ruin it this time around. Now he had the capability of helping all her dreams come to life, and that made him feel good about himself for once.

Sam captured Kate's hand as she rose from the chair. In one smooth motion, he brought her into the haven of his arms. She felt good to him as she leaned against him, her hands resting on his arms as she smiled up at him.

"Miracles," he whispered, catching her mouth and kissing it softly, "happen every day of our lives when I'm with you." Her lips were pliant and sweet beneath his. He caressed her mouth and murmured against it, "And I want to stay in your life and show them to you every single day, Kate Donovan—for the rest of our lives…."

* * * * *

HAWK'S WAY: JESSE

Joan Johnston

For my friends, Sally, Sherry and Heather—
the Square Table at JJ's.

Chapter 1

The hairs prickled on the back of Honey Farrell's neck. She was being watched. Again. Surreptitiously she scanned the room looking for someone—anyone—she could blame for the disturbing sensation that had plagued her all evening. But everyone in the room was a friend or acquaintance. There was no one present who could account for the eerie feeling that troubled her.

Her glance caught on the couple across the room from her. How she envied them! Dallas Masterson was standing behind his wife, his hands tenderly circling Angel's once-again-tiny waist. Their three-month-old son was asleep upstairs. Honey felt her throat close with emotion as Dallas leaned down to whisper into his wife's ear. Angel laughed softly and a pink flush rose on her cheeks.

Honey saw before her a couple very much in love. In

fact, she had come to the Mastersons' home this evening to help them celebrate their first wedding anniversary. Honey found it a bittersweet event. For, one year and one month ago, Honey's husband, Cale, had been killed saving Dallas Masterson's life.

Honey felt her smile crumbling. A watery sheen blurred her vision of the Texas Rangers and their wives chattering happily around her. Mumbling something incoherent, she shoved her wineglass into the hands of a startled friend.

"Honey, are you all right?"

"I just need some air." Honey bit down on her lower lip to still its quiver as she hastened from the living room.

The overhead light in the kitchen was blinding, and Honey felt exposed. Shying from the worried look of another Ranger's wife, who was putting a tray of canapés into the oven, Honey shoved her way out the back screen door.

"Honey?" the woman called after her. "Is something wrong?"

Honey forced herself to pause on the back porch. She turned back with a brittle smile and said, "I just need some air. I'll be fine."

The woman grinned. "I suppose it's all the speculation about you and Adam Philips. Has he proposed yet? We're expecting an announcement any day."

Honey gritted her teeth to hold the smile in place, hoping it didn't look as much like a grimace as it felt. "I—could we talk about this later? I really do need some air."

She waited until the other woman nodded before

pulling the wooden door closed behind her, abruptly shutting out the noise and the painful, though well-intentioned, nosiness of her friends and neighbors.

The early summer evening was blessedly cool with a slight breeze that made the live oaks rustle overhead. Honey sank onto the back porch steps. She leaned forward and lifted the hair off her nape, shivering when the breeze caught a curl and teased it across her skin as gently as a man's hand.

She quickly dropped her hair and clutched her hands together between her knees. She felt bereft. And angry. *How could you have left me alone like this, Cale? I'm trying to forget what it was like to be held in your arms. I'm trying to forget the feel of your mouth on mine.* But seeing Angel in Dallas's arms tonight had been a vivid reminder of what she had lost. And it hurt. It was hard to accept Cale's untimely death and go on with her life. But she was trying.

At least she had learned from her mistake. She would never again love a man who sought out danger the way Cale had. She would never again put herself in the position of knowing that her husband welcomed the risks of a job that might mean his death. Next time she would choose a man who would be there when she needed him. Inevitably Cale had been gone on some assignment for the Texas Rangers whenever a crisis arose. Honey had become adept over the years at handling things on her own.

If her friends and neighbors got their wish, she wouldn't be on her own much longer. Only this time she had chosen more wisely. The man who had brought her to the party tonight, Adam Philips, was a country doctor. Adam would never die from an outlaw's bullet, the way Cale had. And Adam was reliable. Punctual almost to a fault. She would be able to count on him through thick and thin.

That was a definite plus in weighing the decision she had to make. For the good-natured gossip at the party about her and the young doctor was founded in fact. Adam Philips had proposed to her, and Honey was seriously considering his offer. Adam was a handsome, dependable man in a safe occupation. He liked her sons, and they liked—perhaps *tolerated* was a better word to describe how they felt about him. There was only one problem.

Honey didn't love Adam.

Maybe she would never love another man the way she had loved Cale. Maybe she was hoping for too much. Maybe it would be better to marry a man she didn't love. That way her heart could never be broken again if—

The kitchen door rattled behind her. Afraid that someone would find her sitting alone in the dark and start asking more awkward questions, Honey rose and headed toward the corner of the house where the spill of light from the kitchen windows didn't reach. She almost ran into the man before she realized he was there.

He was leaning against Dallas's Victorian house, his booted foot braced against the painted wooden wall, his Stetson tipped forward over his brow so his face was in deep shadow. His thumbs were stuck into the front of his low-slung, beltless jeans. He was wearing a faded Western shirt with white piping and pearl snaps that reflected the faint light of a misted moon.

Honey felt breathless. She wasn't exactly frightened, but she was anxious because she didn't recognize the man. He might have been a party guest, but he wasn't dressed for a party. He looked more like a down-on-his-luck cowboy, a drifter. It was better not to take a chance. Honey slowly backed away.

With no wasted movement, the cowboy reached out a hand and caught her wrist. He didn't hold her tightly, but he held her, all the same.

Honey stood transfixed by the feel of his callused fingers on her flesh. "I'll scream if you don't let go," she said in a miraculously calm voice.

The cowboy grinned, his teeth a white slash in the darkness. "No you won't."

There was a coiled tension in the way he held his body that she recognized. Cale had been like that. Ready to react instantly to any threat. Suddenly her curiosity was greater than her fear. She stopped straining against his hold. Instantly his grasp loosened, but he didn't let go.

"I've been standing out on the front porch watching you through the window, waiting for a chance to talk to you," the drifter said.

So, she wasn't crazy. Someone *had* been watching her all evening. His eyes weren't visible beneath the brim of his hat, but she felt the hairs rise on her nape. He was watching her right now. She ignored the gooseflesh that rose on her arms as he caressed her wrist with his thumb.

"I'm listening," she said. Regrettably the calm was gone from her voice.

"I know you're having some trouble handling things all by yourself at the ranch and—"

"How could you possibly know what's going on at the Flying Diamond?"

"Dallas told me how things are with you."

She exhaled with a loud sigh. "I see." He was no stranger then, although just who he was remained a mystery.

"It wouldn't have been hard to tell you've got problems just by looking at you."

"Oh? Are you some kind of mind reader?"

"No. But I can read people."

She remained silent, so he continued, "That frown never left your brow all evening."

Honey consciously relaxed the furrows of worry on her brow.

"Judging from the purple shadows I saw under your eyes, you aren't sleeping too well. You aren't eating much, either. That dress doesn't fit worth beans."

Honey tugged at the black knit dress she was wearing. Undeniably she had lost weight since Cale's death.

"Not that I don't like what I see," the cowboy drawled.

Honey felt a faint irritation—laced with pleasure—when his grin reappeared.

"You're long legged as a newborn filly and curved in all the right places. That curly hair of yours looks fine as corn silk, and your eyes, why I'd swear they're blue as a Texas sky, ma'am."

Honey was mortified by her body's traitorous reaction as his eyes made a lazy perusal of her face and form. She felt the heat, the anticipation—and the fear. She recognized her attraction to the man even as she fought against it. This tall, dark-eyed drifter would never be reliable. And he had *danger* written all over him.

"Who are you?" Her voice was raspy and didn't sound at all like her own.

"Jesse Whitelaw, ma'am." The drifter reached up with his free hand and tugged the brim of his Stetson.

The name meant nothing to her; his courtesy did nothing to ease her concern. She stared, waiting for him to say why he had sought her out, why he knew so much about her when she knew nothing about him.

He stared back. She felt the tension grow between them, the invisible electrical pulse of desire that streaked from his flesh to hers. Unconsciously she stepped back. His hold on her wrist tightened, keeping her captive.

His voice was low and grated like a rusty gate. "Dallas told me about your husband's death. I came here tonight hoping to meet you."

"Why?"

"I need a job."

The tension eased in Honey's shoulders. She released a gust of air she hadn't realized she'd been holding. Despite what he'd said, the way he'd looked at her, he hadn't sought her out to pursue a physical relationship. She couldn't help the stab of disappointment, when what she ought to feel was relief. At least now she knew how to deal with him.

"I can't afford to hire anyone right now," she said. "Especially not some down-on-his-luck drifter."

The smile was back. "If I wasn't down on my luck, I wouldn't need the job."

She couldn't hire him, but she was curious enough about him to ask, "Where did you work last?"

His shoulders rolled in a negligent shrug. "I've been…around."

"Doing what?" she persisted.

"A little cowboying, some rodeo bull riding, and… some drifting."

Bull riding. She should have known. Even Cale had never ridden bulls because he had thought it was too dangerous. *Drifting.* He was a man who couldn't be tied to any one place or, she suspected, any one woman. The last thing she needed at the Flying Diamond was a drifting cowboy who rode bulls for fun. Not that she could afford to hire him, anyway.

Just today she had discovered over fifty head of cattle missing—apparently rustled—from the Flying Diamond. That loss would cut deep into the profits she had hoped to make this year. "I can't hire anyone right now," she said. "I—"

The back door opened, revealing the silhouette of a large man in the stream of light. "Honey? Are you out here?"

She recognized Dallas, who was joined at the door by Angel.

"Are you coming in?" Dallas asked Honey.

"Yes. Yes, I am." She took advantage of Dallas's interruption to slip from the drifter's grasp. But he followed her. She could feel him right behind her as she stepped onto the porch.

Honey turned to the stranger to excuse herself and gasped. The harsh light from the kitchen doorway revealed the man's features. She was suddenly aware of his bronzed skin, of the high, broad cheekbones, the blade of nose and thin lips that proclaimed his heritage.

"You're Indian!" she exclaimed.

"The best part of me, yes, ma'am."

Honey didn't know what to say. She found him more appealing than she cared to admit, yet the savage look in his eyes frightened her. To her dismay, the drifter put the worst possible face on her silence.

His lips twisted bitterly, his grating voice became cynical as he said, "I suppose I should have mentioned that my great-grandfather married a Comanche bride. If it makes a difference—"

Honey flushed. "Not at all. I was just a little surprised when I saw… I mean, I didn't realize…"

"I'm used to it," he said. From the harsh sound of his voice it was clear he didn't like it.

Honey wished she had handled the situation better. She didn't think any less of him because he was part Indian, even though she knew there were some who would. She turned back to Angel and saw that the young woman had retreated into the safety of Dallas's arms.

"I came outside for some air," Honey explained to Dallas. "And I met someone who says he's a friend of yours."

Dallas propelled Angel ahead of him onto the back porch and pulled the kitchen door closed behind him. "Hello, Jesse. I wasn't expecting you tonight."

Jesse shrugged again. "I got free sooner than I thought I would. Anyway, I could have saved myself the trip. Mrs. Farrell says she can't afford to hire anyone right now."

Dallas pursed his lips in disapproval. "I don't think you can afford not to hire someone, Honey."

"I'm not saying I don't need the help," Honey argued. "I just don't have the money right now to—"

"Who said anything about money?" Jesse asked. "I'd work for bed and board."

Honey frowned. "I really don't—"

"If you're worried about hiring a stranger, I'll vouch for Jesse," Dallas said. "We went to Texas Tech together."

"How long ago was that?" Honey asked.

"Fifteen years," Dallas admitted. "But I'd trust Jesse with my life."

Only it wouldn't be Dallas's life that would be at stake. It was Honey's, and those of her sons, Jack and Jonathan. "I'll think about it," she said.

"I'm afraid I need something a little more definite than that," Jesse said. He tipped his hat back and said, "A drifting man needs a reason to light and set, or else he just keeps on drifting."

Honey didn't believe from looking at him that Jesse Whitelaw would ever settle anywhere for very long. But another pair of hands to share the load, even for a little while, would be more than welcome. There was some ranch work too heavy for her to handle, even with her older son's help. Honey brushed aside the notion that she would be alone with a stranger all day while the boys were at school. It was only a matter of weeks before her sons would be home for summer vacation.

She took a deep breath and let it out. "All right. When can you start?"

"I've got some things to do first."

Honey felt a sense of relief that she wouldn't have to face him again in the near future. It evaporated when he said, "How about bright and early tomorrow morning?"

Honey sought a reason to keep him away a little longer, to give herself some time to reconsider what she was doing, but nothing came to mind. Anyway, she needed the help now. There was vaccinating to be done, and she needed to make a tally of which cattle were missing so she could make a more complete report to the police.

Also she needed to add some light to improve security around the barn where she kept General, the champion Hereford bull that was the most important asset of the Flying Diamond.

"Tomorrow morning will be fine," she said.

The words were barely out of her mouth when the kitchen door was thrust open and another silhouette appeared. "I've been looking everywhere for you. What are you doing out here?"

Adam Philips joined what was quickly becoming a crowd on the back porch. He strode to Honey's side and slipped a possessive arm around her waist. "I'm Adam Philips," he said by way of introduction to the stranger he found there. "I don't think we've met."

"Jesse Whitelaw," the stranger said.

Honey watched as the two men shook hands. There was nothing cordial about the greeting. She didn't understand the reason for the animosity between them; it existed nonetheless.

"Are you ready to come back inside?" Adam asked. He had tightened his hold on her waist until it was uncomfortable. Honey tried to step out of his grasp, but he pulled her back against his hip.

"I think the lady wants you to let her go," Jesse said.

"I'll be the judge of what the lady wants," Adam retorted.

The drifter's eyes were hard and cold, and Honey felt sure that at any moment he would enforce his words with action. "Please let go," she said to Adam.

At first Adam's grip tightened, but when he glanced over at her, she gave him a speaking look that said she meant business. Reluctantly he let her go.

"It's about time we headed home, don't you think?" Adam said to Honey.

Honey was irked by Adam's choice of words, which insinuated that they lived together. However, she didn't think now was the moment to take him to task. The drifter was still poised for battle, and Honey didn't want to be the cause of any more of a scene than had already occurred.

"It is getting late," she said, "and I've got a long day tomorrow. It was nice meeting you, Jesse. I'll see you in the morning."

Honey anticipated Adam's questions and hurried him back inside. It took them a while to get through the kitchen, which now held several women collecting leftover potluck dishes to be carried home.

"Aha! I expect you two were out seeing a little of the moonlight," one teased.

"We'll be hearing wedding bells soon," another chorused.

Honey didn't bother denying their assumptions. They

might very well prove true. But it was hard to smile and make humorous rejoinders right now, because she was still angry with Adam for his caveman behavior on the back porch.

When they reached the living room, a Randy Travis ballad was playing. "Dance with me?" Adam asked. His lips curved in the charming smile that had endeared him to her when they first met. Right now it wasn't doing a thing to put her in a romantic mood. However, it would be harder to explain her confused feelings to Adam than it would be to dance with him. "Sure," she said, relenting with a hesitant smile.

At almost the same moment Adam took her into his arms, she spied the drifter entering the living room. He stayed in the shadows, but Honey knew he was there. She could feel him watching her. She stiffened when Adam's palm slid down to the lowest curve in her spine. It wasn't something he hadn't done before. In the past, she had permitted it. But now, with the drifter watching, Adam's possessive touch felt uncomfortable.

Honey stepped back and said, "I'm really tired, Adam. Do you think we could go now?"

Adam searched her face, looking for signs of fatigue she knew he would find. "You do look tired," he agreed. "All right. Do you need to get anything from the kitchen?"

"I'll pick up my cake plate another time," she said. She felt the drifter's eyes on her as Adam ushered her out the front door to his low-slung sports car. He opened the door for her and she slid inside. Protected by the darkness within the car she was able to look back toward the house without being observed. She felt her nape prickle when she caught sight of the drifter standing at the front window.

Honey knew he couldn't see her, yet she felt as though his eyes pinned her to the seat. They were dark and gleamed with some emotion she couldn't identify. She abruptly turned away when Adam opened the opposite door and the dome light came on.

Adam put a country music tape on low, setting a romantic mood which, before Honey had met the drifter, she would have appreciated. Right now the mellow tones only agitated her, reminding her that Adam had proposed and was waiting for her answer. He expected her to give him a decision tonight. To be honest, she had led him to believe her answer would be yes. They hadn't slept together; she hadn't been ready to face that kind of intimacy with another man. But she had kissed him, and it had been more than pleasant.

"Honey?"

"What?" Her voice was sharp, and she cleared her throat and repeated in a softer tone, "What?"

"Are you sure you want to hire that drifter?"

"I don't see that I have much choice. There's work to be done that I can't do myself."

"You could marry me."

The silence after Adam spoke was an answer in itself. Honey knew she shouldn't give him hope. She ought to tell him right now that she couldn't marry him, that it wasn't right to marry a man she didn't love. But the thought of that drifter, with his dark, haunting eyes, made her hold her tongue. She was too attracted to Jesse Whitelaw for her own good. If she were free, she might be tempted to get involved with him. And that would be disastrous.

But was it fair to leave Adam hanging?

Honey sighed. It seemed she had sighed more in the past evening than she had in the past year. "I can't—"

"You don't have to give me your answer now," Adam said. "I know you still miss Cale. I can wait a little longer. Now that you have that hired hand, it ought to make things easier on you."

They had arrived at the two-story wood frame ranch house built by Cale's grandfather. Adam stopped his car outside the glow of the front porch light. He came around and opened the door and pulled her out of the car and into his arms.

Honey was caught off guard. Even so, as Adam's lips sought her mouth she quickly turned aside so he kissed her cheek instead.

Adam lifted his head and looked down at her, searching her features in the shadows. Something had changed between them tonight. He thought of the stranger he had found with Honey on the Mastersons' back porch and felt a knot form in his stomach. He had always known that his relationship with Honey was precarious. He had hoped that once they were married she would come to love him as much as he loved her. He hadn't counted on another man coming into the picture.

Honey kept her face averted for a moment longer but knew that was the coward's way out. She had to face Adam and tell him what she was feeling.

"Adam, I—"

He put his fingertips on her lips. "Don't say anything. Just kiss me good night, and I'll go."

Honey looked up into his eyes and saw a tenderness that made her ache. Why didn't she love this man? She allowed his lips to touch hers and it was as pleasant as she remembered. But when he tried to deepen the kiss, she backed away.

"Honey?"

"I'm sorry, Adam. It's been a long day."

He looked confused and even a little hurt. But she had tried twice to refuse his proposal and he hadn't let her do it. Maybe her response to his kiss had told him what she hadn't said in words. Then he smiled, and she could have cried because his words were thoughtful, his voice tender. "Good night, Honey. Get some rest. I'll call you next week."

He would, too. *Good old reliable Adam.* She was a fool not to leap at the chance to marry such a man.

Honey stood in the shadows until he was gone. When she turned toward the house she saw the living room curtain drop. That would be her older son, Jack. He kept an eagle eye on her, which hadn't helped Adam's courtship. She called out to him as she unlocked the door and stepped inside.

"Come on down, Jack. I know you're still awake."

The lanky thirteen-year-old ambled back down the stairs he had just raced up. "He didn't stay long," Jack said. "You tell him no?"

"I haven't given him an answer."

"But you're going to say no, right?"

She heard the anxiety in Jack's voice. He wasn't ready to let anyone in their closed circle and most certainly not a man to take his father's place. She didn't dare tell him how she really felt before she told Adam, because her son was likely to blurt it out at an inopportune moment. She simply said, "I haven't made a decision."

Honey put an arm around her son's shoulder and realized he was nearly as tall as she was. *Oh, Cale. I wish you could see how your sons have grown!* "Come on," she said. "Let's go make some hot chocolate."

"I'd rather have coffee," Jack said.

She arched a brow at him. "Coffee will keep me awake, and I need all the rest I can get."

Jack eyed her and announced somberly, "School will be out in about three weeks, Mom. I don't think I can do any more around here until then."

"You don't have to," she said. "I've hired a man to help out."

"I thought we couldn't afford hired help."

"He'll be working for room and board."

"Oh. What's he like?"

Honey wasn't about to answer that question. She couldn't have explained how she felt about the drifter right now. "He'll be here in the morning and you can ask him all the questions you want."

From the look her son gave her, she suspected Jack would grill the drifter like a hamburger. She smiled. That, she couldn't wait to see.

Jesse Whitelaw had another big surprise coming if he harbored any notions of pursuing Honey on her home ground. Her teenage son was a better chaperon than a Spanish duenna.

Chapter 2

Honey yawned and stretched, forcing the covers off and exposing bare skin to the predawn chill. She scooted back underneath the blanket and pulled it up over her shoulders. She was more tired than she ought to be first thing in the morning, but she hadn't slept well. For the first time in over a year, however, it wasn't memories of Cale that had kept her awake.

The drifter!

Honey bolted upright in her bed. He was supposed to show up bright and early this morning. She glanced out the lace curtains in her upstairs bedroom and realized it was later than she'd thought. Her sons would already be up and getting ready for school. She tossed the covers away, shivering again as the cold air hit flesh exposed by her baby doll pajamas. She grabbed Cale's white terry cloth robe and scuffed her feet into tattered slippers before hurriedly heading downstairs.

Halfway down, she heard Jonathan's excited voice. At eight he still sounded a bit squeaky. Jack's adolescent response was lower-pitched, but his voice occasionally broke when he least expected it. She was already in the kitchen by the time she realized they weren't talking to each other.

The drifter was sitting at the kitchen table, a cup of coffee before him. Honey clutched the robe to her throat, her mouth agape.

"Catch a lot of flies that way," the drifter said with a lazy grin.

Her jaws snapped closed.

"Good morning," he said, touching a finger to the brim of his Stetson.

"Is it?" she retorted.

His skin looked golden in the sunlight. There were fine lines around his eyes and deep brackets around his mouth that had been washed out by the artificial light the previous evening. He was older than she'd thought, maybe middle thirties. But his dark eyes were as piercing as she remembered, and he pinned her with his stare. Honey felt naked.

She gripped the front of the masculine robe tighter, conscious of how she was dressed—or rather, not dressed. She thrust a hand into her shoulder-length hair, which tumbled in riotous natural curls around her face. She wondered how her mascara had survived the night. Usually it ended up clumped on the ends of her eyelashes or smudged underneath them. She reached up to wipe at her eyes, then stuck her hand in the pocket of the robe. It wasn't her fault he'd found her looking like something the cat dragged in.

Honey didn't want to admit that the real reason she resented this unsettling man's presence in her kitchen so early in the morning was that she hadn't wanted him to see her looking so…so mussed.

"What are you doing here?" she demanded.

He raised a brow as though the answer was obvious. And it was.

"I let him in," Jack said, his hazel eyes anxious. "You said the hired hand was coming this morning. I thought it would be okay."

Honey took several steps into the room and laid a hand on her older son's shoulder. "You did fine. I'm just a little surprised at how early Mr. Whitelaw got here."

"He said we can call him Jesse," Jonathan volunteered.

Honey bristled. The man had certainly made himself at home.

"Jesse helped me make my sandwich," Jonathan added, holding up a brown paper bag.

Honey's left hand curled into a fist in the pocket of the robe. "That was nice." Her voice belied the words.

"Jesse thinks I'm old enough to make my own lunch," Jonathan continued, his chest pumped out with pride.

Honey had known for some time that Jonathan could make his own sandwich, but she had kept doing it for him because the routine morning chore kept her from missing Cale so much. She was annoyed by the drifter's interference but couldn't say so without taking away from Jonathan's accomplishment.

"Jesse rides bulls and rodeo broncs," Jack said. "He

worked last at a ranch in northwest Texas called Hawk's Way. He's gonna teach me some steer roping tricks. He's never been married but he's had a lot of girlfriends. Oh, and he graduated from Texas Tech with a degree in animal husbandry and ranch management."

It was hard for Honey not to laugh aloud at the chagrined look on Jesse's face as Jack recited all the information he'd garnered. The drifter had been, if not grilled, certainly a little singed around the edges.

The shoe was on the other foot as Jack continued, "I told him how you haven't been coping too well since Dad—well, this past year. Not that you don't try," he backtracked when he spied the horrified look on his mother's face, "but after all, Mom, the work is pretty hard for you."

Honey was abashed by her son's forthrightness. "I've managed fine," she said. She didn't want Jesse Whitelaw thinking she needed him more than she did. After all, a drifter like him wasn't going to be around long. Soon enough she'd be managing on her own again.

She stiffened her back and lifted her chin. Staring Jesse Whitelaw right in the eye she announced, "And I expect I'll still be managing fine long after you've drifted on."

"The fact remains, you need me now, Mrs. Farrell," the drifter said in that rusty gate voice. "So long as I'm here, you'll be getting a fair day's work from me."

The silence that followed was uncomfortable for everyone except the younger boy.

In the breach Jonathan piped up, "Jesse thinks I should have a real horse to ride, not just a pony."

"I'm sure Jesse does," Honey said in as calm a voice

as she could manage. "But I'm your mother, and until I decide differently, you'll stick with what you have."

"Aww, Mom."

This was an old argument, and Honey cut it off at the pass. "The school bus will be here in a few minutes," she said. "You boys had better get out to the main road."

Honey gave Jonathan a hug and a quick kiss before he headed out the kitchen door. "Have a nice day, sweetheart."

Jack was old enough to pick up the tension that arced between his mother and the drifter. His narrowed glance leapt from her to Jesse and back again. "Uh, maybe I ought to stay home today. Kind of show Jesse around."

Honey forced herself to smile reassuringly. "Nonsense. You have reviews for finals starting this week. You can't afford to miss them. Jesse and I will manage fine. Won't we?"

She turned to Jesse, asking him with her eyes to add his reassurance to hers.

Jesse rose and shoved his chair under the table. "Appreciate the offer," he said to Jack. "But like your mom said, we'll be just fine."

"Then I better run, or I'll miss the bus." Jack hesitated another instant before he sprinted for the door. Honey would have liked to hug Jack, too, but at thirteen, he resisted her efforts to cosset him.

A moment later they were alone. Jesse was watching her again, and Honey's body was reacting to the appreciation in his dark eyes. She rearranged the robe and pulled the belt tighter, grateful for the thick terry cloth covering. She felt the roses bloom on her cheeks and hurried over to the stove to pour herself a cup of coffee.

Too late she realized she should have excused herself to go upstairs to dress. If she left now without getting her coffee, he would know she was running scared. There was absolutely no reason for her to feel threatened. Dallas wouldn't have recommended Jesse Whitelaw if she had anything to fear from him. But she couldn't help the anxiety she felt.

"Would you like another cup of coffee?" she asked, holding up the pot.

"Don't mind if I do, Mrs. Farrell," Jesse said.

"Please, you might as well call me Honey."

"All right… Honey."

Her name sounded far more intimate in that rusty gate voice of his than she was comfortable with. She stared, mesmerized for a moment by the warmth in his dark eyes, then realized what she was doing and repeated her offer.

"More coffee?"

He brought his cup over, and she realized she had made another tactical error. She could actually feel the heat from his body as he stepped close enough for her to pour his coffee. She turned her back on him to pour a cup for herself.

"Those are fine boys you have." Jesse moved a kitchen chair and straddled it, facing her.

She leaned back against the counter rather than join him at the table. "In the future, I'd appreciate it if you don't come inside before I get downstairs," she said.

"I wouldn't have come in except Jack said you were expecting me."

"I was—that is—I didn't expect you quite so early."

That was apparent. Honey's bed-tossed hair and

sleepy-eyed look made Jesse want to pick her up and carry her back upstairs. He wasn't sure what—if anything—she was wearing under the man's robe. From the way she kept tightening the belt and clutching at the neck of the thing, he was guessing it wasn't much. His imagination had her stripped bare, and he liked what he saw.

It was too bad about her husband. From what he'd heard, Cale Farrell had died a hero. He supposed a woman left alone to raise two kids wouldn't be thinking much about that. At least he was here to help her with the ranch work. Not that he would be around forever—or even for very long. But while he was here, he intended to do what he could to make her life easier.

He knew it would be easier for her if he didn't let her know he was attracted to her. But he wasn't used to hiding his feelings for a woman. The way he had been raised, part of respecting a woman was being honest with her. Jesse planned to be quite frank about his fascination with Honey Farrell.

He liked the way she'd prickled up last night, not at all intimidated by him. He liked the way she had stood her ground, willing to meet him eye to eye. He bristled when he thought of her with any other man—especially that Philips character. Jesse wasn't sure how serious their relationship was, but he knew Honey couldn't be in love with Philips. Otherwise she wouldn't have reacted so strongly to *his* touch.

At any rate, Jesse didn't intend to let the other man's interest in Honey keep him from pursuing her himself. Which wasn't going to be easy, considering her opinion of drifters in general, and him—a half-breed Comanche—in particular. His look was challenging as he asked, "What did you have in mind for me to do today?"

Honey had been watching Jesse's fingers trace the top rail of the wooden chair. There was a scar that ran across all four knuckles. She was wondering how he'd gotten it when his fist suddenly folded around the back of the chair. "I'm sorry—what did you say?"

"I asked what you wanted me to do today."

"There are some steers that need vaccinating, and the roof on the barn needs to be repaired. Some fence is down along the river and a few head of my stock have wandered onto the mohair goat ranch south of the Flying Diamond. I need to herd those strays back onto my land. Also—"

"That'll do for starters," Jesse interrupted. He rose and set his coffee cup on the table. "I'll start on the barn roof while you get dressed. Then we can vaccinate those steers together. How does that sound?"

Honey started to object to him taking charge of things, but she realized she was just being contrary. "Fine," she said. "I'll come to the barn when I'm dressed."

She waited for him to leave, but he just stood there looking at her. "What is it? Did I forget something?" she asked.

"No. I was admiring the view." He flashed a smile, then headed out the kitchen door.

Honey ran upstairs, not allowing herself time to contemplate the drifter's compliment. He probably didn't spend much time around respectable women. He probably didn't realize he shouldn't be blurting out what he was thinking that way. And she shouldn't be feeling so good about the fact the hired hand liked the way she looked.

She was grateful to discover that her mascara had been clumped, rather than smudged. She took the time to wash her face and reapply a layer of sun-sensitive makeup. It was a habit she'd gotten into and had nothing to do with the fact there was now a man around to see her. Honey dressed in record time in fitted Levi's, plaid Western shirt, socks and boots.

Even so, by the time she reached the barn, Jesse was already on the roof, hammer in hand. He had his shirt off and she couldn't help looking.

Jesse had broad shoulders and a powerful chest, completely hairless except for a line of black down that ran from his navel into his formfitting jeans. His nipples provided a dark contrast to his skin, which looked warm to the touch. She could see the definition of his ribs above a washboard belly. His arms were ropy with muscle and already glistened with sweat. Here was a man who had done his share of hard work. Which made her wonder why he had never settled down.

It dawned on her that the drifter had chosen the most dangerous job to do first. He was standing on the peaked barn roof without any kind of safety rope as though he were some kind of mountain goat. How could he be so idiotically unconscious of the danger!

She started up the ladder he had laid against the side of the barn and heard him call, "No need for you to come up here."

She looked up and found him hanging facedown over the edge of the roof. "Be careful! You'll fall."

"Not likely," he said with a grin. "I grew up rambling around in high places."

"I suppose you had the top bunk in an upstairs bedroom," she said with asperity.

Jesse thought of the high canyon walls he had scaled as a youth on his family's northwest Texas ranch and grinned. "Let's just say I spent a lot of time climbing when I was a kid and leave it at that. By the way, I found the spot that needs to be patched. I brought the shingles up with me, but I didn't see hide nor hair of the roofing nails."

"I put them away. I'll get them for you." Honey headed back down the ladder and into the barn. As she passed General's stall, she patted the bull on the forehead. She and Cale had raised him from birth, and though he had a ring in his nose, he would have followed her around without it.

"Hi, old fella. Just let me get these nails for Jesse and I'll let you out in the corral for a while."

The barn was redolent with the odors of hay, leather and manure. Rather than hold her nose, Honey took a deep breath. There was nothing disagreeable to her about the smell of a ranch—or a hardworking man. Which made her think of the hired hand standing on the roof of her barn.

Honey didn't want to be charmed by Jesse Whitelaw, but there was no denying his charm. Maybe it was his crooked grin, or the way his eyes crinkled at the edges when he smiled, creating a sunburst of webbed lines. Or maybe it was the fact his dark eyes glowed with appreciation when he looked at her.

"Hey! Where are those nails?"

Honey jumped at the yell from above. "I'm getting them!" She grabbed the box of nails and headed back into the sunshine. Jesse had come to the edge of the roof and bent down to take the nails as she climbed the ladder and handed them up.

When he stood again, a trickle of sweat ran down the center of his chest. As Honey watched, it slid into his navel and back out again, down past the top button of his jeans. It was impossible to ignore the way the denim hugged his masculinity. It took a moment for Honey to realize he wasn't moving away. And another moment to realize he was aware of the direction of her gaze. Honey felt a single curl of desire in her belly and a weak feeling in her knees. Her fingers gripped the ladder to keep from falling. She was appalled at the realization that what she wanted to do was reach out and touch him. She froze, unable to move farther up the ladder or back down.

"Honey?"

Jesse's voice was gruff, and at the sound of it she raised her eyes to his face. His lids were lowered, his dark eyes inscrutable. She had no idea what he was thinking. His jaw was taut. So was his body. Honey was afraid to look down again, afraid of what she would find.

She felt her nipples pucker, felt the rush of heat to her loins. Her lips parted as her breathing became shallow. Honey knew the signs, knew what they meant. And tried desperately to deny what she was feeling.

"Honey?" he repeated in a raw voice.

Jesse hadn't moved, but if possible, his body had tautened. His nostrils flared. She saw the pulse throb at his temple. What did he want from her? What did he expect? He was a stranger. A drifter. A man who loved danger.

She wasn't going to get involved with him. Not this way. Not any way. Not now. Not ever.

"No!" Honey felt as though she were escaping some invisible bond as she skittered down the ladder, nearly falling in her haste.

"Honey!" he shouted after her. "Wait!"

Honey hadn't thought he could get off the roof so fast, but she had no intention of waiting around for him. She started for the house on the run. She was terrified, not of the drifter, but of her own feelings. If he touched her…

Honey was fast, but Jesse was faster. He caught her just as she was starting up the front steps and followed her onto the shaded porch. When Jesse grabbed her arm to stop her, momentum slammed her body back around and into his. He tightened his arms around her to keep them both from falling.

Honey would have protested, except she couldn't catch her breath. It was a mistake to look up, because the sight of his eyes, dark with desire, made her gasp. Jesse captured her mouth with his. His hand thrust into the curls at her nape and held her head so she couldn't escape his kiss.

Honey wished she could have said she fought him. But she didn't. Because from the instant his lips took possession of hers, she was lost. His mouth was hard at first, demanding, and only softened as she melted into his arms. By then he was biting at her lips, his tongue seeking entrance. He tasted like coffee, and something else, something distinctly male. His kiss thrilled her, and she wanted more.

It was only when Honey felt herself pushing against Jesse that she realized he had spread his legs and pulled her into the cradle of his thighs. She could feel his arousal, the hard bulge that had caught her unsuspecting attention so short a time ago. She heard a low, throaty groan and realized it had come from her.

Jesse's mouth mimicked the undulation of their bodies. Honey had never felt so alive. Her pulse thrummed, her body quickened. With excitement. With anticipation. *It had been so long.* She needed—craved—more. How could this stranger, this drifter, make her feel so much? Need so much?

At first Honey couldn't identify the shrill sound that interfered with her concentration.

Pleasure. Desire. Need.

The sound persisted, distracting her. Finally she realized it was the phone.

Honey hadn't been aware of her hands, but she discovered they were clutching handfuls of Jesse's black hair. His hat had fallen to the porch behind him. She stiffened. Slowly, she slid her hands away.

"The phone," she gasped, pushing now at his shoulders.

Honey felt Jesse's reluctance to release her. Whether he recognized the panic in her eyes, or the presumption of what he had done, he finally let her go. But he didn't step away. Honey had to do that herself.

"The phone," she repeated.

"You'd better answer it." It was clear he would rather she didn't. His body radiated tension.

Honey stood there another moment staring, her body alive with unmet needs, before she turned and raced inside the house. For a second she thought he would follow her, but from the corner of her eye she saw him whirl on his booted heel and head toward the barn.

She was panting by the time she snatched the phone from its cradle. "H-hello?"

"Honey? Why didn't you answer? Is everything all right?"

Dear Lord. It was Adam. Honey held her hand over the receiver and took several deep breaths, trying to regain her composure. There was nothing she could do about the pink spots on her cheeks except be grateful he wasn't there to see them.

At least there was one good thing that had come from the drifter's kiss. Honey knew now, without a doubt, that she could never marry Adam Philips. The sooner she told Adam, the better. Only she couldn't tell him over the phone. She owed him the courtesy of refusing him to his face.

"Honey, talk to me. What's going on?" Adam demanded.

"Everything's fine, Adam. I'm just a little breathless, that's all. I was outside when the phone started ringing," she explained.

"Oh. I called to see if your hired hand showed up."

"He's here."

There was a long pause. Honey wasn't about to volunteer any information about the man. If Adam was curious, he could ask.

"Oh," Adam said again.

To Honey's relief, it didn't appear he was going to pursue the subject.

"I know I said I wouldn't call until next week," he continued, "but an old school friend of mine in Amarillo called and asked me to come for a visit. His divorce is final and he needs some moral support. I'm leaving today and I don't know when I'll be back. I just wanted to let you know."

Good old reliable Adam. Honey rubbed at the furrow on her brow. "Adam, is there any chance you could come by here on your way out of town? I need to talk to you."

"I wish I could, but I'm trying to catch a flight out of San Antonio and it's going to be close if I leave right now. Can you tell me over the phone?"

"Adam, I—"

Honey felt the hair prickle on the back of her neck. She turned and saw that Jesse had stepped inside the kitchen door.

She stared at him helplessly. She swallowed.

"Honey? Are you still there?" Adam said.

"I'll see you when you get back, Adam. Have a good trip."

Honey hung up the phone without waiting to hear Adam's reply. She stared at Jesse, unable to move. He had put his shirt back on, but left it unsnapped so a strip of sun-warmed skin glistened down the middle of his chest. He had retrieved his Stetson and it sat tipped back off his forehead. His thumbs were slung into the front of the beltless jeans. He had cocked a hip, but he looked anything but relaxed.

"The repairs on the roof are done," he said. "I wanted

to make sure it's all right with you if I saddle up that black stud to round up those steers that need vaccinating."

"Night Wind was Cale's horse," Honey said. "He hasn't been ridden much since—"

Naturally Jesse would want to ride the wildest, most dangerous horse in the stable. And why not? The man and the stallion were well matched.

"Of course, you can take Night Wind," she said. "If you wait a minute, I'll come with you."

"I don't think that's a good idea."

She didn't ask why not. He could use the distance and so could she. "All right," she said. "The steers that need to be vaccinated are in the west pasture. Come get me when you've got them herded into the corral next to the barn."

He tipped his hat, angled his mouth in that crooked smile and left.

Honey stared at the spot where he had been. She closed her eyes to shut out the vision of Jesse Whitelaw in her kitchen. It was as plain as a white picket fence that she wasn't going to be able to forget the man anytime soon.

At least she had a respite for a couple of hours. She realized suddenly that because of Jesse's interruption she hadn't been able to refuse Adam's offer of marriage.

Horsefeathers!

She should never have kissed Jesse. Not that she had made any commitment to Adam, but she owed it to him to decline his offer before he found her in a compromising position with some other man. And not that she intended to get involved with Jesse Whitelaw, but so far, where that drifter was concerned, she hadn't felt as though things were under control. The smart move was to keep her distance from the man.

That shouldn't be a problem. No problem at all.

Chapter 3

The black stud had more than a little buck in him, which suited Jesse just fine. He was in the mood for a fight, and the stud gave it to him. By the time the horse had settled down, Jesse had covered most of the rolling prairie that led to the west pasture. It wouldn't take long to herd the steers back to the chutes at the barn where they would be vaccinated. Only he had some business to conduct first.

Jesse searched the horizon and found what he was looking for. The copse of pecan trees stood along the far western border of the Flying Diamond. He rode toward the trees hoping that his contact would be there waiting for him. He spotted the glint of sun off cold steel and headed toward it.

"Kind of risky carrying a rifle around these parts with everyone looking out for badmen, don't you think?" Jesse said. He tipped his hat back slowly, careful to keep his hands in plain sight all the time.

"Don't know who you can trust nowadays," the other cowboy answered. "Your name Whitelaw?"

Jesse nodded. "From the description I got, you'd be Mort Barnes."

The cowboy had been easy to identify because he had a deep scar through his right eyebrow that made it look as if he had come close to losing his eye. In fact, the eye was clouded over and Jesse doubted whether Mort had any sight in it. The other eye was almost yellow with a black rim around it. Mort more than made up for the missing eye with the glare from his good one. Black hair sprouted beneath a battered straw cowboy hat and a stubble of black beard covered his cheeks and chin.

Jesse evaluated the other man physically and realized if he had to fight him, it was going to be a tooth and claw affair. The cowboy was lean and rangy from a life spent on horseback. He looked tough as rawhide.

"Tell your boss I got the job," Jesse said.

Mort smiled, revealing broken teeth. The man was a fighter, all right. "Yeah, I'll do that," Mort said. "How soon you figure you can get your hands on that prize bull of hers?"

"Depends. She keeps him in the barn. He's almost a pet. It won't be easy stealing him."

"The Boss wants—"

"I don't care what your boss wants. I do things my way, or he can forget about my help."

Mort scowled. "You work for the Boss, you take orders from him."

"I don't take orders from anybody. I promised I'd steal the bull for him and I will. But I do it my way, understand?" Jesse stared until Mort's one yellow eye glanced away.

"I'll tell the Boss what you said. But he ain't gonna like it," the cowboy muttered.

"If he doesn't like the way I do things he can tell me so himself," Jesse said. "Meanwhile, I don't want any more cattle stolen from the Flying Diamond."

The look in Mort's eye was purely malicious. "The Boss don't like bein' told what to do."

"If he wants that bull, he'll stay away from here. And tell him the next time one of his henchmen shows up around here he'd better not be carrying a gun."

Mort raised the rifle defensively. "I ain't ridin' around here without protection."

Jesse worked hard not to smile. It was pretty funny when the badman thought he needed a gun to protect himself from the good guys.

"Don't bring a gun onto the Flying Diamond again," Jesse said. "I won't tell you twice."

It was plain Mort didn't like being threatened, but short of shooting Jesse there wasn't much he could do. The outlaw had kept a constant lookout, so he spotted the rider approaching from the direction of the ranch house when there was no more than a speck of movement in the distance.

"You expectin' company?" Mort asked, gesturing toward the rider with his gun.

Jesse glanced over his shoulder and knew immediately who it was. "Dammit. I told her I'd come get her," he muttered. "It looks like Mrs. Farrell. Get the hell out of here and get now!"

Mort grinned. "Got plans of your own for the Missus, huh? Can't say as I blame you. Mighty fine lookin' woman."

Jesse grabbed hold of Mort's shirt at the throat and half pulled the man out of the saddle. The look in Jesse's eyes had Mort quailing even though the outlaw was the one with the gun. "That's no way to talk about a lady, Mort."

The outlaw swallowed hard. "Didn't mean nothin' by it."

Jesse released the man's shirt. He straightened it with both hands, carefully reining his temper. "Back up slow and easy and keep that rifle out of the sunlight. No sense me having to make explanations to Mrs. Farrell about what you're doing here."

Mort wasn't stupid. What Jesse said made sense. Besides, the Boss would skin him alive if he got caught anywhere near Mrs. Farrell. "I'm skedaddlin'," he said.

Without another word, Mort backed his horse into the copse of pecans and out of sight. Jesse whirled the stud and galloped toward Honey to keep her from coming any closer before Mort made good his escape.

Why hadn't she waited for him at the ranch, as he'd asked? Damned woman was going to be more trouble than he'd thought. But she was sure a sight for sore eyes.

Her hair hung in frothy golden curls that whipped around her head and shoulders as she cantered her bay gelding toward him. She ought to be wearing a hat, he thought. As light-skinned as she was, the sun would burn her in no time at all. He remembered how her pale hand had looked in his bronzed one, how soft it had felt between his callused fingers and thumb. Never had he been more conscious of who and what he was.

Jesse hadn't known at first what it meant to be part Indian. He had learned. *Breed. Half-breed. Dirty Injun.* He had heard them all. What made it so ironic was the fact that neither of his two older brothers, Garth and Faron, nor his younger sister, Tate, looked Indian at all. He was the only one who had taken after their Comanche ancestors.

His brothers hadn't understood his bitterness at being different. They hadn't understood the cause for his bloody knuckles and blackened eyes. Surprisingly, it was his half-English, half-Irish father who had made him proud he was descended from a warrior people, the savage Comanche.

That knowledge had shaped his whole life.

Jesse had often wondered what would have happened if he had been born a hundred years earlier; he often felt as barbaric as any Comanche. He had not been able to settle in one place, but needed to wander as his forebears had. While it was still a ruthless world he lived in, the conventions of society had glossed over the ugliness so it was not as apparent. Except, he had chosen a life that brought him into daily contact with what was cruel and sordid in the modern world. And forced him daily to confront his own feral nature.

Jesse no longer apologized for who and what he was. He had not tied himself to any one place, or any one person. He had never minded being alone or even considered the loneliness and isolation caused by his way of life. Until he had met the woman riding toward him now.

His eyes narrowed on Honey Farrell. He wished he could tell her about himself. Wished he could explain how she made him feel, but he couldn't even tell her who he really was. Nevertheless, he had no intention of letting the circumstances keep them apart. It wasn't honorable to keep the truth from her, but he consoled himself with the thought that when this was all over, he would more than make it up to her.

It was unfortunate she didn't—couldn't—know the truth about him, but he convinced himself that it wouldn't matter to her. He would make her understand that they belonged together. And who—and what—he was would make no difference.

"Hello, there!" Honey called as she rode up to Jesse. "There was a phone call for you after you left."

Jesse took off his hat, thrust his hand through his too-long black hair and resettled the Stetson. "Can't imagine who'd call me," he said. His family had no idea where he was—and hadn't known for years.

"It was Dallas."

Jesse frowned. "Any particular reason for the call?"

"He invited you to dinner tonight." Honey didn't mention that Dallas had invited her to dinner as well. She had tried to refuse, but Dallas had put Angel on the phone, and Honey had succumbed to the other woman's plea for company.

Honey felt that same inexplicable tension she always felt around Jesse. Her gelding sidestepped and their knees brushed. That simple touch produced goose bumps on her arms. She was grateful for the long-sleeved Western shirt that hid her reaction. She stared off toward the copse of pecans in the distance, avoiding Jesse's startled glance.

And spotted a glint of sunlight off metal.

"There's someone in the trees behind you," Honey said in a quiet voice. "I think he has a gun."

Jesse said a few pithy words under his breath. "Don't let him know you see him. Help me get these steers moving toward the barn."

"Do you think it might be one of the rustlers?" Honey asked as she loosened the rope from her saddle.

"Don't know and don't care," Jesse said. "That's a matter for the police. Best thing for us to do is get ourselves and these cattle out of here."

There was no discussion as they used whistles and an occasional slap with a lasso to herd the steers back toward the barn. When they were a safe distance away, Honey kneed her gelding over to join Jesse.

"I've lost a lot of stock to rustlers since Cale died," Honey said. "I suppose they don't believe I'm any threat to them. But I didn't think they'd dare let themselves be seen in broad daylight. I'll call the police when we get back to the house and—"

Jesse interrupted. "There's no need for that. I'll tell Dallas about it when I call to accept his dinner invitation."

Honey frowned. "I guess that'll be okay. Uh… I suppose I should have mentioned I've also been invited to dinner. Would you mind if I got a ride with you?"

Jesse kept the dismay he felt from his face. He had hoped to use the time he was away from the ranch to do some other business without Honey being any the wiser.

Having her along meant he would have to curtail his plans. But he couldn't think of a good reason to refuse her a ride that wouldn't raise suspicion. "Sure," he said at last. "Why not? What time do you want to leave?"

"Around six, I suppose. That'll give me time after we finish with the vaccinating to get cleaned up and make some supper for Jack and Jonathan."

"That sounds fine. Meanwhile, until those rustlers are caught you'd better stay close to home."

Honey glanced at Jesse to see if he was serious. He was. "I have a ranch to run," she said.

"I'm here now. If there's work that needs to be done away from the house, I can do it."

"You're being ridiculous. I don't think—"

"No, you aren't thinking!" Jesse interrupted in a harsh voice. "What's going to happen if you chance onto those rustlers at the wrong time? They've killed before and—"

"Killed! Who? When?"

Jesse swore again. He hadn't meant to alarm her, just keep her safe. "A rancher near Laredo was found shot to death last month."

"Oh, my God," Honey whispered. "Surely it wasn't the same rustlers who took my cattle!"

"What if it is? Better safe than sorry. You stay around the ranch house." It came out sounding like the order it was.

Honey bristled. "I'm in charge here. And I'll do as I please!"

"Just try leaving," he said. "And we'll see."

"Why, of all the high-handed, macho cowboy talk I ever heard—"

Jesse grabbed the reins and pulled her gelding to a halt. "These guys aren't fooling around, Honey. They've killed once. They've got nothing to lose if they kill again. I wouldn't want anything to happen to you."

The back of his gloved hand brushed against her cheek. "I don't intend to lose you."

Honey's heart missed a beat. He was high-handed, all right, but when he spoke to her in that low raspy voice and looked at her with those dark mysterious eyes, she found herself ready to listen. Which made no sense at all.

"How does a drifter like you know so much about all this?" she asked.

"Dallas filled me in," he said. When she still looked doubtful, he said, "Ask him yourself at dinner tonight."

"Maybe I will."

The entire time they vaccinated bawling cattle, Honey said nothing more about the dinner at Dallas Masterson's house. She was thinking about it, though, because she realized Jesse would have to use the upstairs bathroom to clean up. She had yet to explain to him that she planned for him to sleep in a room in the barn that hired hands had used in the past.

She decided to confront him before the boys got home from school, in case he decided to argue. They were both hot and sweaty from the work they'd been doing, so it was easy to say, "I could use some iced tea. Would you like some?"

"Sounds good," he replied. "I'll be up to the house in a minute. I have a few things to put away here first."

Honey was glad for the few moments the delay gave her to think about how to phrase what she wanted to say. She took her time in the kitchen, filling two glasses with ice and sun-brewed tea. She wasn't ready when he appeared at the screen door, hat in hand.

"May I come in?"

His request reminded her that she had met Jesse Whitelaw less than twenty-four hours earlier. It seemed like a lot longer. Like maybe she had known the cowboy all her life. It left her feeling apprehensive. She avoided his eyes as she pushed the screen door wide and said, "Sure. I've made tea for both of us."

He moved immediately to the glass of tea on the table and lifted it to his lips. She watched as he tipped the glass and emptied it a swallow at a time. Rivulets of sweat streamed down his temples, and his hair was slick against his head where his hat had matted it down. He smelled of hardworking man, and she was all too aware of how he filled the space in her kitchen.

Jesse sighed with satisfaction as he set the empty glass on the table. The sound of the ice settling was loud in the silence that followed as his eyes found hers and held.

"I think I have time to look at whatever fence you have down before I have to get ready for supper," Jesse said. "If you'll just head me in the right direction."

"Certainly. There are a few things we need to discuss first." Honey threaded her fingers so she wouldn't fidget. "When I offered you room and board I wasn't thinking about where I'd put you. There's a room at the rear of the barn I can fix up for you, but you'll have to use the bathroom in the house."

Jesse worked to keep the grimace off his face. It would be a lot more difficult explaining how her prize bull had been stolen from the barn if he was sleeping there. “Are you sure there isn’t somewhere in the house I could sleep? I don’t need much.”

Honey chewed on her lower lip. “There is a small room off the kitchen.” She pointed out the closed door to him. “It’s awfully tiny. I’ve started using it for a pantry. I don’t think—”

Jesse opened the door and stepped inside. The room was long and narrow. Wooden shelves along one wall were filled with glass jars of preserves, most likely from the small garden he had seen behind the house. An iron bed with a bare mattress stood along the opposite wall under a gingham-curtained window. A simple wooden chest held a brass lamp and an old-fashioned pitcher and bowl for water.

“This’ll do fine,” he said.

“But—”

He turned and she was aware of how small the room was, or rather, how he filled it. She took a step back, away from the very strong attraction she felt. “The room in the barn is bigger,” she argued. “You’d have more privacy.”

He grinned. “I suppose that’s true, if you don’t count the livestock.”

“I have to come in here sometimes to get food from the shelves,” she explained.

“You could knock.”

“Yes, I suppose I could.” It was hard to argue with logic. Yet Honey didn’t want to concede defeat. Otherwise, she was going to find herself with the hired hand constantly underfoot. She made a last effort to convince him the barn was a better choice. “The boys sometimes make a lot of noise. Morning and evening. You won't get much peace and quiet if you stay here."

"I expect I'll be going to bed later and getting up earlier than they will," he replied.

Honey sighed. This wasn't working out as she had planned at all. Somehow she had ended up with this part-savage stranger, this drifter, living under her roof. She wasn't exactly frightened of him, but she was uneasy. After all, what did she really know about him?

He seemed to sense her hesitation and said, "If you don't feel comfortable with me in the house, of course I'll sleep in the barn."

There it was, her chance to avoid coping with his presence in the house. She opened her mouth to say "Please do" and instead said, "That won't be necessary. I'm sure this will work out fine."

At that moment the kitchen screen door slammed open and Jonathan came racing through. "Hi, Mom! Hi, Jesse! I'm missing cartoons!" He was through the kitchen and gone before Honey could even gasp a hello.

A few moments later Jack appeared at the door. He didn't greet his mother or the hired man, simply dropped his books on the kitchen table and headed straight for the cookie jar on the counter. He reached inside and found it empty. "Hey! I thought you were going to bake some cookies today."

"I didn't have time," Honey apologized.

He opened a cupboard, looking for something else to eat.

Honey saw Jesse's jaw tighten, as though he wanted to say something but was biting his tongue. Perhaps Jack wasn't as courteous as he could have been, but from what Honey had gathered from the mothers of Jack's friends, it was typical teenage behavior. She was used to it. Apparently Jesse wasn't.

Jack seemed oblivious to them as he hauled bread, peanut butter and jelly out onto the counter and made himself a sandwich.

Honey watched Jesse's expression harden. She wasn't sure whether to be more vexed and annoyed by Jack's conduct, or Jesse's reaction to it.

Jack picked up his sandwich, took a bite that encompassed nearly half of it, and headed out the kitchen door toward the den and the television.

"Do you have any homework?" Honey asked.

"Just studying for tests," Jack said through a mouthful of peanut butter. "I'll do it later."

Honey hadn't realized Jesse could move so fast. Before Jack reached the kitchen door, the hired hand blocked his way.

"Just a minute, son."

Jack stiffened. "You're in my way."

"That was the general idea."

Jack turned to his mother, clearly expecting her to resolve the situation.

Honey wasn't sure what Jesse intended, let alone whether she could thwart that intention. For her son's sake, she had to try. "Jesse—"

"This is between me and Jack," Jesse said.

"I don't have anything to say to you," Jack retorted.

"Maybe not. But I've got a few things to say to you."

Jack balled his fist, turning the sandwich into a squashed mess. "You've got no right—"

"First off, a gentleman greets a lady when he comes

into the room. Second, he doesn't complain about the vittles. Third, he asks for what he needs from a lady's kitchen, he doesn't just take it. Fourth, he inquires whether chores need to be done before he heads for the bunkhouse. And finally, he doesn't talk with his mouth full."

Jack swallowed. The soft bread felt like spiny tumbleweed as it grated over the constriction in his throat. This was the kind of dressing-down his father might have given him. The kind of talking-to he hadn't had for more than a year, since his father's death. He resented it. Even though he knew deep down that the hired hand was right.

Jack angled his face to his mom, to see what she was going to do about the drifter's interference. He felt sick in the pit of his stomach when he saw how pale her face was. Jack turned from his mother and confronted the hired hand. He let the hostility he was feeling show in his eyes, but for his mother's sake, struggled to keep it out of his voice. "Maybe I was wrong," he conceded.

Jesse continued to stare at the boy and was pleased when the gangly teenager turned to his mother and gritted out, "Hello, Mom. Thanks for the sandwich."

Jack looked down at the mess in his hand and grimaced.

"You can wash your hands in the sink," Honey said.

Jesse stepped aside to allow the boy to pass and in doing so, glanced at Honey. Her dark blue eyes were afire with emotion, but it wasn't gratitude he saw there. Obviously he had stepped amiss. He clenched his teeth over the explanation for his actions that sprang to mind. She didn't look as though she wanted to hear reason.

Jesse and Honey stared at each other while Jack washed his hands. He turned from the sink, still drying his hands with a dish towel, and asked his mother, "Are there any chores that need to be done before supper?"

Since Cale's death, Honey had taken the responsibility for almost all the ranch chores her husband had done in the evening. When Jack offered, she realized there was work that still needed to be done in the barn that she would appreciate having Jack's help completing. "You can feed the stock," she said. "Also, I let General out into the corral. Would you bring him back inside the barn for the night?"

"Sure, Mom. Anything else?"

"That's all I can think of now."

Without looking at Jesse again, Jack pushed his way out the screen door and let it slam behind him.

The tension was palpable once the two adults were alone.

Jesse started to apologize for interfering, then bit his tongue. He had been hard on the boy, but no more so than his father had been with him. A tree grew as the sapling began. Now was the time for Jack to learn courtesy and responsibility.

"I don't quite know what to say," Honey began. "I don't agree with your methods, but I can't argue with the results. Maybe I've been too lax with Jack the past few months, but he took Cale's death so hard, I..."

Jesse heard the tremor in her voice and took a step toward her. As soon as he did, she squared her shoulders and lifted her chin.

"It hasn't been easy for any of us," she said in a firmer voice. "But we've managed to get along."

Jesse heard "without your help" even though she didn't say the words. So be it. This was the last time he would get involved. If she wanted to let the boy walk all over her, that was her business. It was just fine with him.

Like hell it was.

"Look," he said. "I can't promise I won't say anything more to the boy. We have to work together, after all. But I'll try not to step on any toes in the future. How does that sound?"

"Like the best compromise I'm going to get," Honey replied with a rueful smile.

"Guess I'll go work on that fence."

"I'll take my bath early," she said. "That way the bathroom will be free when you get back."

"Fine."

He had to walk by her to get to the door. Honey marveled at how small any room got with the two of them in it. She stepped back until she pressed against the counter, but their bodies still brushed. Jesse hesitated just an instant before he continued past her. He didn't look back as he pushed his way out the screen door. But she noticed he caught the door and kept it from slamming on his way out.

Honey heaved a sigh—of relief?—when she had the kitchen to herself again. She wished she didn't need Jesse's help so much on the ranch, because she wasn't at all sure she could handle having him around. His presence was already changing everything. She was beginning to feel things that she hadn't ever expected to feel again.

Nothing could come of her attraction to Jesse. He

was a drifter. Sticking around wasn't in his nature. When the mood struck him, he would be moving on. And she would be left alone. Again.

She had best remember that when the yearning rose to let him get close.

Chapter 4

Honey scooted down, settled her nape on the edge of the free-standing, claw-footed bathtub and closed her eyes. Her entire body was submerged and steam rose from water that lapped at the top edge of the tub. There was no shower in the house, only this aged white porcelain tub. She smiled when she imagined what Jesse's reaction was going to be when he confronted this monstrosity.

It was easy to blame the absence of a modern shower on the lack of extra money over the years she and Cale had been married. But the truth was, Honey loved the old-fashioned deep-bellied tub, with its brass fixtures and lion's paw legs. Instead of putting in a shower, she and Cale had expanded the capacity of the water heater so it was possible to fill the giant tub with steaming hot water all the way to the top.

Honey had laced the scalding water with scented bath oil, and the room reeked of honeysuckle. She was reminded of hot baths she and Cale had taken together. Honey crossed her arms and caressed her shoulders, smoothing in the bath oil. And imagined how it would feel if Jesse…

Abruptly Honey sat up, sloshing water over the edge of the tub. Her eyes flew open and she looked around her. Her daydreams had seemed so real. For a moment it had seemed as though that man was here. In her tub. With her. His hands—never mind where his hands had been! And his mouth—Honey shivered in reaction to the vivid pictures her mind had painted.

"Horsefeathers!" she muttered.

Honey lunged up, splashing water on the floor, and grabbed for a terry cloth towel. She wrapped herself in it, then reached down to pull the plug. And felt a spurt of guilt. The water heater would fill the tub once—but not twice. Her remorse didn't last long, and a smile slowly appeared on her face. Jesse Whitelaw could stand to cool off a little. A nice cold bath ought to help him along.

Honey was in her bedroom and had almost finished dressing when Jesse knocked at her door.

"Hey, there's no shower in that bathroom," he said.

"I know." Honey tried to keep the grin out of her voice.

He muttered something crude under his breath, then said, "Where are the towels?"

"The linens on the rack in the bathroom are yours to use."

Honey heard the water run for a short while, then

stop. She left her bedroom and stood outside the bathroom door listening. There was a long silence, followed by a male yelp and frantic splashing. "This water's like ice!" he bellowed.

"I know," she said loud enough to be heard through the door. By now her grin was huge.

Jesse muttered again.

"I'm going downstairs to fix some dinner for Jack and Jonathan. Enjoy your bath."

Her laughter followed her down the stairs.

Jesse shivered, but not from the cold. It was the first time he'd heard Honey laugh, and the sound skittered down his spine. His lips curled ruefully. At least now he knew she had a sense of humor.

He soaped a rag and washed himself vigorously, as though that could obliterate his thoughts of her. But Honey Farrell had gotten under his skin. Every breath he took filled his lungs with the honeysuckle scent she had bathed in. Everywhere he looked there were reminders that he had invaded her feminine domain.

The pedestal sink was cluttered on top with all sorts of female paraphernalia—powder and lipstick and deodorant and suchlike—except where she had cleared a tiny space for his things.

Jesse cursed a blue streak as he rinsed himself with the icy water, then grabbed a towel and stepped out onto the deepest pile rug he had ever felt beneath his feet. It was decorated with whimsical daisies—as was the towel he had wrapped around his hips. If his brothers could see him now, they would rib him up one side and down the other.

He quickly pulled on clean briefs and jeans, then

slung the towel around his neck while he shaved. He debated whether to leave his straight edge razor and strop in the bathroom, then decided that as long as she had left the space for him, he might as well use it. When he saw his things beside hers, he pursed his lips thoughtfully. It was as though an unfinished picture had been completed.

He spread the damp towel over the rack and put on the shirt he had brought into the bathroom with him. He had hoped the steam from a hot shower would ease some of the wrinkles out of it. Since he'd ended up taking a cold bath, he had no choice except to shrug into the wrinkled shirt.

Jesse started to borrow Honey's hairbrush but changed his mind and finger-combed his hair instead. It would hang straight once it dried no matter what he did with it now.

Jesse came down the stairs quietly and stood at the kitchen door undetected by the trio at the table. Honey was serving up her younger son's dinner. Her face was rosy, probably from all that hot water she'd bathed in, he thought with a silent chuckle. He was glad to see she wasn't wearing black again, but he thought the pale green was wrong for her.

She ought to be wearing vivid colors—reds and royal blues—that were as full of life as she was. He liked the way the dress clung to her figure, outlining her breasts and defining her slim waist and hips. She looked very much like a woman, and he felt the blood surge in his loins at the sight of her.

He watched unnoticed as Honey brushed a lock of hair off Jonathan's forehead. She put a hand on Jack's shoulder as she set the salt and pepper before him. Then she found another reason to touch Jonathan. Jesse wondered if Honey had any idea what she was doing. He felt his body tauten with the thought of her touching him like that.

Jesse's family members were fiercely loyal to each other, but they weren't much for touching. He could count on one hand the number of times his mother had caressed him in any way. He hadn't realized until now just how needful he was of Honey's touch and the feel of her hands on his body.

"Oh, there you are!" Honey froze with her hand outstretched for the butter dish. She wondered how long Jesse had been standing there. He had a way of watching her that she found totally unnerving. His dark, hooded gaze revealed a hunger that took her breath away, but there was a yearning, almost wistful expression in his eyes as well.

"Are you ready to go?" he asked.

Honey took a good look at what the hired hand was wearing and frowned. She wondered what kind of life Jesse Whitelaw had led when this was all he had to wear to dinner. His jeans were clean but worn white at the stress points and seams. The faded Western shirt was frayed at collar and cuffs and badly creased. His leather belt was dark with age and had a shiny silver buckle she felt sure he had earned as a prize at some rodeo. He wore the same tooled black leather boots he had worn all day; the scuff marks showed the hard use they'd had.

She almost offered to iron his shirt, then changed her mind. Somehow she knew he wouldn't appreciate the suggestion. Besides, if he had really been concerned about his appearance, he could have asked for the iron himself. "I'm ready anytime you are," she said.

The ride to Dallas's place in Jesse's pickup truck—which was barely two years old and in surprisingly good shape compared to his clothing—took barely an hour. Because of the long, uncomfortable silences between inane bits of conversation, it felt a lot longer.

Even in the modern West, a man was still entitled to his privacy. Thus Honey didn't feel she could ask Jesse about himself. That left a myriad of other subjects, not one of which came readily to mind.

The silence was deafening by the time Jesse said, "How long have you known Dallas and Angel?"

Honey grabbed at the conversational gambit like a gambler for a deck of cards. "I met Dallas about four years ago when he and Cale started working together on assignments for the Texas Rangers. Dallas introduced me to Angel a little over a year ago, about the same time she and Dallas met each other."

"How did the two of them meet?" Jesse asked.

"You know, they never said. Every time I asked, Angel blushed and Dallas laughed and said, 'You wouldn't believe me if I told you.'"

"How did you and that Philips guy meet?" Jesse asked.

That was more personal ground. Honey hesitated, then grinned and admitted, "Dallas invited me on a double date with Adam and Angel. By the end of the day, Dallas ended up with Angel, and Adam and I were a couple."

"How serious are things between you and Philips?"

Honey shot a quick look at Jesse, but his expression was bland. "I don't think that's any of your business."

"I think maybe it is."

"I can't imagine why—"

"Can't you?" His piercing gaze riveted her for a moment before he had to look at the road again.

Honey's pulse began to speed. She grasped at the opportunity to put the hired hand in his place once and for all. "Adam has asked me to marry him," she said.

A muscle jerked in Jesse's cheek. "You don't love him," he said curtly.

"You can't possibly know whether I love him or not."

He cocked a brow and his lips drew up cynically. "Can't I?"

Honey turned to stare out the window, avoiding his searching look.

"Are you going to marry him?"

"I—" Honey considered lying. Perhaps if she told Jesse she was committed to another man, he would leave her alone. But she couldn't use Adam like that—simply to keep another man at arm's length. "No," she admitted.

"Good."

Nothing else passed between them for the few minutes it took to traverse the length of the road from the cattle guard at the entrance to Dallas's ranch to the Victorian ranch house. At least, nothing in words. But Honey was aware of the portal the drifter had forced open between them.

"I won't ever hurt you," Jesse said in a quiet voice.

"You can, you know," she said in an equally quiet voice.

His lips flattened. "I don't want you to be afraid of me."

"Then leave me alone."

"I can't do that."

"Jesse..."

The Mastersons' porch light was on, and Jesse pulled the truck up well within its glow. He killed the engine and turned to look at Honey. "Is it your husband?" he asked bluntly.

Honey felt the pain that always came with memories of Cale. "Cale is dead."

"I know that. Do you?"

Honey gasped and turned to stare at Jesse. "What do you want from me?"

"More than it seems you're willing to give."

Jesse's sharp voice cut through her pain, and Honey realized she was angry. "You can hardly blame me," she said. "I'm not in a hurry to get my heart torn out again."

"Who says you have to?"

Honey snorted inelegantly. "That sounds pretty funny coming from a man like you. How many women have you loved and left, Jesse? How long should I plan on you hanging around? And what am I supposed to do when you're gone? I'd have to be a fool to get involved with you. And whatever else I might be, I'm no fool. I—"

Honey broke off when she saw Angel come running out onto the porch to greet them. She flashed Jesse a look of frustration and quickly stepped out of the truck and headed up the porch steps.

"It's good to see you again, Honey," Angel said as the two women hugged. She didn't offer her hand to the drifter and kept her distance. "Dallas is putting the baby to bed. He'll be down in a minute. Won't you both come inside?"

She stepped away from Jesse and held the door. Honey saw the other woman actually shiver as Jesse passed by her. Honey wondered what it was about the drifter that caused Angel to shy away from him. Was it possible that Dallas had told her something about Jesse? Something sinister?

Honey shook her head and dismissed the possibility. She didn't know much about Jesse, but she didn't see him as a villainous figure. Probably there was something in Angel's own past that was causing her to react so strangely to Dallas's friend.

Dallas had none of his wife's reservations. He greeted Jesse warmly and shook his hand. "I'm glad you could come on such short notice," Dallas said. "I thought maybe we could talk about old times, maybe get reacquainted. How are your brothers and your sister?"

Honey's eyes widened and she stared at Jesse as though she had never seen him before. "You have a family?"

Jesse grinned. "Two older brothers and a younger sister."

"Where?" Honey asked.

"At the family ranch, Hawk's Way, in northwest Texas near Palo Duro Canyon."

So, Jesse wasn't as much of a footloose drifter as he had led her to believe. He had some roots after all.

"Would anyone like something to drink?" Angel asked.

"Whiskey and water," Jesse said.

"Iced tea for me," Honey said.

"Dallas?"

"I'll join Jesse and have a whiskey, but without the water, Angel."

Honey sat on the Victorian sofa and Dallas took the leather chair that was obviously his favorite spot in the living room. Jesse joined Honey on the narrow sofa. It barely held the two of them, and Jesse's jean-clad leg brushed against her as he sat down.

Honey jerked away, then looked up to see if Dallas had noticed her reaction. He had. He looked concerned, but Honey wasn't about to explain the sexually fraught situation to him. Honey grimaced and folded her hands together in her lap. It was going to be a long evening.

Or it might have been if Angel hadn't been there. Honey had always liked Angel and had an affinity with the other woman that she couldn't explain. She did her best throughout the spicy Mexican meal to focus her attention on Angel and ignore Jesse Whitelaw. She wasn't totally successful.

It bothered Honey that Angel never got over her odd behavior around Jesse. Angel never quite relaxed, and her eyes were wary every time she looked at him. In fact, it bothered Honey enough that she mentioned it when she and Angel went upstairs to check on the baby after supper, leaving the men to stack the dishes in the dishwasher.

"You don't seem to like Jesse Whitelaw," Honey said bluntly.

Angel refused to meet her gaze, focusing instead on the baby sleeping in the crib. "It's not that I don't like him, it's just…"

"Just what? Has Dallas told you something about him? Something I should know?"

"Oh, no!" Angel reassured her. "It's nothing like that. It's just..."

Honey waited while Angel searched for the words to explain her aversion to the drifter.

"When I was much younger, I had a bad experience with some Indians." What Angel wasn't able to tell Honey was that she had seen the tortured remains of a Comanche raid in 1857. But no one except Dallas knew Angel had traveled through time to reach this century. So Angel was forced to explain how she felt without being able to give specific details.

"Whenever I look at Jesse," she said, "I see something in those dark eyes of his, something so savage, so feral, it reminds me of that time long ago. He terrifies me." Angel visibly shivered. "Aren't you afraid of him?"

"Sometimes," Honey admitted reluctantly. "But not in the way you are." Honey felt certain Jesse posed no physical threat to her. The wild, savage looks that frightened Angel only served to make Jesse more intriguing to her. "I find him attractive," she confessed. And that was more frightening than anything else about the drifter that she might have admitted.

Their talking woke the baby, but Honey couldn't be sorry because she had been dying for a chance to hold the little boy.

"Aren't you a handsome boy, Rhett," Honey cooed as Angel laid the baby in her arms. "Can we take him downstairs?"

Angel seemed hesitant, but Honey urged, "Please?"

"All right." Angel had to face the fact that her fears

of Jesse were misplaced in time. She might as well start now.

Dallas and Jesse stopped talking abruptly when the women came downstairs with the baby.

"Look," Honey said, holding Rhett so Jesse could see his face. "Isn't he something?"

Jesse wasn't looking at the child, he was looking at the glow on Honey's face. It was something, all right! She looked radiant and happier than he had ever seen her. He couldn't help imagining how she would look holding their child in her arms.

He frowned, wondering where that idea had come from. He wanted Honey, but babies had a way of tying a man down. Still, he considered the idea and felt things he hadn't anticipated. Pride. Protectiveness. And fear.

Was Honey still young enough to carry a child without any danger to her health? She didn't look over thirty, but he knew she had to be older because Jack was thirteen.

"How old were you when Jack was born?" Jesse asked.

Honey was surprised by the question. "Eighteen. Cale and I married right out of high school."

That made her thirty-two. Three years younger than he was. Maybe the better question was whether he was too old to be a father. He hadn't realized until just now how much he wanted a child of his own someday. Maybe he'd better not put it off too much longer.

"Do you wish you had more children?" he asked Honey.

She never took her eyes off the baby's face. Jesse watched her fingers smooth over the tiny eyebrows, the plump cheeks, the rosy mouth and then touch the tiny fingertips that gripped her little finger. "Oh, yes," she breathed.

She looked up at him and his heart leapt to his throat. Her eyes were liquid with feeling. Suddenly he wanted to be gone from here, to be alone with her.

Honey saw the fierce light in Jesse's eyes but knew she had nothing to fear. The fierceness thrilled her. The light drew her in and warmed her. Jesse Whitelaw was a danger to her, all right. But only because he had the power to steal her heart.

Honey was never sure later how they managed to take their leave so quickly, but she was grateful to be on her way home. In the darkness of the pickup cab she could hug her thoughts to herself. It was only after they had gone several miles that she thought to ask, "Did you tell Dallas about that suspicious man I saw on my property today?"

There was only the slightest hesitation before Jesse replied, "Yes. He said he'd look into it."

"Did you have a good time tonight?"

"I had forgotten how much Dallas and I have in common," he said.

"Oh?" She hadn't thought the two of them were much alike at all. "Like what?"

Jesse was quiet so long Honey didn't think he was going to answer. At last he said, "I can't think of any one thing. Just a feeling I had." He couldn't say more to Honey without raising questions that he wasn't prepared to answer.

"How did you like Angel?"

"Fine." *When she wasn't cringing from me.* He

couldn't say that to Honey, either. He wasn't sure what it was about him that frightened Angel Masterson. He only knew she was terrified of him. His lip curled in disgust. She had probably heard stories about the savage Comanche. A hundred years ago his forebears had been savage. Perhaps Angel had been a victim of Comanches in another life.

Jesse shrugged off the uncomfortable feeling he got when he remembered Angel's fear of him. There was something about her that bothered him as much as he bothered her. If he stuck around long enough, maybe someday he would find out what it was.

"Jesse? Is something wrong?"

He hadn't realized he was frowning until Honey spoke. He wiped the expression off his face and said, "No. I'm okay."

"Can I ask you something?"

"Anything."

"Why didn't you tell me you have a family?"

Jesse shrugged. "It didn't seem important."

Family not important? Honey shook her head in despair. Everything she learned about Jesse confirmed him as a loner. She had to stay away from him if she wanted to survive his eventual leave-taking heart-whole.

"Now I want to ask a question?" Jesse said.

"What?"

"Why did you marry so young?"

"I was in love." She paused. "And pregnant."

That wasn't the answer he had been expecting, but it didn't really surprise him. He could imagine her youthful passion. He had tasted a little of it himself.

"Were you ever sorry?"

How could she answer that? Maybe she regretted losing some of her choices. But she didn't regret having Jack. As for having to marry…

"I met Cale when I was fourteen years old and fell in love with him at first sight," she said. "I never wanted to be anything but Cale's wife, the mother of his children, and to work by his side on the Flying Diamond."

Honey had never put her feelings into words, but it made her loss seem even greater when she realized that her whole life had been focused on Cale. Now that Cale was gone, she was forced to admit that they had never had the partnership she had imagined when she married him. Those youthful dreams were gone. The children were only hers to love for a little while before they grew up and left her. All she would have in the end was the Flying Diamond. Except now the Flying Diamond was being threatened as well.

"I wish someone would catch those rustlers," she said, expressing her fears aloud. "About the only thing that's keeping the ranch afloat with the losses I've had is the service fees I get for General. I sure can't afford to lose any more stock."

He thought of the devastation she would feel when the bull was stolen, but pushed it from his mind. "You won't be losing any more cattle," Jesse said and then could have bitten his tongue.

"How can you be so sure?"

He shrugged. "Just a feeling I have."

One of those uncomfortable silences fell between them. Honey chewed her lower lip, wondering whether she ought to ask a question that had been on her mind lately. She saw the two-story ranch house come into sight and realized she would lose the opportunity to speak if she didn't do it now.

"Were you ever married?" she asked.

Jesse's brow rose at the personal nature of the question. "No."

"Why not?"

His dark eyes glittered in the light from the dashboard as he turned to her and said, "Never found the right woman."

Honey shivered at the intensity of the look he gave her. On a subconscious level she was aware they had arrived at the house, that he had turned off the car engine, and that this time he had parked the truck in the shadows away from the front porch light.

"Honey?"

His voice rasped over her like a rough caress. She felt his need but wasn't sure what to do. She leaned toward him only a fraction of an inch. It was all the invitation he needed.

Jesse's hand threaded into her hair and tugged her closer. Their mouths were a breath apart but he didn't close the distance.

"Honey?"

He was forcing her to make a choice.

Honey drew back abruptly at a loud tapping on the window.

"Hey, Mom! You guys coming inside or what?" Jack shouted through the glass.

Honey closed her eyes and took a deep breath. Oh Lord. She had forgotten about her overprotective teenage son. He hadn't done anything quite this blatant with

Adam, but apparently he recognized Jesse as a greater threat. He wasn't far wrong. She didn't understand the strength of her attraction to the hired hand, but she realized now she would be a fool to underestimate it.

She glanced at Jesse to see how he was handling the interruption and was surprised to see a smile on his face.

"I'm glad you're finding this so amusing," she said.

"If what I suspect is true, Jack hasn't allowed you much privacy with Philips. I have to be eternally grateful to him for that."

"You don't seem too worried that he's going to get in your way."

Jesse grinned. "Nope."

"Why not?"

"Because I don't intend to let him."

Right there, with Jack staring aghast through the window, Jesse took her in his arms and kissed her soundly. Then he reached across her and opened the truck door on her side, gently nudging Jack out of the way.

"Why don't you escort your mom inside, Jack. I've got some things I have to do."

Honey stepped out of the truck without thinking and stood with Jack as Jesse backed the truck and headed down the road that led off Flying Diamond property.

When the truck was gone, Jack confronted his mother in the faint light from the porch.

"Why'd you let him kiss you, Mom?"

"Jack, I—" Honey didn't know what to say.

"You're not gonna marry him or anything, are you?"

That she could answer more easily. "No, I'm not

going to marry him." He wasn't going to be around long enough for that.

"Then why'd you kiss him?" Jack persisted.

"I like Jesse a lot, Jack. When two adults like each other, kissing is a way of expressing that feeling. When you're a little older, you'll understand."

"Well, I don't like it," Jack said. "And I don't like him, either."

Honey thought of how hard it was for her son to accept another man in Cale's place, and to share his mother, whom he'd had to himself for the past year. "You know, Jack, just because I kissed another man doesn't mean I'll ever love your father any less. Or you and Jonathan, either."

"Oh, yeah? Well, Dad wouldn't like it."

"Dad would understand," Honey said quietly. "He wouldn't want us to stop living because he's not here with us. You're going to keep growing, Jack, and changing. Dad wouldn't have wanted you to stay a little boy. He'd want you to grow into the man you're destined to be.

"And I don't think he would necessarily want me to spend the rest of my life alone, without ever loving another man."

Jack jumped on the one word that stuck out in all she'd said. "Are you saying you're in *love* with that drifter?"

"No." *But I could be.*

Honey put her hand on Jack's shoulder, but he shrugged away from her. She ignored the snub as they headed up the porch steps and into the house. "Let's just take each day one at a time, shall we? I hope you'll give Jesse the benefit of the doubt. I don't love him, but I do like him, Jack. I'd appreciate it if you could try to get along with him."

"I'll try," Jack said. "But I'm not promising you anything."

"That's all I can ask," Honey said.

After she had sent Jack to bed, Honey stood at the lace-curtained window in her bedroom and looked out into the dark.

Where are you Jesse Whitelaw? What brought you here? And what do you want from me?

It was three in the morning before Honey heard the front door open and close. Jesse was back. She sat up, thinking to confront him about where he had been. Then she lay back down.

He wasn't her husband. He wasn't accountable to her. And it was none of her business what he had been doing. Or with whom.

Honey closed her eyes. When Cale died she had made up her mind never to let another man break her heart. She lay on her side and pulled the covers up over her shoulder. She was going to put that drifting man out of her mind once and for all.

Maybe Jack was right. From now on, she would keep a little more distance between herself and the hired hand.

Chapter 5

Jesse had known he was heading into deep water the first time he touched Honey Farrell. But it had been impossible to ignore the woman. There was something about her that called to him. He had no business getting involved with anyone, not with the life he led. Yet he hadn't been able to control the desire for her that rocked him whenever she was near. His attraction to her was as strong now, three weeks after he had first laid eyes on her, as it had been that first night. Once having tasted Honey, having touched her, it was an exercise of will to keep his distance from her.

He had been a fool to take that room off the kitchen. He could have found a way to steal General without arousing suspicion even if he were living in the barn. It was rough enough seeing Honey every morning for breakfast, without knowing that he didn't have the right to hold her the way he wanted.

As it turned out, he had ended up seeking out the room in the barn at odd times—like now—for the privacy it offered him. Jesse crossed his arms behind his head and lay back on the bunk. The room offered few amenities. The bed was hard and the walls were unadorned wooden slats. It smelled always of leather and hay. But at least here he could get away from her to think. Right now he had a lot to think about.

Something had happened this morning that he wasn't sure he wanted to remember, but he was quite sure he would never forget.

He had woken at the break of dawn, since he and Honey had agreed that he should have use of the bathroom first each morning. As he climbed the stairs wearing no more than jeans and socks, scratching his bare chest, he distinctly heard the water running. He had wondered what Honey was doing up so early. Over the past three weeks she had kept her bedroom door closed until he had bathed and shaved and headed back downstairs to make coffee. Then she would bathe and join him to finish making breakfast before the boys awoke.

Jesse had been curious enough about the change in routine to continue to the bathroom door. He knocked, but there was no answer.

"Honey?"

When she didn't respond, he tried the door. It wasn't locked, so he cautiously opened it. He wasn't sure what he expected, but what he found was disturbing.

Water was lapping at the edge of the tub, threatening to overflow. Honey was lying back with her nape against the edge of the tub. Her face was angled away from him. Her hair was wet and slicked back to reveal the plane of her jaw. In the steam-fogged room she provided an almost ethereal vision. He stood transfixed, staring at her.

"Honey?"

Concerned when there was still no response he stepped forward and knelt beside the tub. He gasped at his first glorious sight of her naked body. Before desire could take hold, he caught sight of her face, frozen in a mask of agony. Certain that something was seriously wrong, he rose to shut off the water and in the same deft move reached for a towel to wrap around her.

When he lifted her from the water, her eyes remained closed. Her face was frozen in a tragic pose like some marble statue. He picked her up in his arms and, rather than stay in the steamy room, headed for the open door down the hall that led to her bedroom. She offered no resistance, which made him even more concerned. Once inside, he shoved the door closed with his shoulder and carried her over to the canopied bed.

He wondered if her husband had slept with her in this frilly room, but decided she must have redone it since his death. It was a feminine place now, with the lace canopy overhead and lace curtains at the windows. It smelled of some flower, which he finally identified as the same honeysuckle scent he had breathed so often in the bathroom.

He tried to lay her on the bed but she grasped him around the neck, refusing to let go. He sat down on the bed and pulled her farther into his arms.

It was then that he realized she was crying. Sobbing,

actually. Only there was no sound, just the heaving of her body and the closed, distorted features on her face.

"It's all right," he crooned. "You're all right. I'm here now."

Her grip tightened around his neck and her nose nuzzled against his throat. She moaned once, and the silent sobbing began again.

Jesse felt his throat swell with emotion. His arms tightened around her, as though he could protect her from whatever was causing her pain. Only he hadn't a clue as to why she was so distraught.

"It's all right, Honey. Nothing can hurt you. I'm here. You're fine."

He meant what he said. He wouldn't allow anyone or anything to harm her. Jesse tightened his arms possessively, only to feel her struggle against his hold. Which reminded him he had no right to feel such feelings. They were virtual strangers. He knew little about her; and she knew nothing, really, about him.

He loosened his hold, caressing her bare shoulders in preparation for moving them apart. As soon as he tried to separate them, she clutched at him and buried her face even deeper against his chest. He was perfectly willing to hold her all day, if that was what she needed. He settled himself more comfortably, putting his stockinged feet on the bedspread, to wait out her tears.

She cried herself to sleep.

Jesse watched the sun rise with a sleeping woman in his arms. He had always wondered what it would be like to settle down, to have a woman of his own, to wake like this with her softness enfolded in his arms.

His life hadn't allowed such a luxury. Lately he had begun to wonder whether he ought to think more seriously about finding a wife.

He had bitter experience already with one woman who hadn't been able to handle the kind of life he led. She had worried and begged and cried for him to change his ways. But he hadn't been able—or willing—to give up the life he had planned for himself. It had been a bitter separation, and he had learned that he could hurt, and be hurt.

That had been nearly ten years ago. He hadn't allowed himself to fall in love again. Or to dream about a permanent woman in his life.

Until he had met Honey.

Jesse brushed back a drying wisp of curl from Honey's brow. He had no idea what it was about this woman that made her different from every other. She was like the other half of him; with her he felt whole. He worried about what would happen when she knew the truth about him.

Maybe it wouldn't matter.

Jesse grimaced. It would matter.

At least the boys weren't around this morning. He shuddered to think what Jack would have said if he caught Jesse in Honey's bedroom—no matter how innocent the circumstances. Fortunately, since yesterday had been the last day of school, Jack had gone off to an end-of-school party and stayed the night with friends. Jonathan was spending the first six weeks of summer vacation with Honey's mother and father.

Jesse felt Honey stir in his arms and thought how well the name fit her, for she flowed around him, her softness conforming to all his hard planes. He smoothed the damp hair as best he could. "How are you feeling?"

She stiffened in his arms. "Jesse? What are you doing here?"

"You don't remember?"

She frowned. "No…yes…oh."

He watched an endearing pink blush begin at her neck and rise to her face as she realized she was naked under the towel. It had slipped some since he had carried her into the room. Now it exposed a rounded hip and teased him with the edge of one honey-brown nipple. He found the sight enchanting.

She tried to ease herself away.

"There's no sense worrying now," he said. "I've already seen everything there is to see. But I would like to hear what had you so upset."

Her shoulders sagged. For a moment he thought she wasn't going to tell him. When she did, he wished she hadn't.

"Yesterday would have been my fourteenth wedding anniversary. I couldn't get Cale out of my mind all night. I guess I was hoping to soak the memories out of my system—the sad ones, anyway."

"Did it work?"

Her face was surprisingly serene when she answered, "I think maybe it did. I feel better anyway. Thanks for being there. I hadn't realized how much I needed…someone…to hold me."

Once Jesse was reassured that Honey was no longer in pain, it left him free to acknowledge the other feelings that arose from holding her in his arms. And to pursue them.

"I wouldn't be honest if I didn't say I'm enjoying this," he said. "You're a beautiful woman, Honey." He felt his body tighten and knew she must feel the swell of arousal beneath her.

Honey tried to sit up, but Jesse kept her where she was. "No need trying to pretend you didn't hear what I said. I've kept my distance the past three weeks, but it hasn't been easy. I want you, Honey. I don't want to fight what I'm feeling anymore."

"How can you say something like that when you know I've spent the night crying over another man?"

"Cale is dead, Honey. You're entitled to your memories of him. But I won't let him come between us."

"There is no *us!*" Honey protested. "You're a drifter, Jesse. Here today and gone tomorrow. I can't—"

His voice was fierce because he feared she was right. "We have today," he said. "I can't offer you a tomorrow right now. Believe me, if I could, I would."

He could see that she wanted him, that she was tempted to take today and say to hell with tomorrow. He wished he could make promises, but a man in his line of work couldn't do that. So he held his tongue, his jaw taut as he waited to hear her answer.

"If it were only me," she began, "I might be willing to accept what you have to offer. But I have two sons. I have to think of them. You're a drifter, Jesse. You could never stay in one place long enough to be the father they need."

"What if I said I could?" She lifted her blue eyes to him and he saw they were filled with hope…and despair.

"I'd like to believe you. But I can't."

"So you're posting a No Trespass sign?" he asked.

"I didn't say that."

"Then what are you saying?"

"I have to think about it," she retorted. She looked up into Jesse's dark eyes seeking answers for her confused feelings. His gaze was intent, his lids hooded, his mouth rigid, tense with desire.

Suddenly she was aware again of her half-naked state and of the hard male body beneath her. Jesse put a hand on her bottom and shifted her so she was lying with the heart of her pressed to the heat of him.

She gasped. Honey had forgotten the pleasure of a man's hard body pressed against her softness.

"Ah, sweetheart, that feels so good," Jesse murmured.

She clutched at his shoulders, afraid to move lest she succumb to the pleasure or have to give it up. She closed her eyes and laid her head against his chest. He felt strong, and she felt secure in his arms, as though she could have no more worries if they faced the world together.

He was offering himself for a while. For the moment. Honey realized suddenly that she was seriously considering his offer. She didn't want to fall in love with him. That way lay disaster. When he left he would break her heart. But she couldn't deny that when she was with him she felt safe and, curiously, loved. It was a feeling she'd had with no other man since Cale's death.

She would be a fool to live for today; she would be a fool to give up today for the hope of tomorrow. But maybe the time had come for acting a little foolish. Knowing her decision was made, Honey relaxed and nuzzled her face against Jesse's throat.

He felt her acquiescence. Her body flowed once more like honey, hot and smooth. His blood began to thrum.

Honey suddenly felt herself being rolled over onto her back. Jesse lay on top of her, his hips pressed tightly into the cradle of her thighs, so there was no mistaking his intention. He levered himself onto his palms and she felt herself quivering as he took a long, lazy look at the breasts he had exposed.

"You're so beautiful," he rasped.

He lowered his mouth so slowly that Honey felt the curl of desire in her belly long before his mouth reached the tip of her breast. She anticipated his touch, but the reality was stunning. The warmth. The heat. The wetness of his tongue. The sharp pain as his teeth grazed the crest, and then the strong sucking as he took her breast into his mouth. It was almost more pleasure than she could bear.

Honey was frantic to touch his flesh, and her fingernails made distinct crescents in his back as his mouth captured hers and his tongue ravaged her.

Honey shuddered as his hand cupped her breast. He kneaded the tip between his callused finger and thumb, causing a feeling that was exquisite. There were too many sensations to cope with them all. The roughness of his hands, the wetness of his mouth, the heaviness of his lower body on hers. She was lost in sensation.

With Cale, they would have rushed to fulfillment. But when she reached for the metal buttons of Jesse's fly, his hand was there to stop her. It seemed he had not nearly had his fill of touching and tasting. He held her hand tight against the bulge in his jeans for a moment, then laid her palm against his cheek.

"Touch me, Honey. I need you to touch me."

And she did. Her fingertips roamed his face as though she were a blind woman trying to see him for the first time. She found the tiny scar in his hairline and the spiderweb of lines beside his eyes. The thickness of his brows. The petal softness of his eyelids and his feathery lashes.

She searched out the hollow beneath his cheekbone and the strength of his jaw. The long, straight nose and beneath it the twin lines that led to his lips, soft and damp and full.

He nipped her fingertips and made her laugh until his teeth caught the pad between her fingers and thumb. His love bite chased waves of feeling down her spine.

She used lips and teeth and tongue to trace the shell shape of his ear and was rewarded with a masculine groan that fought its way up through clenched teeth. She was lost in an adventure of discovery, so she wasn't aware, at first, of similar forays Jesse was making.

He nibbled at her neck and laved the love bites with his tongue. Honey felt her whole body clench in response. His hands entwined with hers, and he held them down on either side of her head so she couldn't interfere with his sensual exploration. His lips traced the length of her collarbone and slipped down to the tender skin beneath her arm. He bit and suckled until Honey was bucking beneath him.

"Jesse, please," she begged. She couldn't have said herself whether she wanted him to stop or go on.

Jesse certainly had no intention of stopping. He was fascinated by the woman under him. By her scents and textures and tastes. She smelled of honeysuckle, but her taste was distinct, a woman taste that was meant for him and him alone. Her skin was like satin, or maybe silk, smooth and alluring. He couldn't touch her enough, couldn't taste her enough.

His mouth found hers again, and he brought their bodies into alignment, feeling the moist heat of her through the denim that still separated them. He wanted her. How he wanted her!

He released her hands to reach down toward his Levi's, but her hand was there before him.

"Let me."

Her eyes were lambent, heavy-lidded, the blue almost violet with desire. His loins tightened. He couldn't speak, so he nodded curtly.

She took her own damn sweet time with it. A button at a time he felt himself come free until she was holding him, surrounding him with her hand.

He hissed out a breath. "Damn woman. You're going to kill me with kindness."

Honey smiled seductively. "Then you'll die smiling, cowboy."

The crooked grin flashed on his face and was gone an instant later as she led him toward the female portal that awaited him.

He paused long enough to rasp out, "Are you protected?"

She nodded at the same time he thrust himself inside her. *Hot. Wet. Tight.* The feelings were astounding, and he groaned as he seated himself deep within her body.

For a moment he didn't move, just enjoyed the feeling of being inside her, of having joined the two of them as one. *Right. It felt right. And good.*

"Honey, dammit, I—" He wanted to wait even longer, arouse her more, until she couldn't talk or even breathe. It was soon apparent she was as aroused as he. Her hands shoved his jeans down and she grasped his buttocks as her legs came up around him. He took his weight on his hands, leaving him free to caress her lips and breasts with his mouth.

Jesse felt a frenzy of uncontrollable need for this woman, at this moment in time. "Honey, I can't—"

He needn't have worried that he was leaving her behind. He felt the convulsions deep inside her and knew she had reached the same pinnacle as he. He threw his head back, teeth clenched against the agony of pleasure that swelled through him as he spilled his seed. He was unaware of the exultant cry that escaped him at that ultimate moment.

Honey felt the tears steal into the corners of her eyes as Jesse slipped to her side and pulled her into his arms. She held on to him tightly, afraid to admit the awesomeness of what had just happened between them. It wasn't what she had expected. The pleasure, yes. But the feeling of belonging… That, she couldn't explain and didn't want to contemplate.

"Honey? Did I hurt you?"

She felt his lips at the corners of her eyes, kissing away the tears. "No," she said. "You didn't hurt me."

"Then, why—?"

"I don't know," she admitted in a choked voice. Another tear fell.

He pulled her into his embrace. In a low voice, that rusty-gate voice, he said, "It felt right, Honey. It felt good. Don't be sorry."

"I'm not," she said. And realized she wasn't. Cale was dead; she was alive. She didn't fool herself. What she and Jesse had just experienced was rare. It hadn't even happened all the time with Cale. That must mean that she felt more for the drifter than even she had previously perceived. She wasn't ready yet to examine those feelings. She wasn't sure what she would find. She certainly wasn't ready to confront them head-on.

Honey changed the subject instead. "Jack will be showing up soon," she whispered.

"Yeah. I'd better get out of here." He grinned and slicked his hand through hair damp with sweat. "I could really use a bath."

Honey arched a brow. "Are you bragging or complaining?"

His eyes were suddenly serious as he said, "I got exactly what I wanted. Are you saying you didn't want it, too?"

"No. I'm not saying that."

He searched her eyes, trying to discern her feelings. First and foremost among them was confusion. Well, he could identify with that. Perhaps what they both needed now was time and distance. Especially since he could feel himself becoming aroused again simply by her nearness. "I'd better get that bath."

He pulled his Levi's back on and buttoned them partway, knowing he was just going to pull them off again down the hall, then turned back to look at Honey.

She had grabbed the towel and was using it to cover herself.

"I think I find you even more enticing half-clothed than when you're naked," he warned.

Honey clutched the towel closer, accidentally revealing even more skin. She was helpless to resist him if he touched her again.

Jesse considered making love to her again, but his common sense stopped him. Any moment Jack might return home. While he hadn't allowed her son's objections to prevent him from pursuing Honey, he didn't want to confront Jack coming from her bedroom, either. He didn't want the boy thinking any less of his mother because of her relationship with some drifter. When the time was right, he would tell them all the truth and let Honey decide whether she wanted anything more to do with him—or not.

He finished his bath and went downstairs to make coffee, as usual. Shortly thereafter he was joined by Honey, fresh from her bath and looking even more alluring with her hair curling in damp tendrils around her face. She was wearing the same man's robe she had worn the first day he had arrived. He wondered if she had done it on purpose, to remind him that she had belonged to another man. He wanted to cross the room and pull her into his arms, but the wary look on her face held him apart.

"I started coffee," he said, to break the uncertain silence.

"How about eggs and bacon this morning?" she asked, heading for the refrigerator.

He let her pass by him without reaching out, but his nostrils flared as he caught the scent of honeysuckle from her hair. He watched her do all the normal things she had done for the past three weeks, as though nothing momentous had happened between them in the bed upstairs.

Then he saw her hands were trembling and realized she wasn't as calm as she wanted him to believe. He didn't think, just closed the distance between them. He had put his hands on her shoulders when a noise behind him froze them both.

"Hey, what's going on here?" Jack said belligerently, shoving open the kitchen door and letting himself in.

Jesse turned to face Honey's older son, but he didn't take his hands from her shoulders. "Your mom's making breakfast."

"That's not what I mean and you know it," Jack retorted.

Jesse saw the tension in the boy's shoulders, the suspicion in his eyes. There was no purpose to be served by aggravating him. He let go of Honey's shoulders, picked up the pot of coffee from the stove and returned to the table to pour himself a cup.

Jack watched with hostile eyes from the doorway, then marched over to stand before the hired hand.

Jessie had been expecting Jack to confront him, but he wasn't prepared for the bluntness of the boy's attack.

"You stay away from my mother. She doesn't want anything to do with you."

"That's her decision, isn't it?"

"I can take care of things around here now that school's out!" the boy said. "We don't need you."

Jesse heard the pain beneath the defiant words. "From what I've seen, your mother can use another helping hand."

"You can never replace my father!" Jack said. "He was a Texas Ranger, a hero. You're nothing, just some drifter who rolled in like tumbleweed. Why don't you go back where you came from?"

"Jack!" Honey was appalled at Jack's attack on Jesse. "Apologize," she ordered.

"I won't!" Jack said. "I meant every word I said. We don't need him here."

"But we do need him," Honey contradicted. "I can't do it all, Jack. Even though you're a big help, there are jobs you can't do, either. We need a man's help. That's why Jesse is here."

Honey realized immediately that she had used the wrong appeal with her son. He was a youth on the verge of manhood, and she had reminded him that despite the change in his voice and his tall lanky body, he was not yet a man.

"Fine!" he retorted. "Keep your hired hand. But don't expect me to like it!"

With that he shoved his way out the screen door and headed for the barn. Without breakfast. Which, knowing Jack's appetite, gave Honey some idea just how upset he was.

Honey felt the tears glaze her eyes. "I'm sorry that happened."

Jesse put his hands on her shoulders to comfort her. "He'll be all right."

"I wish I could be as sure of that as you seem to be."

"Don't worry, Honey. Everything will work out fine. You'll see."

But as he lay in the bunk in the barn, he felt a knot in his stomach at all the hurdles that would have to be crossed if he was ever to claim this woman as his own.

Chapter 6

Jesse found Jack in the barn brushing General. He stuck a boot on the bottom rail of the stall door and leaned his forearms on the top rail.

"You and that bull seem to be good friends," Jesse said.

The boy ignored him and continued brushing the bull's curly red coat.

Jesse tipped his hat back off his brow. "When I was a kid about your age my dad gave me a bull of my very own to raise."

"I was eight when Dad bought General," Jack said. "He wasn't much to look at then, but Dad thought he was something pretty special. He was right. General's always been a winner." Jack seemed embarrassed at having said so much and began brushing a little harder and faster.

"Sounds like your dad was something pretty special, too," Jesse said.

"You're nothing like him, that's for sure!"

"No, I expect not," Jesse agreed. "I do have one thing in common with your father."

Jesse waited for the boy's curiosity to force him to continue the conversation.

"What's that?" Jack asked.

"Feelings for your mother."

Jack glared at him. "Why can't you just leave her alone?"

How could he explain what he felt for Honey in words the boy would understand? Jesse wondered. What did one say to a thirteen-year-old boy to describe the relationship between a man and a woman? It would be easier if he could tell the boy he was committed in some way to Honey. But Jesse had never spoken of "forever" with Honey, and he wasn't free to do so until his business here was done.

"I wish I had an easy answer for your question," Jesse said quietly. "But I don't. Will it help if I say I'll try my damnedest never to do anything that'll hurt your mom?"

Abruptly Jack stopped brushing the bull. "She's never gonna love you like she loved Dad. You're crazy if you think she will. There's no sense in you hanging around. Now that school's out, I can handle things. Why don't you just leave?"

"I can't," Jesse said simply.

"Why not?"

"Your mother needs my help." *And I still have to steal this bull.*

Jack's body sagged like a balloon losing air. "I wish Dad was still alive," he said in a quiet, solemn voice.

Jesse retrieved a piece of hay from the feed trough and began to shred it. "My father died when I was twenty," he said. "Bronc threw him and broke his neck. I didn't think anything could hurt so much as the grief I felt losing him. I missed him so much, I left home and started wandering. It took a few years before I realized he was still with me."

The boy's brow furrowed, revealing the confusion caused by Jesse's last statement.

Jesse reached out to scratch behind the huge bull's ears. "What I mean is, I'd catch myself doing something and remember how my dad had been the one to teach it to me. My father left me with the best part of himself—the memories I have of everything he said and did."

Jack swallowed hard. His teeth gritted to stop the tremor in his chin.

"Your mom won't ever forget your dad, Jack. No more than you will. No matter who comes into her life, she'll always have her memories of him. And so will you."

Jesse wasn't sure whether his words had caused any change in Jack's attitude toward him, but he didn't know what else to say.

The silence deepened and thickened until finally Jesse said, "You're doing a fine job grooming General, boy. When you get done, I could use some help replacing a few rotted posts around the corral."

Jesse turned and left the barn without waiting for a reply from Jack. Fifteen minutes later, Jack appeared at his side wearing work gloves and carrying a shovel.

The two of them labored side by side digging out several rotten posts and replacing them with new ones.

Honey could hardly believe her eyes when she looked out the kitchen window. She forced herself to remain inside and give Jesse and Jack time alone together. When several hours had passed and they were still hard at work, she prepared a tray with two large glasses of iced tea and took it out to the corral.

"You both look thirsty," she said.

Jesse swiped at the dripping sweat on his neck and chest with a bandanna he had pulled from his back pocket. "I am. How about you, Jack?"

Honey was amazed at the even, almost cordial sound of her son's voice as he said, "I feel dry enough to swallow a river and come back for more."

Both males made short work of the tall glasses of iced tea. Honey flushed when Jesse winked at her as he set his glass back on the tray. She looked quickly at Jack to see how he reacted to Jesse's flirtatious behavior. Her son shrugged…and grinned!

She turned and stared in amazement at Jesse. What on earth had he said to Jack to cause such a miraculous reversal in her son's attitude? Honey frowned as the two shared a look of male understanding. Whatever it was, she ought to feel grateful. And she did. Sort of.

Honey tried to pinpoint what it was that bothered her about Jack's acceptance of the drifter. Her forehead wrinkled in thought as she slowly made her way back to the house. She wasn't pleased with the conclusions she reached.

So long as Jack found the drifter a threat and an interloper, it had been easier for Honey to justify keeping Jesse at an emotional arm's length. She had realized there was no sense letting herself get attached to him if one of her children clearly abhorred him. Jack's sudden acceptance of Jesse left her without a piece of armor she had counted on. Now, with her defenses down, she was extremely vulnerable to the drifter's entreaties.

Halfway to the house, the phone started ringing. Honey was breathless from running when she finally answered it.

"Honey? Did I catch you outside again?"

"Oh, Adam. Uh, yes, you did. When are you coming home?"

"I am home. Are you free to go out tonight?"

Honey thought about it for a moment. Clearly she needed to be sure Jesse wasn't anywhere around when she told Adam she couldn't marry him. Going out was probably not a bad idea. "Sure," she said at last. "What time should I meet you and where?"

"I'll pick you up."

"That isn't necessary, Adam. I—"

"I insist."

It was clear he wouldn't take no for an answer. Rather than argue, she agreed. "All right."

"See you at eight, Honey."

Honey almost groaned aloud at Adam's purring tone of voice when he said her name. It was not going to be a pleasant evening. "At eight," she confirmed.

When Jesse and Jack came into the house for supper they found only two places set at the table. It was the most subtle way Honey could think of to say that she was going out for the evening. From the look in Jesse's eyes, subtlety wasn't going to help much.

It was Jack who asked, "Aren't you going to eat with us?"

"No. Adam is taking me out to supper."

Identical frowns settled on two male faces. It had apparently dawned on Jack that his mother had not one, but two suitors. Honey would have laughed at the chagrined expression on her son's face if the situation hadn't been so fraught with tension.

Jack looked warily at Jesse. "Uh… Adam is mom's… uh…friend," he said by way of explanation.

"That's what your mom said," Jesse agreed.

Jack relaxed when it appeared Jesse wasn't upset by the situation. He turned to his mother and asked, "Are you going to tell Adam tonight that you won't marry him?"

Honey clutched her hands together, frustrated by the situation Jack had put her in. The gleam of amusement in Jesse's dark eyes didn't help matters any. She simply said, "Adam deserves an answer to his proposal. And yes, I intend to give it to him tonight."

"And?" Jack prompted.

"After I've given Adam my answer, I'll be glad to share it with you," she said to Jack. "Until then, I think you should sit down and eat your supper."

Honey escaped upstairs to dress, where she managed to consume most of the two hours until Adam's expected arrival at eight.

Shortly before Adam was due to arrive, Jack knocked on her door and asked if he could spend the night with a friend.

"What time will you be home tomorrow morning?" Honey asked.

"Well, me and Reno were thinking maybe we'd go tubing tomorrow. I figured I'd stay and have lunch with him and spend the afternoon on the river."

"Jack, I don't think—"

"It's the first Saturday of summer vacation, Mom! You aren't gonna make me come home and work, are you?"

Jack knew exactly what to say to push her maternal guilt buttons. "All right," she relented. "But I don't think you can make a habit of this. I'm depending on your help around the ranch this summer."

"Believe me, Mom, it's just this once."

Moments later Jack came by with his overnight bag thrown over his shoulder to give her a quick, hard hug. Then he scampered down the stairs and out through the kitchen. She heard the screen door slam behind him.

If Honey thought she had managed to avoid a confrontation with Jesse by staying in her room until the very last minute, she was disabused of that notion as soon as she descended the stairs. He was waiting for her at the bottom.

"You told me you aren't going to marry that Philips guy," Jesse said.

Honey postponed any response by heading for the living room. She brushed aside the lacy drapery on the front window and looked for the headlights of Adam's sports car in the distance. No rescue there. She turned and faced Jesse, who had followed her into the room and was standing behind the aged leather chair that had been Cale's favorite spot in the room.

"I've never given Adam an answer to his proposal,"

Honey said. "He deserves to be told my decision face-to-face."

"Tell him here. Don't go out with him."

Honey felt a surge of anger. "I may not be willing to marry Adam, but I care for him as a person. I agreed to go to dinner with him, and I'm going!"

She watched Jesse's eyes narrow, his nostrils flare, his lips flatten. His anger clearly matched her own. But he didn't argue further.

Neither did he leave the room. When Adam arrived five long minutes later, he found Jesse comfortably ensconced in Cale's favorite chair idly perusing a ranching magazine.

Jesse looked up assessingly when Adam entered the living room, but he didn't rise to greet the other man. He kept his left ankle hooked securely over his right knee and slouched a little more deeply into the chair, concentrating on the magazine.

"Don't be too late," he said as Adam slipped an arm around Honey to escort her out the door. Jesse smiled behind the magazine when the other man stiffened.

His smugness disappeared when Honey replied with a beatific smile, "Don't wait up for me."

Jesse would have been downright concerned if he could have heard what passed between Honey and Adam in the car on the way to the restaurant.

"That hired hand sure made himself at home in your living room," Adam complained before too many minutes had passed.

Honey sighed in exasperation. "It wasn't what it looked like."

"Oh?"

"He was trying to make you feel uncomfortable," Honey said.

"He succeeded. I wouldn't have been half as upset if it weren't for the things I know about him."

"You've only seen him twice!" Honey protested. "You don't know anything about him."

"Actually, I did some checking up on him."

"Adam, that really wasn't necessary." Honey didn't bother to keep the irritation out of her voice. Men! Really!

"Maybe you'll change your mind when you hear what I have to say."

Honey arched a brow and waited.

"Did you know he's got a criminal record?"

"What? *Jesse?*" Honey felt breathless, as though someone had landed on her chest with both feet. "Dallas vouched for him."

"Dallas obviously covered for his friend. The man's been arrested, Honey." He paused significantly and added, "For rustling cattle."

Honey leapt on the only scrap of positive information Adam had given her. "*Arrested.* Then he was never convicted?"

Adam released a gusty breath. "Not as far as I could find out. Probably had a good lawyer. It was only by chance that there was any record of the arrest. Don't you see, Honey? He might even be one of the rustlers who've been stealing your stock. He probably moved in so he could look things over up close."

"I lost stock long before Jesse showed up around here," Honey said coldly. "I refuse to believe he's part of any gang of rustlers."

But she couldn't help thinking about the night Jesse had been gone until three in the morning. Where had he been? What had he been doing? And Jesse hadn't wanted her to call the police when she had spotted someone suspicious on her property. He had said he would rather tell Dallas about it. Had he?

Adam had given her a lot to think about, and Honey was quiet for the rest of the journey to the restaurant in Hondo. Hermannson's Steak House was famous for its traditional Texas fare of chicken-fried steak and onion rings. A country band played later in the evening, and she and Adam danced the Texas two-step and the rousing and bawdy Cotton-eyed Joe.

Adam was always good company, and Honey couldn't help laughing at his anecdotes. But she was increasingly aware that the end of the evening was coming, when Adam would renew his proposal and she would have to give him her answer. She felt a somberness stealing over her. Finally Adam ceased trying to make her smile.

"Time to go?" he asked.

"I think so."

She tried several times in the car to get out the words *I can't marry you.* It wasn't as easy being candid as she wished it was.

Adam wasn't totally insensitive to her plight, she discovered. In fact he made it easy for her.

"It's all right," he said in a quiet voice. "I guess I knew I was fooling myself. When you didn't say yes right away I figured you had some reservations about marrying me. I guess I hoped if I was persistent you'd change your mind."

"I'm sorry," Honey said.

"So am I," Adam said with a wry twist of his mouth. "I suppose it won't do any good to warn you again about that drifter you hired, either."

"I'll think about what you said," Honey conceded. She just couldn't believe Jesse had come to the Flying Diamond to steal from her. She had to believe that or die from the pain she felt at the thought he had simply been using her all this time.

The inside of the house was dark when they drove up, but it was late. Honey was grateful that she wouldn't have to confront Jesse tonight about the things Adam had told her.

"Good night, Adam," Honey said. She felt awkward. Unsure whether he would want to kiss her and not willing to hurt him any more than she already had by refusing if he did.

Adam proved more of a gentleman than she had hoped. He took her hand in his and held it a moment. The look on his face was controlled, but she saw the pain in his eyes as he said, "Goodbye, Honey."

She swallowed over the lump in her throat. She hadn't meant to hurt him. "I'm sorry," she said again.

"Don't be. I'll survive." Only he knew how deeply he had allowed himself to fall in love with her, and how hard it was to give up all hope of having her for his wife.

Slowly he let her hand slip through his fingers. He came around and opened the car door for her and walked her to the porch. As he left her, his last words were, "Be careful, Honey. Don't trust that drifter too much."

Then he was gone.

Honey let herself into the dark house and leaned back against the front door. Her whole body sagged in relief. She had hurt a good man without meaning to, though she didn't regret refusing his proposal.

"You were gone long enough!"

The accusation coming out of the dark startled Honey and she nearly jumped out of her shoes.

"You scared me to death!" she hissed. "What are you doing sitting here in the dark?"

"Waiting for you."

As her eyes adjusted to the scant light, she saw that Jesse was no longer sitting. He had risen and was closing the distance between them. Escape seemed like a good idea and she started for the stairs. She didn't get two steps before he grasped her by the shoulders.

"You didn't bring him inside with you. Does that mean you've told him things are over between you?"

"That's none of your—"

Jesse shook her hard. "Answer me!"

Honey was more furious than she could remember being at any time since Cale's death. How dare this man confront her! How dare he demand answers that were none of his business! "Yes!" she hissed. "Yes! Is that what you wanted to hear?"

Jesse answered her by capturing her mouth with his. It was a savage kiss, a kiss of claiming. His hands slid around her and he spread his legs and pulled her into the cradle of his thighs. He wasn't gentle, but Honey responded to the urgency she felt in everything he did. Against all reason, she felt a spark of passion ignite, and she began to return his fervent kisses.

"Honey, Honey," he murmured against her lips. "I need you. I want you."

Honey was nearly insensate with the feelings he was creating with his mouth and hands. He made her feel like a woman with his desire, his need. She shoved at his shoulders and whispered, "Jesse, we can't. Jack is—"

"Jack's spending the night with friends," he reminded her.

He grinned at the stunned look on her face as she realized that her youthful chaperon was not going to come to her rescue this time.

Without giving her a chance to object, Jesse swept her into his arms in a masterful imitation of Rhett and Scarlett and headed upstairs.

"What do you think you're doing?" Honey demanded.

"Taking you to bed where you belong," Jesse said.

"We can't do this," Honey protested.

Jesse stopped halfway up the stairs. "Why not?"

There was a long pause while Honey debated whether to confront him with the accusations Adam had made. "Because… You'd never lie to me, would you, Jesse?"

It was dark so she couldn't see his face, but being held in his arms the way she was, she felt the sudden tension in his body.

"I'd never do anything to hurt you, Honey."

"That isn't exactly the same thing, is it?"

There was enough light to see his smile appear. "That's one of the things I like about you, Honey. You don't pull any punches."

"I think you'd better put me down, Jesse," she said.

Slowly he released her legs so her body slid down

across his. She was grateful for the way he held on to her, because her feet weren't quite steady under her. Her nipples puckered as he slowly rubbed their bodies together.

"You want me, Honey," he said in his rusty-gate voice.

"It would be hard to deny it without sounding like a fool," she said acerbically.

His mouth found the juncture between her neck and shoulder and blessed it with tantalizing kisses. Honey gripped his arms to keep from falling down the stairs as his mouth sought out the tender skin at her throat and followed it up to her ear. Her head fell back of its own volition, offering him better access. Her whole body quivered at the sensations he was evoking with mouth and teeth and tongue.

A hoarse, guttural sound forced its way past Honey's lips. "Jesse, please."

"What, Honey? What do you want?"

Honey groaned again, and it was as much a sound of pleasure as of despair. "You," she admitted in a harsh voice. "I want you."

Jesse lifted her into his arms and carried her the rest of the way upstairs.

Chapter 7

Honey felt the heat of the man beside her and reached out to caress the muscular strength of a body she now knew as well as her own. When Jesse stirred, Honey withdrew her hand. She didn't want to awaken him. Last night had been magical. She didn't wish to rouse from the night's dream and face the reality of day.

Jesse looked younger in the soft dawn light, though still something of a rogue with the stubble of dark beard that shadowed his face. She rubbed her cheek against the pillow, noticing that her skin was tender where his beard had rubbed again—and again. As were her breasts, she realized with chagrin.

He hadn't been gentle, but then, neither had she. Their lovemaking had blazed with the feelings of desperation that had followed them upstairs to the bedroom.

Honey understood her own reasons for feeling that

she had to reach for whatever memories she could make with Jesse before he was gone. She had no idea why Jesse had seemed equally desperate. Had he already made up his mind to leave her? Did he already know the day when their brief interlude would come to an end?

She touched her lower lip, which was tender from the kissing they had done, the love bites he had given her. She must have bitten him, as well. There was a purplish bruise on Jesse's neck, put there in a moment of passion, she supposed. She didn't remember doing it, and she was embarrassed to think what he was going to say when he saw it. She hadn't left such a mark on a man since she'd been a teenager, playing games with Cale.

Honey winced. She hadn't thought of Cale once last night. Jesse hadn't left room for thought. He had spread her legs and thrust inside her, claiming her like some warrior with the spoils of battle. And what had she done? She had allowed it. No, that wasn't precisely true. She had *reveled* in his domination of her. She had opened herself to Jesse and allowed him liberties that Cale had never enjoyed.

And she wasn't even sorry.

Honey had never needed a man so much, or felt so much with a man. She didn't understand it. What made Jesse so different from Adam? Why couldn't she have chosen a man who would give her the security she needed in her life? Why did she have to love—

Honey stopped her thoughts in midstream, appalled by the word that had come to mind. *Love.* Was that why the lovemaking had been so thrilling? Was she in love with Jesse Whitelaw?

It was unfair to be forced to evaluate her feelings

when she was staring at the object of her desire. Because she loved the way Jesse's raven-black hair fell across his brow. She loved the way his dark lashes feathered onto bronze cheeks. She loved his mouth, with the narrow upper lip and the full lower one, that had brought her so much pleasure.

She loved the weight of his body on hers when they were caressing each other. She loved the feel of his skin, soft to the touch, and yet hard with corded muscle. She loved the way his flesh heated hers as his callused fingertips sought out her breasts and slid down her belly to the cleft between her thighs.

She loved the feel of their two bodies when they were joined together as a man and woman were meant to be. She loved his patience as he brought her to fulfillment. She loved the lazy-lidded satisfaction in his eyes when she cried out her pleasure. And she loved the agonized pleasure on his face as he followed her to the pinnacle of desire they had sought together.

Honey refused to contemplate the other facets of Jesse's character that appealed to her. They were many and varied. It was painful enough to know that she loved him this way. Because where there was love, there was hope. And Honey was afraid to hope that the drifter would be there in the days to come. She wasn't sure her memories would be enough when he was gone.

Honey knew she couldn't stay in bed any longer without turning to Jesse yet again. Rather than be thought a wanton, she slipped quietly from beneath the covers, grabbed a shirt, jeans, socks and boots and headed downstairs to dress in the kitchen.

She didn't make coffee, certain the smell would wake

Jesse, and wanting more time alone. Honey headed outside to feed the stock. Maybe she could subdue her unruly libido with hard work. She entered the barn and was immediately assailed with familiar smells that comforted and calmed her. She headed for General's stall and stopped dead at the sight that greeted her. Or rather, didn't greet her.

At first Honey refused to believe her eyes. She gripped the stall where General was supposed to be with white-knuckled hands. Had she left General outside in the corral all night? She was appalled at her thoughtlessness.

Honey ran back outside, but the bull was nowhere to be seen. She hurried back to examine the stall, thinking he might have broken the latch. But it was still hooked.

Staring didn't make the bull appear. He was gone. *Stolen!*

Honey felt despair, followed by rage at the one suspect for the theft who was still within her reach. Purely by instinct, she grabbed two items from the barn as she raced back to the house. She made a brief stop in the kitchen before marching determinedly up the stairs.

Jesse came roaring to life, drenched by the bucket of icy water Honey had thrown on him. "What the hell are you doing, woman?"

He leapt out of bed like a lion from its den, roaring with anger. He was naked, and she had never seen him look so powerful. Or so seductive to her senses.

He grabbed for her and she stepped out of his way. "You bastard!" she hissed.

"Honey, what the hell—"

"Don't come any closer." She held up the buggy whip she had found in the barn, a relic of days gone by. "I'll use this," she threatened.

"What's going on here?" Jesse demanded. "It's a little late for outraged virtue."

"Outraged virtue! You low-down mealymouthed skunk!" she raged. "You stole my bull!"

She wanted him to deny it. With all her heart she yearned for him to say he was innocent. But the dark flush she could plainly see working its way up his naked flesh from his powerful shoulders, to his love-bruised neck, landing finally on his strong cheekbones, was as blatant a statement of guilt as she had ever heard.

"How could you?" she breathed, more hurt now than angry. "I trusted you." Then the anger was back, and she wielded the whip with all the fury of humiliation and pain she felt at his betrayal. "I trusted you!"

The whip landed once across his shoulders before he reached out and jerked it from her hands. He threw it across the room and pulled her into his arms.

Honey fought him, beating at him with her fists and kicking at him with her feet until he threw her down on the soaking-wet bed where he subdued her with his weight.

"Stop it, Honey! That's enough!"

"I hate you!" she cried. "I hate you! I hate you!"

She burst into gasping sobs and turned her head away so he wouldn't see the tears she cried over him. She lay still, emotionally devastated, as he kissed them away.

"Honey." His voice sounded like gravel. "I'm sorry."

"Where's—my—bull?" she gritted out between clenched teeth.

"In a safe place," he said.

Honey moaned. His words were final confirmation that he had used her, lied to her, stolen from her.

"It's not what you think," he began.

She turned to face him, eyes blazing. "Can you deny that you lied to me?"

"No, but—"

"That you stole General?"

"I did, but—"

She growled deep in her throat and bucked against him.

"If you know what's good for you, you'll lie still," Jesse warned.

Honey froze, suddenly aware of the fact he was naked, and they were in bed. "Don't you dare touch me. I'll fight you. I'll kick and scratch and—"

"If you'll just shut up for a minute, I can explain everything."

"I don't want to hear your excuses, you bastard. I—"

He kissed her to shut her up.

Honey felt the punishment in his kiss, and it was easy to fight his anger with her own, to arch her body against the weight of his, to grip the male fingers threaded through her own and struggle against his domination.

The more she fought, the more her body responded to the provocation of his. He insinuated his thigh between her legs knowing it would excite her. At the same time his mouth gentled and his lips and tongue came seeking the taste of her, dark like honey, rich and full. She fought his strength, but his hands held hers captive on either side of her head while he ravished her.

"Don't," she pleaded, aware she was succumbing to

the desire that had never been far below the surface. "Don't."

She was helpless to deny him. He was stronger than she. To her surprise, he stopped kissing her and raised himself on his elbows so he could look at her.

"Are you ready to listen now?"

She turned her head away and closed her eyes.

He shoved one of her hands back behind her and held it there with the weight of his body while he grabbed her chin with his now-free hand and forced her to look at him.

"Open your eyes and look at me," he commanded.

When she didn't, his mouth came down hard on hers. "Open your eyes, Honey. I'm going to keep kissing you until you do."

Faced with that threat, her eyes flashed open and she glared at him.

His dark eyes burned with fury. His mouth was taut. A muscle jerked in his cheek. "There is an explanation for everything," he gritted out.

"I'll bet!" she retorted.

"Shut up and listen!"

She snorted. But she stayed mute.

He opened his mouth and closed it several times. *Searching for more lies,* Honey thought. He closed his eyes and when he opened them again, she saw regret.

"I don't know how to say this except to say it," he began.

She waited, wondering how she could bear to hear that the man she had spent the night making love to, the man she had begun to think herself in love with, was part of a gang of murdering rustlers.

He took a deep breath and said, "I'm a Texas Ranger. I'm working undercover to catch the leader of the gang of rustlers that's been stealing from ranches in this area."

Honey couldn't believe her ears. Her first reaction was relief. *Jesse wasn't a thief!* The very next was anger—make that fury. *He had lied to her!* It was a lie of omission, but a lie all the same to keep her ignorant of his true identity. Finally there was hopelessness. Which was foolish because she had never really had much hope that the drifter would settle down. Now that she knew Jesse was a Texas Ranger, the situation was clear. *He would leave her when his job was done.* Not that it really mattered. She would never repeat the mistake she had made with Cale.

"Honey? Say something?"

"Let me up."

"Not until I explain."

"You've said enough."

"I didn't want to lie to you, but Dallas—"

"Dallas was in on this? I'll kill him," Honey muttered.

Jesse was pleased by the fire in her eyes after the awful dullness he had seen when he had told her the truth. Or at least as much of the truth as he could tell her.

"Dallas was under orders, too," Jesse continued. "The Captain thought it would be better if you were kept in the dark. Because of…" His voice trailed off as he realized he couldn't tell her the rest of it. "I mean… I guess he thought you would understand, having been the wife of a Texas Ranger, why it was necessary."

"I understand, all right," Honey said heatedly. "You used me without a thought to the pain and anguish it would cause."

"How much of what you're feeling is the result of losing General and how much the result of my deceiving you?" Jesse asked in a quiet voice. "General would have been returned within a day or so at the most and no harm done. I hadn't counted on what happened between us, Honey."

"You never should have touched me."

"I know," he said.

"You should have left me completely alone."

"I know," he said.

"Why didn't you?"

"Because I couldn't. I didn't know I would find the other half of myself here, now, under these circumstances."

Honey swallowed over the lump that had suddenly risen in her throat. She closed her eyes to shut out the tenderness in his dark-eyed gaze.

"I love you, Honey."

When her eyes opened they revealed an agony she hadn't ever wanted to feel again. "Don't! Don't say things you don't mean!"

"I've never meant anything more in my life."

"Well, I don't love you!" she retorted.

"Who's lying now, Honey?"

"This can never work, Jesse. Even if you could settle down, and I'm not sure you can, you're a Texas Ranger."

"What does that have to do with anything?"

"I don't want to spend my life worrying about whether you're going to come home to me at the end of the day. I had no choice with Cale. But I have one now. And I choose not to live my life like that."

"I can't—won't—change my life for you," Jesse said, disturbed by the narrow lines she was drawing.

"I'm not asking you to," Honey said.

"Where does that leave us?"

"You've got a job to finish. I assume you're going to meet with the rustlers and exchange General for a great deal of money?"

He grinned crookedly. "That was the plan."

"Then I suggest you go to work."

Jesse sobered for a moment. "Things aren't over between us."

She didn't argue with him. There was no sense in it. As soon as his job was done he would be leaving. She felt the pain of loss already. Even if he had been the drifter he first professed to be, he would have been moving on sooner or later. She had always known Jesse wouldn't be hanging around. Only now his leaving had a certainty that allowed her to begin accepting—and grieving—his loss.

She searched his features, absorbing them, cataloguing them so she would remember them. Her eyes skipped to the body she had adored last night, and she noticed a huge red welt on his right shoulder that had previously been hidden by the pillow.

"Oh, my God, Jesse. Look what I've done to you!"

Jesse gasped as she reached out and touched the spot where the horsewhip had cut into his flesh.

She pushed at his chest. "Let me up, Jesse. I need to get some salve for that before it gets any worse than it is."

Honey didn't know what she would have done if he hadn't let her up just then. She was feeling so many things—remorse and embarrassment and love. And the love seemed to be winning out. She didn't want to care for this man. It would only hurt worse when he left.

Jesse took advantage of the time Honey was out of the room to put on his pants and boots. When she came back he was sitting on the edge of the bed shirtless, waiting for her.

Honey laid the things she had brought back with her on the end table beside the bed, then sat down beside Jesse to minister to the wound.

He hissed in a breath of air when she began dabbing at the raw flesh with warm water. "I know this must hurt," she soothed.

As she worked, Jesse wasn't nearly so aware of the pain as he was of the care she was taking of him. It had been years and years since there had been a woman in his life to care for him. His mother had died when his sister, Tate, was born, leaving Tate to be raised by a father and three older brothers. He had been how old? No more than eleven or twelve.

He luxuriated in the concern Honey showed with every gesture, every touch. She cared for him. He felt sure of it. Even though she denied him in words, her gentleness, her obvious distress over his injury, gave her away. He meant to have her—despite the reservations she had voiced.

It had never occurred to him that she would demand that he leave the Rangers. He relished the danger and excitement of the job. There must be a way he could have Honey and the Texas Rangers, too. He would just have to find it.

"When are you going to meet with the rustlers?" Honey asked.

"Sometime tonight."

Honey bit her lip to keep from begging him not to go. She had learned her lessons with Cale. Her pleas would be useless. Instead she said, "Promise me you'll be careful."

He took her hand from his shoulder and held it between both of his. "Don't worry about me, Honey." He flashed her a grin. "I've been doing this a long time. I know how to take care of myself. Besides, I'm not about to get myself killed when I've got you to come back to."

"Jesse..."

He reached up and caught her chin in his fingertips, drawing her lips toward his. "Honey..."

Warm. Wet. Tender. His mouth seduced her to his will. His hand curled around her nape and slid up into her hair. Suddenly she was sitting in his lap, her hands circling his neck, and his mouth was nuzzling her throat.

"I can't get enough of you," he murmured. "Come back to bed with me, Honey."

She was tempted. Lord how she was tempted!

"Forget about General. Forget about the Texas Rangers. Don't think about—"

Honey tore herself from his grasp and stood facing him. Her breasts ached. Desire spiraled in her belly. It was hard to catch her breath. But catch it she did long enough to say, "No, Jesse. This has to stop. Right now. You can stay here long enough to finish your business. Until then...just leave me alone."

Jesse was equally aroused and frustrated by the interruption of their lovemaking. "You're being foolish, Honey."

"So now I'm a fool on top of everything else," she retorted. "You're making it very easy to get you out of my life, Jesse."

He thrust a hand through his hair, making it stand on end. "That came out wrong," he admitted. "You know what I mean."

He rose and paced the floor like a caged wolf. "We're meant to be together. I feel it *here*." He pounded his chest around the region of his heart. "You're only fighting against the inevitable. We *will* spend our lives together."

"Until you get shot?" she retorted. "Until I bury you like I buried Cale? No, Jesse. We aren't going to be together. I need someone I can rely on to be around for the long haul. You aren't that man."

"That remains to be seen," he said through clenched teeth.

Jesse wasn't prepared for the tears that gathered in Honey's eyes. He watched her blink hard, valiantly fighting them. It was clearly a losing battle, and they spilled from the corners of her eyes.

"It's over, Jesse. I mean it." She dashed at the tears with the back of her hand. *"I won't cry for you."*

He watched her eyes begin to blaze with anger as she battled against the strong emotions that gripped her—and won. The tears stopped, and only the damp streaks on her face remained to show the pain she was suffering.

He felt her retreating from him even though she

hadn't moved a step. "Don't go, Honey. I need you." He paused and added, "I love you."

"You lied to me. You used me. That's not the way people in love treat each other." She choked back the tears that threatened again and said, "You should have told me the truth. You should have trusted me. You should have given me the choice of knowing who you really are before I got involved with you. That's what I can't forgive, Jesse."

She turned and left the room, shoulders back, chin high, proud and unassailable. He had never wanted her more than he did in that moment, when he feared she was lost to him.

He sank down onto the bed and stared out through the lace-curtained window. He had to admit his excuse for keeping Honey in the dark about why he had come to the Flying Diamond had sounded feeble even to his ears. He could see why she was angry. He could see why she felt betrayed.

But there was no way he could have told her the real reason she hadn't been let in on his identity: every shred of evidence against the rustlers, every outlaw trail, led straight back to the Lazy S Ranch—and Adam Philips.

Chapter 8

"Did you steal the bull?" Mort asked.

"Yes," Jesse replied.

"Then where is it?" the rustler demanded.

"In a safe place."

"The Boss is waiting for that bull," Mort said. "You were supposed to bring it here." Mort spat chewing tobacco toward the horse trailer he had brought to transport the bull, and which would apparently be leaving empty.

"Plans change," Jesse said.

Mort's eyes narrowed. "What's that supposed to mean?"

Jesse stared right back at the grizzle-faced cowboy. "I've decided to renegotiate the terms of our agreement."

"The Boss ain't gonna like that," Mort warned ominously.

"If he doesn't like it, I can find another buyer for the bull," Jesse said.

"Now hold on a minute," Mort sputtered. "You can't—"

"Tell your boss to be here at midnight tonight," Jesse interrupted. "I'll be waiting with the bull, but I'll only deal with him in person. Tell him the price is double what we agreed on. In cash—small bills."

Mort was clearly alarmed by Jesse's ultimatum. "You're making a big mistake."

"If he wants the bull, he'll come."

It wasn't a subtle method of getting to the top man, Jesse thought, but it inevitably worked. Greed was like that. Of course he would have to watch out for the also inevitable double-cross. There was always the chance that bullets would start flying. He hoped he'd have enough backup to ensure that the guys in the white hats won.

Mort drove away grumbling, and Jesse got into his pickup and headed in the opposite direction from the Flying Diamond. He felt confident that his business for the Rangers would soon be finished. Then he could concentrate on what really mattered—his relationship with Honey. First he had to see Dallas to confirm the details of their plan to capture the brains behind the brawn tonight.

Jesse might have had second thoughts about how soon things were going to be wrapped up if he had known that his visit with Mort Barnes had been observed by another very interested party.

Honey was sweeping off the front porch when Adam Philips drove up later that same afternoon. She felt a momentary pang of guilt, but it was quickly followed by relief that she had ended their relationship. Considering they were no longer romantically involved, she couldn't imagine why Adam had come calling.

Honey laid the broom against the wooden wall of the house—noticing that it badly needed another coat of white paint—and stepped over to the porch rail. She held a hand over her brow to keep the sun out of her eyes. "Hello, Adam," she greeted him cautiously. "What brings you out here today?"

It wasn't anything good, Honey surmised after one look at the grim line of Adam's mouth. His features only seemed to get more strained as he left the car and headed up the porch steps toward her.

"Have a seat," Honey said, gesturing toward the wooden swing that hung from the porch rafters. She set a hip on the porch rail, facing the swing.

Adam sat down but abruptly jumped up again and marched over to stand before Honey. "How much do you really know about that man you hired to help around here?"

"Not a lot," Honey admitted with a shrug. "He has a degree in ranch management and—"

"Did it ever occur to you to wonder why a man with a degree in ranch management is content to work as a mere hired hand?" Adam demanded.

Honey stared at him. It hadn't, of course. She hadn't questioned anything about Jesse's story. Which was why his revelation that he was a Texas Ranger had caught her so much off guard. It was clear Adam was still suspicious of Jesse's motives. But there was no reason for him to be. "You don't have to worry about Jesse," she said.

"What makes you so sure?"

"Because he's a Texas Ranger."

"What?" Adam looked stunned.

Honey grinned. "He's working undercover to catch the rustlers who've been stealing cattle around here. I don't think he'll mind that I told you, but keep it under your hat, okay?"

Adam gave her a sharp look. "Did you know all along that he was a Texas Ranger?"

"I only found out myself this morning," she admitted.

Adam stuck his thumbs into the pockets of his Levi's. He pursed his lips and shook his head ruefully. "Looks like I've been a real fool. I thought that he—Never mind. I'll be going now. I've got some calls to make before dark."

"Adam," Honey called after him.

He stopped and turned back to her. "Yes, Honey?"

"Don't be a stranger."

A pained expression passed fleetingly across his face. He managed a smile and said, "All right. But don't look for me too soon, all right?"

"All right. Goodbye, Adam."

Honey worked alone the rest of the afternoon. She was grateful for Jack's absence because it gave her time to come to terms with Jesse's revelation that he was a Texas Ranger. Equally fortunate, she was spared Jesse's presence as well. He had left earlier to run some errands and hadn't returned.

Maybe it was better that they didn't spend too much time alone. Last night had been a moment out of time, almost too good to be true. It had certainly been too perfect to expect it to last. If only…

Honey thought about what she would have to give up to have Jesse in her life. Having a partner to share the responsibility of the ranch and to be there when she needed him, for one thing. She had sworn when Cale died that she would never marry another man who didn't put her needs, and the needs of the Flying Diamond, at least on an equal footing with his profession.

Although Adam's work as a doctor would have taken him away on occasion, his free time would have been devoted to her. He was wealthy enough to have hired a local man, Chuck Loomis, whose ranch had gone bust, to manage the Lazy S. Honey knew Adam also would have hired the help necessary to take care of the Flying Diamond and preserve it as a heritage for her sons.

Over the past fourteen years, Honey had fought the steady demise of her ranch. But her efforts alone—while Cale had been off fighting badmen—hadn't been enough to make all the repairs needed. The Flying Diamond was a shabby shadow of what it had been in the years when Cale's father had devotedly nurtured it.

She owed it to her sons to marry someone who could help her bring the Flying Diamond back to its former glory. Jesse could help her make it happen if he devoted himself full-time to running the ranch. But Honey couldn't imagine him being willing to leave the Texas Rangers for any reason, least of all because she asked it of him.

Even if she swallowed her pride and shouldered all the burdens of the Flying Diamond, she would still have to face the constant fear of losing Jesse to an outlaw's bullet. She couldn't bear the constant strain of not knowing whether he would come home to her at the end of the day.

The case Jesse was working on right now was a good example of what she could expect if he didn't quit the Rangers. He had told her the men he was hunting weren't just rustlers, they were murderers. They had killed a rancher in Laredo. If they ever found out a Texas Ranger had insinuated himself in their organization… Honey shuddered at the thought of what would happen to Jesse.

She hadn't forgotten what it felt like when she'd heard that Cale had been killed in the line of duty. She didn't ever want to suffer through that kind of anguish again. In the few weeks he had been around, Jesse had made a place for himself in her life and in her heart. She didn't want to contemplate how she would suffer if something went wrong and he was killed.

"Penny for your thoughts?"

Honey nearly fell backward over the porch rail. Jesse reached out and caught her, pulling her into his embrace. Honey's arms circled his broad shoulders and she looked into his amused face.

"Nearly lost you," he said. "What were you daydreaming about?"

She wasn't about to admit she had been worrying about him. "I was just thinking what good weather Jack has for tubing on the river."

"You mean he's not home yet?"

"No," she said, embarrassed by how breathless her voice sounded. Honey flushed at the intent look on Jesse's face as it suddenly dawned on him that they had the place to themselves. She swallowed hard and said, “Where have you been all day?”

“Doing business for the Texas Rangers,” he admitted. “But I’m all yours now.”

The leer on his face made it plain what he hoped she would do with him.

Honey was tempted to start a fight, or do whatever else was necessary to make Jesse angry enough to leave her alone. On the other hand, she was also very much aware of the sensual lure he had thrown out to her. Their time together was coming to a close. It was hard to say no when he was here, wanting her, desiring her, with his eyes and his voice and his body.

He reached out and tugged on the waistband of her jeans. The top button popped free.

“Don’t even think it,” she warned.

“You can read my mind?”

“Enough to know you’re crazy.”

“Probably certifiable,” he admitted. “But if you don’t tell, I won’t.”

He made growling sounds and bit her neck, sending a frisson of fire through her veins.

She grabbed Jesse’s face to try to make him stop whatever tantalizing thing he was doing to her throat with his tongue, but he caught her hands and forced them behind her. Twining their fingers together, he used them to pull her between his widespread legs where his arousal was evident.

“Jesse,” she protested with a breathless laugh. “We can’t. It’s broad daylight.”

“There’s no one to see,” he said, thrusting against

her and causing her to groan as her body responded to the urgency of his.

She was running out of excuses for him not to do what she so desperately wanted him to do. "Jack might come home."

"Then we'll just have to go where he won't find us," Jesse murmured conspiratorially.

Honey thought he meant her bedroom, but he obviously had other ideas. She gasped when he threw her over his shoulder and headed for the barn.

"Not the barn!" she hooted.

"Why not the barn?" he said with a grin.

"Hay itches."

He stopped and rearranged her in his arms so he could see her face. "Sounds like you speak from experience."

The color rose on Honey's cheeks. When Jesse laughed she hid her face against his throat.

He murmured in her ear, "If you feel any itches anywhere I'll be glad to scratch them."

Honey giggled like a schoolgirl. She felt so carefree! If only it could always be like this, laughter and loving, with no thought of the future to spoil it. Honey nibbled on Jesse's ear and heard him hiss in a breath of air.

"Keep that up, woman, and we won't make it to the barn," he warned.

Honey was feeling in a dangerous mood. She teased his ear with her tongue, tracing the shell-like shape of it. She shrieked when Jesse teasingly threatened to drop her.

At the barn door he stopped and stood her before him so he could look at her.

When Honey caught sight of his face she knew she was playing with fire. His dark eyes were heavy-lidded, his features taut with desire. His nostrils flared and his hands tightened on her flesh. Her whole body tensed in response to his obvious sexual hunger.

Her fingertips caressed his cheekbones and slid up from his temple into the thick black hair at his nape. "I want you, Jesse."

Her words were like a match on tinder. Jesse's mouth came down on hers, his tongue thrusting in a mirror image of that age-old dance between men and women. Her fingers clutched at his hair, forcing his hat off his head. She grabbed hold of him as though to keep from flying off into the unknown. For nothing Jesse did to her from then on was like anything that had ever happened to her before.

His mouth found her nipple through her thin cotton shirt, rousing her to passion. His hand slid down the front of her jeans and cupped the heat and heart of her. He urged her hand down to the hard bulge that threatened the seams of his Levi's. He thrust against her, his desire a stronger aphrodisiac than any shaman's love potion.

They stood just inside the barn door, and Jesse molded them together belly to belly as he backed her out of the sunlight and into the shadows. "It's time you and I had a talk about what happens when you tease a man," Jesse rasped, pressing her up against the barn wall with his body.

He insinuated his thigh between her legs and lifted her so she could feel the heat and pressure of his flesh against that most sensitive of feminine places. Meanwhile he cupped a breast in one hand while the other captured her nape to hold her still for the onslaught of his mouth and the invasion of his tongue.

"Honey," he rasped. "I can't get enough of you, the feel of you, the taste of you."

Honey was overwhelmed. She couldn't breathe. She couldn't move. She could only respond to the sensations that assaulted her. Her knees collapsed and Jesse had to hold her upright.

Abruptly he left her and she leaned against the rough wooden walls, legs outstretched, while he grabbed a clean saddle blanket and spread it hurriedly over the fresh, crackling straw in an empty stall at the back of the barn.

She felt his urgency as he returned to lift her into his arms and carry her to the blanket, laying her down carefully before mantling her with his body.

Honey looked up into eyes that were narrowed in concentration on her, fierce, dark eyes that should have frightened her but only made her wild with anticipation.

Slowly, slowly, Jesse began unbuttoning her shirt. His mouth caressed her flesh as he exposed it, until he reached the button on her Levi's. The button hardly made a sound as it fell free, but her zipper grated noisily as he slid it down. His mouth followed where his hands had led and soon he was nuzzling at the very apex of her thighs.

Honey reached for whatever part of him she could grasp, but when he nipped her through her silken panties her nails curved into the muscles of his back.

"Jesse!"

He sat up to pull off her boots and then his own. She

yanked off her socks and then his, grinning at the sight of his long naked feet. He started to unsnap his shirt, but she stopped him.

"Let me."

She offered him the same enjoyment he had given her, exposing his bronze skin one snap at a time and caressing it with her lips and tongue. Intrigued by his distended nipples she forayed across his chest to nibble gently on one.

His whole body tensed, and he held himself motionless while she tested his control. He didn't last long. A moment later she found herself flat on her back, Jesse astride her.

"Play with fire and you can get burned, woman."

He unsnapped the front clasp of her bra and brushed it aside as he took one of her nipples in his mouth to tease it with his tongue. Honey arched upward with her hips and encountered the hardness of his arousal.

She grasped his buttocks to pull him close and spread her legs to accommodate him more fully. Jesse returned the pressure as she gently rubbed herself against him.

Abruptly Jesse freed himself from her grasp and began stripping her. She was equally urgent in her efforts to undress him until moments later they stared at each other in the filtered sunlight.

"God, you're beautiful," he said reverently.

Honey felt herself flushing with pleasure at the compliment. She knew he wasn't merely mouthing the words. His delight was mirrored in his eyes.

"I'm glad I please you."

The gentle touch of his mouth on hers was like a paean to a goddess. He honored her. He revered her. He desired her. His lips and mouth and tongue adored her. The kisses that began at her mouth continued downward to her throat, found their way to her breasts, then to her belly and beyond.

Honey stiffened and reached out a hand to grip his shoulder. She hadn't expected this. She wasn't sure whether she wanted it.

Jesse raised his eyes to hers. "I want to taste all of you," he said.

In all the years they had been married, Cale had never loved her this way. It was the most intimate of kisses. And it required complete trust. Jesse was aware of that, and he awaited her consent. Honey was wired as tight as a bowstring, anxious to please him, afraid she wouldn't, afraid of the unknown. Of that forbidden pleasure.

She had always wondered what it would feel like, always wondered whether it truly brought the immeasurable ecstasy that made it something to be whispered about. All she had to do was trust Jesse enough to allow him to love her as he so clearly wanted to do.

She opened her mouth to agree, but no sound came out. She swallowed hard and slowly nodded her head.

Jesse's quick grin surprised her. "You won't be sorry," he said. Just as quickly the grin disappeared. "You only have to say the word and I'll stop. This is supposed to please us both. All right?"

Honey nodded again.

She was surprised when he rose and kissed her on the mouth again. He took his time kissing his way back down her body, but she knew where he was heading.

By the time he got there she was more aroused than she could ever remember being.

For Jesse had not relied on his mouth alone to make that journey. His callused hands had smoothed across her flesh, finding her breasts and teasing them, taunting her by rolling her nipples between fingers and thumb. He had caressed ribs and hipbones and the length of her back from her nape to the dimples at the curve of her spine. She was sure she would find impressions of his fingers on her buttocks where he had lazily learned the shape of them.

Finally he lifted her in his hands while his tongue teased her. She gasped as her body tautened. She grabbed handfuls of the wool blanket to keep from touching him, lest he think she wanted him to stop. For she didn't. Oh, no, she did not!

Honey felt the ripples building, felt her inner flesh clenching, felt the muscles in her thighs tighten until she could not move. And still he kissed her. Loved her. Teased her with his mouth and tongue.

She moaned and writhed in pleasure. Her body arched toward him and at last her hands reached for him, clutching at his shoulders as though he could save her from the cataclysmic—wondrous, astounding, remarkable—things her body threatened to do.

Honey did not want to let go of what little control she had left. There was no hiding the strong muscular contractions as she began climaxing beneath him. Excited, animal sounds came from her throat as she convulsed with pleasure.

Jesse met her eyes and watched the agony of ecstasy that she could not hide from him.

When it was over, she turned her face away from him. Her throat was swollen with emotion and tears stung her eyes.

"Honey?"

She heard the anxiety in his voice and tried to reassure him. But no sound would pass over the lump in her throat. She reached out and grasped his hand.

He lay down beside her and brushed a sweat-dampened lock of hair from her brow. "Are you all right?"

She nodded jerkily.

"You're not acting all right," he said.

She hid her face in his throat and clutched him around the waist.

He continued smoothing her hair and rubbing her back gently. She couldn't see his face, but she could feel from the tension in his body that he was troubled. She wanted to reassure him that she was all right, but she was simply so *overwhelmed* by what had happened that words did not seem sufficient to explain how she felt.

Eventually her breathing calmed and her throat relaxed. "It was so…"

Jesse put a finger under her chin and forced her eyes up to meet his. "So what?"

"Beautiful," she whispered.

He hugged her hard then and rocked her back and forth. "I'm glad," he said. "I'm so glad. I was afraid—"

"It was wonderful," she said. Then, shyly, "I only hope you're going to give me the pleasure of returning the favor."

He grinned. "Someday soon," he promised. "Right now, there's something more I want from you."

"What's that?"

"This."

He nudged her knees apart and sheathed himself easily in her still half-aroused body.

When he kissed her again, Honey found the taste of herself still on his lips. She gave back to him that which he had given her. She was far beyond rational thought by that time, only wanting to join herself with him in any way she could.

Honey touched Jesse's body everywhere she could reach as he sought to bring her to a second pinnacle of pleasure. She wasn't really conscious of how she caressed him, but moved her hands in response to the way he arched his sinewy body beneath her, the way he moved toward her touch or away from it. By sheer luck she found a spot—the crease where belly met thigh—that made him shudder with pleasure.

Jesse did not allow her time to tarry. He lifted her legs up over his thighs and took them both on a journey of delight. After she had fallen off the world yet again, he poured his seed into her, his head arched back in ecstasy, every muscle taut with unspeakable pleasure.

Afterward, they both slept. It was nearly dark by the time Honey wakened. Jesse's head rested on his hand and he was staring down at her as though memorizing her features.

"It's late," she said.

"We'd better get dressed," he agreed.

Neither of them moved.

"After tonight, I'll be finished with my work here," Jesse said at last.

Honey closed her eyes to hide the myriad emotions vying for dominance. "When will you be leaving?"

"Honey, I…"

She opened her eyes. "I'll miss you," she admitted. She reached up to touch his mouth with a fingertip. Was she responsible for the sensuous look of his swollen lower lip?

He took her hand in his and kissed each finger. "I love you, Honey. Will you marry me?"

Honey was so shocked her mouth fell open.

He nudged at her chin with a bent finger. "Catch a lot of flies that way," he teased in a husky voice.

But Honey saw how his hand trembled when he took it away. It was clear that despite his levity he cared a great deal about how she answered. She was so tempted to say yes! But it wasn't fair to marry Jesse without expressing the reservations she harbored.

"Are you willing to quit the Rangers?" she asked.

"Are you making that a condition of your acceptance?" he answered in a sharp voice.

Honey took a deep breath and said, "Yes, I think I am."

He was on his feet an instant later, pulling on his pants. "That's totally unreasonable, Honey, and you know it!" he ranted.

She was suddenly embarrassed to be naked when he was dressed. She grabbed at her shirt and stuck her arms into the sleeves. Honey searched for her panties and found them across the stall. She turned her back on Jesse to step into them and was conscious of the silence as she did. Over her shoulder she discovered him ogling her bottom.

She yanked her panties on and dragged her jeans over

her legs. "I don't see what's so unreasonable about wanting a husband who'll be around to help run this ranch!"

"I'd be around!" he insisted.

"In between assignments," she retorted. "You forget, I've already been married to one Texas Ranger. You're as bad as Cale."

"Don't tar me with the same brush."

"How are you different?" she demanded. "You can't deny you take the same foolish, dangerous chances with your life that he did. And look what happened to him! I couldn't bear it if—"

Honey cut herself off and went searching for her socks.

Jesse grabbed her by the arms and forced her to face him. "I know you love me," he began.

"That isn't the point," Honey interrupted.

"Then you do love me?"

He stood there waiting for an answer. Honey grimaced and admitted, "I love you but—"

Jesse cut her off with a hard kiss. "Then all the rest is small stuff. We can work it out."

"You're not listening to me," Honey said, her voice rising as she felt control of the situation slipping away. "I won't marry you, Jesse. Not unless you're willing to give up the Rangers."

His mouth thinned in anger. "You're asking the impossible."

"Why is it impossible? There are other challenges in life besides hunting down outlaws."

"Like what?"

"Like raising kids. Like making a success of this ramshackle ranch. Like growing a garden. Like spending the afternoon making sweet, sweet love to your wife."

He captured her in his arms and nuzzled her throat. "The last part of that certainly sounds promising."

Honey remained stiff in his embrace, fighting the tears that threatened. *"Listen to me,"* she pleaded. "I'm fighting for our life together."

His head jerked up and he glared down at her. "So am I," he insisted. "You're asking me to give up what I *am.*"

Honey shook her head sadly. "No, Jesse. It's just a job. You can quit."

"And if I won't?"

She pushed at his shoulders, forcing him to release her. "Then I guess this is goodbye."

His lips flattened. "You don't mean that."

Her chin lifted and her shoulders squared. "Goodbye, Jesse."

She turned and marched barefoot from the barn, leaving Jesse to stare at her stiff back. "Damned fool woman," he muttered. "Can't expect me to give up everything for her. She's crazy if she thinks I will. No woman is worth that kind of sacrifice."

It was a sober and contemplative man who left the barn. The best thing to do was put the situation with Honey out of his mind and concentrate on his rendezvous with the rustlers. It wouldn't do to let himself get distracted. Honey was right about one thing. A Texas Ranger led a dangerous life. He had to pay attention to what he was doing tonight or he might end up getting himself killed. He snorted in disgust. He would hate like hell to prove Honey right about the dangers of his job.

Chapter 9

Because of all she had been through with Jesse, Honey hadn't given Jack a thought for the past twenty-four hours. In fact, she had spent most of that time in a euphoric haze. Memories of Jesse's lovemaking had preoccupied her in the morning, and their interlude in the barn, his proposal and their subsequent quarrel had kept her agitated until well after dark. It wasn't until nearly nine o'clock Saturday evening that she realized how late Jack was in returning home and began making inquiries.

Honey was aghast when she discovered Jack had not spent the night with a friend—or even made plans to do so. He hadn't gone tubing on the Frio, either! Jack had never lied to her before. She couldn't imagine where he could have gone last night, unless…

The worst conclusion to be drawn from the facts

came first: *Jack had run away from home.* Honey suddenly remembered how hard Jack had hugged her last night before he left the house, how intently he had looked into her eyes. She hadn't paid much attention to the hug except to be pleased by it because Jack so seldom indulged in such sentimentality these days. Now his hug took on ominous significance. *Jack had been saying goodbye!*

Honey's heart began thudding heavily. Her palms tingled. She felt light-headed. Her knees went weak and she had to sit down before she fell down.

Things had been rough for the past year since Cale's death, but surely not bad enough for her son to want to escape the situation. Jesse's appearance had injected a note of tension in the household, but Jack seemed to have made his peace with Jesse the day they worked together on the corral.

But maybe Jack had only been pretending things were all right. Maybe he had resented the hired hand much more than he had let on. Maybe having his mother courted by two men at the same time was more strain than he could handle. But he didn't have to run away!

To Honey's chagrin, the first person she thought of to help her hunt for Jack was Jesse Whitelaw. But shortly after their argument in the barn, Jesse had gotten into his pickup and driven away. Honey didn't know where. And she didn't care.

Honey snickered in disgust. Who was she trying to kid? She cared. She already missed Jesse and he hadn't even left the Flying Diamond. At least, she didn't think he was gone for good. His things were still in the small room off the kitchen. She knew because she had checked.

Honey shuddered to think that the man she loved had been in any way responsible for her son running away from home. What an awful mess her life had become!

Well, she would just have to straighten it out. Jack had to learn he couldn't run from his problems, that he had to confront them head-on and resolve them. And Jesse, well, he could stand to learn a lesson or two about not running from problems himself. She was just the woman to instruct them both!

Deciding she could use reinforcements, Honey picked up the phone and called Dallas Masterson. Angel answered.

"Is Dallas there?" Honey asked.

"I'm afraid he's gone for the evening. Some Ranger business," Angel said.

Honey had completely forgotten about General and the trap Jesse was supposedly laying for the rustlers. Was that where he was tonight? Was his life in danger even now?

"Honey, are you okay?" Angel asked, concerned by the long silence.

Honey sank back into a kitchen chair. "I don't think so."

"What's wrong? Can I help?"

"Jack's missing," Honey said. "And I don't have the first clue where to look for him."

"I'll be right over," Angel said.

"What about the baby?"

"I'll bring him. He'll be fine riding in the car while

we look for Jack. Don't go anywhere till I get there. I won't be long."

"I'll use the time to call some more of Jack's friends. Maybe they'll have some idea where he is," Honey said.

Angel was as good as her word, and a short while later she drove into the yard. Honey came running out and jumped into the passenger's side of the car.

"Do you have any suggestions where we can start looking?" Angel asked.

"No," Honey said. She bit down on her lower lip to still its tremor. "We might as well start on the Flying Diamond. Maybe he—" Honey stopped herself from saying *had an accident;* it was a possibility she didn't want to consider. It was almost better believing he had run away.

They searched the Flying Diamond in vain. Jack was nowhere to be found. Honey was getting frantic. It was nearly midnight. *Where was her son?*

"I don't know where to look from here, except to check whether he might have gone to see Adam at the Lazy S," Honey said at last.

"Dallas told me to stay away from the Lazy S tonight. There's something going on at that corral where your boys practiced roping earlier this spring."

"As I recall, there's a pen for livestock," Honey said, thinking aloud. "So that's where Jesse hid General!"

"What are you talking about?" Angel asked.

"Last night Jesse stole General."

"What!"

"It's a long story. Anyway, he said he'd put him somewhere safe. I'm betting he meant the pen at that roundup corral on the southern border of the Lazy S. If Dallas told you to stay away from there tonight—"

"—because of Ranger business—"

"—then chances are that's where they both are right now." Honey hissed in a breath of air. "Jack couldn't have suspected...he wouldn't have gone... Jack just couldn't..."

"Jack couldn't what?" Angel asked.

Honey had a terrible feeling of foreboding. "We have to get to that corral," she said. "Hurry!"

"Dallas specifically said to stay away from there," Angel protested.

"Jack's there!" Honey said.

"How do you know?"

"Call it a mother's instinct if you like, but he's there, all right, and he's in trouble! Let's go!"

Jack hadn't liked lying to his mother, but sometimes there were things a man had to do. Protecting his mother was one of those things. So he had told her he was spending the night with a friend and asked if it was all right to spend the following day tubing on the Frio River. In reality, he planned to spend the entire time spying on Jesse Whitelaw.

Jack had grudgingly given Jesse the benefit of the doubt after their talk in the barn. By the end of a day spent working with the hired hand, he had felt a secret admiration for the cowboy. Then he had overheard Jesse on the phone after dinner, making plans to rent a stock trailer.

At first Jack supposed his mother had sold some cattle. When Jesse mentioned something about "restraints for the bull," Jack got suspicious. There was only one bull on the Flying Diamond, and General wasn't for sale. Jack felt sick.

He had secretly been dreaming about what it would be like if Jesse Whitelaw became his stepfather. He had imagined lots of days like the one they had spent together working to repair the corral. Jesse had treated him as an equal. He had respected him as a person. Working with Jesse hadn't been a chore, it had been fun.

Now Jack saw Jesse's behavior as a phony act to lull him and his mother into complacency, so they wouldn't interfere when Jesse stole the one thing of true value left on the Flying Diamond. Jack felt like a fool. The more he thought about it, the angrier he got, until there seemed only one course of action open to him. He would catch Jesse Whitelaw red-handed. He would put the deceitful drifter in jail where he would have plenty of time to regret having underestimated a gullible, trusting, thirteen-year-old boy.

Jack had packed an overnight bag and hugged his mom goodbye as though he were spending the night with friends. Instead, he had hidden himself where he could stand guard on the barn. Sure enough, about an hour after his mother left the house with Adam Philips, Jesse Whitelaw had backed a stock trailer up to the barn and let down the ramp.

At first Jack had been tempted to confront the drifter. But even at his age he knew discretion was the better part of valor. He thought about running to the house to call the police, but figured Jesse would be long gone before anyone could block the roads leading from the Flying Diamond.

So while Jesse was in the barn with the bull, Jack had snuck under a tarp lying in the back of the pickup truck pulling the stock trailer. It was all very easy, and Jack was pleased with how clever he had been. Surprisingly, Jesse had taken the bull to the roundup corral on the southern edge of the Lazy S.

Jack knew he ought to go right to his mother with what information he had, but he was afraid she would let Jesse go because of her soppy feelings for the drifter. So while Jesse was unloading the bull into one of the stock pens, Jack left the truck and hid inside a nearby tin-roofed shed, figuring he couldn't go wrong staying with General. Besides, if he left, the bull might be gone by the time he got back with the authorities.

Jack was nearly discovered when Jesse came inside the shed to get hay for the bull. Apparently the theft had been more well thought out than Jack had realized. To Jack's dismay, when Jesse left the shed he dropped a wooden bar across the door. *Jack was trapped!*

His first instinct was to call out. Fear kept him silent. There was no telling what the drifter would do if he knew he had been found out. Jack remained quiet as the truck drove away. Surely Jesse would return soon. All Jack had to do was wait and be sure he got out of the shed undetected when it was opened again.

Jack had spent a long, uncomfortable night on a pile of prickly hay. He had finally fallen asleep in the wee hours of the morning and only wakened when the sun was high in the sky. He was relieved to see through a knothole in the wooden-sided shed that General was still in the stock pen, but he was also confused. Surely someone should have come to collect the bull by now.

All day long, Jack waited expectantly for Jesse to return. It was late afternoon by the time he realized the exchange would likely be made after dark. He was hot and hungry and thirsty and dearly regretted not having called the police when he had first had an inkling of what Jesse intended.

Jack wondered whether his mother had checked up on him and uncovered his lies. He consoled himself with the thought that she wouldn't really start to worry until after dark. Only the sun had fallen hours ago. Where was she? Why hadn't anybody come looking for him? Where was Jesse? *Where was everybody?*

Jesse hunkered down in the ravine where Dallas was hidden so he wouldn't be spotted talking to the other Ranger. "Is everything set?" he asked.

"The local police have the entire area covered like a glove," Dallas reassured him.

"I just hope Adam steps into the trap," Jesse said.

Dallas shook his head. "He isn't going to be the one who shows up here tonight. You'll see. I'd stake my life on it."

Jesse arched a disbelieving brow. "You're still sticking by the man, even with all the evidence we have leading to the Lazy S? With all we've discovered about how his ranch has floundered lately? With everything we know about how bad Adam Philips's finances have gotten over the past year?"

Dallas nodded. "I know Adam. He just can't be involved in something like this. There's got to be another explanation."

"For your sake, I hope you're right," Jesse said. But

he wouldn't mind if Adam Philips ended up being a villain in Honey's eyes. Maybe then she would start to see Jesse in a more positive light.

That woman was the most stubborn, bullheaded, downright maddening creature Jesse had ever known. How he had fallen so deeply in love with her was a mystery to him, but the fact was, he had. Now the fool woman was refusing to marry him unless he left the Rangers. Damn her willful hide!

He couldn't possibly give up an honor he had striven so hard to achieve. Why, the Rangers were an elite group of men. Independent. Fearless. Ruthless when necessary. He was proud to be part of such an historic organization. It was unfair of Honey to ask him to make such a sacrifice.

Yet he could see her side of the issue. Over the weeks he had worked on the Flying Diamond, he had gotten a glimmer of how little time Cale Farrell had devoted to the place. It wasn't just the roof that needed repair, or a few rotten corral posts that had to be replaced. The whole ranch showed signs of serious neglect.

It was apparent that because of Cale's commitment to the Rangers, the brunt of the ranch work must have fallen on Honey's shoulders. Not that they weren't lovely shoulders, but they weren't strong enough to support the entire weight of an outfit the size of the Flying Diamond.

Jesse had seen dozens of opportunities where better management—and plain hard work—would have improved the yield of the ranch. The Flying Diamond had land that could be put to use growing feed. Expanded, Honey's vegetable garden could easily provide for the needs of the ranch. And it wouldn't be a bad idea to invest in some mohair goats. The money from the mohair harvest could be applied to supporting the cattle end of the ranch.

If he stayed on as a Ranger, Jesse wouldn't have much time to invest in the ranch. He could expect to be called away on assignments often. Honey would be left to take care of things. As she must have been left for most of her married life, Jesse suddenly realized.

He had never heard Honey complain once about the burden she had carried all these years. And he was only thinking in terms of the ranch. Honey had probably borne most of the responsibility as a parent as well. She had done a good job. Jack and Jonathan were fine boys that any man would be proud to call sons.

Jesse felt a tightness in his chest when he remembered the look he and Jack had shared at the end of the day they had spent working together. Jesse had never known a stronger feeling of satisfaction. He had truly felt close to the boy. It was hard to imagine walking away from Jack and Jonathan. It was impossible to imagine walking away from Honey.

All his life Jesse had somehow managed to have his cake and eat it, too. Honey was asking him to make a choice. He just didn't know what it was going to be.

Jesse saw the truck lights in the distance and checked the revolver he had stuck in the back of his jeans. It wasn't particularly easy to get to, but then, he was hoping the show of force by the police would reduce the chance of gunplay. He stood by the corral waiting as the tractor-trailer truck pulled up. The engine remained running. It was Mort Barnes who stepped into the glare of the truck headlights.

Jesse stiffened. He saw his efforts to finally uncover the man in charge going up in smoke. "Where's your boss?" he demanded.

Mort grinned, though it looked more like a sneer. "I'm the boss."

"I don't believe you," Jesse said flatly.

Mort revealed the automatic weapon in his hand and said, "I'll take that bull."

Jesse didn't hesitate. He threw himself out of the light at the same instant Mort fired. Instead of running for cover, Jesse leapt toward the rustler. Blinded by the headlights, Mort didn't see Jesse until he had been knocked down and his gun kicked out of his hand, disappearing somewhere in the underbrush.

Moments later, Jesse straddled Mort on the ground, with a viselike grip on the rustler's throat and his gun aimed at the rustler's head. "I told you I'm only going to deal with your boss."

"Why you—" Mort rasped.

"You can release Mort," a voice said from the shadows on the other side of the truck, "and drop the gun. I'm here."

Jesse didn't recognize the man who stepped into view, his automatic weapon aimed at the center of Jesse's back. But it wasn't Adam Philips. Jesse dropped his gun. Then he released Mort and stood to face the newest threat. "Are you the boss of this outfit?"

"I am," the man said. "I can't say it's a pleasure to meet you, Mr. Whitelaw. Actually, you've thrown a bit of a corkscrew into my plans. If you'll just step over to that shed, we can finish our business."

"You brought the money?" Jesse asked.

"Oh, no. All deals are off. I'm simply offering you a chance to get out of this alive. Are you going to walk over there peacefully, or not? I've already killed once. I assure you I won't hesitate to do so again."

Jesse was pretty sure the Boss intended to kill him anyway, but he was counting on Dallas to make sure he got out of this alive. Meanwhile, he had best keep his wits about him. He took his time sliding away the board that held the shed door closed, giving Dallas plenty of time to get everybody into position. Once Jesse was inside the shed and, he hoped, before the Boss man shot him, Dallas would move and it would all be over.

The instant Jesse released the door, a blur of movement shot past him. The escaping body was caught by Mort. Jesse's blood froze when he saw the gangly teenager the rustler was wrestling into submission.

"What the hell are you doing here?" Jesse rasped.

"Waiting for you!" Jack retorted. "You won't get away with this, you know. I'll tell them everything. They'll catch you, and you'll go to jail forever."

"Dammit, Jack, I—"

"Hey!" Jack was eyeing the man holding the gun on Jesse. "I know you! You're the foreman of the Lazy S. What're you doing here, Mr. Loomis?"

"Dammit, Jack," Jesse muttered. Now the fat was in the fire.

"You got any more surprises hidden around here?" Loomis asked Jesse.

"Look, the kid being here is as much a surprise to me as it is to you," Jesse said.

Jesse closely watched the man Jack had identified as Mr. Loomis and saw his mouth tighten, his eyes narrow. By identifying the Boss and making threats of going to the law, Jack had signed his own death warrant. Jesse forced himself not to glance out into the darkness. Adam's foreman was suspicious enough already. Dallas would realize that the boy's presence complicated things and make new plans accordingly.

"Both of you get into the shed," Loomis said, gesturing with the gun.

Jack spied the gun for the first time, and his eyes slid to Jesse's, wide with fright.

"It's all right," Jesse said in a voice intended to calm the youth. "They're just going to lock us up in the shed."

Jesse's last doubts that Loomis intended killing them both ended when Mort chuckled maliciously and said, "Yeah, you two just mosey on inside."

Jack struggled against Mort's hold, and the outlaw slapped him hard. "Quit your bellyachin' and get movin'."

Jesse had decided to use the distraction Jack was creating to make a lunge for Loomis's gun, when a pair of headlights appeared on the horizon.

"I knew it was a trap!" the outlaw snarled. Loomis swung the gun around to aim it at Jack and fired just as Jesse grabbed at his hand, pulling it down.

Jesse grunted as the bullet plowed into his thigh, but he never let go of his hold on Loomis's wrist. He swung a fist at the foreman's face and heard a satisfying crunch as it connected with the man's hooked nose. Loomis managed to fire once more before Jesse wrenched the gun away, but the bullet drove harmlessly into the ground.

Moments later, the area was swarming with local police and Texas Rangers. It soon became apparent to Jack from the way Dallas Masterson greeted Jesse, that the drifter wasn't going to be arrested by the Texas Rangers *because he was one!*

"What idiot turned on those headlights?" Jesse demanded. "Damned near got us killed!"

Jesse's head jerked up when he heard the sound of a woman's voice beyond the arc of light provided by the semi's headlights. "Who's that?"

Dallas grinned. "The idiot who turned on the headlights."

Jesse only had a second to brace himself before Honey threw herself into his arms. Her eyes were white around the rims with fright. Her whole body was shaking.

"I saw what happened. You saved Jack's life! I heard shots. Are you hurt?" She pushed herself away to look at him and saw the dark shine of blood on his leg. "My God! You've been shot!" She turned to the crowd of men scattered over the area and shouted, "Where's a doctor? Why haven't you taken this man to the hospital?"

Jesse pulled her back into his arms. "It's all right, Honey. It's just a little flesh wound. I'll be fine."

Jack stepped into the light and stood nearby, afraid to approach his mother and the drifter…who wasn't really a drifter after all.

Honey saw her son and reached out to pull him close. "Are you all right? You're not hurt?"

"I'm fine," Jack mumbled, feeling lower than a worm for having caused so much trouble.

"You're damned lucky not to be dead!" Jesse said.

Jack glared at Jesse. "If you'd just told me the truth in the first place, none of this would have happened. I spent a whole day in that stupid shed for nothing!" He turned to his mother and said, "I'm hungry. Is there anything at home to eat?"

Honey gaped at Jack and then laughed. If her son had started thinking about his stomach, he was going to be just fine.

Dallas had left briefly and now joined them again. "I've got a car to take you to the hospital, Jesse."

"I'll see you at home, Honey," Jesse said.

Now that she knew Jesse was all right, Honey forced herself to step away from him. If anything, this episode only proved what she had known all along. She didn't want to be married to a Texas Ranger. "I'll let you in to get your things," she said. "But I expect you to find somewhere else to spend what's left of the night."

Jesse didn't argue, just limped away toward the car Dallas had waiting.

But Jack wasn't about to let the subject alone. "He saved my life, Mom."

"I suppose he did."

"You can't just throw him out of the house like that."

"I can and I will."

"If you want my opinion, I think you're making a mistake," Jack said.

"I didn't ask for your opinion," Honey said. "Besides, you've got a lot to answer for yourself, young man."

Jack grimaced. "I can explain everything."

"This I've got to hear."

Angel interrupted to say, "I can give you both a ride home now."

"Let's go," Honey said. She put her arm around Jack and dared him to try to slip out from under it. "It's been a hectic night. Let's go home and get some sleep."

"But I'm hungry!" Jack protested.

"All right. First you eat. Then it's bed for both of us."

But hours later—just before dawn—when Jesse Whitelaw returned, Honey was sitting in the kitchen, coffee cup in hand, waiting for him.

Chapter 10

Honey didn't move when the kitchen door opened, just waited for Jesse to come to her. Her eyes drifted closed when his hands clasped her shoulders. She exhaled with a soughing sigh. He didn't give her a chance to object, just hauled her out of the chair, turned her into his arms and held her tight.

Honey's arms slipped around his waist and clutched his shirt. Her nose slipped into the hollow at his throat and she inhaled the sweaty man-scent that was his and his alone. She wanted to remember it when he was gone. And she *was* going to send him away.

"We have to talk," Jesse whispered in her ear.

Honey gripped him tighter, knowing she had to let him go. "I think I've said everything I have to say."

"I haven't." His lips twisted wryly. "I think this is where I'm supposed to sweep you into my arms and carry you off to the bedroom," he said. "But I don't think my leg could stand the strain."

Honey realized all at once how heavily he was leaning on her. "Come sit down," she said, urging him toward a kitchen chair.

"Let's find something a little more comfortable," he said. "Getting up and down is a pain. I'd like to find someplace I can stay awhile."

She slipped an arm around his waist to support him while he put an arm across her shoulders. Slowly they made their way to the living room, where he levered himself onto the brass-studded leather couch. He winced as she helped him lift both legs and stretch out full-length. She knelt beside him on the polished hardwood floor.

Jesse took one of her hands in both of his and brought it to his lips. He kissed each fingertip and then the palm of her hand. He laid her hand against his cheek, bristly now with a day's growth of beard, and turned to gaze into her eyes.

"Let me stay here tonight," he said.

"Jesse, I don't think—"

"We have to talk, Honey, but I can barely keep my eyes open."

"You can't stay here," she said. If he did, she would be tempted to let him stay another night, and another. Before she knew it, he would be a permanent fixture. "You have to leave," she insisted.

He smiled wearily. "Sorry. I'm afraid that's out of the question. Can't seem to get a muscle to move anywhere." His eyes drifted closed. "I have some things to say…"

He was asleep.

Honey stared at the beloved face before her and felt her heart wrench in her breast. How could she let him stay? How could she make him go?

She sighed and rose to find a blanket. After all, it was only one night..She would be able to argue with him better once she had gotten some sleep herself.

The homemade quilt barely reached from one end to the other of the tall Ranger. Jesse's face was gentle in repose. There was no hint of the fierceness in battle she had seen, no hint of the savage passion she had experienced. He was only a man. There must be another—not a Ranger—who would suit her as well.

She leaned down slowly, carefully, and touched her lips to his. A goodbye kiss. She walked dry-eyed up the stairs to her bedroom. It looked so empty. It felt so forlorn. She lay down on the bed and stared at the canopy overhead. It was a long time before she finally found respite in sleep.

The sun woke Honey the next morning. It was brighter than bright, a golden Texas morning. Honey stretched and groaned at how stiff she felt. Then she froze. Where was Jesse now? Was he still downstairs sleeping? Had he packed and left? Was he dressed and waiting to confront her?

Honey scrambled off the bed and ran across the hall to the bathroom. She took one look at herself and groaned. Her face looked as if she'd slept in it. She started the water running in the tub as hot as she could get it and stripped off her clothes. There was barely an inch of liquid in the claw-footed tub by the time she stepped into it. She sank down, hissing as the water scalded her, then grabbed a cloth and began soaping herself clean.

It never occurred to her to lock the bathroom door. No one ever bothered her when she was in the bathroom. Her eyes widened in surprise when the door opened and Jesse sauntered in. He was shirtless, wearing a pair of jeans that threatened to fall off, revealing his navel and the beginning of his hipbones.

She held the washcloth in front of her, which didn't do much good, not to mention how silly it looked. "What are you doing in here?" she demanded indignantly.

"I thought I'd shave," Jesse said. "We might as well get used to having to share the bathroom in the morning." He turned and grinned. "That is, unless I can talk you into adding a second bathroom. One with a *shower?*"

"What's going on, Jesse?"

He soaped up his shaving brush and began applying the resulting foam to his beard. "I'm shaving," he answered. "Looks like you're taking a bath." He grinned.

Honey tried ignoring him. She turned her back on him and continued washing herself. She was feeling both angry and confused. *He has no right to be doing this! Why doesn't he just go?* If Jesse had changed his mind about leaving the Rangers he would have told her so last night. This was just another ploy to get his own way. She wasn't going to let him get away with it.

Honey covered herself with the washcloth as best she could while she reached for a towel. Just as she caught it with her fingertips, Jesse slipped it off the rack and settled it around his neck.

"I need that towel," she said through gritted teeth.

"I'll be done with it in a minute," he said. "I need to wipe off the excess shaving cream."

Honey was tempted to stand up and stroll past him naked, but she didn't have the nerve. What if Jack was out there? *Jack!*

"Where's Jack?" she asked.

"Sent him out to round up those steers we vaccinated and move them to another pasture."

"And he went?"

"Don't look so surprised. Jack's a hard worker."

Honey's brows rose. "I know that. I didn't think you did."

"Jack and I have an understanding," Jesse said.

"Oh?"

"I told him this morning that I was going to marry you and—"

"You what!" Honey rose from the water like Poseidon in a tempest. Water sluiced down her body, creating jeweled trails over breasts and belly.

Jesse didn't know when he had ever seen her looking more beautiful. Or more angry.

"Now, Honey—"

"Don't you 'Now, Honey' me, you rogue. How could you tell my son such a thing? How could you get his hopes up when you *know* I'm not going to marry you!"

"But you are," Jesse said.

Honey was shivering from cold and trembling with emotion. Jesse took the towel from around his neck and offered it to her. She yanked it out of his hand and wrapped it around herself.

"I'd like to play the gallant and carry you off to the

bedroom to make my point, but—" He gestured to the wounded leg and shrugged. "Can't do it."

Honey made a growling sound low in her throat as she marched past Jesse to the bedroom. Actually she had to stop marching long enough to squeeze past him in the doorway, and she had to fight him for the tail end of the towel as she slid by.

"Just have one more little spot I need to wipe," he said, dabbing at his face.

"Let go!" she snapped. She yanked, he pulled, and the ancient terry cloth tore down the middle. "Now look what you've done!"

Tears sprang to Honey's eyes. "You're ruining everything!"

"It's just a towel, Honey," Jesse said, misunderstanding her tears. He tried to follow her into the bedroom, but she shut the door in his face. And locked it.

"Hey, unlock the door."

"Go away, Jesse."

"I thought we were going to talk."

"Go away, Jesse."

"I'm not going to leave, Honey. You might as well open the door."

"Go away, Jesse."

Jesse put a shoulder against the door, just to see how sturdy it was, and concluded that at least the house was well built. His bad leg wouldn't support him if he tried kicking it in. Which was just as well. Honey wasn't likely to be too impressed with that sort of melodrama.

"I'm leaving, Honey," he said.

No answer.

"I said I'm leaving."

Still no answer.

"Aren't you going to say goodbye?"

"Goodbye, Jesse," she sobbed.

"Jeez, Honey. This is stupid. Open the door so we can talk."

She sobbed again.

Jesse's throat constricted. She really sounded upset. Maybe this wasn't the best time to talk to her after all. He had some chores he could do that would keep him busy for a while. Surely she couldn't stay in there all day. He'd catch her when she came down for some coffee later.

Honey heard Jesse's halting step as he limped his way down the stairs. So, he was leaving after all. Honey got into bed and pulled the covers over her head. She didn't want to think about anything. She just wanted to wallow in misery. She should have taken the part of him she could get, the part left over after he'd done his duty to the Rangers. It would have been better than nothing, certainly better than the void he would leave when he was gone.

Then she thought of all the time she would have to spend alone, with no shoulder to share the burden, no lover's ear to hear how the day had gone and offer solace, and her backbone stiffened. She deserved more from a relationship than half measures. She had to accept the fact that Jesse had made his choice.

Honey didn't notice the sun creeping across the sky. She had no knowledge of the fading light at dusk. She never even noticed the sun setting to leave the world in darkness. Her whole life was dark. It couldn't get any blacker.

Meanwhile, Jesse had spent the day waiting patiently for Honey to come to her senses. At noon, he prepared some tomato soup and grilled cheese sandwiches, planning to surprise her with his culinary expertise. He ended up sharing his bounty with Jack, who ate all the sandwiches and dumped the soup with the comment, "Mom makes it better."

When Jesse had explained to Jack that he needed some time alone with Honey, Jack was more than willing to go spend the night with friends again. In fact, Jesse was embarrassed by the lurid grin on the teenager's face when he agreed not to come home too early the next morning.

"Does this mean Mom has agreed to marry you?" Jack asked.

"I haven't quite talked her into it yet," Jesse said.

"But you will."

"I'm sure going to try," Jesse said grimly.

"Don't worry," Jack said, slapping Jesse on the shoulder. "I think Mom loves you."

But as Jesse was discovering, the fact that Honey loved him might not be enough to induce her to marry him. Jack left late in the afternoon. Jesse tiptoed up the stairs and listened by Honey's bedroom door, but there was no sound coming from inside. He decided he was just going to have to outwait her.

It was nearly ten o'clock that evening before he finally decided she wasn't coming out anytime soon. He knocked hard on her bedroom door. "All right, Honey. Enough's enough. Come on out of there so we can talk."

He heard the sound of rustling sheets and then a muffled "Jesse?"

A moment later the door opened. Her hair looked as sleep-tousled as it had the first morning he had come to the Flying Diamond. Her blue eyes were unfocused, confused. She tightened the belt on the man's terry cloth robe she was wearing, then clutched at the top to hold it closed.

"Jesse?" she repeated. "Is that you?"

"Of course it's me. Who did you think it was?"

"I thought you left," she said.

"Why the hell would I do that?" Jesse felt angry and irritable. While he'd been cooling his heels downstairs all day, she'd been up here *sleeping!* "If you're through napping, maybe we could have that talk I mentioned earlier."

"You want to talk?" Honey was still half-asleep.

"Yes, by God, I want to talk! And you're going to listen, do you hear me?" Jesse grabbed hold of her shoulders and shook her for good measure.

The moment Jesse touched her, Honey came instantly awake. This was no dream. This was no figment of her imagination. A furious Jesse Whitelaw was really shaking the daylights out of her.

"All right, Jesse," she said, putting her hands on his arms to calm him. "I'm ready to listen."

At that moment there was a knock on the kitchen door and a familiar voice called up the stairs, "Honey? Are you home?"

Good old reliable Adam.

Honey ran past Jesse as though he wasn't even there,

scrambled down the stairs and met Adam at the door to the kitchen.

He looked tired and frazzled. Honey avoided meeting his eyes, because they still held too much pain.

"I just wanted to let you know that I found some of your stolen cattle on my property," he said. "I'll have some of my cowhands drive them over here tomorrow."

Adam's eyes flickered to a spot behind Honey. "It seems I misjudged you, Whitelaw," Adam said. "I had no idea Chuck Loomis was using my ranch as a base for a statewide rustling operation. I owe you an apology and my thanks." He stuck his hand out to Jesse, who slid a possessive hand around Honey's waist before he reached out to shake it.

Honey felt the tension between the two men. They would never be close friends, but at least they wouldn't be enemies, either.

"I'll be going now," Adam said.

"Are you sure you're all right?" Honey asked.

"My business affairs are in a shambles and I need a new ranch manager, but otherwise I'm fine," Adam said with a self-deprecating smile.

"I'll let you out," Honey said. But when she tried to leave Jesse's side, he tightened his grasp.

Adam saw what was going on and said, "I can see myself out. Goodbye, Honey."

Honey saw from the look on Adam's face that he wouldn't be coming back anytime soon. She felt his sadness, his loneliness. Somewhere out there was a woman who could bring the sparkle back into Adam's life. All Honey had to do was keep her eyes open and help Adam find that special someone.

When the kitchen door closed behind Adam, Jesse took Honey's hand in his and ordered, "Come with me."

He limped his way back up the stairs, down the hall and into her room. Once inside, he turned and locked the door behind them. "I've got something important to say to you, Honey, and it can't wait another minute."

Honey could see Jesse was agitated. While he talked, she led him over to the bed and sat him down. She kneeled to pull off his boots, then lifted his feet up onto the rumpled sheets.

"Are you more comfortable?" she asked.

"Yes. Don't change the subject."

"What is the subject?" Honey asked, climbing into the other side of the bed.

"You're going to marry me, Honey. No ifs, ands, or buts."

"I know," she said.

"No more arguments, no more—What did you say?"

"I said I'll marry you, Jesse."

"But—"

"I shouldn't have tried blackmailing you into quitting your job. I know how much being a Ranger means to you. It isn't fair to ask you to give that up." She smiled. "I'll manage."

Jesse couldn't have loved Honey more than he did in that instant. How brave she was! What strength she possessed! And how she must love him to be willing to make such a concession herself rather than force him to do it. What she couldn't know, what he hadn't realized himself until very recently, was that it was a sacrifice he was willing to make. He loved being a Ranger; he loved Honey more.

Jesse wanted the life she had offered him, a life working side by side with the woman he loved. Raising kids. Running the ranch. Loving Honey.

Jesse swallowed over the lump in his throat. It was hard to speak but he managed, "I love you, Honey." He gently touched her lips with his, revering her, honoring her.

She moved eagerly into his arms, but he held her away.

"There's something I have to tell you," he said.

He saw the anxiety flicker in her eyes and spoke quickly to quell it. "Before I came back here this morning, I resigned from the Texas Rangers."

Honey gasped. "You did? Really?"

"I did. Really."

Honey didn't know what she had done to be rewarded with her heart's desire, but she saw only rainbows on the horizon. Here was a man she could lean on in times of trouble, a man with whom she could share her life, the happiness and sorrow, the good times and the bad.

"I can't believe that this is really happening," Honey said. "Are you sure, Jesse?"

"Sure of what?"

"That you won't be sorry later. That you won't have regrets. That you won't change your mind and—"

"I won't change my mind. I won't have regrets or be sorry. Being a Ranger made it easy to avoid looking at my life as it really is. I've been drifting for years looking for something, Honey. I just didn't know what it was. I've found it here with you and Jack and Jonathan."

"What's that?"

"A place where I can put down roots. A place where

my grandchildren can see the fruits of my labor. A home."

Honey didn't know what to say. She felt full. And happy. And by some act of providence she and the man she loved just happened to be in bed together.

"Where's Jack?" she asked.

Jesse grinned. "He's spending the night with a friend."

Honey arched a brow provocatively. "Then we have the whole house to ourselves?"

"Yes, ma'am. We sure do."

"Then I suggest we make use of it."

Jesse arched a questioning brow. "The whole house?"

"Well, we can start in the bedroom. But the desk in the den is nice. There's the kitchen table. And the tub has definite possibilities." Honey laughed at the incredulous look on Jesse's face.

"You'll kill me," he muttered.

"Yeah, but what a way to go," Honey said.

Hours later, Jesse was leaning back in a tubful of steaming water, his nape comfortably settled on the edge of the claw-footed tub. Honey was curled against his chest, her body settled on his lap.

"I didn't think it could be done," he murmured.

"You're a man of many talents, Mr. Whitelaw."

He grinned lazily. "May I return the compliment?"

"Of course." Honey leaned over to lap a drop of water from Jesse's nipple. She felt him stiffen, and gently teased him until his flesh was taut with desire.

Jesse groaned, an animal sound that forced its way past his throat. "Honey," he warned, "you're playing with fire."

She laughed, a sexy sound, and said, "There's plenty of water here if I wanted to put it out…which I don't."

A moment later he had turned her to face him, her legs straddling his thighs. He grasped her hips and slowly pulled her down, impaling her.

Honey gasped.

He held her still, trying to gain control of his desire, wanting the pleasure to last. She arched herself against him, forcing him deeper inside the cocoon of wetness and warmth.

"You feel so good, Honey. So damn good."

"May I return the compliment?" she said in a breathless voice. She grasped his shoulders to steady herself as she rocked back and forth, seeking to pleasure him and finding the pleasure given returned tenfold.

Jesse reached out to cup her breasts, to tease the nipples into peaks, to nip and lick and kiss her breasts until Honey was writhing in pleasure. He found the place where their bodies met and teased her until she ached with need. Their mouths joined as his body spilled its seed into hers.

Breathless, Honey sought the solace of his embrace. He held her close as the water lapped in waves against the edge of the tub.

"I can't believe it," she said as he pulled her close and tucked her head beneath his chin. "Oh, the things we can do to improve the ranch! I have so many plans, so many ideas!"

Jesse chuckled. "Whoa, there, woman. One thing at a time."

She looked up at him and grinned. "What shall we do first?"

"First I think we ought to do some planting."

"What are we going to grow?"

"Some hay. Some vegetables. Some babies."

Honey laughed with delight. "Let's start with the babies."

Jesse fell in love all over again. It was amazing how sheer happiness made Honey glow with beauty. His heart felt full. His chest was so tight with feelings it hurt to breathe. He didn't have to drift any longer. He had found his home. Where he would spend each night with his woman. Where he would plant seeds—of many kinds—and watch them grow.

* * * * *

SPECIAL EXCERPT FROM

HARLEQUIN®

ROMANTIC suspense

Parting ways broke both attorney Simone Black's and Dr. Paul Reilly's hearts. Now Paul desperately needs Simone's help when he discovers something fatally wrong in the medications provided by a major pharmaceutical company. Can these two find their way back to each other while bringing down a very powerful enemy?

Read on for a sneak preview of Reunited by the Badge, *the next book in Deborah Fletcher Mello's To Serve and Seduce miniseries!*

"I appreciate you coming," he said.

"You said it was important."

Paul nodded as he gestured for her to take a seat. Sitting down, Simone stole another quick glance toward the bar. The two strangers were both staring blatantly, not bothering to hide their interest in the two of them.

Simone rested an elbow on the tabletop, turning flirtatiously toward her friend. "Do you know Tom and Jerry over there at the bar?" she asked softly. She reached a hand out, trailing her fingers against his arm.

Her touch was just distracting enough that Paul didn't turn abruptly to stare back, drawing even more attention in their direction. His focus shifted slowly from her toward the duo at the bar. He eyed them briefly before turning his attention back to Simone. He shook his head. "Should I?"

"It might be nothing, but they seem very interested in you."

Paul's gaze danced back in their direction and he took a swift inhale of air. One of the men was on a cell phone and both were still eyeing him intently.

"We need to leave," he said, suddenly anxious. He began to gather his papers.

"What's going on, Paul?"

"I don't think we're safe, Simone."

"What do you mean we're not safe?" she snapped, her teeth clenched tightly. "Why are we not safe?"

"I'll explain, but I think we really need to leave."

Simone took a deep breath and held it, watching as he repacked his belongings into his briefcase.

"We're not going anywhere until you explain," she started, and then a commotion at the door pulled at her attention.

Don't miss
Reunited by the Badge *by Deborah Fletcher Mello*
available October 2019 wherever
Harlequin® Romantic Suspense
books and ebooks are sold.

www.Harlequin.com

Copyright © 2019 by Deborah Fletcher Mello

HRSEXP0919

Need an adrenaline rush from nail-biting tales (and irresistible males)?

Check out **Harlequin Intrigue®**, **Harlequin® Romantic Suspense** and **Love Inspired® Suspense** books!

New books available every month!

CONNECT WITH US AT:

Facebook.com/groups/HarlequinConnection

 Facebook.com/HarlequinBooks

 Twitter.com/HarlequinBooks

 Instagram.com/HarlequinBooks

 Pinterest.com/HarlequinBooks

ReaderService.com

ROMANCE WHEN YOU NEED IT

SGENRE2018R

SPECIAL EXCERPT FROM

HARLEQUIN®

INTRIGUE

Waking in the middle of a war zone, Jane Doe has no memory of who she is or who she can trust. When she meets former elite Force Recon member Gus Walsh, she finds that trusting him is her only chance at finding answers.

Read on for a sneak preview of Driving Force, *the fourth installment of the thrilling Declan's Defenders series by* New York Times *and* USA TODAY *bestselling author Elle James.*

CHAPTER ONE

She struggled to surface from the black hole trying to suck her back down. Her head hurt and she could barely open her eyes. Every part of her body ached so badly she began to think death would be a relief. But her heart, buried behind bruised and broken ribs, beat strong, pushing blood through her veins. And with the blood, the desire to live.

Willing her eyes to open, she blinked and gazed through narrow slits at the dirty mud-and-stick wall in front of her. Why couldn't she open her eyes more? She raised her hand to her face and felt the puffy, blood-crusted skin around her eyes and mouth. When she tried to move her lips, they cracked and warm liquid oozed out on her chin.

Her fingernails were split, some ripped down to the quick, and the backs of her knuckles looked like pounded hamburger

HIEXP0919

meat. Bruises, scratches and cuts covered her arms.

She felt along her torso, wincing when she touched a bruised rib. As she shifted her search lower, her hands shook and she held her breath, feeling for bruises, wondering if she'd been assaulted in other ways. When she felt no tenderness between her legs, she let go of the breath she'd held in a rush of relief.

She pushed into a sitting position and winced at the pain knifing through her head. Running her hand over her scalp, she felt a couple of goose egg–sized lumps. One behind her left ear, the other at the base of her skull.

A glance around the small cell-like room gave her little information about where she was. The floor was hard-packed dirt and smelled of urine and feces. She wore a torn shirt and the dark pants women wore beneath their burkas.

Voices outside the rough wooden door made her tense and her body cringe.

She wasn't sure why she was there, but those voices inspired an automatic response of drawing deep within, preparing for additional beatings and torture.

What she had done to deserve it, she couldn't remember. Everything about her life was a gaping, useless void.

The door jerked open. A man wearing the camouflage uniform of a Syrian fighter and a black hood covering his head and face stood in the doorway with a Russian AK-47 slung over his shoulder and a steel pipe in his hand.

Don't miss
Driving Force *by Elle James,*
available October 2019 wherever
Harlequin® books and ebooks are sold.

www.Harlequin.com

Copyright © 2019 by Mary Jernigan

HIEXP0919